LEGION
⊙ XXII ⊙

BELLATRIX

LEGION
⊙ XXII ⊙

BELLATRIX

SIMON TURNEY

HEAD
of ZEUS

An Aries Book

First published in the UK in 2023 by Head of Zeus
This paperback edition first published in 2023 by Head of Zeus,
part of Bloomsbury Publishing Plc

9 7 5 3 1 2 4 6 8

A catalogue record for this book is available from the British Library.

ISBN (PB): 9781801108980
ISBN (E): 9781801108959

Cover design by Ben Prior
Map design by Jeff Edwards

Printed and bound in Great Britain by
CPI Group (UK) Ltd, Croydon CR0 4YY

Head of Zeus
5–8 Hardwick Street
London EC1R 4RG

WWW.HEADOFZEUS.COM

For Andy, Michelle, Anne and Brian

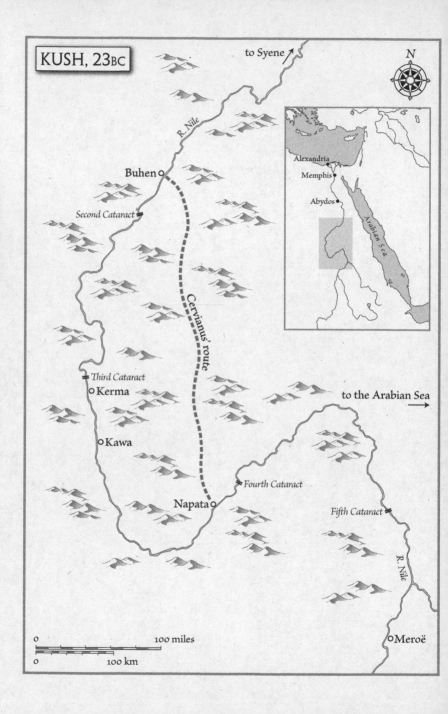

I

INTO EMPTINESS

Cervianus watched with a sinking feeling as the last ranks of the legion filed away along the riverbank, the vanguard already nothing more than a cloud of dust in the far distance. With no support wagons, the legion moved surprisingly swiftly and would be gone from sight within moments. A last look afforded him a fleeting glimpse of the cavalry of the Nome of Sapi-Res riding around the rear of the column and out as scouts. Somewhere among the white clad cavalry was his friend Shenti. Would he ever see him again?

The blast from the cornu drew his attention once more to his immediate surroundings. The First and Second cohorts stood ready on the rocky bluff overlooking the Nile, the steel- and bronze-clad legionaries already sweltering and suffering under the merciless heat of the southern sun. Not a man among them smiled or relaxed into their stance; every face was a bleak reflection of the daunting journey ahead. Nasica and Draco gave the traditional rousing speech and briefing at first light and, even having left out more than half the concerns Cervianus had raised, their oration had hardly eased the minds of the men.

It had been particularly hard to say goodbye to Shenti.

Without his advice and knowledge of the people and lands of Aegyptus, Cervianus was in no doubt that he would have fallen foul of something or someone by now. The loss of his support and aid would be keenly felt in the next week.

A week!

The thought of spending a full day and night in the harsh conditions of the great desert filled him with dread. Seven or more of them? Madness. And seven was a conservative estimate. Seven days would be the task if the two cohorts were somehow able to keep up a good, steady marching speed. For every pace they dropped each hour, the journey would extend. Ulyxes had frightened him by actually calculating the numbers, but he'd thankfully forgotten the details.

With a sigh, he watched the men in front moving off at a solid pace, the optio's staff drumming on bronze greaves with a threatening rap, making sure the men marched in good order. A quick final glance at the disappearing bulk of the legion moving away up the Nile, and he began to stomp forward in time with the others, leaving the low bluff above the river and heading toward the rocky mounds ahead.

The trail the native scouts had located for Vitalis passed not along the open, dusty flat land near Buhen, but into hilly, dry lands toward the south. Ulyxes had complained that the terrain was considerably harder and it would have been easier keeping to the open desert, but Cervianus knew better and had enlightened him that morning as they'd prepared their kit.

While it was considerably easier to walk on the flat ground Ulyxes favoured, the wind would be able to whip the sand up around them constantly, choking the men and covering the trail, hiding the route and likely sending them off course into the deep desert to die. There would be times on this more-than-two-hundred-mile trek where such terrain was unavoidable, but the nomads who had originally forged the track had known their lands and had utilised the rocks and valleys as best as possible to give them at least some protection from the worst of the elements.

But who would protect them against those very nomads?

That was the question that still caused Cervianus' heart to skip a beat. He could almost stoically accept the decision to march the cohorts into the barren waste, with all its inherent dangers, had it not been for the fact that they all knew that these lands belonged to the black-clad head-takers who had horrified the legion at Buhen.

Settling into the pace, Cervianus shifted his furca pole into a slightly more comfortable position and tried not to dwell on the enemy who could be waiting around any corner or lurking in any crevice they passed.

Each man carried a much more specialised pack than the standard legionary marching kit. Gone were the sudis stakes, entrenching tools, cooking utensils and spare clothing. Food would be eaten cold or cooked over a small fire if any wildlife should be unfortunate enough to cross their path. No bread would be baked on this journey. Instead, extra hard tack had been added and the bulk of the weight carried by each man consisted of extra blankets against the sudden drop in temperature during the night and the life-preserving stores of water, the most precious commodity they could attain now.

Nasica had sensibly, if disobediently, waited for the tribune's column to leave, and then requisitioned two dozen of the horses and camels that accompanied the baggage train that would wait at Buhen for their return. Despite Vitalis' orders that they travel without animals, for speed and flexibility, Nasica and Draco had listened intently last night to Cervianus' list of dangers and needs and had decided that the expedient acquisition of a few of the faster pack animals would be a sensible idea, even though half their load would be their own food.

Cervianus had rolled his eyes at the idiocy of Ulyxes finding places among his kit to secrete the decorative daggers they had removed from the stores in Nicopolis. So much had happened in the past few weeks that their very existence had gone clear from Cervianus' mind until he found his friend cramming them in among water packs and blankets. Still, should they actually, against all the odds, make it through this, it would be better that the incriminating evidence stay with them than be found among the kit by those who stayed at Buhen. How awful it would be to survive a march across the most forbidding place in the world only to be beaten for theft upon their return!

Cervianus glanced across at his friend and received a crazed grin in return. Ulyxes never ceased to amaze him with his optimistic attitude in the face of horrible hardships. Turning back, he faced the direction of march and scanned the terrain. The track they followed was barely traceable in the grey-brown nightmare landscape. How the scouts could even identify that this was a trail at all amazed him. The column of men wound their way up the slope from their starting point by the river and into a strange world of humps of land, formed by dark grey or deep umber rocks, displaying jagged points or lines of strata as they rose from the grit. It looked to him as though this were an impromptu graveyard for giant petrified tortoises.

The defiles and dips between them could contain anything.
The sand was already in his boots and rubbing his feet raw.

The day stretched on as the legion moved. By the time they
stopped for the main break at around an hour before noon,
the men were already heartily sick of the journey. Ulyxes had
calculated their pace and distance and had announced with a
jolly laugh that they had managed fifteen miles in the morning
and that, if Nasica could keep them to the same pace, they
should manage thirty miles a day, a pace that could see them at
Napata in the predicted seven days, eight at the most, putting
them at their destination an estimated five days before the rest
of the army.

One look around at the men collapsed on their shields,
rubbing their feet and wincing, made the likelihood of that
actually occurring miserably apparent. The pace would slacken
only a little this afternoon, but Cervianus could see ahead.
Tomorrow morning, the strain of what they had achieved
today would begin to tell. After a night's rest, the muscles
would seize, especially given the bone-chilling cold of a desert
night. Blisters and grazes would come up and burst, leaving
men's feet and shoulders raw and painful.

No. Tomorrow they would be lucky if the pace dropped by
only a third.

The noon break was well received by the men of the cohorts,
even though it involved sitting in the lee of dusty rocks and
trying to hide from the roasting sun, eating cold, hard biscuit
with a mere dribble of water, rather than the meat, bread and
soured wine they would normally consume on campaign.

And then, all too soon, the worst of the day's heat passed

and Nasica and Draco, with their optios, put out the calls, gathering the men ready for the march once again.

The mounds of grey and brown began to blend into one another as the hours wore on, dust causing the men to gag, weariness and uneven ground leading to stumbles and falls, each one rewarded with a jab from an officer's vine staff and a lash from his tongue. Along the line men reached surreptitiously for their water packs, taking mouthfuls of the precious liquid to stave off the parching dryness of the journey. The officers barked out orders and threatened such men with discipline, knowing how little spare water there would be, even if they kept good time.

Cervianus watched the man in front secretly emptying the last dregs of his first waterskin, the torrents running down the sides of his chin and soaking into his mail shirt with the hiss of evaporating liquid... no man would dare touch the metal rings of their armour now for fear of burning. The fool. That water was almost two days' supply and he'd finished it in less than a day. If the whole force thought like that, rations would be out half way through the march and no one would ever find the desiccated husks of the two Roman cohorts, dead in the deep desert sands.

The end of the first day was greeted with a cheery attitude. The men gave thanks to their favourite deities, mostly those traditional Celtic lords of the Gauls, but with the occasional Roman, Greek or even Syrian god among them. The cheeriness waned as men relaxed and realised that their sense of achievement that rose from surviving the life-sucking day was a false relief, given the small proportion of the journey this one day actually represented.

As the great disc of Ra lost the worst of its power and began to fall toward the western desert, the cohorts made their camp for the night. No fortifications would be dug and raised here. Even if they'd brought the sudes to form a fence and the tools for trenching, no rampart formed of shifting sand would ever hold, and no ditch could be cut through the rough, rocky ground. Besides, the men were in no state at the end of the day to begin the construction of a military-standard marching camp.

Instead, the cohorts pitched their tents as best they could, so close together that a man could hear his counterparts snoring, turning and flatulating three tents over. Around the small camp of one hundred and twenty-eight tents, four watch fires blazed, awaiting the arrival of full darkness, each smaller than its attendants would have liked, the fuel mostly garnered from the parched plants that grew very sparse and rare, brown and wilted, and from the dried dung of the animals that travelled with them. A watch group of one contubernium of men tended each fire.

The night was nerve-wracking for all of them, though mostly for Cervianus. Predators and scavengers howled and hissed and padded in the night, hidden in the darkness just out of the range of the fire light: noises to loosen the bowels of even the hardiest soldier. But Cervianus was aware of the less obvious dangers that filled the day and night out here, too.

The temperature, when it dropped, did so almost suddenly. The stones and gritty ground held some of the sun's warmth for a time after the golden glow retreated beyond the horizon, but the desert night leeched that retained heat in a heartbeat, leaving the land barren, hard, dry and bone-chillingly cold. More than one man that first night wished he'd been wounded enough to stay with the others at Buhen, even knowing the likelihood that the black-garbed killers would return for them.

* * *

It was, Cervianus reflected the next morning, the least comfortable night he had ever spent on campaign. Somehow the unbearable heat of the day made the awful chill of the night that much worse.

The morning sun came up to find an army that was already largely awake, most of the men having slept fitfully at best. It transpired that the watch fires had died in the heart of the night, the quantity of fuel for them so low and pathetic that the men had even burned scraps of tunics and cloaks to keep them going as long as they could.

The morning was sullen and quiet as each man contemplated what they had endured that previous day and during the night that had sapped them of yet more strength and rested them little. By the time the tents were stowed and the men began to march, Cervianus had tended to over a hundred minor injuries, grazes, boils and blisters, treated three men for sunburn resulting from having been less than careful the previous day, and even been called on to examine one of the horses that danced wildly and seemed to be favouring one of its rear legs. The beast was strong and had clearly suffered a minor leg injury yesterday, but might be able to keep pace. Cervianus' supplies of amagdalinum oil, mosulum and terminthos resin were already shockingly depleted after one day.

Nasica and Draco had the calls put out for muster on that second, miserable morning, and gave out the watchwords for the day, despite the fact that the very idea of leaving the unit long enough to need a returning password was unfathomable. The officers gave words of encouragement, reminding them that they had travelled more than an eighth of the way already, and reiterated warnings about covering themselves to prevent sunburn and sunstroke and not to over-consume water rations. Finally, all things in order, the cohorts marched on.

Nasica set the pace once again, though today it slackened noticeably to a speed that would likely cover twenty miles in one day. The previous day had been a morale-building exercise. Despite the dangers of pushing the men so hard in these conditions, having covered such a good slice of the distance in the first day hammered a small glimmer of hope into the despairing façade of the cohorts.

The terrain was depressingly familiar as the morning wore on and the sun climbed in both height and intensity. The humps and mounds of grey rock continued, each and every one seeming so familiar that they could easily be circling in the forbidding land were it not for the sense of direction afforded by the merciless sun.

At the first pause that morning, Cervianus had been close enough to the officers, treating one of the signifers for a burn mark caused by his own white-hot, sun-heated bronze standard, to overhear the supposedly private conversation as the two most senior centurions consulted the scouts.

Would they soon be moving into easier terrain?

Would there be a source of fuel for watch fires?

Were they nearing any known areas of nomad activity?

The scouts shrugged and replied in their sparse, stilted Latin that there would be two more days of the rocks before they moved out into the shifting sands. There would be small areas of dry foliage here and there among the rocks; certain plants that they spoke of, whose names were unfamiliar to Cervianus, apparently had the ability to reach down further than any normal flora and draw the tiny moisture from the deep earth below the barren surface. The scouts would locate such areas as they travelled and lead forage parties to them while the cohorts paused for breath.

As for the nomads, the scouts could say nothing. The dangerous inhabitants of this forbidding land were an unknown quantity even to their neighbours. They could be hundreds of miles away, or they could be lurking in the valley behind the next rock. There was simply no predicting them.

And the journey continued.

The endless dust cloud and mounds of barren rock joined the frying heat, the parching dryness, and the danger of head-taking psychopaths at the top of Cervianus' list of things he most hated in the world.

The noon break of the second day was muted and quiet, missing the feeling of relief of the previous one. The men sat in silence and ate the dry, dull, hard rations, sipped their water, or gulped it if they were stupid, and silently prayed to every deity they could think of that this nightmare journey would end soon and well.

Listening to the odd comment to very much the same pattern, Cervianus bit his tongue to prevent himself from giving them a hint of the truth: that they had had it easy so far. Things were going to become a great deal worse in the coming days. The pace and the rations and the discomforts they were feeling now were luxuries compared with what yet awaited them.

It was therefore something of a relief when, as the sun began to descend on that second day and a forage party returned with desiccated, dead leaves and bark and piles of dried dung, the horse that had hurt its leg that first day finally succumbed to its weakness and became lame, hobbling and collapsing onto three knees, one leg buckling and splaying out at a horrible angle.

There had not even been a discussion. No orders were needed, and certainly no encouragement.

In the flash of an eye, three legionaries were around the beast, knocking it onto its side and slashing its throat swiftly, putting it out of its misery in preparation for helping lessen their own. Nasica had Cervianus carefully checked over the remaining seven horses and six camels, confirming that the rest of the pack animals were healthy, and then gave the order to make camp where they were.

The watch fires doubled that second night as cooking fires and the mouth-watering smell of roasting meat made men salivate. The water and food from that horse's burden was redistributed among the other beasts and men and by the time darkness truly fell, the bones of the horse retained not enough meat to tempt even the hungriest of men. The carcass was discarded some three hundred paces from the watch fires and the men's mood lifted just a fragment at the small, cooked morsels that had accompanied their night's biscuit ration, the meat divided up fairly and leaving little more than a tasty mouthful for each man.

That night, the sounds from beyond the firelight were the stuff of nightmare, enough to cause even the bravest of legionaries to pull his blanket up over his head and block his ears. Scavengers had come to pick clean the bones of the horse and the noises they made were simply shocking.

The third morning, the reality of the journey began finally to set in. The pace had slackened again, just a touch. Perhaps a mile or two less, but it spoke volumes; even the officers couldn't keep up the tortuous pace. Cervianus tried not to think about how much slower they were now travelling and how long, if the pace kept slowing, this trek might take. Would they arrive to find that Vitalis had already taken Napata? Would they arrive at all?

There was hardly a word spoken that morning, and Nasica set them off on their march with no commands, reminders or words of encouragement.

The third day was the change for the men of the First and Second cohorts. Some men, having over-consumed their own water ration, attempted to draw extra from the remaining animals, an act that drew the ire of the officers. Those men who had had the lack of foresight to rush through their allotment found that the third day, the worst so far for heat, dryness and despair, would be their first day with no water, barring the sip that would come with lunch and the evening meal, such as they were.

Men began to succumb to the heat and conditions, much as Cervianus had predicted in the privacy of his own head. Though the cohorts marched on throughout the morning and past the noon break without losing a single man or animal, the strain and hardship began to show plainly on many a face and it came as a surprise to the capsarius that the full complement of men stood after the meal to begin the march anew for the afternoon.

Another morning and noon spent tending burst, bloodied blisters, grated by sand and filled with dust, soured Cervianus, who knew that the only respite from his tending of such small irritations would come when the real trouble began.

He didn't have to wait long.

Perhaps an hour into the afternoon march, there was a sudden shout of pain and bellows of alarm and consternation from somewhere back in the column. Biting his cheek in anticipation, Cervianus was already running, his hand unbuckling his bag before the optio found his voice to order it.

One of the legionaries from the Second cohort sat on the rocky ground, his face pale and waxy, his eyes panicked and wild, lips trembling. Half a dozen legionaries close by, the column having stopped abruptly, were gathered in a tight circle. Cervianus was about to investigate when his question was answered for him.

The six soldiers turned and one held out the source of the trouble with distaste. The snake was only a foot long at most. It had been a mottled two-tone brown with an interesting pattern, though that pattern was hard to make out in its current condition. The half-dozen soldiers had stamped on it repeatedly, smashing its skull to pieces and flattening it until its guts squeezed out of the side.

"That's a sand viper. You could just have thrown it away."

The legionary stared at him. "Bloody thing got off lightly."

Cervianus crouched by the wounded man. "What happened?"

"Bit me... on the ankle as I was marching. Never even saw it!"

The capsarius grasped the man's leg and hauled it up to eye height, causing the man to tip backwards, where he lay in the dust in a panic, his eyes searching for any other dangerous reptile nearby.

"You probably trod on it and it struck instinctively. Good; got it early enough. These things can be lethal if it's not dealt with immediately. We've a sub-species back home that I've studied. Cleopatra supposedly killed herself with one of these."

The soldier holding the snake flung it out across the desert.

"That bitch died of a sword blow from a Roman-loving hand. Don't listen to folk tales, capsarius!"

Ignoring the man, Cervianus rummaged in his pack.

"Suck the bloody poison out," the snake-killing legionary demanded.

Cervianus ignored him and quickly applied a tourniquet around the man's lower leg, using his index finger to measure the discoloured veins that led away from the bite and positioning the tie just beyond them.

"Come on!" shouted the man.

Cervianus, rummaging once more in his bag and not looking up, shook his head as he pulled out jars, poultices and his surgical tools.

"Sucking it out is dangerous for both of us. I could cause an infection that could lose him his leg or his life as surely as the venom itself, and I could accidentally take in a little of the venom and bring about my own demise. This is quick and simple, so leave me to work."

Without further comment, he drew a sharp blade from his surgical kit and cut a neat, circular chunk from the man's leg around the bite itself, scything through the greeny-black veins that carried the life-threatening venom and creating a hole almost an inch across. The patient shrieked at the cut, but the slicing was so quick and accurate that by the time he screamed, it was already over. Blood poured out of the open wound and Cervianus put his thumb over the discoloured area and began to push the blood out of the veins into the wound, as though squeezing something from a bag.

A few moments passed as the discolouration faded and the legionary panted in pain. Finally, Cervianus leaned back, dipped into his bag and retrieved his ephedron, pouring a small quantity into the wound. The legionaries, watching intently, drew an impressed breath as the bleeding visibly slowed almost to a stop on contact with the strange remedy.

Nodding at the progress of the wound, he untied the tourniquet and retrieved a poultice and binding, along with a jar marked "erica", from his pack. Smearing the paste from the jar onto the poultice, he applied it to the wound and began binding it. The legionaries around him nodded in appreciation.

Finishing, Cervianus slumped back and dug around in his bag again, drawing out two more containers. "Here are asplenium and melia. Mix them in with a small amount of water at each meal and consume them. It will help catch anything that was left in the system and should repair any ill effects already caused."

The man grinned, wincing at the pain in his leg.

"Don't be too pleased. Remember you've got to march on that leg."

"I'll manage, mate. I'll manage."

Cervianus nodded encouragingly and stood, turning to walk back to his own unit. The man might make it, but the odds were against it. Not from the snake bite, of course. That had been dealt with quickly enough that it hadn't had time to set in and he was pretty sure he'd got all the venom out, but the man would weaken with the wound and would probably be unable to match the marching speed of his compatriots, whatever he thought now. Unless his friends helped him, he would gradually fall behind and neither Nasica nor Draco, nor any of the other centurions, would advocate a slower pace just to accommodate one man.

Sand vipers.

Only one of so many dangers in this damned land. He would

have to speak to Nasica and see what he could suggest. Where there was one of these creatures, there would be many more and, if not caught with extreme alacrity, the bite of one would simply be fatal.

The first real danger had presented itself.

The third evening brought new changes, challenges and dangers. As the sun began to sink, the two cohorts finally moved to the southern edge of the rocky terrain. Ahead, down below, a vast swathe of golden brown stretched out as far as the eye could see, undulating like the waves of the sea. Nothing broke the monotony of the landscape. Not a rock or bush dotted that forbidding terrain.

Nasica gave the order to make camp here in a depression between three of the larger mounds, each maybe a hundred feet in height, making the most of the cover before they moved out into the open, shifting sands. The campsite was well chosen, sheltered from the elements and with good watch sites on the three mounds that gave a view in every direction.

As had become the norm, one of the centurions selected the watch and handed out the password and the men erected their tents as tightly packed as they could in the flat space while those watchmen made their way up to the three hummocks.

The day had produced precious little in the way of combustible materials and, given the fact that a single light could have been seen for more than thirty miles across those sands below, Nasica decided to forego the watch fires. They could only have been kept burning for an hour or so with the sparse fuel anyway.

With the watch in position the men slumped and ate their

dry biscuit rations, supping their meagre water. There were few words spoken and Cervianus, as was his wont, moved among the tents, tending to the small wounds and blisters of the men, treating the sunburn and heatstroke that was becoming increasingly common.

And finally the sun's rays left the world, the watch now having to rely on the light of the crescent moon and myriad stars. The legionaries of the two cohorts moved into their tents subdued and early and nestled into their blankets, trying not to pay too much attention to the noises of the rocky desert, with its scavengers and predators, beyond the camp.

Cervianus lay on his back, staring up at the bare leather of the tent, listening to the breathing of the others who shared the accommodation. Ulyxes, Fuscus, Suro and Petrocorios he knew well, of course. The three who had been drafted in after Buhen to replace Evandros, Batronus and Vibius, on the other hand, had barely spoken yet. He'd heard their names, of course, in passing, but his own recall for petty things was considerably poorer than Ulyxes'.

The three men had marched, eaten and slept alongside them, but the atmosphere in the two cohorts was hardly conducive to social bonding at the moment. Cervianus sighed. Besides, the chances were that not all of the contubernium would even make it across the desert. Cultivating friendships just in time to watch them die a slow, dry and painful death seemed such wasted effort.

His mind wandered and he lay there contemplating the change in the attitude of the cohort in the past few weeks. With Evandros and Batronus, the ringleaders of his misery, gone, the influence against him had quickly dissipated to nothing and left a unit with camaraderie and cohesion, much as any normal contubernium. Even Petrocorios, who had never been his greatest fan, had proved to be a reasonable and pleasant enough fellow when he wasn't under the sour influence of the two departed thugs.

He frowned in the darkness. Perhaps it *would* be better to try and draw the three men more into their confidence? Certainly there might come a time when they would need them.

He lay in silence until he drifted off to sleep.

The dreams that assailed him were peculiar and, as he woke with a start, he called out the name of the crocodile god without being able to remember for the life of him why. Indeed, as he lay there in the darkness, wondering what time it was, even the sharpest, clearest images of his night-time imaginings faded into fuggy confusion.

He lay for some time silent and still, hoping to slip back into sleep unassailed by the vivid images, but the arms of Morpheus steadfastly refused to enfold him and he lay, shifting regularly on the uncomfortable ground, until finally he was so wide awake that sleep was beyond hope.

Finally, driven by a combination of the sheer boredom of lying awake in his blankets and the growing need to relieve himself, Cervianus shuffled out of his covers and rose, smoothing down his tunic and retrieving the cloak that formed part of his bedding. Stepping lightly over Ulyxes and the tall new recruit with the braided blond hair, he made his way to the tent's entrance and reached down to fasten his caligae.

The tents were getting closer together every night, if that were at all possible, and, as he lifted aside the flap and stepped out the front, Cervianus found himself staring directly at the flap of another contubernium's tent. Glancing left and right, he saw the leather edifices were so close that one could hardly move but to shuffle along the narrow alleyway onto which the two rows opened.

The air was cold enough for his breath to frost and the capsarius shivered, pulling his cloak tightly around him and wishing the Twenty Second had retained the Gaulish long-trousers known as braccae as part of their unit traditions.

Making his way along, he left the confines of the tightly packed tents with a breath of relief and strolled across to the designated "piss patch". No entrenching tools meant no purpose-constructed latrines. The answer was to designate areas that were far enough away from the tents to keep the worst reek at bay, and that sloped away from any habitation, just in case.

Carefully, not wanting to stray actually into the designated area and soak his boots, Cervianus wandered across the dusty ground, his teeth chattering involuntarily. The ridiculous extremes of temperature in this place were truly astounding.

Stopping where he hoped was right, he pulled up his tunic and opened the cloak enough to relieve himself, shivering again at the sudden waft of freezing cold air on his privates. A cloud of white breath stuttered from his lips and rose into the dark air. Fascinated by the sight, he let his pee fall where it may and raised his eyes to watch the cloud of steam rise. It twisted back upon itself, changing shape and billowing, despite the lack of a breeze, shining in the starlight against the dark shape of the nearest hummock and then the blackness of the star-studded sky.

He stopped. His bladder suddenly clenched.

Another, smaller burst of frosty breath escaped his mouth as he glanced back at the gently curved boundary between the hill and the night sky.

"That can't be right?" He kept his voice to a whisper as he addressed himself in a nervous tone.

Urination forgotten, he tucked himself away and lowered his tunic again, turning to look around the camp.

The other two hills that formed the boundary looked exactly the same:

Quiet...

Peaceful...

Empty!

With a lead weight in the pit of his stomach, Cervianus began to stride along the edge of the tented encampment. The wrongness of the situation insinuated itself as he broke into a jog and then a run.

No watchers.

No guards.

No movement.

No noise.

There was the gentle dull murmur of a camp at night, for certain. The sounds of snoring, coughing, farting and the low rumble of occasional, hushed conversation. A few of the men would be awake; in a camp of near a thousand men, it was inevitable. But with the outside temperature so unwelcoming, none of them would leave their tents unless they had to.

But that was all. The sound of his own breathing and of the men in the tents.

His worst fears proved to be wholly accurate as he reached the end of the tent lines at a run and came to an abrupt halt.

The animal-tethering area was empty.

Thirteen beasts of burden, all gone. As his mind reeled, he glanced to the side, to the small pen where their packs had been stored.

All gone, of course.

"To arms!"

He was already racing up the slope toward the low hill as he raised the alarm. Behind him, the camp erupted in activity as men emerged from their tents, blinking, their hands already grasping swords as their colleagues clambered out from their blankets.

The gritty sand slipped and crumbled under his boots as he ran, his leg muscles screaming at him as he reached the steeper reaches of the slope. It was only as he began to level out on the top of the mound that he realised he hadn't brought his sword with him. He was unarmed and unarmoured and, while trained as a legionary just like every other fighting man in the camp, he was tall and gangly and entirely unsuited to unarmed combat, as a number of unfair beatings had made clear over the years.

Slowing, realising the danger in which he'd placed himself, he crept up toward the crown of the peak, only rising to his full height as he took in the scene before him.

Eight bodies lay scattered around the top, their arms and armour still on them, their blankets and packs nearby.

Eight bodies.

But no heads.

Without paying too close attention to the grisly sight of the watchmen, he stepped past to get the best view he could from the hill.

There was no sign of movement out in the flat land below. He fancied he could make out a narrow trail disappearing off across the sands, though that might have been a figment of his overactive imagination, fuelled by what was occurring around him.

The swine had simply picked off the three watch units with apparent ease and without a sound. They had blithely walked into the Roman camp and stolen the animals and supplies. It was almost unbelievable. How had they managed all this without raising even a shout from someone?

The camp below was now in chaos and he turned to see that men had run up the other slopes, checking out the equally empty summits and undoubtedly finding the same grisly scenes.

Turning, he ran back down the slope, other soldiers hurtling toward him and stopping as they saw him descending.

"What's up?"

"Are they dead?"

"Did they kill anyone?"

Ignoring the questions of the others, he ran on, the soldiers turning and following on close. He made for the empty animal pen, a space that was open due to the lack of materials to form a fence, but where heavy rings had been driven into the rock to tether beasts in one small area. The rings shone mockingly in the moonlight.

Close by, next to the empty storage area, several officers were in deep discussion, while one more centurion and two optios were directing men into small patrols and sending them out from the camp. One of the officers was Nasica, as could be seen from the sheer bulk of the ox-like veteran commander.

The senior centurion looked up almost instinctively as Cervianus with his small entourage approached.

"You've been up there?"

"Yes, sir."

"Tell me."

Draco appeared from one of the tents and joined the other officers, his face grim.

"Sir," Cervianus reported, salute forgotten and the oversight ignored, "the contubernium up there was wiped out. Seems to have happened in a matter of moments. All eight men died without drawing a sword. Their heads were taken."

Nasica nodded. "I thought as much. No doubt the other hills will tell the same story. Perhaps they've been waiting for us to have a night with no fires to watch for them."

Draco shook his head. "I think they waited until we were not far from half way and were screwed whatever we did."

Nasica looked at him and frowned. Draco folded his arms.

"They took most of the food and water and all the animals. They've left us with a handful of supplies only. Even at a top-speed march we're still three or four days from Napata, but now we're also three days from Buhen. There's no point in turning back and we don't have enough water for the whole army in either direction. They've effectively all but destroyed our chances of making it across the desert."

Cervianus swallowed nervously. "I think I may have seen tracks leading out across the desert below."

One of the lower centurions slapped his fist into the palm of his hand. "If that's true, then we should pursue them. We can retrieve the animals and the water."

Nasica and Draco shared a look and the senior centurion turned to the third officer.

"We'll never catch them or find them. They know this country like the back of their hand and we're novices out here. Besides, in an hour winds will have come and gone and wiped the tracks clean. Then we'd be lost in the dunes somewhere.

No. We stay on course and drop to appropriate rations accordingly."

Draco cleared his throat. "It gets worse, sir. Looks like they got to one of the outlying tents."

"Really?" Nasica frowned. "This strikes me more as a raid calculated to allow us to die slowly, rather than a direct attack. Why would they risk tipping us off if they weren't prepared for a full fight?"

"Perhaps they simply saw an opportunity. But they didn't take these heads. I think they must have poisoned them or something."

Cervianus narrowed his eyes and cleared his own throat. "Respectfully, sir, could I see the bodies?"

Draco shrugged and pointed to the tent from which he had emerged a moment ago and where two legionaries stood by the entrance, ashen faced. Cervianus steeled himself, wondering whether he should go back for his bag, and strode across to the tent, nodding to the soldiers and stepping inside.

It took a moment for his eyes to adjust to the darkness within and he realised at an impatient breath behind him that the two senior centurions had followed him.

There were only seven forms inside.

"Seven men?" Cervianus mused quietly.

"Not every century is fully up to strength," Draco noted quietly. "What did the bastards do to them?"

Cervianus shook his head as he leaned toward the nearest body. Now his eyesight had adjusted, he could see at first glance that all seven bodies seemed to show the same symptoms. With a start, he shuffled backwards. Grabbing one of the bodies by the foot, he hurried backwards from the tent, dragging the dead legionary unceremoniously behind him.

"What are you doing?" demanded Nasica.

"Back up, sir. Get away from the tent."

The centurions did as they were bid, and the three men stepped out into the starlight, Cervianus still dragging the pale body in its green tunic.

"Explain yourself."

Cervianus dropped the body ten feet from the tent and began to examine it closely all over. Nasica and Draco looked down in a mix of worry and disapproval as other officers and men began to approach and crowd around.

The body was a waxy, pale colour, its lips blue and a froth of pink foam around the mouth, dried on to the skin. The eyes were wide open and staring blankly with terror up at the stars.

"*Soldier*," demanded Nasica impatiently, but Cervianus had found what he was looking for, a smug satisfaction at the speed of his diagnosis somewhat tempered by the unfortunate circumstances.

"Here, sir." He gestured to marks on the man's arm. There were three puffed up, raised areas, each with a black centre.

"What are we looking at, Cervianus?" urged Draco.

"Scorpion stings, sir. Remember I told you about the deathstalker scorpion? This sort of land is its natural habitat."

Nasica nodded, frowning.

"You also told us they were very rarely fatal in a healthy man."

Cervianus nodded. "One, yes, sir. This man was stung three times. Even a bull would have succumbed to that. Three in quick succession, and each one causes paralysis, so the man probably didn't even get to cry out as he woke up."

He tried not to imagine the terror of waking up to a pain

that had rendered you immobile and helpless, only in time to feel it happen twice more. The lurching of your system; the pain in every nerve; the heart failing. The sheer terror. He failed, going pale and stepping unconsciously a few paces further away from the victims' tent.

Draco waved his arm toward the structure. "But there are *seven* of them? That's a busy bloody scorpion!"

Cervianus shrugged. "It's said that they live in colonies. They're a surprisingly social creature." He became aware of the strange and sour look that comment drew from the officers. "I mean that they live together in a group. Those poor bastards pitched their tent on one. There's two big rocks in the corner near the doorway. That's probably it. There could have been a dozen or more of the things in there. That's why I backed out rather quickly."

Nasica stared. "This is not a good night. I'm glad we don't have an animal to sacrifice, 'cause I'd hate to see the auguries right now!"

Draco nodded. "What do we do, sir?"

The commander stood silent for a moment, his arms folded, tapping his lip. "We preserve water and strength. We march at night now without a stop. As soon as the sun starts to sink, we move off and we don't stop until it puts in an appearance in the morning. That should give us half a day at a time of solid marching. The men should need less water without the sun's heat, and the marching speed can be kept up a little more. We can camp down during the day and the watch will have a better idea of what's coming."

His gaze flickered up to that tent and back.

"Nothing we can do about snakes, scorpions or anything like that, but we'll do what we can. I'm damned if I'll let the tribune get to Napata first and have any cause to take issue with us."

Cervianus nodded. The decision was a sensible one, though he felt sure, privately, that the tribune would find fault with them anyway for one reason or another.

"Sound the muster and take down the tents," Nasica ordered. "We need to inform the men of the situation, and then we'll make use of tonight to get underway."

Cervianus looked down at the pale body beside him.

Thirty-one men dead in one night and without a sound or a fight.

Not for the first time, he wished he'd been slower in stopping that arrow at Buhen.

The night's journey was drawing to a close as the fourth day neared its dawn.

The column of silent, sullen and worried legionaries had traipsed for eight hours through the darkness, keeping up a remarkable turn of speed, given the terrain. The events of the previous night had sickened and angered the men and the desire to be as far away as possible from those rocks and their dangers, both two-legged and eight, had given enough impetus to the march that they had easily matched the strong speed of the first day.

But now, as golden fingers crept up over the eastern horizon, men were beginning to flag once more.

With the acknowledged presence of the dangerous snakes and scorpions, the legionaries had defaced their tunics and scarves, tearing strips from them to tuck into their sandal-boots, filling any gaps and protecting the bare flesh from stings and bites. The move had had the unsought but very welcome side effect of rendering the gritty sand less troublesome and preventing further blisters and sores.

Cervianus had heard that those units who fought with Caesar up in cold, wet Gaul had taken to wearing socks, or even the Gallic enclosed boots. He wondered how much more sensible it would have been to adopt those traditions in these conditions too.

The cohorts had stopped around two hours ago for a hard biscuit and a tiny sip of water – all that was permitted – but far from improving morale, the extremely restricted rations sent an extra wave of misery through the men.

A few of the more bureaucratic officers had begun to discipline their men for the destruction of their uniforms. Nasica and Draco, despite their reputations as the toughest and strictest of the officers in the Twenty Second, could plainly see the truth of their legionaries' complaints and were more sensible, counselling leniency among the centurionate for such minor infractions.

The land gradually changed colour underfoot from the dismal grey of the night-time desert to the brown and then the gold of the daytime.

There was a brief discussion at the head of the column, and the senior officers decided to continue on for a while yet, as long as the sun was still low and cool. Groans and moans arose from the legionaries as the column set off once more in the glow of the crimson sun that hovered, almost touching the eastern desert.

Cervianus found that his feet were beginning to feel heavier and heavier and wondered how long they might keep up this pace. If they could do so, and it may well be that Nasica was aiming for this, then they could even reach their destination and leave this awful desert within the next three days.

For the first time on this journey, a worrying thought occurred to him. Were the scouts truly as trustworthy as the officers apparently believed? They were locals of southern Aegyptus, after all. What if they felt more allegiance to the head-taking desert nomads than their Roman overlords? Were they leading the cohorts in the correct direction, or out into the open desert to die? Cervianus realised that he was starting to feel minor panic rising and forced himself to push it back down. If the scouts were going to betray them, they would have done it last night when the nomads came. He was being foolish.

"Look."

He turned at Ulyxes' voice and saw that the man was pointing upwards. Following his gesture, he spotted half a dozen large birds circling overhead.

"The vultures have started early," the shorter man said calmly.

Cervianus nodded, trying not to let the panic rise again. "They think men will die today. So do I."

Ulyxes laughed. "You morbid pillock."

One of the three new recruits, marching in the four-abreast line in front, looked over his shoulder. "He's right, though, Ulyxes. We'll lose men today."

"Piss off, Maros. You're as bad as he is."

The man shrugged and turned back.

The cohorts marched on across the endless sea of identical dunes, following some invisible trail that only the native scouts could identify. Already, before the sun rose, they had lost sight of the rocks behind them and now nothing could be seen in any direction except mile upon mile of forbidding, blistering sand.

Over an hour passed as the sun rose higher and higher, every inch adding to its scorching heat. Men began to sweat and groan. The mail shirts and pilum tips soon became too hot to touch and the march was constantly accompanied by the yelp of men who burned themselves on their own equipment.

Cervianus had decided to stop treating such minor burns yesterday, when he realised just what a dent such activity was making in his supplies. The capsarius of the Second cohort, an unimaginative little man with a lazy eye, was still treating them against Cervianus' advice. The man would be out of his more basic remedies before the desert march was over, let alone the campaign.

Finally, as the sun hit its most sweltering, the cornu at the head of the column rang out its call and the column came to a halt. Two more blasts and the cohorts shifted into parade ranks. Nasica, Draco and three other centurions stood at the front, along with the First cohort's chief signifer and the three scouts.

Cervianus looked the signifer up and down with a professional eye. The man was not well. The standard continually dipped and wove. Though he had discarded the lion skin he traditionally wore draped over his helmet and shoulders, the sheer extra weight of the heavy standard was almost bringing him to his knees. A quick glance cast around and Cervianus realised that the other standard bearers were all in a similar state, their burdens being that much heavier and hotter than those of the legionaries.

"Here we camp for the day," Nasica shouted out across the units. The men sagged with relief. "We will erect the tents in standard formation and set watch every ten paces around the perimeter in units of four. Eat your rations sparingly since, even if we make best time, we now have only just enough to see us through. As soon as the sun's worst heat is gone, we'll be moving on. Centurions to me."

The commander fell into quiet discussion with Draco, and the optios turned to their units while their centurions made their way out front.

"Sir?"

Nasica turned at the voice and spotted Cervianus with a raised arm. "Capsarius?"

Cervianus swallowed nervously. "Sir, the tents will be too hot for the men in this sun. They'll just cook."

"They'll survive," commented Draco darkly.

"But sir," he repeated, taking a deep breath and addressing the primus pilus directly, "the men are suffering with heat exhaustion. Confining them to enclosed leather tents will lead to illness and dehydration. You could lose dozens of men over the rest stop."

Nasica beckoned to him, and Cervianus strode out of the ranks to where the officers were gathering.

"Go on?"

"I'm just thinking, sir, that the tents could be used instead to fashion a sun shade. That would keep the heat off, but allow the breeze to circulate."

The commander nodded thoughtfully and turned to one of the other centurions. "Sensible. Make it happen."

Cervianus dithered for a moment.

"Anything else, soldier?"

A pause... probably long enough. Just another moment.

"Soldier?" Nasica repeated irritably.

Behind the officer, the First cohort's signifer collapsed in a heap and Cervianus was already rushing toward him. The senior centurions gave him a quick look but turned away. Insubordination came in varied levels, but small leeway had to be given in the circumstances. Nasica paid him no further attention as he crouched by the unconscious standard bearer, the gleaming pride of the unit lying, half buried, in the sand.

The man was suffering from heatstroke and while he was far from the first man to succumb on this journey, he was the first today, since the loss of the pack animals and the supplies. Cervianus reached for his canteen and tipped a few mouthfuls of water into the signifer's mouth. Turning, he bellowed back toward his unit.

"Ulyxes? Fuscus?"

The two men, who were busy unpacking leather tent flaps, gave a quick questioning glance to the optio for approval. The officer gave them a curt nod and they ran over, still carrying their burden. Cervianus looked up as they approached.

"Get that tent flap up here as a sunshade."

Ulyxes and Fuscus shared a glance, shrugged, and began to erect the temporary shelter so that the shade fell on the signifer.

One of the centurions nearby that Cervianus only knew by sight leaned toward him. "Don't waste water," he snapped.

Cervianus glanced up at him angrily. "He needs to be cooled as fast as possible, both inside and out. If not, he may well die, sir."

The officer, unable to find a suitable reply and unwilling to order anything that might cost the life of a standard bearer, turned away grumpily to pay attention to what was happening among the other commanders.

Cervianus tipped a little of the water over the signifer's maroon, sunburned face and, as soon as the shade had been erected, began to remove the man's mail shirt and tunic, allowing his skin access to the air beneath the shade.

"Give me a hand."

Ulyxes and Fuscus knelt and began helping strip the man down to his loincloth.

"Never thought I'd be trying to help a bloke get naked." Ulyxes grinned. "Women, yes, but not a bloke."

Fuscus sniggered. "Hope he's not dreaming of something good. I'd hate to get a surprise when we get his tunic off!"

The laughter drew the attention of several of the gathered centurions, who glowered at them but soon turned back to what was being discussed. Cervianus, satisfied his patient was now out of immediate danger, began rummaging in his bag for his salves, amagdalinum oil, lily root and Cypriot rosewax. The good-natured, slightly off-colour humour of his tent mates washed over him, but he found that, without intending to do so, his mind had wandered, his ears defocusing from the immediate scene and honing in on the nearby conversation of the officers.

"A crossroads?"

It was Draco's voice.

"Yes. Meet for nomad trail."

A scout.

"Back: Buhen. Down: Napata. Sunfall: Soleb. Sunrise: Evangliz."

Cervianus saw Nasica turn a befuddled expression on one of the others. A centurion who clearly had a good grasp of the topography spread his hands.

"We know about the Buhen to Napata trail. Apparently the

one that crosses it here runs from Soleb on the Nile to Limen Evangelis, an old Greek port city on the coast of the Persian Sea."

Nasica nodded thoughtfully. "We must be alert then. This place is not the empty barren place it appears. We could have company at any time. Possibly even company willing to share its water."

One of the other centurions cleared his throat and when he spoke, his voice was low. "Sir, the trail to the east goes to a trading port. We could have the cohorts back in civilisation and be heading by boat to Alexandria before you could—"

Nasica rounded on him, interrupting him mid-flow. "If you finish that sentence, I will have no choice but to charge you with insurrection, Cassius."

The silence that followed was mute witness to how many of the twelve centurions gathered there agreed with Cassius in the privacy of their heads.

Nasica's jaw set firm.

"We are Roman officers, bound by oath and honour to follow the directions of our commander. The next man who utters a breath of revolution I will break myself. Do you understand?"

There were muted nods. Nasica was the rock upon which the centurionate of the Twenty Second anchored their hopes and their pride. As long as the man stood in command, the legion would continue on its appointed task.

"I understand there are rumblings of protest among the men. It is natural for a soldier to complain of hardship. However, complaining is as far as I will allow it to go. I don't give a damn where the east and west trails go, we are bound for Napata to the south and until I receive word from the tribune that we are to turn about and head elsewhere, we will continue on course. Besides, it may very well be further to this port than it is to Napata."

The centurions lapsed into further discussions of plans and resources, and Cervianus turned his attention to his work again.

"That Cassius is right," Ulyxes muttered.

"Shut up," hissed Fuscus, beating Cervianus to it.

"You know I'm right. Nasica may be all noble and invincible, but that doesn't mean he's always right. Rome expects obedience, but it doesn't expect *blind* obedience! Vitalis has ordered his legion to their death, and Nasica's determined to make it happen."

"Will you keep your voice down," snapped Cervianus, sharing a glance with Fuscus.

Ulyxes nodded.

"Alright, but the time's coming when we're all going to have to make a decision between the eagle and our own lives, you mark my words."

Cervianus opened his mouth to reply, but a commotion interrupted him and drew his attention. The centurions had also halted mid-discussion and were looking back to the men, who were busy assembling their shelters.

A scuffle had broken out somewhere near the centre, and the sounds of violent fighting could be heard clearly over the worried silence of the rest of the men. Even as Cervianus and his friends stared, the fracas spread, violence erupting at the front of the assembled legionaries. An optio bellowed for order and was knocked clean from his feet with the pointed butt of a pilum thrust out from somewhere in the melee.

Leaving their now-stable patient in the shade, Cervianus

and his companions rose and paced back toward the rest of the men, while the centurions strode down toward the mess.

Perhaps twenty or thirty men in the forward centre of the massed soldiers had stopped constructing their shade and were engaged in merrily beating one another to a pulp. The optio lay unconscious with a broken nose some five paces from the fray; other optios ran toward the trouble.

"STAND TO!" bellowed Nasica as the centurions approached the lines.

The effect of that all too familiar voice was impressive. More than half the trouble stopped immediately, bleeding and bruised men coming to attention.

The slowing of the trouble gave the other optios space to work and three of them, accompanied by their more obedient men, marched into the centre of the crowd and pulled the combatants apart.

The centurions waited in a huddle for the last fighters to be dragged from each other, kicking and shouting.

"What is the meaning of this?" barked Nasica.

The silence across the army was so taut it felt as though it might snap at any moment.

"I will have an *answer*!" bellowed the primus pilus.

One of the optios in the centre, who had been instrumental in separating the combatants, turned and pushed the man he held forward, one arm still round the fighter's throat while the other forced his elbow up behind his back. Nodding at one of his men, he escorted the beaten man out to the front. His aide hauled another legionary out behind them.

"I believe these two started it, sir."

Nasica nodded.

"Speak!" he snapped at the two bruised and bloodied soldiers.

"He stole my waterskin, sir!" one of the men pleaded.

"No I pissing didn't!"

The two men started pulling at the arms that held them tight, trying to reach one another, anger and spittle on their faces.

"SILENCE!" roared the commander, and the two men stopped and went limp.

"Every man has a water ration. If you lose it that's your problem. If it's taken from you or there's a dispute, you bring it to the attention of your optio or centurion…"

The primus pilus's face took on a thunderous look that made even Cervianus, standing on the periphery and uninvolved, reel back.

"You do NOT start fighting among yourselves. Do you understand?"

The legionaries nodded, swallowing nervously.

"The rest of you get on with putting the shelter up. You two, come here!"

Narrowing his eyes, Draco, keen-sighted as ever, pointed at a man in the crowd wielding a pilum.

"And you!"

The optio and his man pushed the two somewhat reticent fighters out toward the centurions, while the pilum-wielding man marched out behind. Their arms suddenly released, the two bruised, blood-soaked men came to attention nervously. The third soldier saluted, slightly apart from them.

Nasica glanced at Draco and raised his eyebrows.

"He's the one," Draco replied confidently.

The primus pilus nodded and addressed the two bloody men.

"You two shame the entire legion. Every man here, including the officers, is short of water and food. We're all weary, but there is no excuse for your behaviour."

He turned to the optio.

"Take these men's rations of water and distribute them among the rest."

The two soldiers' faces fell, suddenly aware of what their hastiness had earned them.

"See if you can make it to Napata dry," Nasica snapped. "If you have friends, perhaps they'll give you some of theirs. Perhaps not. That's not our concern. Get back to your ranks and if I ever see your faces again outside a parade or a battle, you'll regret it."

The two men, a mix of hopelessness and, curiously, relief, turned and rushed back to their unit.

The man with the pilum stood alone now and the sudden realisation that he was surrounded by all of the senior officers sank in.

"You," Draco said in a quiet, almost lilting voice.

"Sir!"

"You had the audacity to hit an officer in the face with your weapon."

"No sir," the man said desperately. "It wasn't me, sir."

"Yes it was," Draco said quietly.

"Look sir. No blood, sir." The man held the butt of the weapon up to show a clean, if sand-covered tip.

Draco shook his head and looked to Nasica for approval. The primus pilus nodded once and Cervianus' centurion, known throughout the Twenty Second as a martinet and an unforgiving man, gestured to the optio, who stepped forward and wrenched the pilum from the man's grip.

"Take this man out two hundred paces from camp, point him east, and make sure he keeps walking until he's out of sight."

The optio saluted and, while the condemned man yelped in panic, still protesting his innocence, marched him out toward the edge of the rapidly assembling camp.

Cervianus watched, sickened, as the optio had two more legionaries join him in marching the man out into the desert.

Still, while it may seem cruel, there was a strong likelihood that the rest of them would be going the same way in the next few days.

With a last, wistful look out toward that indiscernible trail that led to the Ptolemaic seaport, he sighed and returned to the mass of men to prepare the noon meal.

II

DESERT

Despite the best intentions to keep up the pace and shorten the rest of the horrendous journey, the next night again saw a decline in the marching speed of the cohorts. Once the sun had descended toward the endless rippling sands, the officers had called the men to order to begin the march again, and the legionaries had assembled wearily with faces devoid of hope or humour.

An inventory carried out during the day's rest had driven the men further into despair as the rations proved to be far sparser than even initial estimates. At best there was enough water for two more days, with three days' journey left. Worse: given the decreasing pace and the inability of the men to keep to the scant rations they had been allocated, the chances were that the trek would extend to at least four days, while the water would run out some time tomorrow.

Even with Cervianus' suggested sun shade helping during the day, heatstroke had continued to manifest and, given the need to preserve water supplies, the officers had forbidden the capsarii the use of spare water for treating such illness.

The result was unpleasant.

As the cohorts began this morning's march, they left another twenty-some men at their makeshift camp, some buried beneath piles of sand that would do little to keep scavengers from finding and devouring them; others had been left alive, if barely so: conscious only on the most rudimentary level, the effects of the sun and their own boiling body temperatures driving them into fever and madness. One man had taken his own life while on watch, plunging his pugio into his chest and collapsing with a relieved sigh to the sand.

And so the men of the Twenty Second plodded on at a slow, painful pace across the endless grey sands and beneath the twinkling stars. Early in the night's journey, men had already begun discarding their pila, furca and helmets, some even going so far as to abandon their mail shirts to the shifting sands. If the officers saw such activity, they jumped on it, disciplining their men, but more often than not they saw nothing.

Cervianus, having left his own helmet somewhere in the first two miles, could quite sympathise. The weight of the armour and equipment made the march slow and difficult. During the prime of the day, the metal heated to untouchable levels, burning men when they were careless. During the night, it plunged to freezing temperatures, even so far as to become frost-coated.

A similar effect began to cost men early on. The first soldier to fall by the wayside was a legionary from the Second cohort, his body having lost so much strength that he began to suffer horrible knotting in his arm and leg muscles. He was unable to walk or even stand. Cervianus had examined him and been forced to conclude that without additional food, rest and water supplies, the man would only continue to weaken until he could no longer move at all.

He had seen the sympathy in the faces of the man's friends, and even Nasica, as he had given the command to move on, had seemed stricken. To lose men and comrades in battle was an expected factor of life in the army. To lose them on a march simply because their legs could no longer propel them was heart-wrenching.

The man had screamed and shouted to his friends as they turned and marched on, the cries tearing through the souls of every man as they left their colleague to die, alone and immobile in the desert.

Cervianus hardened himself. He had warned Nasica and Draco that this sort of thing would happen and yet, despite having spent the past two days expecting and preparing for this, he felt horribly responsible as he closed his ears to the wailing and traipsed on.

By the third hour of the night-time march, four men had fallen, two from the cramps and two from the awful effects that the alternating blistering heat and bone-chilling frost had on the system. One of the men fell in agony, his toes having become black and brittle, unable to march a step further.

The signifer in whom he had invested so much energy earlier collapsed twice, shaking and pale, a waxy sheen to his skin, but managed both times to pull himself back up and move on, one of his friends offering to shoulder the burden of the standard for a while. The signifer refused, the honour of his position and of the unit resting heavy in his arms. The friend had to make good on his offer, though, as the moon reached its zenith and the signifer fell for the third and final time, his eyes rolling up into his head.

More and more men collapsed as they travelled, the instances becoming so commonplace that in the end only the man's friends paused, desperately urging them to go on, fear and sympathy crowding their features. The officers no longer delayed and Cervianus and his counterpart from the other cohort no longer checked for reasons.

Men were dying of thirst, exhaustion and repeated shocks to the system. Others, the worst cases of all to watch, simply had not the strength to go on and gave up, collapsing to the sand and falling by the wayside, where they would slowly sink into unconscious misery and wait for the desert cats and vultures to descend and begin to tear them apart.

The sun rose on the fifth day to find a ragged column of desperate, hollow-looking men, part-armoured and dragging their feet through the interminable sands as though they wore lead boots.

Nasica called a halt in the lee of a long, sloping dune. The grey-gold incline displayed strange lines and ridges, almost like farming terraces, but which had been left by the winds. A small rocky hollow at the base held three scrubby, brown-green bushes and a gnarled tree, mute evidence of the existence of water at some level.

While the majority of the men went about wearily and hopelessly raising the sun shade, a party of twenty men were assigned to dig down at the bushes in the hope of bringing the elusive water to light, and the officers ran a headcount, the men calling off names to their optio's roster. No watch was to be set today. There seemed little point.

Cervianus and Ulyxes, assigned to the digging, listened with trepidation and growing sadness as the ominous silences in the roll call announced the names of the dead; silences that were all too frequent. Though he could only name the men of his own cohort and even then not more than half of them, Cervianus found himself each time, as the optio repeated the name in the hope that the man had merely misheard, remembering and muttering the rough time and the cause of the man's death. Almost a third of those mentioned by the optios of the First cohort he could remember, and the fact sickened him.

Next to him Ulyxes, who had retained his helmet, used it as a shovel to shift load after load of gritty, dark sand, occasionally feeling it bash off the roots of the ancient tree.

"Garbantes," Cervianus said bleakly. "Remember that one? His mates tried to drag him for a while, but his legs had just given up."

Ulyxes glanced across at him. "You're doing yourself no favours, Titus. Stop thinking about the ones we've lost and concentrate on the ones that are still answering."

Cervianus snorted. "It's as well to remember those we've lost. Bear in mind that some of those men ten miles back are still alive and awake, on their own, watching the birds circling and hearing the predators coming. I only hope they're dead by the time the scavengers start..."

He tailed off, but Ulyxes shook his head. "Every man has a knife, so no one needs to end like that. Stop brooding and be positive."

Cervianus stopped scooping the sand with his hands. "Be *positive*? Are you insane? What is there to be positive about?"

"The fact that we're both still alive and relatively healthy's a start, wouldn't you say? The fact that we're less than three days from Napata and the Nile if the scouts are accurate. We can still make it."

Cervianus snarled and turned back to his digging. "This is pointless. There might be water here but if there is, it's so far down we'll never find it. The bushes are dead and the tree's not in good shape. We could dig down fifty feet and still not find more than soggy sand."

Ulyxes shook his head again. "For the love of Damona, will you try not to be so bloody depressing?"

"Shut up and dig. The sooner we prove there's no water, the sooner we can go sit under the shade and not eat and drink."

Despite their best efforts and the ever-positive comments of Ulyxes, Cervianus proved to be correct. Whatever water there was here was too deep to excavate with mere hands and helmets. The dampness of the sand as they dug attested to the existence of the source of plant life, but there was just no real way to access it without major engineering. After an hour of ceaseless work by the small party, Draco pronounced the exercise a failure and pulled them away to rest.

The headcount came back and, though the officers were hardly advertising the losses, one of the men nearby overheard their conversation and like wildfire the news spread across the makeshift camp that sat sizzling under the rising sun.

The cohorts still being slightly under-strength, despite all Nasica's transfers, the number of men that had left Buhen counted eight hundred and eighty-two. The raid in the rocks and the scorpion attacks the other night had cost them thirty-one men, dropping the number to eight hundred and fifty-one. Twenty-four had been left at camp yesterday, and the roll call this morning had brought the number of men present to seven hundred and sixty-three.

Cervianus collapsed back and breathed out his unhappiness. Sixty-four men lay in the sand somewhere along the estimated twenty-five miles they had covered last night. Almost three men a mile, and among those two in every three would still be awake and contemplating the fate that faced them.

The mind boggled at the attrition rate. And it would only get worse. Another day of rations far below the healthy minimum, cases of fatal heatstroke and heat cramps, exhaustion and simple surrender to despair. Then in twelve hours another march into the darkness as the temperatures plummeted and frost formed on men's eyebrows and moustaches, their breath pluming white in the frigid moonlight.

Tomorrow would be worse. The casualty rate would likely double. That would be a hundred and thirty men, give or take. Following those estimates and allowing for two further days of travel at least before they neared their goal, the day after would see almost three hundred men fall.

Cervianus whistled though his teeth at the sheer magnitude of the folly that had set them on this path. They would be lucky if there were many more than three hundred of them alive two sunrises from now. And if their speed had slowed enough to mean an extra day? Well then not a single man would likely see the Nile again.

He sighed.

A few short weeks ago he had been clinging to the side of a ship, grinning like an excited child visiting a toy-maker. Alexandria with all its wonders had lain spread out before him, promising him marvels and delights. A chance to read in one of the remaining library buildings. A visit to the palace where the hated Antonius and his Ptolemaic consort had breathed their last. Possibly even the chance to climb the great Pharos lighthouse and gaze out over the Mare Nostrum. And all the wonders of Aegyptus that spread down the Nile.

And it had all led to this: lying beneath an inadequate sunshade with a rapidly diminishing doomed force of men as his life's blood gradually boiled and his sweat leeched every last ounce of strength from his muscles. Would it be tomorrow that he finally collapsed and fell to the sand? If it was, would he have the strength of character to take his pugio and cut his own throat before the cats came to tear out his innards or the vultures descended to peck his eyes?

He became aware that both Ulyxes and Fuscus were staring at him. The short, incorrigible legionary was grinning.

"What?"

"You are a pessimistic sod. Stop calculating the odds. I've already done it to the last man. Time to cheer up and start trying to think positive."

Cervianus rounded on him angrily. "Will you *stop* telling me to be positive? There's nothing to be positive *about*. If we prepare ourselves for the worst, nothing that's coming will shock or disappoint us. There's a more than good chance that we're all going to die out here."

Ulyxes' grin widened. "Then you won't need your cash."

"*What?*" Cervianus was genuinely baffled by the comment until Fuscus held up a pair of bone dice behind him.

"Come on. Lose what you can't spend anyway."

"If you remember I had my pay reduced anyway," grumbled the capsarius, turning over.

"I'll wager my water stash," wheedled the stocky, moustachioed man.

"Then you'd be even more stupid and die all the sooner."

Fuscus stared at Cervianus' back. "Leave him. We'll fleece some of the buggers from the Second cohort. They don't know about your creepy skill with numbers."

Cervianus felt the gap open up behind him and fill with depressing silence as the two men left to run their gambling game. He waited until they were gone and rolled onto his back, his blankets doing little to make the lumpy, gritty ground comfortable.

The leather tent flaps that formed the shelter above them left the air beneath stifling and warm. The sun was visible as a bright glow through part of the leather, already reaching high toward its apex. Men lay all around beneath the shelter, groaning and muttering in quiet, somewhat negative conversation. He could hear whispered, hopeless, yet fervent prayers being uttered to a number of powerful gods and goddesses.

None of the Aegyptian ones, though.

Interesting how some of the men still followed Taranis and Teutates and numerous other Gaulish deities brought to Galatia by their ancestors; others had adopted the Greek gods worshipped by the neighbouring states and kingdoms. Yet more had already begun to favour the Roman gods so invested in the legions, though this was a short and easy leap from the masters of Olympos. Some even worshipped Syrian, Phoenician or Armenian gods.

And yet no one seemed to have thought to devote their prayers to those gods who held court over the very land that was killing them. Of course, perhaps that was a good thing, given how the gods seemed to have abandoned the Twenty Second. The priest at Ambo had said that Sobek would not protect them here, nor would Horus be able to save them. Did that mean that they would also actively chastise them?

He shook his head irritably. Every week in this country dragged him further away from reason and deeper into the idiotic world of the superstitious. Gods had better things to do than play games with his life. Grumbling, he sat up, feeling suddenly light-headed with the movement. It was beginning, then.

The light-headedness came from too much sweating and not enough intake of water and food. He knew the signs; had seen them a dozen times or more on men now somewhere back amid the dunes, struggling to protect themselves with useless, wasted muscles from the circling predators.

Perhaps it would be tomorrow.

Still. Exercise would help a little. To sink into immobility would allow the cramps to get to work. Keeping himself supple and making sure he didn't seize up might mean the difference between death tomorrow and an extra day of misery. Carefully, steadying himself, he stood, swaying a little. Closer to the leather cover, the air around his head was like an oven, making it difficult to breathe. He felt panic closing in from the combination of light-headedness, shaky legs and the inability to take in a good, solid breath.

Forcing himself to stay calm, he strode to the edge of the shelter and peered out into the bright, golden world where the merciless disc of Ra fried the sand below to the extent that if he stood still and quiet, he was sure he could hear it sizzle.

Taking a shallow breath, since that was all there was to take, he stepped out from the shade and onto the sunlit sand. The stifling heat of the shelter was no better or worse than the conditions outside. As soon as he moved out of the shelter, the sun, high in the sky, began to pound his head and make his skin sizzle just like the sands. The heat of the ground reflected up at his legs made walking extremely unpleasant, while sinking into the roasting sand as he moved made the going difficult.

Still, he persevered.

For some reason, Ulyxes' boyish optimism had driven him to the very precipice of annoyance and threatened to push him over. He was aware deep down that his pessimism served little purpose other than to allow him to wallow in misery and self-pity, and someone deliberately trying to prevent that made it all the more necessary.

Despair was like that, he mused, as he wandered out into the sand, the heat battering his scalp. It became desirous – necessary, even. Once you crossed some hidden line, it stopped making you feel bad and became a security blanket, like a very personal friend. Misery was addictive. He stared out into the endless gold, wondering whether recognising his addiction would begin to break it.

No. He decided not.

Instead, he would spend some time alone, away from the distractions of the men sheltering together from the life-sapping rays of the sun. Taking another breath, he strode out across the sand, making his way not toward anything in particular, but rather away from the men of the two cohorts. It occurred to him that he could save himself a great deal of effort by simply walking out into the sands and lying down, waiting for death to take him. Would it be any better to spend a day or two marching in discomfort first?

Happy that his depression had taken a solid hold once more, he found a small dip in the sand, formed where a scattering of dark grey rocks had held the sand back. Staggering forward onto the slope, he shuffled down into the low bowl, losing sight of the world of men. Here, things were strangely quiet and comforting. Half a dozen rocks surrounded him and a circular horizon of gold framed a perfect blue sky, the sun itself hidden from sight in this dip.

He liked it here.

He might stay.

It would be a good place to wait for the end.

He leaned back on the sand and closed his eyes.

"Thought it was you."

Cervianus opened his eyes and blinked.

He'd drifted off.

Where was he again?

Tumbled, strange images of dark, shattered statues and animals with out-reaching paws began to fade instantly into the perfect circle of blue framed in gold.

And now also with a figure.

He squinted.

Petrocorios, with his flat nose and heavy jaw, black moustache and missing tooth, grinned down at him.

"What are *you* doing here?" Cervianus demanded irritably. He had almost gone. It had been so peaceful and pleasant.

"Saw you walking away. There's no guards, so I thought someone had best check on you. You alright? You look like you've been asleep for hours: all bleary, like. It's only been a few dozen heartbeats, you know?"

Cervianus nodded. "I was… I don't know. I think I was relaxed for the first time in weeks; since before we got to Syene. I was having a really peaceful dream, but I can't remember what it was about now." He stood and stretched. The light-headedness had gone and his muscles felt a little more rested. "Funny, though. I feel better. Just a couple of moments' sleep and I actually feel quite good. I'm surprised you came to find me, though."

His tent mate reached down a hand, offering to help him back up the slope. "I'm not your enemy, Cervianus. I think, in the circumstances, anything other than trying to help one another is petty to the point of dangerous, don't you?"

Cervianus smiled. "Let's get back to camp. I've not had my rations yet and Ulyxes was going to gamble his water. I'm feeling lucky."

He grasped Petrocorios' outstretched hand and pulled himself up and out into the bright sunlight. The pair paused and then turned, making their way back toward the camp and civilisation.

The sand slid and shifted under their boots as they left and it tumbled down the sides of one of the black rocks, revealing shapes. Etched long ago by a forgotten hand, the image of a falcon-headed man stood above glyphs carved in a language native to the desert and unknown even by the people of Aegyptus.

Horus watched them leave.

And on the horizon, a dark band began to rise.

Despite the bright sunlight, the intense, stifling heat beneath the leather shelter and the general feeling of hopelessness, men slept and slept well. It was in the nature of the Roman legionary to face death and get on with the task in hand professionally and without faltering. It mattered not that most of the men believed they would never see civilisation again; facing the struggle fresh after a solid sleep improved their chances.

Cervianus lay on his side, propped up on an elbow and watching with fascination, sleep evading him despite several attempts. Ulyxes sat opposite him with Fuscus and Petrocorios. The other two also sat in rapt enthralment, watching Ulyxes.

The stocky man, his brow furrowed in concentration and tongue protruding from the corner of his mouth, was drawing lines and markers with a stick on an area of sand that he had carefully smoothed out. Somehow it had not occurred to Cervianus that his friend's perfect recall could apply to such things as cartography. If only he'd been able to study a map before they began this journey, they would hardly have had any use for the scouts.

And the route map that was rapidly taking shape on the ground before him was a thing of beauty. The detail was astounding. Ulyxes had not only marked the major landmarks they had passed en route, but had actually drawn in the individual hummocks in the hilly grey land, carefully added every angle of course change, and noted each stopping point.

Fuscus whistled through his teeth.

Apparently Cervianus had been alone in his knowledge of Ulyxes' talent; the man had told no one else, perhaps believing they would shun him for his differences.

"That's amazing."

Ulyxes shrugged. "There's no skill in it. It's purely a matter of memory."

"Still…" Fuscus perused the makeshift map. "So can you work out how long there is to go?"

The cartographer shook his head.

"Sadly not. It's nice enough as a drawing, but piss all use otherwise. I've not seen a map, so I don't know how far the river or Napata are. I don't think even Nasica will have seen a map. We've been relying on native scouts."

Cervianus frowned. "But we can work it out." He sat up. "Can you remember how far Vitalis said the journey was?"

Ulyxes gave him a scathing look. "What do you *think*? Yes I can remember. He said..." the soldier frowned as he dug deep into his memory, "'Following the Nile along its great curve, the legion will have to march approximately four hundred miles to reach Napata.' Then he added: 'That track, though hard and forbidding, is a little over half the distance of the river route.'"

Cervianus nodded. "So if we take as a rough estimate four hundred miles for the other eight cohorts, it's a fair assumption that *this* journey would be around two hundred and fifty miles."

"I guess so."

"Well look at your map. You've marked the first night's spot clearly. I figure we moved thirty miles that first day, so we should be able to work out how many we've actually moved in total from that."

Ulyxes shook his head. "*Thirty-five* the first day. Draco announced when he believed we'd passed the thirty mark and we went on a while after. In fact, if you look..."

He started gesturing at points on the sandy map with his stick. "First day: thirty-five miles from the Nile near Buhen to this point. Second: twenty-five to here. Third: only twenty to this point, but then we started marching at night and we managed another thirty-five. So by the time we stopped that morning we'd totalled one hundred and fifteen miles. We only managed twenty-five yesterday from here to here."

Cervianus sighed and sagged.

"One hundred and forty then. Still around a hundred miles to go. That's further than I'd estimated even pessimistically."

"Three days at our best pace so far," agreed Ulyxes.

"The whole army will have fallen from exhaustion and thirst before then."

The four of them leaned back, staring despondently at the map, which clearly demonstrated the inability of the legion to reach their goal. It was only as they fell silent that they became aware of the commotion at the far end of the shelter. Voices were being raised in panic and men were leaping up, rousing their sleeping friends.

Ulyxes looked up. "What's going on?"

"Come on," Cervianus urged, grasping his medical bag tight, and the four men rose, stepping out to the edge of the shelter. Men were now rising everywhere and, despite Cervianus' extra height, he couldn't see past the mass of bodies to identify the source of the commotion.

"This way," Petrocorios gestured, striding out of the shelter and into the bright sunlight, trying to gain a view round the edge of the camp. The others followed him onto the golden sands and turned to the east, their mouths falling open in circles of horrified astonishment.

"What is *that*?" Fuscus breathed.

Despite the unmarred deep blue of the sky, the horizon had changed. When camp had been set, the eastern skyline had undulated gently, a gold and brown line against the azure. Not so, now. Somehow a distant, hazy mountain range seemed to have risen at the periphery.

"How…?"

But it wasn't mountains. The mass of purple-brown was moving, roiling like a heaving sea.

Billowing.

Rolling.

And approaching.

"What *is* it?" Fuscus repeated.

"I don't know, but I don't think I like the look of it."

"Magic," breathed Petrocorios.

"What?"

"Those head-hunting bastards. This is *their* land; *their* magic!"

Cervianus treated him to a scathing glance, despite the panic going on around them. "Don't be absurd. Whatever it is, it's something natural."

"Don't start denying the gods again, Cervianus. Remember last time? Vulcan and the parade ground?"

"Oh be quiet."

But even Cervianus, restating a natural origin for the wall of roiling purple despite his friends' fears, was beginning to feel nervous and slightly unsure. Beneath his feet he could feel a rumbling, and a quick glance showed that the sand was vibrating and shifting beneath his feet as though in response to thousands of marching feet. A low, menacing rumble was growing in power at the edge of their hearing.

"Sounds like cavalry charging," Fuscus said, his eyes wide.

"Magic," repeated Petrocorios, glancing nervously sidelong at Cervianus. "We used to keep you at arm's length for a reason!"

Ulyxes gave him a light punch in the arm. "This is nothing to do with Cervianus."

A small, lithe figure ducked out of the press of men and approached them. Suro, always the quietest and least assuming member of their contubernium, grasped Fuscus by the shoulders.

"It's a storm. The scouts are shouting in panic."

"*That's a storm?*"

They looked out again at the thing rolling across the landscape toward them. It seemed impossible but, now that he looked carefully, it was moving in the same way as winter squalls back home in Galatia, when they picked up discarded leaves and whirled them around.

But to an astounding degree.

"Sand and wind. That's all it is: sand and wind." He frowned. Why were the scouts so panicked over sand and wind?

"Whatever it is it sounds like a cavalry charge and I don't think I want to be in it," Suro replied. "The scouts dropped to the ground and started covering themselves with blankets. They seem to be pretty bloody scared of it."

Cervianus frowned. "They're hiding under covers?"

Suro nodded.

"Well, they're locals. They seem to know what to do. Let's get to it."

Without the need for further urging, Ulyxes, Petrocorios, Fuscus and Suro began helping him separate two of the leather tent sections from the shelter. In moments they had the two ten-foot by eight-foot leather panels freed.

Petrocorios tapped Cervianus on the shoulder. "Your little hiding place!"

"What?"

"Out there! Where you went earlier. We can get down in there and cover ourselves."

Blinking in surprise for a moment, Cervianus nodded. "Come on, then."

Briefly scanning the sand beyond the camp, trying to identify where it was he had previously hidden, he spotted the location and beckoned, heading out at a run, grasping one end of a leather panel.

As they pounded across the soft, gritty sand, covering the two hundred paces or so to the small dip he had discovered by accident, Cervianus turned to peer at the approaching storm. The roiling wall of sand was closing on them with an alarming speed, moving faster than any cavalry charge. His eyes widened at the sheer dimensions of the storm. Presenting one huge churning wall of grit, it reached as far as the eye could see to either side and must have been a hundred feet tall, filling the sky and blotting out the light.

The ground was now shaking and bucking beneath their feet and the rumbling noise grew to tremendous proportions. As they ran, Fuscus lost his footing when the sandy desert jumped beneath him, throwing him to one side. Suro paused for a moment to haul him back to his feet and they turned, glanced once at the approaching horror, and ran for dear life after Cervianus.

Correcting his path slightly, the capsarius saw the edge of the hole and, the noise and shaking all around him, the light beginning to dim, threw himself head first into it, ignoring the dangers of the rocks that held back the sand and formed the ditch.

Behind him, the other four men arrived at a run, each leaping into the dip, Cervianus howling with pain as they landed in a pile: a tangle of arms and legs, all on top of him. His cry was lost, however, in the deafening roar of the storm, now almost on top of them.

As Suro and Fuscus pulled the leather tent sections over the top and shuffled them around so that they effectively created a lid to the pit, the last thing they heard from the world of men was the screams and cries of pain and alarm from the camp, loud enough to be heard even over the tumult of the deadly sandstorm.

The world was small, dark and enclosed and smelled of sweat and fear. Cervianus struggled in the hot, fetid darkness, extricating himself from the tangle of bodies in the pit. The ground shook constantly, sand sliding down the slopes of the pit and half burying him so that he was continually forced to dig himself out and clamber on top.

Above him, he could hear and feel Suro and Fuscus supporting the makeshift leather roof with their strong backs, grunting and swearing at the weight and pressure bearing down on them, the supporting pillars of this tiny space that might well become their tomb.

The noise was intense and mind-numbing, sounding like the spirits of a million lemures, returned from the underworld to howl and taunt the living, backed by thunder reminiscent of a thousand hoof beats.

None of the five could say how long they remained there, crouched and folded, painfully tight and uncomfortable in the pit. It seemed like hours or even days as the terrible force raged overhead, destroying everything it could, scourging the desert clean. Cervianus had to admit that it was hard to believe it was nature and not the work of the gods as they endured, seemingly forever.

They also couldn't say how long it had been over before they realised as much. The noise had gone and the shaking of the ground gradually died away, the last few sand grains trickling down to Cervianus at the bottom.

"Is it over?" Fuscus sounded disbelieving.

"I think so. We should check."

With a great deal of effort, Suro and Fuscus heaved the leather covers to one side, the accumulated two-foot depth of sand above falling in on top of them in a choking cloud and coating the five men.

"Nice one," grumbled Petrocorios as they began to stretch and examine their surroundings. The stones that held back the sand and formed the dip were barely visible at all now under the extra coating of grit.

Strangely, the sky above was once more crystal-clear blue, unmarred and perfect.

"Does that seem odd to anyone else?"

The others mumbled their agreement with Ulyxes as the five men crawled up the side of the sandy pit, dragging the heavy leather tent segments behind them.

The empty sky reached from horizon to horizon, the only sign of the storm a distant band of purple far to the west, barely an inch high from this distance. The ground was clear and flat, all sign of their passage wiped clear by the howling gales.

Hearts in their mouths, they turned to the camp.

Or rather, to where the camp had been.

The devastation appeared almost complete. Of the shelter of leather tent sections there was no sign. Here and there men wandered as though lost. An optio stood in the centre of the wreckage, bellowing out names. The ground around the camp appeared to be rippled and undulating and, with a sickness that filled his stomach, Cervianus realised that each ripple or mound was a body beneath a heavy covering of sand.

"Shit!" Ulyxes exclaimed, echoing the thoughts of his companions.

"That's it," Fuscus sighed. "We all thought we were done for yesterday. This confirms it. We're well and truly screwed now."

Petrocorios nodded and glanced at Cervianus. "It may be nature to you, but to me that says the gods that abandoned Vitalis are trying to wipe us from their land."

Cervianus stared. It was a seductive point of view in spite of everything. "But look. We survived. All five of us. And others have, too. There may be more than you think."

Slowly and in disbelief, the five men approached the scene, taking in the sheer horror of what had happened around them. Men lay either fully covered or half buried in the sand and where their faces were visible, they displayed terror, their eyes wide and filled with detritus, their mouths open in an "O" of panic, sand wedged deep in their throats, their teeth abraded by the grit.

There was little sign of any of the equipment or arms and armour. Here and there, men struggled to their feet, coughing and gagging, spitting out dust and staggering with shaky legs.

"What in Hades?"

They turned at Fuscus' voice and followed his gaze.

A body they passed, half buried in sand, was burned black and red, sizzling, smoke rising from the flesh. The sand around its head reflected the perfect sky like glass. They stared at the bizarre and grisly spectacle.

"I suppose it was a flash in the storm."

"Jupiter clearly didn't like him!"

"A thunderbolt in the middle of that?"

"As though the rest isn't enough?"

They lapsed into a silence filled with the muted sounds of

men trying to piece together their lives, the gentle hiss of the burned corpse, and the plaintive call of the optio searching for his men.

Unbelievably, amid the chaos, the sound of a cornu rang out, calling a muster. Shaking their heads, the small group of survivors made for the musician, trying not to notice the innumerable dead around them.

Standing like a rock, fully armoured, though helmetless, as though the storm had raged around him but dared not touch him directly, was Nasica. His cornicen and a man carrying the gleaming standard stood nearby. Slowly, like the survivors of a battle, men staggered through the sands and converged on the senior centurion, shaking their heads at the madness of the situation. Nasica waited until several dozen men had reached him. Among them were three optios and two centurions.

"Right. You're going to split into three groups. Those on my left: go through the camp and find me every survivor, whether he's healthy or wounded. Those on my right: gather together every remaining piece of armour and every weapon you can. Locate every waterskin and pack of rations. Gather them all in one place and start to stockpile. The rest of you are on corpse duty. We can't build a pyre so you'll have to raise a mound over them."

The men, despondent and weary, went about their tasks without comment, grateful in the chaos to be given a purpose and have an attainable goal. Cervianus turned to join the scavenging party with the others, but Nasica singled him out.

"Capsarius? You and your friend come here."

Blinking, he and Ulyxes staggered across to the primus pilus, their tent mates giving them a curious look before heading off in search of the water supplies.

"Sir?"

"You'll need to set up a treatment centre. There are still a few tent sections you can use. Get some helpers and treat anything you can. I think you'll find that most of them are either as healthy as they'll get or plain dead and beyond hope, but you'll find a few." He gestured behind him with a thumb. "Draco for a start. Broken arm you can splint."

Glancing behind the primus pilus, Cervianus was surprised at how relieved he was to see the centurion. For all the man's harshness, the idea of facing the coming days without him was not a pleasant one. Draco gave him a stern look.

"What are you faffing for, Cervianus? Get your arse moving. There are men in more desperate need than me. And you, Ulyxes. Get the tent sheets together."

Ulyxes grinned. "Yessir."

Cervianus cleared his throat. "Sir?"

Nasica glanced at him. "Yes?"

"Can I ask what we're going to do? Ulyxes and I worked out our route and figure we're about a hundred miles yet from the river."

Nasica nodded, narrowing his eyes. "You two have some idea where we are?"

Ulyxes nodded. "Got a good mental map, sir."

"Once you're done with the wounded, come and see me. The scouts are either dead or scarpered, so I'm on the lookout for help."

"But sir, a *hundred miles*!"

Nasica nodded. "Once I have a headcount of healthy men, all the equipment together, and the dead tended to, we march."

"Sir?"

"We march for Napata and we don't stop until we're wading

in the Nile. No night's sleep. Just quarter-hour rests and food breaks as required. We can be there in just over a day if we move at full pace and don't stop."

Cervianus stared at the man. Clearly the primus pilus was mad, but the strange thing was: he found he was grinning. With men like Nasica and Draco leading them, could it be possible? Could they actually make it?

He laughed and saluted.

"Stop pissing about and get to work!" barked Draco, cradling his arm as he struggled to his feet.

The death toll of the sandstorm had been lower than initial fears. Once the men that had fled and found tiny areas of shelter in the same manner as Cervianus and his friends had been located and returned to the fold, and those buried by sand but still alive and breathing were excavated, the funerary mound that was raised covered two hundred and nine men. A horrifying figure for any time outside the most fraught of battles, for sure, but still better than they had all feared.

And so of the eight hundred and eighty-two men that had begun the dangerous march, five hundred and fifty-four men remained. Before they set off once again, the losses among the centurionate and the optios were assessed and Nasica reorganised the centuries from twelve seriously under-strength units to seven almost full ones, two of those commanded by optios field-promoted to the centurionate.

The greatest toll so far was to the signifers, weighed down so heavily by their extra burdens. One of the newly promoted centurions had advocated disassembling the standards and discarding the staff, dispersing the decorations among the men, but Nasica would hear nothing of it. They may be down by almost half their number, starving and thirsty and marching through endless wastes, but while there was a man left able to carry the weight, the standards of the cohorts and centuries would go on, gleaming in the sunlight.

It was perhaps miraculous that the entirety of Cervianus' contubernium had pulled through the storm intact, although Maros, one of the recent additions, seemed to be suffering from a deep, rattling cough that Cervianus suspected would become more complicated in time as the dust worked on him. A number of the men who had survived the storm were, to his trained ear, suffering with sand-filled lungs and living on an extremely limited lifespan.

Dead men walking.

Still, it was a tribute to the power and influence of Nasica and Draco that not only did the men begin to march on in good order, but the army's spirits were surprisingly high. They had survived, in most men's minds, every possible threat a land could throw at them, and yet here they were, closing on their goal.

Nasica's belief that they could make the river in one solid march with no sleep break was an infectious one. Moreover, with the loss of men, the stores of water they had managed to locate and preserve would stretch a great deal further. In fact, the survivors had not been on the luxury of only *half* rations since before the nomad raid, and welcomed the increase.

The column marched at a brisk pace under the watchful eye of Nasica and his officers, managing to maintain order even in the roasting temperature of the afternoon. Strangely, the horrible storm that had ravaged the army had made the simple tortuous heat of the desert sun seem feeble by comparison and complaints were few and quiet.

Within half an hour the scene of so much destruction was far behind and the mound of Roman dead out of sight and therefore out of mind for most. After a pause to take a swig of the precious rations when the sun began to sink toward the horizon, an enterprising man with a pleasant baritone began a traditional marching song for the Twenty Second, the musical tale of a merchant from Ephesus who was tricked into losing everything, but was then press-ganged by the army and found ways to wreak revenge on his tormentors.

But even with the slight increase in rations and the sheer unassailable authority of the commanders, morale could not stay so high for long. Complaints increased in number and volume as the sun sank beneath the western desert, turning the sand to blood and draining the life and colour from the world.

The night settled in with the usual bone-chilling cold. A brief pause to wrap cloaks and blankets around them and to adjust their equipment, settling their shields on their backs on a carrying strap, and the men marched on into the grey emptiness, their spirits failing and sinking with every cold step.

Men began to fall away by the side of the trail once more, the first collapsing, shivering and pale as the moon neared its zenith, but others following on soon after. A halt was called at some time during the infernal night for food, and the men tucked hungrily into the dry biscuit rations that were rapidly dwindling to nothing. By the time the first pale touches of dawn reached the eastern horizon, Cervianus had estimated the dead during the night at twelve. A horrible thing, for sure, but fewer than he'd expected.

As the great disc of Ra began its ascent, so the mood of the men continued to darken. The direction of the march took them up a long, slow incline, where the sand gave way to rocks and chunks of rounded, wind-smoothed stone. Looking ahead, the men could see the rise marching out in front seemingly endlessly and groans rippled through the force.

The rays of the partially visible early morning sun to the east cast long spears of light between the hills and hummocks of sand, much of the landscape still in the shade. It was a strange and eerie sight, even after days of witnessing it.

Cervianus, along with Ulyxes, marched near the front, close to Nasica, who occasionally paused to confer with the stocky legionary, drawing details from his phenomenal memory. The shape of a rock they had seen an hour before could be all-important as they passed by to be sure they were continuing on course.

The capsarius sighed and leaned close to his friend. "Just 'cause we're heading in the direction that we were before the storm, it doesn't mean that's the *right* way. The trail could turn and we'd never know without the scouts."

"We're heading almost due south. You can tell by the stars, so stop panicking."

"This isn't panic," Cervianus snapped. "This is despair. How do we know south is the right direction?"

"Kush is to the south," his friend replied calmly.

"Oh come on. That's idiotic. Ancyra is somewhere to the north, but the chances of hitting it by turning round and marching in a straight line are infinitesimally small!"

"Quiet!" barked Nasica, a dozen paces ahead and with the hearing of a hawk.

Cervianus fell gloomily silent.

Despite his earlier burst of optimism, the truth of the situation was beginning to settle in once more.

The words of the priest from Ambo continued to rattle around the inside of his skull as they had time and again since his "heroic" act at Abu, mocking the tribune's decision to march them south into the desert.

What was Vitalis thinking?

Of *course* pain and death awaited them in Kush. If they even *got* that far, that was. Haroeris had warned them not to go; had turned his back on them, just as Sobek had. Would the Roman gods help if the local ones couldn't? Would Taranis look after his good Galatian stock?

Cervianus bit irritably on his tongue. A month ago he would have laughed at people thinking like this, but the image of his dream way back at Thebes rose up in the fug of his thoughts and immediately pushed his derision aside: the gods of Aegyptus leaning toward him, reaching out in desperation; supplication. Thoth and Sobek and the great lion-headed warrior-goddess Sekhmet. Others behind them, too.

He frowned.

That was something that hadn't occurred to him before: the gods wanted something from him. Why would they turn away from him if they wanted something from him?

No.

The gods had turned their back on *Vitalis*, but they still wanted something from *Cervianus*. Perhaps things would become clearer in time. There would be—

He stopped as he almost walked into the back of the legionary in front. No call had gone up from the musician, but Nasica had his hand raised to halt the column in silence. In confusion, Cervianus' head whipped this way and that, trying to ascertain the reason for the sudden halt. And then he saw it.

They had reached the summit of the enormous rocky mound and the view in every direction was breathtaking, made all the more so by the early touches of dawn as streaks of gold made their way between the dunes of sand, crawling like probing fingers across the grey world.

It was not the awesome beauty of the land that caught their attention, though.

It was what lay to the south and west.

Their path had clearly diverged at some point from the scouts' trail, and they had not come out of the desert as planned, directly to the north of Napata. Below and ahead, the welcome sight of the Nile had been almost invisible in the night, lost in the endless grey until the first light of the sun caught it and picked it out like a shimmering silvery ribbon curving off to both sides.

The golden rays fell upon the water, twinkling and dancing on the ripples, making the green reeds at the bank glow with an other-worldly colour. The sight of the great, life-giving river was enough to silence each and every man and send half a thousand prayers of thanks up to the heavens.

They had emerged perhaps three or four miles north-east of the Kushite settlement for which they had been aiming, but were afforded a perfect campaign-planner's view from the hillside. Napata was a city in two parts. The sprawl of mud-brick housing of poor quality alongside occasional larger, higher-status buildings covered a wide area from the dust of the desert to the bank of the river, with no walls and no defences that they could see, ripe for invasion and looting.

But despite everything, it was neither the life-saving Nile nor the sign of civilisation that the town represented that drew their attention.

Napata was *more* than a city.

It was the religious centre for the Kushite world, and that importance was clearly indicated by the scale of the religious compound to the west. Some half a mile from the inhabited area, a walled enclosure surrounded whitewashed buildings of beautiful construction, reminiscent in many ways of the temples of Aegyptus with their pylons, hypostyle halls and enormous statues.

Forgetting the undefended and equally indefensible civil settlement entirely, and concentrating on the religious complex, their eyes scanned the fortified enclosure briefly before being drawn inexorably to the great mountain at its rear.

The breath caught in every throat as the men of the Twenty Second saw the enormous plateau of gold-red rock that towered over the complex, a large, powerful and impressive temple at its base, marching out from the base of the rock between the surrounding buildings, forming a monumental centre and clearly dominating the compound.

The light of the rising sun hit the brilliant white of the painted temple walls and lit both them and the great red bulk of the mountain to dazzling effect. It was simply beautiful.

Cervianus found himself instantly torn.

In the same way as he'd been desperate to see the great sights of Aegyptus that had been described by so many Greek travellers, he suddenly found that this place of which he'd heard nothing held as much fascination, if not more.

He didn't want to sack this place. He wanted to *explore* it; to drink in its beauty and breathtaking power. He wanted to wander among those temples and into the great complex at the base of the mountain. Had the gods of Aegyptus been pleading for him to come here? The Kushites worshipped them too, after all. Had they wanted him to do something here? To... what?

He shook his head.

To explore this place...

"Shouldn't be too much trouble," a voice said not far from his ear. He turned to see that Draco had come forward to consult with Nasica and the two centurions were carefully weighing up the complex and the civil settlement.

"Town's a waste of time. Has to be the religious compound if we want a defensible base. Wall's not much for what it is, but it's still enough to make a direct assault difficult and costly," Nasica replied. "Given the number of men we've lost getting here, I want to preserve as many as possible and I'm in no mood to besiege a wall."

Draco nodded professionally. "We'll have to do some planning, sir."

"Indeed. But not yet. Whatever we do, I think we'll have to do it at night, and the lads deserve a rest."

Draco nodded again. "The day down by the river, then?"

The primus pilus smiled. "I could use a wash myself."

With a nod, Draco returned to his position and the commander held up his hand and then dropped it in the signal to march. Suddenly excited and purposeful, the men fell into step readily and began the descent from the great rocky mound. The officers changed the angle of march once again so that the cohorts made their way down the eastern slope, quickly losing sight of their objective, and remaining hidden from the enemy.

The descent seemed to take forever as they moved down toward the lush valley of the Nile, though in truth the journey took a little less than an hour. Gradually, the rocky surface dissipated, leaving just gritty sand that stopped almost abruptly perhaps half a mile from the river itself.

Cervianus frowned as they moved from the endless, mind-numbing brown into the most welcome green of the Nile. Much like areas of the river valley away to the north in the civilised land of Aegyptus, this place was farmed. Strips of green plantation spoke of a settled culture. Somehow, given the descriptions from the Roman officers back in the north and from Shenti, of course, and most of all the memory of the screaming, bloodthirsty warriors they had faced at Abu Island and Buhen, he had expected the lands of the Kushites to be...

He wasn't sure what. But not to be green farmland, for certain. This was supposedly a warrior culture.

He sighed as the cohorts made their way between green fields and along the side of small irrigation canals. This place was, in truth, little different from Shenti's homeland. The cavalry decurion had accused the Kushites of stealing his culture. Had they done so to such an extent that they were barely distinguishable from their northern neighbours when you got right down to it?

Cervianus was beginning to feel distinctly uneasy about all of this. The realisation on the hilltop that this was a city of temples to the very gods that had taken such a personal interest in him had shaken him to the core. The realisation that they were about to assault that religious centre and turn it into a legion's campaign base sent a shiver of something up his spine.

But now, added to that the sudden realisation that, although they had warriors and dreams of conquest, these people also had farms and houses and all the ordinary things that ordinary people expected to have, and Cervianus suddenly felt cold.

For the first time, he realised what he was.

He was an invader.

Worse even than the Kushites. They had sacked southern Aegyptus and taken loot and slaves, yes. They had committed atrocities by any civilised standard, but these people were the poor cousins of that ancient kingdom to the north. These people had ruled Aegyptus for a hundred years and been ruled by the pharaohs in their turn. This was a land whose history and culture was intertwined with that of Aegyptus and had been for millennia. What happened between these two nations was tied up in thousands of years of mutual control and familiarity. The Twenty Second brought with it only the perspective of outsiders.

Rome was here and would not merely loot, but conquer. Rome would not take slaves as booty back to the north and leave them as Kush had; Rome was here to enslave the entire nation of Kush forever and to rape their lands.

Could that be what the gods were pleading with him for? Rome had already taken their northern lands, statues of Octavian being raised in places of import alongside the deities of that ancient kingdom; Isis being carved as a Roman matron. Were they pleading with Cervianus to save the one place that was still truly theirs from oblivion?

A conversation long forgotten suddenly reared in his mind. Sentius, the man wounded by the crocodile, had wondered back in Thebes at the future of the province; had foreseen Rome tearing down the great temples of Aegyptus and raising Roman ones in their place as they had in Galatia: pedimented, colonnaded houses for the gods, constructed according to a design common from Hispania to Syria and from Germania to... well, to Aegyptus if that was the case.

Despite the rising warmth of the morning, Cervianus shivered.

"Ulyxes?"

"Mmm?"

The pair closed ranks as they stomped on across the green toward the thirst-quenching river.

"I'm a little concerned about Napata."

"Don't be. It's got a big enough wall for sure, but Nasica's planning on going in quietly at night, I think, anyway."

Cervianus shook his head. "I don't mean concerned about *how* we'll take it." He lowered his voice and spoke through clenched teeth. "I mean concerned about whether we *should* take it!"

"What?"

The capsarius sighed. "This is a religious centre, a place of temples and priests. It's not like storming a fortress full of screaming warriors. This is desecration in its simplest form."

Ulyxes nodded thoughtfully. "Maybe. But I don't think the primus pilus is the kind of man to go angering gods, do you? It's quite possible to take Napata without damaging the temples."

"Perhaps."

Again, Nasica's hand went up in front to call the column to a halt.

"Alright, lads. We're going to stop here for the day. Make the most of the water. Drink, bathe and recover. As soon as you've slaked the worst of your thirst, I want details to tear up these reeds and start constructing a shelter before the sun rises too high. No point in us surviving a trek across the open desert for everyone to collapse from the heat right next to the river."

A ripple of low laughter spread throughout the men.

"Go. Enjoy yourselves. Watch for crocodiles and any locals. If you see anyone here not in Galatian green, bring him to me at sword point. I want you all reporting in half an hour to put shelters together and set the watch."

With a cheer, the five hundred and forty men of the desert cohorts ran to the water, heedless of any dangers, throwing themselves into the brown, silty torrent of the Nile, diving beneath the surface and then bursting through the rippling water like playful dolphins, spitting out jets like fountains.

Cervianus strode down to the riverbank alongside Ulyxes, who was busy struggling out of his mail shirt. "I can't believe we made it. And half a day sooner than we thought."

Ulyxes nodded. "I told you to try and be positive. Come on. Let's get soaked!"

III

ASSAULT ON NAPATA

Cervianus glanced to left and right as the muscles bunched in his calves. Ulyxes bore an expression of intense concentration, head lowered, looking for all the world as though he were about to take part in a race at Olympia. Fuscus simply looked bored.

The last reflected glow of the sun had left the rocks and dust and turned the world a uniform grey over an hour ago, but Nasica was patient and clever, leaving any movement until he'd had plenty of opportunity to study their objective.

There were guards at the Napata complex. That much had become clear during the afternoon reconnaissance when twenty men had removed their armour, wet their tunics and rolled in the dust and finally approached the holy compound crawling on their bellies, all but invisible from more than a hundred paces.

The guards were armed differently from the Kushites they had faced at Syene and Buhen. *They* had been barely armoured, if at all, and their arms were a random assortment of weapons.

Cervianus had come to suspect that those men had been the standard warrior caste of the kingdom, though he was rapidly reappraising the situation. It may well be that those they had faced up in Aegyptus were a rabble or conscript army left to maintain a border the Kushite queen knew she would lose. Certainly the men who patrolled the walls at Napata were of a different class altogether.

The soldiers of Napata, for these deserved a more civilised term than "warriors", wore clean white linen all over, including leggings and sleeved tops, though the torso was further covered with a mail shirt of a quality that clearly matched, if not surpassed, those of the legion. Their spears were long, with wide leaf-blades, the swords belted at their waists lengthy and straight, and the shields on their free arms made of animal hide and wood. These were clearly a well-trained and well-equipped force, fiercely loyal to the rulers of Napata.

The guards passed back and forth along the perimeter wall of the complex, not a strong defensive force, but keeping every area covered and leaving no gaps for approach, undoubtedly with many men in reserve. The walls themselves were stout and low, perhaps twenty feet tall and with a small parapet, but enough to present a solid obstacle to an under-strength force with no artillery or engineer support. It had taken only moments for Nasica to discount any assault on the wall or attempt to breach a gate.

That left the only approach that was not defended by the wall.

The great mountain that stood on the northern side of the compound with the impressive temple at its base was the only feasible stealthy way in. That would mean inevitably that patrols of Kushite guards would also stride across the plateau's surface, protecting their holy place, though likely they would be fewer than below, access by that route being so steep that only a madman would try it...

... or eighty madmen.

The mountain's façade that towered over the complex was rocky, jagged and, above all, precipitous, presenting a very challenging point of entry to the religious site below, but getting up to the mountain would be far easier than scaling the well-guarded walls while being stuck with spears from above. The northern slopes of the great hump, unlike the vertical face of the south, angled more gently down toward the desert. It would be a muscle-straining climb with a few steep places, but much safer in the long run.

Cervianus rolled his shoulders ready. Entirely unarmoured, and lacking his shield, he was equipped only with sword and pugio, his tunic and skin matted with dried mud and dust to make them less visible, the only difference between him and the others the medical bag slung on his back.

Ulyxes, however, had a sack tucked into his belt that swung with a heavy weight as he moved. No one seemed to have noticed the strange addition to his apparel, or at least no one had commented on it. The ways of the dangerously unpredictable Ulyxes made nothing he did a surprise. He'd not confided in Cervianus what the bag was, but to the capsarius it was perfectly clear. Five very expensive, very decorative and very stolen officers' pugios would weigh about that amount, and there was no way Ulyxes would leave the incriminating evidence back below to be pawed through by someone else.

Cervianus rolled his eyes. The man was clearly mad. He should have just discarded them somewhere back in the desert for ease and forgotten about them.

"Ready!" a deep voice uttered nearby.

A quick examination of the cohorts' men had led Nasica to the inescapable conclusion that, although his First century took pride of place in the legion, stocked with the prime fighters available, Draco's Second century seemed to be manned almost entirely by athletic men with wirier builds, much more suitable for this assault than the bear-shouldered killers of the First. And so the primus pilus had selected the Second for the dubious "honour" of the sneak assault, mixing in half a dozen of the less bulky men from his own century to bring up the numbers.

Draco's pride had swelled briefly until he realised that his splinted and bound arm would prevent him from actually leading the attack. With a stoic nod hiding his disappointment, he had backed down in place of his superior and taken command of the secondary force of the remaining nine centuries, leaving Cervianus and his contubernium under the direct command of the primus pilus.

Nasica had a totally different style of command to Draco, possibly because of his unique position as chief centurion of the entire legion. While Draco kept his eye on every move among his men and controlled each action, his soldiers played carefully like pieces in a game of latrunculi, Nasica seemed to give his men freedom and leeway, expecting them to know instinctively what to do and where to be.

Strangely, it appeared to work. The half-dozen men here who had served under Nasica throughout their time were in position or moving before he even gave the order. It was fascinating to watch. The bull-necked man with the massive fists and lantern jaw was the quintessential Roman centurion. Men like him were the backbone of the army that had won Rome half the world and would win the rest given the chance.

Behind him, someone must have seen the signal that the other centuries were in place, and Nasica's deep, gravelly voice spoke quietly.

"Go."

The Second century burst into animated life on the order of the commander and Cervianus ran without another glance to his side; he knew his companions were there and would keep pace with him. Three men to the right, he could almost feel the powerful and comforting presence of the primus pilus.

The pounding of the men's feet on the gravel was lost to him as the blood pumped in his ears, thudding around his head and matching the increase in his rate of breathing. In silence, apart from the drumming of footsteps, the century left the shelter of the curious rocks they had crouched behind and ran across the open dirt toward the lowest slopes of the mountain.

They had delayed long enough for Draco to lead the remaining centuries around in a wide arc and settle into hiding behind a few of the numerous funerary monuments that lay to the west of the city, a necropolis for the holy city and almost a mockery of those of Aegyptus.

These pyramids were fascinating to Cervianus. In the same way that the Kushites seemed to have absorbed the culture of Aegyptus in so many other ways, so they had adopted even their methods of dealing with death. The pyramids of Napata were far more numerous than those of Memphis, though much smaller and more vertiginous, as though they had been designed by men that had only seen the great tombs of the pharaohs from a distance and had misunderstood the scale.

Draco and his men would lurk there until they received three signals.

In a way, despite his adherence to the rational, Cervianus was quite grateful to be performing a dangerous assault rather that hiding in the dark among the houses of the dead. All too often these days he seemed to be prey to the unexplained and the downright creepy and that small forest of pointed mausolea promised nightmares.

He shivered as he ran.

It took three dozen heartbeats to cross the open ground from their cover and reach the shelter of the larger boulders at the base of the mountain. A low ridge of jagged rock spread from here to their left, where the sloping sand built up, creating a ramp to the next section of the ascent.

Cervianus dived into the shelter of the ridge, ducking out of sight of anyone at the top of the mountain. Ulyxes dropped to the sand next to him and Nasica, just beyond, began to use hand signals to pass out the next set of orders.

In addition to the gestures to split into two groups, one moving to each end of the ridge to begin the assault, he also mimed the presence of four guards on the next slope above the second ridge. Cervianus shook his head. The primus pilus must have the eyes of a hawk. He himself had kept his eyes locked on the mountain as they'd run across the open space, not down at the ground as most had, and the nearest figures *he'd* seen moving were on the very summit.

Barely pausing for breath, Nasica nodded to the men and then turned and made his way toward the sandy ramp. Briefly, Cervianus looked at Ulyxes questioningly. No one had explained how the two groups were going to be split. Nasica seemed to have assumed they would work it out and was already pushing for the second stage of the approach. Ulyxes shrugged and pointed after the primus pilus. For those used to Draco's regimented approach to command, this was hard to get used to.

Perhaps ten men reached the sandy slope ahead of the friends, scrambling with difficulty up the bank, their breath coming in gasps with the exertion. Cervianus, however, glanced at Ulyxes and pointed to the right-hand edge of the slope. Here, where the sand bank gave way to the low cliff, staggered chunks of rock jutted out, almost like high, wide steps, only partially submerged by the sand. It would certainly be easier going.

Ulyxes nodded and then looked up over Cervianus' shoulder. The capsarius turned and nearly jumped as he discovered Nasica immediately behind him, his approach so silent that Cervianus hadn't known he was anywhere near. The primus pilus nodded at them and then at the steps and, turning, made more arcane hand gestures to the others. The remaining men, now beginning the ascent at the lower end of the sandy ramp, began to angle toward them and the steps.

Without waiting for a further acknowledgement, Nasica made for the rocks, Cervianus and Ulyxes at his heels. While there were, undoubtedly, easier paths to the top of the mountain, there would be few this easy that were as well hidden from above. Clambering up from one rocky shelf to the next, the three men quickly climbed to the top of the first ridge, a gentle slope of perhaps forty feet separating them from the second.

Now, the primus pilus was all activity. No longer pausing to gather his men, he turned and gave a number of new hand signals to those who could decipher them and made straight for a narrow crevice in the second ridge.

This would be the first critical moment since they had crossed the open ground below unnoticed. Above these rocks, unseen by anyone other than Nasica, four guards patrolled. Cervianus and Ulyxes tore off up the slope after the centurion, the heavy bag at the shorter legionary's side swinging wildly and smacking into his leg as he ran. Cervianus was grateful that his own medical bag had a long enough strap to hang over his shoulder on his back, safe and out of the way.

Behind them, half a dozen more legionaries reached the top of the first ridge and scrambled silently up the slope toward them. Nasica ducked into the shadows of the crevice and peered up. A narrow defile ran at a steep gradient up through the rocks to the top of the second ridge.

The primus pilus turned to the two men with him and made a number of silent hand signals that looked for all the world to Cervianus to be an impression of a lopsided and possibly ill swallow in mid-flight. The centurion turned and pounded on up the slope, his enormous tree-trunk legs working like machines. He hadn't even broken a sweat.

Cervianus, salty perspiration pouring down his forehead in sheets, turned to Ulyxes and shrugged questioningly. Ulyxes grinned and gave him a wild, crazy-eyed look. The man clearly also had no idea what Nasica was expecting of them but, just as clearly, didn't care. Cervianus sighed. It had been a surprisingly long time since Ulyxes had punched anyone and a fracas was clearly long overdue.

Gritting his teeth, Cervianus watched as his friend turned and began to scramble up the slope behind Nasica and, taking a deep breath, he followed suit just as the first of the men behind them reached the entrance to the crevice.

The going was considerably harder here, where darkness added to the dangers and difficulties. More than once, Cervianus' footing went awry and his boot slipped, raining sand and gravel down below with a noise that sounded thunderously loud in the silence. Each time both Ulyxes and Nasica turned back and flashed angry glances at him, and he could almost hear the swearing and threats of the men below, spoken under their breath as their hair and eyes filled with falling dust.

He almost shouted out as Ulyxes, climbing a particularly steep section of the upper reach of the defile, stopped dead and the capsarius found himself face to face with his friend's backside, his nose all but wedged between the man's buttocks.

Wrenching his head to one side angrily, he peered past Ulyxes to try and identify the reason for the sudden halt. Nasica had come to a stop, watching intently and silently. Beyond him, Cervianus could just see a flash of white at the top: a guard passing the upper end of the crevice. After a moment, the white was gone.

A legionary appeared below Cervianus' heel and glared irritably at the man who had been showering him with grit for the last few moments. He made an unkind gesture that the capsarius judiciously ignored, and they all waited, tensely, watching Nasica. After sufficient time had passed, the primus pilus deemed it safe to move on, and the line of men began to climb again.

The world held its breath. All was silence, despite the effort being expended by each and every man. Quiet reigned high above the holy complex, a silence barely broken as the primus pilus paused, mere inches from the top of the defile, and drew the sword from his sheath with a gentle rasp. Ulyxes followed suit and Cervianus joined them, deeming the remaining ascent easy enough to manage with blade in hand. Below him, others waited yet, too much of a climb ahead to deal with while carrying a weapon. A quick series of hand signals came again from the primus pilus.

In aggravated confusion, Cervianus looked up to Ulyxes for help and his friend grinned, held up four fingers, and slowly drew his finger across his throat. Very helpful. Cervianus could have *guessed* that much; it was the fine details of planning that he was missing out on. He was trying to work out a way to get this across to his friend silently, when it became too late.

A flash of white appeared once more at the top of the crack, and this time Nasica leapt, using the rock he was on as a launch pad and hurtling up into the air on the next ledge. Ulyxes sprang up after him, and Cervianus clambered up the last few steps before bursting out onto the top of the second ridge.

The four guards had idiotically, though usefully for the attackers, stayed close together for company in the long, dull night, rather than spreading out to keep a wide watch as a Roman guard would. The result was their undoing.

Nasica was Mars incarnate as he went to work, and for the first time Cervianus appreciated how this man had survived so many brutal battles, facing an elephant charge without buckling, and why every time a battle ended the man seemed to be coated in blood from head to toe.

It all happened in a fraction of a second. Ulyxes ran for the white-clad guard off to their left, and Cervianus jumped to the right to contain the threat, but by the time they had even managed to plant their feet on the flattish rock at the top of the escarpment, Nasica had already dealt with one man and was onto the second.

It was sheer poetry of death. The primus pilus, his enormous, bulky frame belying his suppleness and agility, had managed to throw his arm around the first man's neck, covering his mouth, and then spin him bodily around with sheer strength until the man was face to face with the centurion, the officer's gladius busily ripping through his chest.

All in less than a heartbeat.

Nasica let go of the man, a splash of blood leaping from the guard's shredded chest cavity as he fell, and hit the second man full in the back, knocking him to the ground and kneeling on top of the prone guard as he drove the sword point into the man's spine between the shoulder blades. The guard may have had a fraction of a second to scream before he died, but any noise he made was spat into the sand beneath his face.

Silence was of the utmost importance this close to the top; that was clear to all concerned, without the need for Nasica's bird impressions. Any noise at this level would mean that all the patrols on the summit would converge on them and be ready.

Ulyxes' target managed only a gasp as the stocky man hit him low and at a run, powering into him from behind and knocking him flat. The man turned his face out of the dirt, spitting blood and sand to draw breath for a warning shout.

And his eyes glazed over.

Ulyxes withdrew his pugio and wiped the blade on the white linen, grinning.

Cervianus mentally kicked himself as he made his move simultaneously with the others. He had instinctively gone right and had, true to form, landed himself with the man furthest away, most prepared and, frankly, the biggest bastard of the bunch.

The white-garbed guard spun at the sound of the movement and saw the chaos and slaughter in the blink of an eye as the gangly, strange-looking northerner sprinted across the rock at him. He opened his mouth to call a warning to the men on the rocks above, but was silenced in sheer surprise as the Roman legionary flung his sword, the weapon spinning in the air and smacking the guard in the face with the flat of the blade.

He staggered.

Cervianus didn't stop. He'd disarmed himself and the blow was little more than a distraction, certainly not enough to cause real damage. All he had now was the element of surprise, a pugio at his belt and the medical bag slung round his shoulder and resting on his back.

He hit the man at a run and the pair went down into the dust, creating a small cloud that obscured the fight for a moment. As he'd run, the capsarius had whipped his scarf over his head and, even as they hit the ground together, he rammed the mud-coated green cloth into the man's mouth, muffling the shout for help.

Desperately, he reached for the dagger at his belt and was horrified to find that it had gone. Glancing down, he realised with shock that the enemy guard had drawn his own damn pugio in the kerfuffle while he was busy dealing with the scarf and was pulling back to stab him in the ribs with it.

Urgently, his hand shot out and grasped the guard's wrist, trying to hold it back. It was immediately clear that the Napatan was far, far stronger than him and, despite his best efforts to hold the dagger at bay, the man's hand was closing on him and it was only a matter of time before the blade plunged into his side. The guard was snarling something in his strange language through the bulk of the scarf that kept him muffled.

Suddenly the guard's other hand was at his throat. Desperately, Cervianus, his eyes rolling, tried to think of what to do. His sword was out of reach, his dagger in the hands of his enemy and inching toward his ribs, and the only other weapon he could think of was his surgical kit in the bag on his back, clearly irretrievable at this point. Desperately, he tried to headbutt the man, but the guard's grip on his throat made it impossible to move his head any closer.

Forcing all the strength he could muster into his left hand to keep the dagger away from his side, he started to see flashing lights in his head as the oxygen-depriving grip on his throat continued to tighten.

Relief was instant. The grip fell away from his neck just as the dagger-hand flopped loose. Cervianus heaved in a deep breath, then another and another, clutching his throat, and then finally reared back to stare at the body of the man beneath him.

One side of the head was matted already with hair and blood, the numerous puncture wounds from the hobnails on the underside of Ulyxes' boot making a pretty, if fatal, pattern.

A hand found his and helped him up.

"You *threw* your sword at him," his friend whispered with a wide grin.

"Didn't know what else to do to keep him quiet."

"You are a prat, you know that?"

They turned as Nasica hissed at them to be quiet. The remaining slope up to the top was considerably more gentle. From here the going was easy and quick. Further arcane hand signals went as over their heads as the previous ones, though a few of the legionaries emerging from the crevice behind them seemed to comprehend and spread out, gathering into individual contubernia as they shuffled into position on the top of the ridge.

Cervianus stepped back as his own tent mates finally joined them, and suddenly realised how near to the cliff edge he was. Though not a martyr to acrophobia, still the immense drop made his head spin as he realised how close he was, and he stepped away from it again with a breath of relief. He hadn't grasped from the journey up the defile just how high they'd climbed. They were now very near the summit. Just a gentle slope.

And more guards waiting on the top, roving the plateau in small groups.

Still, even if there were forty of them, there were eighty legionaries assembling now on the rock ready to rush them. It was distinctly possible, given how high they were, that any shouted warning on the top of the mountain would go unheard in the compound below, but there was always a possibility. Best to remain quiet if possible. Stealth would be difficult on the bare summit, but speed and efficiency would help do the job.

The order given quietly, each man drew both sword and dagger, arming himself as best he could, and began to move quietly yet speedily up the slope toward the mountain's top.

There proved to be fewer patrols than Nasica had anticipated. Ten contubernia of men scattered across the plateau like a fast-spreading disease, their tunics darkened, their skin somewhat muted by the sand and mud they had used for camouflage. The five four-man guard patrols on the top stood no chance, easily identifiable in gleaming white and totally unprepared for this sudden violent assault.

Legionaries ran and spread across the top, bringing silent and painful death to the defenders, who, though they fought like lions, were surprised and outnumbered. Only twice did a shout of alarm go up and both times it was silenced quickly and seemed to have gone unheard below. At least, no extra activity could be heard in the complex.

Better still, as the units began to converge on Nasica at the far end of the plateau, they seemed to have lost only nine men in the surprise attack. The soldiers of the Twenty Second Deiotariana reached the edge and looked down on their goal. Napata's holy centre lay spread out below them in all its glory.

Something made Cervianus shiver as he examined the great religious complex of the Kushites. "Something's wrong," he whispered to Ulyxes.

The shorter man looked across at him, his brow furrowed.

"Don't ask me what," the capsarius added. "There's just something about Napata. We're heading into deep shit here."

"And with no latrine tools." Ulyxes grinned at him.

Cervianus ignored him and looked down at the walled enclosure of temples and other large structures as that same shudder ran up his spine again.

The seventy-three legionaries and officers peered down from the holy mountain, some daring to get closer to the edge than others, until Nasica gave them a quiet but very firm command to step back and stay out of sight, in case the guards far below proved to be over-vigilant.

The ground fell away almost vertically, in a precipice of some hundred and fifty feet to the temple below, which was only partially visible due to an overhang. From here, the walls of the complex marched out to either side of the rock, encircling a collection of magnificent buildings that owed nothing to planning and design in the manner of a Roman or Greek settlement. Napata's religious compound had grown like a living thing, apparently from the great temple at its centre, spreading out gradually, other temples and palaces being constructed over the centuries until finally a forward-thinking ruler had decided to surround them with a perimeter wall.

Scattered around the compound were smaller temples, some in the local reddish-brown stone, others whitewashed and painted with bright colours, yet identifiable as religious edifices from the simple fact that they followed the form of those to the north in Aegyptus. Between them were three larger structures that put Cervianus in mind of villas and palaces, standing alone with tended gardens.

As they stepped back away from the awesome view, Cervianus leaned close to Ulyxes, who was scratching himself surreptitiously, believing no one was watching.

"There must be more than a dozen different temples down there."

"Sixteen," the shorter man replied. "And three of the big palaces. Plus I saw hints of temple fronts right below, almost underneath us, that we can't quite see yet."

They realised that Nasica was watching them with a disapproving face and fell obediently silent. The primus pilus turned his back to the complex below, stepped onto a low mound, and withdrew the pouch at his belt, opening it and withdrawing the flattest and most perfectly-crafted silver mirror Cervianus had ever seen. Four inches across and with rounded corners, the back was cast in a dull lead colour.

The men watched in fascination as the centurion withdrew a cloth and gave the unbelievably flat mirror a careful rub, removing any marks from its journey in the bag. Nasica suddenly became aware of the silence and the fact that the men who were not part of his own century were watching with interest.

"Signalling mirror. Not common issue and not held by the

quartermaster, but if you're ever put in charge of a dangerous patrol, I highly recommend purchasing a good one."

Replacing the cloth, Nasica peered out into the indigo world, identifying the strange, small pyramids that Draco had made for. After a long moment, he nodded to himself, happy that the other centuries were in place, and began to carefully angle the mirror. The moon lay not far from the horizon to the south-west and it was with ease that Nasica caught the beam in the silver surface and reflected it back down to the pyramids. Angling it away twice, he created a series of three flashes. A pause of a few breaths and then a repeat, and he was happy that the watching men below would have seen the signal. Turning, he nodded and replaced the mirror in his pouch.

"Alright, men," the senior centurion said quietly, as the legionaries gathered around him. "We're going to begin the descent. I don't want to hear any talking, whispering, panic or even praying. Silence all the way down. There won't be any guards on the roof of the temples and the chances of there being anyone out in the compound at this time are quite small, but the soldiers on the walls will be alert and this'll all be for nothing if even one of you screams. Any man puts this assault in jeopardy and I'll hunt him down through the mists of Hades to rip his balls off if I have to."

Grins opened up among the men and Nasica nodded again.

"Right. Once you start, keep at least one man's height apart. When you get down as far as the temple roof, go into a crouch and stay still until we're all there. Now go."

At the centurion's command the legionaries made their way out to the cliffs and peered down again, this time not with an eye for the slumbering complex below, but for the descent itself. There were clearly routes down, none of which, in Cervianus' opinion, a sane man would tackle without ropes. The shimmering silver rays lit the rock face, making any movement on it easier for the defenders to spot, but giving the legionaries at least a chance. Without that moonlight, any attempt to descend would be suicide.

The first third of the climb was feasible, the land angling out at almost forty-five degrees in a slope rather than a cliff, routes moving down along shelves and through crevices. Descent would be manageable anywhere along the top above the temple. Then, however, the slope became vertiginous, spurs and spires of rock giving them the only hope of a safe climb. What happened below *that* would remain unknown until they were two-thirds of the way down, due to the overhang that obscured the base of the cliff and the rear end of the temple.

For the first time, the men realised what they were really facing and began silently to question Nasica's decision to enter the compound by the mountain and not simply storm the walls.

"Shit," someone said under their breath as they leaned further out to peer at the lowest levels of the cliff. A man grasped his shoulder and hauled him back and they both turned to see Nasica glaring at them. They fell into an embarrassed silence. The primus pilus, ever a man to lead by example, walked calmly to the brink and, without even pausing to glance down, stepped over into the darkness, disappearing from sight.

The men of the Twenty Second moved to follow and Cervianus turned and stepped onto the slope, biting his lip in anticipation. The first few steps were nerve-wracking, hobnail boots, packed with shredded pieces of tunic since the desert, sliding on loose shale and finding grip only occasionally and with some difficulty.

A skid and a slide brought him to the first drop and he almost went over before righting himself with a wobble and peering down, his heart thumping somewhere in the back of his mouth. The drop he had slid to was only some three feet to another gravel-coated shelf, but beyond that all he could see from this angle was the flat, white roof of the temple far below.

Getting a grip on himself, he stepped back and carefully lowered himself over the edge and down the three feet to the next surface. Along the cliff, Fuscus was watching him and grinning. Cervianus was about to shoot across a scathing reply and then remembered Nasica's look at the last person who had spoken. He mouthed the words "piss off" at his tent mate and then shuffled forward to look for the next move.

All around him people were descending at different speeds, some sliding with apparently careless abandon toward the next set of rocks below them, others very methodically moving a step at a time and carefully planting their feet in safe spots. Nasica was already some ten feet below him, slipping out from a narrow gulley and stepping dangerously close to a precipitous drop before coming to an abrupt halt and changing tack on his continual death-defying descent.

Cervianus bit down hard and tried not to think of the unavoidable result of one full slip from this height. The next ledge led to much more of a drop, some ten or eleven feet, almost to where Nasica had just been. As he watched, another legionary from an unseen position to his right dropped through the void and landed on that narrow ledge lightly, raising a cloud of dust. Cervianus shook his head at the idiocy; that ledge was perhaps four and a half feet wide. Dropping the height of two men onto it was asking for a long, whistling plummet to a very wide, flat death.

He almost leapt as someone nudged him, and his head whipped round to see Petrocorios urging him on, waiting to follow.

Glaring angrily at the man and wishing he could speak in order to impart some acerbic wisdom, Cervianus turned and took a deep breath, willing the fluttering in his belly to cease and his heart to stop pounding like a racehorse at Ancyra's hippodrome.

His eyes closed involuntarily as he dropped the ten or more feet to the ledge, but his fears seemed unfounded as he landed safe and stable, raising a small cloud of dust. He had barely moved on, following the route that Nasica had taken, when first Petrocorios and then a man he didn't recognise dropped to the ledge behind him.

The next hundred heartbeats saw him carefully and nervously negotiating the steep, winding route along which Nasica had blazed a trail, his tent mate close behind. It seemed as though every third step the capsarius took caused him to stumble or slide, bringing him dangerously close to a fall.

He had not realised, until he looked around at the other men, just how supple and strong they appeared to be, even Ulyxes, his speed and care belying his stocky frame as he descended like a lizard on a stone wall and with apparently as much concern. Nasica had chosen his men well and it was difficult not to feel a strong surge of pride in the Second century. At least, it was difficult until he slipped again, his clumsy step clearly labelling him the least stealthy member of this assault.

A glance both up and down told him that he must have come the first fifty feet or more, a fact confirmed as he reached what appeared to be a terrifying overhang, though in truth not more than a few feet.

Here, at last, he was afforded an uninterrupted and clear view of the temple below. And here, for the first time, he realised that the main temple did not, in fact, meet flush with the cliff, but backed into a rocky slope below that connected the two. Other much smaller temples along to the west seemed to be actually partially carved from the great mountain, but the large central one stood apart, some fifty feet from the mass of solid rock, partially embedded in the scree slope. He smiled. That meant that the next forty feet or so was the only truly dangerous section, after which the legionaries would reach the slope into which the temple backed and could use it as a ramp to descend to the roof or the ground.

Perhaps twenty feet below him, Nasica seemed also to be reassessing the situation and paused, wedged into a crack, to withdraw his signalling mirror. With a moment's calculation, he shuffled round so that the pyramids were just in view around the rock's edge and flashed out the next signal to Draco. Cervianus could picture the men already in position below the ancient tombs, ready to move on the third.

Returning his attention to his current predicament, the capsarius glanced left and right until he located a small channel worn through the ledge. Another deep breath and he began to shimmy down it, using his hands to grip the knobbly rock desperately any time his feet failed to find instant purchase.

Infinitesimally slowly, he made his way down the channel, past the horrifying overhang, glancing across once, irritably, to see one of the others nonchalantly vaulting over the edge, swinging by one hand into the rock face beneath where he managed to find a solid handhold.

Some people were show-offs, pure and simple.

Trying not to lose his footing, Cervianus began to work

his way down a zigzag of cracks and jutting chunks of rock, gradually nearing the gentle slope below.

His heart leapt when he heard a stifled gasp of shock as a man ten feet above him lost his grip and plummeted through the air, falling forty feet before he hit the rocky incline. It was a testament to both the man's incredible endurance and Nasica's influence that, as he hit, he managed to bite down on the scream and limit himself to low sobs. Cervianus had heard the leg snap from here.

Slowly, carefully and with a great deal of probing, the men of the Second century negotiated the final stage of the climb and dropped with relief to the slope. Cervianus, his heart leaping with joy as his feet touched the sloping, unsettled ground, immediately rushed over to the pale, agonised man lying on the slope.

The leg was beyond hope; he could see that even on early approach, as the glimmering white of bone protruded from the mangled leg. The man would never walk on that limb again.

The capsarius almost jumped out of his skin as Ulyxes tapped him on the shoulder.

'What?' he mouthed silently at his friend.

Ulyxes pointed at the medical bag and shook his head sadly. Cervianus frowned for a moment and then, realising what his friend was trying to say, shook his own head vigorously, crouching and rummaging in his pack. Suddenly his hands were being grasped and held. He looked up in surprise at Ulyxes, but the shorter man held his arms in place, still shaking his head.

Cervianus turned to look at the badly wounded legionary. For certain his leg was gone, and there were likely other breaks and maybe even life-threatening injuries, but he couldn't countenance the death of a man when he could still save the life.

Desperately he tried to extricate himself from Ulyxes' hold, but the stocky man had a grip of iron. Helplessly, the capsarius watched as Nasica strode across to the soldier and crouched next to him. The primus pilus leaned down close and whispered something into the man's ear. The pale, shocked legionary heaved a deep breath, shook, and finally nodded, all hope fleeing his eyes.

The huge centurion stood, walked around behind the man, who pulled himself up into a seated position, gritting his teeth against the agony of movement. Nasica reached out and put one hand on the man's chin and the other behind his head. Cervianus looked away and winced as he heard the snap. Military expediency. He'd heard it labelled such before but, regardless, it never sat well with him.

By the time Ulyxes had loosened his grip and helped the capsarius to his feet, the entire assault force had assembled on the rocky slope. Still no alarm had been raised and Cervianus had to admit that the fact that only one man had lost his life in the descent was nothing short of miraculous.

Ulyxes smiled sadly at him and leaned close enough to whisper in his ear. "Seems like the gods are with us after all."

Cervianus nodded, trying not to look at the legionary lying on the ground with a leg jutting out at almost as unnatural an angle as his head.

But why? That was the question that swam around his head seeking an answer. If the gods had not wanted the legion to march into Kush, why were they helping now, if indeed that was what they *were* doing and it wasn't all just a case of blind luck?

It was hard not to apply a notion of some sort of divine support, though, given the fact that they had faced a deadly trek across the desert and lived and that now, with only ten men gone, they had infiltrated the holy city's temple complex. He realised suddenly that his mind was wandering and Ulyxes was gesturing to him to pay attention. Glancing around, he realised that Nasica was giving orders once more with his system of arcane hand signals.

Turning, the primus pilus already had his signalling mirror out and was flashing a message toward the pyramids in sharp movements. At this height it was dangerous, the tombs behind which Draco's force waited only just visible over the perimeter wall. Should one guard be looking toward them from that direction now, he might see the signal and raise the alarm.

Nasica pointed toward the west gate of the compound's wall and held up four fingers, each apparently representing a contubernium. Four more were directed down to the dusty streets to hold back any reinforcements sent from the east end of the complex. The remaining two, he pointed to the temple below.

For a moment, Cervianus dithered, caught somewhere between the groups and unsure where to go, but Ulyxes and Petrocorios appeared beside him, grasped his shoulders and turned him toward the temple. The last thing he saw, glancing out toward the pyramids as Nasica replaced his mirror, was a mass of small, dark shadows rushing across the grey sand from the pyramid tombs toward the walls.

This was it.

It had begun.

★ ★ ★

Perfect silent order turned to chaos in the blink of an eye.

Perhaps the gods were not with them after all.

Despite the care, stealth and astounding success of the assault, the entire thing came crashing down around their ears as a man, middle-aged and naked to the waist, shuffled out of the doorway of one of the smaller ancillary buildings in the thoroughfare that led from the great temple down toward the western gate. He had stepped out into the night and, shivering and yawning, turned to see almost thirty spectres in mud, armed with glinting swords, racing down the street toward him, an ox-like man at the head of the group.

He screamed in a surprisingly feminine voice and the alarm went up.

Nasica and his four contubernia had only managed a hundred paces from the temple as the trouble began. Cervianus and the other twelve men with him were stepping quietly across the roof of the great temple toward the open hypostyle hall at the front, while the other men were spreading out into the dusty ground of the compound and taking up a defensive position.

Nasica and his men ploughed on past the man, sacrificing stealth for speed, knocking him aside and not even stopping to deal with him. Their priority was now to get that gate open for Draco and the rest of the cohorts as soon as possible.

Cervianus watched nervously as the men charged on toward the gate, the white-clad guards on the walls converging on the structure for which they were aiming. Within moments a call was being sounded: some huge animal horn by the sound of it, deep and reminiscent of a wounded ox. Men started to appear from the various ancillary buildings, mostly in a state of undress and unarmed, but other guards were starting to put in an appearance from the eastern side of the compound, where a barracks must have been situated.

The capsarius's head snapped back and forth, watching the legionaries and the centurion reacting with professional calm in the sudden bedlam. A hand on his shoulder drew his attention and he turned to see Ulyxes pointing at the courtyard below. Each unit, each man, even, had his task in this assault and it was no good wasting time on monitoring other actions. A man simply had to trust that his fellow soldiers could achieve their objectives while he focused on his own goal.

The great temple at the centre of the complex was of a very familiar design and, as they peered down into the forecourt of the outer hall, Cervianus nodded to himself, mentally picturing the rest of the structure beneath the dusty white roof.

Fuscus, examining the colonnaded walkway around the edge, sighed. "Wish we had native scouts now," he whispered.

"It's a simple Aegyptian design," Cervianus replied, so low as to be almost inaudible.

"What?"

"Most of their temples follow a fairly standard design. I've been in quite a few now."

Fuscus smiled. "That puts you in charge, then. Lead on, Centurion Doom."

Ulyxes grinned and Cervianus considered arguing for a moment, but the simple fact was that he had the best shot at directing them through the temple.

"Alright. There's two ways out of the courtyard," he whispered, grateful now that Nasica wasn't here with his rule of silence and arcane signals. He glanced once up and over the edge of the roof. Bellowed shouts were audible over by the gate some seven hundred paces away, though no sounds of fighting yet. Noises were beginning to erupt across the compound, but it was now time to ignore all that and concentrate on their own plan.

"The outer pylon won't have a door. Despite the sphinx avenue, there's a good field of view from there. I'd say three or four men need to hold that gate in case guards reach the place. We don't want to have to fight our way out too."

Fuscus frowned. "What in Juno's name is a 'pylon'?"

"A gate, Fuscus, for Taranis' sake. From the Greek."

The wiry legionary shook his head in exasperation and turned, pointing at Petrocorios and three others and then gesturing to the great outer pylon. "You four hold the outer gate."

Cervianus closed his eyes, picturing the rest of the structure. "The other exit might have a door, or it might not. It'll lead to another court like this one, but roofed and possibly dark. There might be some sort of religious structure in the middle, but most of it will be columns. Beyond that might be a similar room. If there is one, it'll be a lot smaller, but they might not have added a third hypostyle…"

Fuscus furrowed his brow irritably. "I thought you said you knew these?"

"There might be differences. These are Kushite buildings, after all, not Aegyptian. Besides, even the Aegyptian ones are not all quite the same, despite similarities." Cervianus frowned. "The complicated part starts after that third hall, where there's sanctuaries, offering rooms and all sorts of other little places. A lot of it only priests are allowed in, so we'll have to play that very much by ear."

Fuscus nodded. "Shouldn't be anyone here but priests anyway, surely?"

"Hopefully. Let's go."

Wordlessly, ignoring the chaos that reigned across the complex as solid fighting erupted at the west gate and the men in the streets began to bar access to the guard reserves that were trying to cross the city and become involved in this sudden threat, the thirteen men on the roof scrambled over the edge and hung out into space before dropping the twenty feet into the open courtyard as carefully and quietly as they could.

Like the great temples of the northern Nile, this large colonnaded courtyard was surrounded by intricately designed, painted columns, their colours showing strange in the silvery moonlight, the walls hidden in the shadow behind, displaying carvings of warriors and gods interspersed with the writing of the Aegyptians.

The great pylon gate was almost twenty feet across, opening out onto a view of a sphinx avenue with the various temples and ancillary structures of the complex beyond. In the distance tiny figures moved between the buildings, though it was impossible at this distance to say whether they were Roman or Kushite. Either way, things were happening in the streets.

"What are those doorways?" Petrocorios frowned, pointing to small, squat entrances in the corners of the outer wall.

"They probably lead up to the top of the pylon."

The legionary frowned. Grabbing the other three, he ran toward the pylon and, as they crossed the open court, two men veered off to check out these additional passageways and clear them. The remaining nine legionaries watched as their two companions settled into the darkness to either side of the gateway, watching the open ground outside for potential attackers.

Turning, Cervianus pointed at the doorway to the far side,

toward the great rock. It was perhaps eight or ten feet across and a little higher, the interior dark and menacing.

"Come on."

Swords and daggers out, the capsarius and his eight companions ran through the lines of pillars and into the shadows of the inner doorway where they stopped, leaning against the carved stonework and heaving in breaths while the two friends, at the head of the assault, peered into the darkness.

"All clear." Ulyxes nodded.

He had already begun to move into the dark room, the others close at heel, when Cervianus realised what he had sensed that held him back. The room was dark and silent, but there was a smell of burning pitch and oil.

"Ulyxes… wait!"

As he ducked into the room in a low panic, the torches and lamps that had so recently been doused, creating the heady odour, were reignited. The nine soldiers of Rome skidded to a halt in the centre of a confusing forest of columns as the sudden, blinding light of flickering orange flames danced among the pillars and picked out the images of gods and men on the walls and columns.

The legionaries were not alone. Nor were the occupants of this inner court any kind of priest. Two dozen figures in grey robes stood around the edge in menacing silence, hoods covering their heads and adding to the other-worldly eeriness of the situation. Cervianus' mind reeled. What was going on? Who were these—

And then everything fell into place.

The grey-robed figures Shenti had told him about. Those folk of Aegyptus that believed the world was coming to an end because Rome had arrived and the pharaohs had gone. Had he not been armed in both hands, Cervianus would have slapped his forehead. Where else would they go, these men who held tight to the ancient gods of their land? As Rome settled into the lands of their forefathers, so they had come south into Kush to find the only place their gods were free of the invaders.

With a moment of clarity, Cervianus realised what they had done. Pharaoh had gone and left a hole in their pantheon, but the warrior kings and queens of Kush had once been the rulers of Aegyptus. Their bloodlines held that of the pharaohs. As Rome had annexed Aegyptus and Cleopatra VII, last of the pharaohs, had died, gurgling and thrashing in a palace in Alexandria, these people had made an obvious change in allegiance to the Kandake of Kush.

"Shit."

The legionaries, realising they were surrounded, began to back toward the entrance, pulling together into a tight group. Cervianus turned, but three of the grey figures had already blocked off the door behind him.

"Who are these people?" Ulyxes asked.

"Fanatics. Roman-haters and religious nuts."

"Oh, bloody wonderful," grumbled another man.

Ulyxes shrugged. "Come on lads... get stuck in!"

Without waiting, he turned and launched himself at one of the grey figures who had made the mistake of stepping out in front of the others.

The nature of the fanatics became apparent in that sudden moment of action. Some of them might be priests after all, their shaved heads and painted eyes glowing in the torchlight as their hoods fell away. Some were probably ordinary townsfolk and villagers. They certainly *looked* ordinary. But a few among the crowd, as they let their hoods fall back, raised their hands from beneath their robes and brought forth swords.

Even as Ulyxes plunged his gladius into the unprotected chest of a grey-robed man who didn't have time to throw back his hood, the pugio in his other hand slashing out to his right, keeping another man at bay, the room erupted into pandemonium.

Driven on by Ulyxes' precipitous act, the men of the legion entered the fray, swords and daggers stabbing, slashing and ripping. In a matter of seconds, confusion reigned complete as a number of men bearing torches and lamps fell to random sword blows, their lights dousing as they hit the sandy floor. The level of illumination in the room dropped and the grey-clad figures became less distinct and harder to spot in the flickering gloom. Cries of pain joined curses in at least three languages as the unarmed civilians among the fanatics were the first to fall.

Although they were unable to prevent the Roman invaders cutting them down, the ordinary folk who had fled Aegyptus for this haven of religious peace threw themselves at the legionaries, clawing with fingers, biting, elbowing – doing anything they could to display their hatred and disgust at these legionaries who had chased them down into this sanctum.

Cervianus hated every moment and every act.

The clang and nerve-jangling whine and scrape of metal on metal rose above the clamour of voices in the room as the warriors among the fanatics fought back with a vigour that surprised the attackers.

Cervianus stepped forward as a grey-robed figure with a chiselled, almost unfeasibly long face leapt at him, snarling, his nostrils flaring. The blade in his hand slashed out and the speed and angle surprised the capsarius, who ducked to the side only just in time as the tip ripped a hole in his sleeve and drew a long, angry red line across his upper arm.

Desperately, he thrust out with his pugio, trying to keep the man from drawing the sword back for a second strike. The small, wide dagger caught the gleaming blade and the two weapons slid along one another with nerve-jarring sounds. The enemy sword found the nick in Cervianus' blade that he had been unable to find time to polish out since that larcenous escapade back in Nicopolis. The sliding Aegyptian blade stopped, caught in the dent. Making the most of it, Cervianus pushed the weapon back as he lunged forward with his gladius, the point entering the man's throat where his collarbones met and driving deep for an instant kill. There were distinct advantages in warfare for a man who knew anatomy and was able to keep his cool.

The fanatic, his eyes going wide with shock and agony, slumped back, and Cervianus was almost pulled from his feet as the sword fell with him. Desperately, he fumbled and tried to haul the blade out. Staggering upright again, he suddenly found a grey sleeve around his neck, hauling him back.

Desperately, he stabbed behind him with the pugio and felt the blade enter the man's chest through the ribs at his side. Still the grip held, despite the grunt from behind, and yet another grey figure pounced on him from the front, taking advantage of this suddenly constricted Roman.

Cervianus braced himself for the blow, but Fuscus appeared from somewhere, smashing into the new assailant's side and knocking him out of the way, sword dripping and flashing red in the torchlight as it descended upon the grey man.

The pressure fell away from Cervianus' neck as his attacker's life ebbed and the dying fanatic toppled backwards. Without pausing for breath, the capsarius leapt forward and helped another legionary take down a grey-clad figure. Slowly, the room fell quiet, the chaos and noise dying away with the last gasps and groans of the fanatics.

Cervianus felt sick.

These were not true enemies of Rome; they had not raised arms to defend their homes against the Roman invader. They had taken the route of peace and sense, fleeing south to safety outside the grasp of the Princeps and his armies.

Or so they had thought.

But Vitalis had brought that army south beyond any place he had a right to be and that decision had led to Cervianus drawing a sword in a temple and murdering devout men in cold blood. He found his teeth were grinding.

The legionaries were gathering at the centre in the silence that was broken only by the unpleasant sounds of the dying.

"Let's finish the place off and get out," Fuscus grumbled. "These people are insane."

Cervianus stomped into the group, his eyes burning in the flickering glow of the few remaining lit torches. "No. This is a temple. We couldn't help it with these people, but we don't need to go slaughtering priests."

Fuscus looked up in surprise. "What?"

Cervianus glowered. "*You're* the ones who are always so reverent, the ones who tell me I defy the gods when I simply espouse reason. And here you are in the holiest place south of Aegyptus wanting to cut a bloody swathe through the priests? No. It ends here. We kill guards when we have to or any man who takes arms against us, but we are not here to kill innocent townsfolk or priests. *Do I make myself clear?*"

Even Cervianus was surprised at the raw power and anger in his voice, and Fuscus actually leaned back from him. Ulyxes was suddenly at his side.

"He's right, lads. They should be given the option to surrender. We're not here to invade temples and kill priests."

Slowly, in the silence that followed, Fuscus nodded and smiled weakly at Cervianus. "That it takes *you* to talk sense into me is a good indication of just how screwed up this whole campaign is."

Cervianus heaved a sigh of relief. There were six men standing in the gloomy hallway now, three more legionaries lying among the many grey bodies that were strewn between guttering torches.

Silence descended once more and the men suddenly focused on the noises from outside, behind them. The sounds of fighting were close and loud. Clearly, the west gate had fallen and Draco and the reserves were now inside the compound; forty or fifty men simply could not make that amount of noise.

"Sounds like the place is about to fall," Ulyxes noted with a sigh of relief.

"Good. Then we can get this place tidied up and maybe make a few offerings of apology."

"Come on," Fuscus prompted. "We need to make sure this temple is secured."

Cervianus nodded and the six legionaries crossed the room, their swords glinting menacingly in the flickering flames, crimson spattered across men and weapons alike. The last two men in the small party had collected guttering torches from among the carnage and held them high to light the way ahead.

The next doorway led into an even smaller, darker room, packed tightly with tall, thin columns, each decorated with some strange anthropomorphic carving high above, barely visible in the darkness. Ahead, a small room represented that part of a temple into which Cervianus had thus far been unable to enter. Despite his general disgust at the acts in which he was involved, the capsarius could not help but feel a small thrill of excitement as he strode into the inviolable and secret rooms at the centre of the temple.

"The sanctuary," he whispered.

"Why is there a boat in here?" Ulyxes asked in genuine surprise.

Cervianus peered into the darkness, the gloom receding as his friends brought the torches closer. Small, dark and mysterious doorways led from here in the three other cardinal directions, each revealing nothing but more darkness. The centre of the small sanctuary, however, was dominated by a huge square sandstone block upon which sat a strangely stylised model of an Aegyptian barque, of the variety that could be seen plying the Nile anywhere north of Syene. The centre of the boat held a tall box of stone, a container of some sort.

"It's a model barque." Cervianus shrugged. "I've heard they use them as shrines to the gods."

"Weird lot."

Before Cervianus could stop them, Fuscus and another legionary he didn't know had reached forward and were swinging open the doors on the container.

"Amun," said the capsarius in hushed tones.

"A moon? What?"

"He's the creator of all things. Sort of the Aegyptian version of Uranus and Gaia rolled into one."

"Who the who?" replied Ulyxes his frown of confusion deepening.

"Maybe think of him as Cronus or Saturn. Just think of him as the god at the top of the heap."

Ulyxes nodded. "Gotcha. Tribune of the gods."

"Why has he got a huge knob growing out of his head," asked Fuscus with a grin.

"It's a crown of feathers, not a knob!" snapped Cervianus. "Can we concentrate a little more?"

Ulyxes nodded. "Alright. What now, then? There's no one here, anyway."

Cervianus shook his head and, frowning, placed his finger to his lips. "Shhh."

The general mirth at the creator-god's suggestive crown died away and the men fell silent, apart from a few remaining groans from the dying men two chambers away. But as they stopped talking, it became apparent that that was not the only noise.

Another hushed conversation ended a second or two later, like an echo of their own words.

"What was that?" Fuscus asked quietly.

Ulyxes grinned. "Someone's hiding from us."

"I'd presumed they wouldn't leave a temple of this importance empty of priests and allow the fanatics back there access."

"Split into pairs," Ulyxes muttered. "You two go left, you two go right, and Cervianus and me'll go forwards."

With nods, the men readied their swords and daggers and moved toward the doors, edging closer and then leaping round the corner ready to deal with anything lurking beyond. As the other four disappeared from sight, Cervianus and Ulyxes approached the far door, the room plunging deep into gloom as the others left with the two torches. The pair stood for a long moment in silence, trying to acclimatise enough to pick out a few details by the dim glow coming from two rooms back.

"Have you any idea how idiotic splitting up was?" Cervianus grumbled at his friend. "Quite apart from the darkness, what happens if we suddenly bump into six guards?"

He couldn't see Ulyxes but had the irritating feeling the man was grinning. "Then there'd be three each and decorations to be won."

"Oh shut up."

In the silence, a voice ahead suddenly started saying something but stopped as it realised the cover of their own conversation had died away. The voice spoke in a deep, strange dialect that must be Kushite, and was muffled, as though hiding in a cupboard.

"Go back and get another torch," Cervianus said and Ulyxes, nodding his agreement, ran to the fanatics' room and collected one of the dying flames from the floor, coaxing it into new life with a few huffs and puffs. As Ulyxes returned with the torch, Cervianus discovered that they had entered a small hallway, not unlike the one in Ambo where the priest of Haroeris had accosted him. As well as the door that led from the entrance, three more led off ahead.

Ulyxes looked at the doors. "This is a bloody labyrinth."

Cervianus nodded. "To an extent, but the noises definitely came from ahead. Come on."

The pair crept across the hallway and in through the door opposite, entering a long, narrow room, the walls crowded with images and carvings very familiar to anyone who had seen a temple to the Aegyptian gods. The room was, however, solid with no new doorways.

"Dead end."

Cervianus shook his head. "The talking was coming from this direction. Come on."

Slowly, he crept along the room until he was near the back wall.

"Here," Ulyxes said quietly, gesturing at the walls.

"What?"

"Look at the carvings."

Cervianus examined the indicated area of wall, frowning. "I don't see wha—"

But he did. The walls of the room were covered with a constant flow of hieroglyphics and images; this area was no different but for the fact that there were blank spaces. He stood back and peered at the wall. Blank spaces in a square. Like a door frame.

"So how do we get in there?" Cervianus muttered.

"We don't. They come out to us."

"Why would they do that?"

Ulyxes cleared his throat. "One of you priests in there speaks Latin, or at least Greek, so talk to me."

There was a pregnant pause before a muttering began. Ulyxes gestured to his companion and Cervianus repeated the statement in Greek. After another pause, a tremulous voice issued slowly from behind the stone.

"You violate a sacred place. A curse on you."

Cervianus grumbled. "I'm probably *already* cursed. You need to come out now and surrender to us. The Twenty Second legion is in control of Napata, but we are soldiers and civilised men, not barbarians. We are not here to sack your city or enslave priests. If you come out you will be treated with the respect due your station."

There was another muttered exchange and Ulyxes leaned close and whispered into Cervianus' ear. The capsarius cleared his throat. "And my companion wishes me to warn you that on the count of ten he's going to start having the doorway bricked up. This is a temple. Don't make it a tomb."

A further pause and then slowly, quietly, a grinding noise issued from deep in the stonework. The carved wall slowly opened to reveal five men, blinking in the sudden light. All were shaven-headed and dressed in the fine garments and animal pelts of Aegyptian priests, gold jewellery adorning them, their painted eyes peering out nervously.

"Come on," Ulyxes demanded, gesturing outside with his gladius.

Cervianus readied his weapons. Priests were unlikely to try and fight, but there was always the possibility. As the five men moved out into the open, Ulyxes and Cervianus fell in behind them like prison guards, marching them out into the wider chambers beyond. As they passed the model boat, Fuscus and his companion returned from the side room and grinned.

"You had better luck than us, then."

Cervianus nodded. "I think one of these is probably the high priest of Amun."

Smiling, the four legionaries wandered out, past the carnage of their earlier fight, where the priests viewed the bodies with dismay and distaste, and into the first forecourt. The other two legionaries caught them up from behind as they walked out into the open beneath the stars. The men guarding the pylon gate grinned.

"Looks like you lot had fun. Nasica and Draco are coming along the main street with a load of prisoners. Cheer up, Cervianus. Napata's ours!"

IV

NAPATA

Cervianus peered over the top of the rock. "What in Hades are you doing?"

Ulyxes looked up from the gritty dust at the base of the slope, some ten paces from the edge of the main temple. The helmet in his hands, full of sand and red dust, the makeshift tool with which he had dug the two-foot deep hole that lay in front of him.

"Will you shut up?" the stocky man snapped back. "I'm trying to be quick and secret."

"Then here's a tip. Don't saunter and whistle. It makes you look the guiltiest man in the world. So what are you doing?"

Ulyxes popped up from the natural dip that his exertions were deepening and peered suspiciously around.

"No one is paying any attention other than me, because everyone already knows you're a madman. They probably think you're trying to dig back to Alexandria."

Ulyxes waggled his eyebrows in a way that made Cervianus roll his eyes, and produced a bag from beside him. "We're likely to be here for a while, so it's time to stow the booty."

Cervianus regarded the bag of stolen pugios, shaking his head. "Stop calling it 'booty'. You are not a pirate. Nor is it 'plunder' or 'swag'. Anyway, I'll be glad to see the back of them. Don't know why you didn't just throw them away in the desert. It was Calidius *not* having the daggers that was important, not us *having* them."

Ulyxes smiled.

"Half a year's pay at least I could get for these. I'm bollocksed if I'm just going to throw them away. Besides, that'll probably be all we make from this campaign. Doesn't look like Vitalis wants booty."

"Just bury the things and come back to the square in front of the temple. Draco and Nasica are allocating duties and they'll notice if they get to the end and you're not there."

"What about you?" Ulyxes added.

"I already have a trade, remember? I've set up my temporary surgery and ward in that big white building opposite the Amun temple. Looks like it was a residence for an important man. Even has a bath in it."

"Fabulous. Knowing me I'll get burial detail or prison guard. Or latrine digging."

"At least you're in good practice for that."

Ulyxes glowered at him and got back to work burying the bag of stolen weapons. Cervianus crouched and leaned back against a small boulder.

"Final count's in. Four hundred and eighty-four men, including thirty-two walking wounded and eleven crippled."

Ulyxes nodded soberly. "You say that quite brightly, given that leaves us with not far off half the number of men we had when we left Buhen."

Cervianus shook his head in disbelief. "That's surviving all the dangers of the desert, a killer storm and an assault on one of the most important places in Kush, for Taranis' sake."

The shorter, stocky legionary narrowed his eyes. "Numbers of dead that are acceptable? Now you're starting to sound like Draco."

"Oh come on. I didn't want to do this, you *know* that, but if any force has to take Napata I'm glad it was us and not the main army under Vitalis. Can you imagine the destruction and death then? I'm just glad it's ended in such a civilised way."

Ulyxes simply nodded. It *had* been remarkably sensible in the end. The city guards had fought like lions despite their smaller numbers, and would have fought to the very last man had not the priests that had been captured in the main temple officially surrendered the compound to Nasica. The head priest had ordered the guards to capitulate and within a quarter of an hour the complex was quiet and under control.

Moreover, the leaders and all men of money and influence at Napata all resided in the compound, particularly in the three palatial buildings they had spotted earlier. The capture of the civil leaders placed the occupied settlement itself near the river firmly in their control.

In return for their gracious surrender, Nasica had given them extremely favourable terms, allowing all members of the priestly classes amnesty to go about their ordinary daily business. He had gathered the entire remaining guard force, had them disarmed and roped for transport back after the campaign, and they now sat disconsolate in one of the ancillary buildings re-designated as the stockade. Other than that, he had agreed to take only one villager in four as a slave and to disregard all young children and their parents. They were terms that even Cervianus could find few faults with for their level of humanity.

Draco and Nasica had set up their headquarters in one of the palaces, quartering themselves there and their men in the other two large mansions. All in all, given the level of trepidation that Cervianus had felt about the assault and the self-loathing he had experienced killing religious fanatics in a temple, he was surprisingly calm about the way things had turned out.

Storehouses had been located in the complex that held enough grain and dried meat to keep the men of the Twenty Second going for weeks or even months, and even fruit and some sort of cloying beer had been found. Spirits were high all round.

Cervianus watched Ulyxes fill in the hole, covering the evidence of their storehouse raid, and wondered for a moment how Ulyxes would remember where he'd buried them, before realising and chiding himself.

"You done?"

Ulyxes nodded, brushing the dirt from the inside of his helmet and replacing the liner.

"Going to have to polish and oil this later. Come on. Let's go see what fresh nightmare Draco has dreamed up for me now."

The pair turned and walked past the entrance of the great temple of Amun and toward the diminishing crowd of legionaries receiving their orders from the officers.

The days passed in a blur of relief for the men of the two cohorts. The daily tasks resolved themselves into a mundane and simple round of checking, guarding, polishing, maintaining, eating and bathing. After the weeks of trekking up the Nile, the desert trail, and the intermittent bloodbaths at Syene, Buhen and Napata, the simple humdrum routine was relished by each and every man.

Moreover, the rising spirits of the cohorts had a surprising knock-on effect as their treatment of the locals, both priestly and commoner, and even of the enslaved prisoners, was humane and undertaken with care and restraint.

Patrols were set on the mountain top, remembering the relative ease with which the legion had effected its entry. The walls were strengthened with a standard defensive ditch and lilia pits. All in all, the men began to feel comfortable and safe.

Cervianus strolled slowly around the wide wall walk, supporting a legionary named Celsus who was recovering from a battered head and a slash-wound at the left knee, and recovering well with the aid of the capsarius. Cervianus' counterpart from the Second cohort had disappeared during the desert storm, his body never found, and it was with relish that the tall Galatian took on the authority naturally garnered as the only trained medical man in a unit. Even Draco and Nasica had begun to defer to his opinion where health matters were concerned, and his makeshift hospital gave him virtual autonomy.

Ulyxes, Fuscus and Petrocorios managed, through sheer persistence rather than persuasion, to get themselves assigned as his orderlies, largely in order to free them from the onerous manual labour demanded of the men, as far as Cervianus could see, since they seemed to pay little attention to their actual duties unless he walked around with them, telling them what to do at every turn.

Celsus hissed through his teeth.

"Problem?" Cervianus asked, his face full of professional concern.

"Just the weak knee, sir. Any time I turn and forget to lift the leg it feels like someone's torn the bottom half off."

"Try to make sure you lift it each time and higher every day until it's got full mobility."

"Yes, sir."

Cervianus nodded and smiled and crouched to examine the wound. The stitching had worked well and a dressing was routinely applied with just a careful period each day when it was opened to the air to aid in the healing.

"Looks good. No pus, which I'm pleased about."

He stood again and realised the soldier was paying him no attention, his eyes reaching out across the open sand beyond the wall. Cervianus followed his gaze.

A cloud of dust on the horizon was getting rapidly closer, far too quickly to denote the march of the legion. He was just about to shout a warning when the alarm went up along the wall on the west gate, a cornu blasting out to draw the immediate attention of each and every man. Celsus and his wound almost forgotten, Cervianus peered into the distance, trying to see through the dust before he had to tear himself away and arm for battle. Already the century's cornu was blasting out, calling him and his compatriots to the great square before the Amun temple.

There they were. Figures in silver and white among the dust, mounted and bearing down on the complex. Clearly the guards of Napata had a cavalry wing too. They were far more organised and civilised than Cervianus had initially given them credit for.

If they were just cavalry then the defenders could count themselves safe, tucked behind ditch and wall and with weeks' worth of food. If they had infantry and artillery, things might be very different, however.

Biting his lip, he turned back to Celsus, who was hobbling

along the wall as fast as he could manage, making for the steps down by the west gate. Hurrying, he caught up with the wounded soldier and lent him an arm. The two men shuffled quickly toward the gate, where everything was now a bustle of activity, weapons being hauled up to the top, men falling into position behind the battlements.

They reached the top of the stair, hearing the third call for muster going out. Now, those who were late to the square would be looking at disciplinary action from their officers, though Cervianus' case would likely be overlooked due to his extra duties. Carefully, he helped Celsus step down from the wall as his ears honed in on a conversation nearby.

He stopped sharply and turned.

"What did you say?" he asked the soldier at the wall nearby.

"I think it's our auxilia, sir. Not the enemy."

Cervianus blinked. Making sure his charge was safe and stable, he ran to the wall and narrowed his eyes at the western haze once more. The riders were now close enough to make out details and, as the cloud billowed and thinned in places, he examined them carefully.

Dressed in white linen and with mail shirts they were identical at this distance to the guards that had manned Napata's wall on their arrival but, now that the soldier had pointed it out, it occurred to him that the cavalry of the Nome of Sapi-Res at least wore an almost identical uniform. It was quite understandable, when you thought about it. They were born of very similar cultures, after all, for all Shenti's vehement denunciations.

Then he saw it. The shields became visible, first one and then others. No animal hide patterns here. The shields were deep blue and oval, with the golden eye of Horus emblazoned upon them.

The auxilia.

Cervianus sagged against the stonework with relief. Looking up, he spotted the centurion in charge of the gate guard and turned to the soldier who had caught his attention.

"Best go warn your centurion."

The man nodded and jogged off along the wall, and Cervianus returned his attention to Celsus, helping him slowly down the wall stairs. Before they had reached the dusty ground the cornu above had called the all-clear and the order to stand down was being relayed across the compound.

A cheer went up at the wall top and the gates were being swung open as the two men reached the ground and stood, recovering from their exertions.

The cavalry auxilia rode in through the gate, slowing as they arrived so as not to fill the interior with too much of a dust cloud, and began to rein in, small groups dismounting and leading their mounts by the bridle. Almost a hundred riders entered before the gates were closed again. Leaving Celsus to rest by the wall, Cervianus cast his gaze around and among the cavalry until his gaze fell on one of the officers and his face split into a grin.

"Shenti!"

Smiling wide, he jogged across the dusty ground to where the decurion was dismounting, his horse steaming. The officer turned at the shout and laughed as he saw his friend.

"Thanks be to Sekhmet, whom I personally charged with protecting you. I feared I had seen the last of you."

Cervianus nodded, unable to force the grin from his face. "I feared much the same, but all is apparently well."

Something flitted for a moment across Shenti's face. Doubt? Disappointment? Whatever it was, his friend forced it instantly aside and it was gone before Cervianus could identify it. The decurion handed his reins to one of his men and slung his shield over his shoulder.

"Come. I wish to hear all about your journey and I need a cool drink."

Cervianus laughed. "We have plenty of fruit in the stores and a cistern of clean water. I'll tell you about everything that deserves to be told. And I want to hear about your journey up the Nile, too."

Again that unidentifiable something passed across Shenti's face.

"My journey was uneventful and undeserving of a tale, but come."

Cervianus narrowed his eyes, but that *something* had gone again and his friend was all happy business.

"The rest of the legion is but a few hours behind us. We are the forward scouts only. My commander will report to yours, so I am free."

"Good. Let's find Ulyxes. If anyone has food, wine and soft seating, it'll be him."

Four hours later, the signal went up again, shouts echoing across the compound and cornua blowing out refrains. The remaining eight cohorts of the Twenty Second Deiotariana made their way slowly and with stately grace toward the gate, the auxilia marching or trotting alongside and following on behind.

Cervianus had led Shenti to his makeshift hospital and to the small area he reserved for staff, where he, Ulyxes and Fuscus had recounted the tale of their lengthy journey across the desert, with all its horrors and shocks. Shenti had listened, nodding occasionally as though he had known exactly what to expect from the trek. For the last hour, however, they had relaxed and eaten and drunk in calm, light conversation, the sheer relief of reunion overriding all else; until the signal for the legion's arrival had goaded them into activity, that was.

Cervianus and Ulyxes stopped in the doorway as Fuscus ran past, jamming a helmet on his head. Ulyxes watched as Cervianus and Shenti clasped hands in a traditional gesture, and the two men wordlessly parted to join their own units. Ulyxes jogged alongside the capsarius as they moved to fall in at the centre with their century where Draco waited, eagle-eyed and impatient, his demeanour sourer than usual due to the discomfort and itching he was enduring with his splinted arm.

The last men fell into position, adjusting their equipment just as the vanguard of the legion rounded the nearest building and approached the square. Despite their long journey, Vitalis and his junior tribunes were immaculate, their armour gleaming in the hot sun and blinding to look at.

A quick, surreptitious glance to each side confirmed Cervianus' suspicions. Half the men on the temporary parade ground were without a helmet or without a shield. Most of them lacked a pilum, and their tunics and scarves were of different lengths and colours, bleached by the sun and torn and shredded for bandages, padding and other more trivial uses. They looked like a unit of disordered mercenaries, rather than the pride of Galatia and Rome.

He could picture the senior tribune tutting at the sight already. At least the man had apparently decided against a fanfare for his victorious entry to Napata. It wouldn't have been wholly out of character, but *would* have been highly insulting to the men who had actually won this victory. Instead, calls went up and, as the vanguard came to a halt, the various centuries spread out as room allowed and came to attention.

It had been less than two weeks since the two forces had separated so far to the north, but the difference in the men in that time was astounding. Moving at a standard pace through more temperate conditions and using their tents, the men of the eight newly arrived cohorts were neat and clean, but tanned and tired, the sun's mid-afternoon heat causing them to perspire heavily.

The men who had crossed the desert, on the other hand, had hardened in ways that went beyond the effects of mere weathering. Their skin had already darkened to such an extent that it resembled that of the native auxilia more than their Galatian compatriots. Their brown hair had become golden and the golden almost white. Most impressive of all, despite their shabby appearance, the victors of Napata were lean, muscular and comfortable, barely breaking a sweat even in the worst heat of the day. It was as though they had stared into the very heart of the sun and bested it. Pride flowed through the men. They had not only achieved, but had excelled, and even grown. Cervianus found he was grinning, and he wasn't the only man to do so.

Vitalis and the five junior tribunes behind him dismounted, saluted, and strode purposefully toward Nasica, where he stood to attention at the head of his force.

"Centurion." The tribune nodded a quiet greeting. "Your men look dirty and unkempt, though I am inclined to leniency, given all they must have been through."

Cervianus held his breath. The silence that followed the statement was so absolute that a pin dropping would have crashed to the ground with a tumult. The cords in men's necks stood out as they strained, and lips curled into disdainful sneers. A wrong word now and the whole world could turn upside down. The silence flooded the crowd until Nasica, with visible effort, fought down his own disgust, bit down on the words that crowded his mouth, and stepped forward with a salute.

"May I present to you the captured sanctuary of Napata to the great glory of the Twenty Second Deiotaran legion and the survivors of the desert force under my command."

Cervianus stared. The deliberate omitting of the tribune from the toast of glory was a deeply cutting sleight and could very well be the comment that ignited the simmering hatred that surrounded them. Vitalis either ignored, or more likely failed to even notice, the sleight.

"You are to be commended and congratulated on a job well done, centurion. Your reputation is well deserved and proves the worth of my decision to send you on ahead."

"Thank you, sir."

Cervianus couldn't help but notice that both Nasica and Draco out at the front had discarded their official vine staffs somewhere and that each man's sword hands rested on the pommel of their gladius.

"Report," commanded the tribune officiously.

Nasica straightened, his hands going behind his back, where Cervianus watched them writhing with the desire to strangle the commander.

"There were fewer defenders than anticipated, but of higher quality than the Kushites we have faced so far. We managed to infiltrate the city and open the gates for the main assault. The men of the Second century in my cohort captured the high priests of the complex and the whole place surrendered at that point with no further bloodshed."

Vitalis was nodding, one eyebrow slightly raised. Cervianus felt his nerves twanging.

"In the spirit of the Pax Romana," the primus pilus continued, "we have allowed the priests to continue worship in their temples as before, though I realise we may now need to requisition more of their structures for the men. We have a total of five hundred and twelve healthy slaves in a compound awaiting transport and the population in the town seem to have accepted our presence without the risk of reprisals." He took a deep breath. "This place is eminently fortifiable and will make an excellent base. Welcome to Napata, sir."

Vitalis continued to nod for a moment after Nasica finished, and then straightened.

"I appreciate everything you and your men have done, Nasica. I want a commendation list and, upon our return to Alexandria in due course, I will distribute coronae, phalerae and torcs appropriately. Decorations will also be affixed to the standards for your most excellent actions."

He turned to take in the complex in a wide view. "However, the concessions you have made these people are wholly inappropriate."

Cervianus' heart fell; he'd half seen this coming. The bile rose in his throat as he listened.

"We are here to chastise and conquer, not to ally ourselves with these people. The Kandake of Kush invaded our territory, looted and enslaved. We are here to bring the Roman heel down on her throat and make her wish she had never heard of Aegyptus."

Nasica opened his mouth, but could not force out the words he apparently wanted to use.

Vitalis gestured with one hand, taking in the whole complex. "Execute the population, beginning with the priests and leaders, then the soldiers and the civilians. There will be no slaves taken. I want Napata erased."

Nasica finally found his voice, his face pale and furious. "Sir…"

Vitalis shook his head. "Raze the temples and any structure that cannot be utilised in its current form by the legion. I want the stonework removed and used to add towers to the walls and to create the base for barrack blocks."

The centurion was shaking slightly, and Cervianus closed his eyes. Nasica was at breaking point and here, in this place and at this time, Nasica *was* the legion. Slowly, with infinite patience, the primus pilus straightened, his face emotionless.

"Very well, sir. I will have my optio escort you to the temporary headquarters."

Cervianus watched the look exchanged by Draco and the primus pilus and caught his breath. The cohesion of the legion's command was hanging by a thread and, as always, that thread was Nasica.

Cervianus gripped the unlit torch in his hand so tightly that the knuckles whitened and the hard wood bit into his palm. Around him the men of his contubernium walked in tight-lipped, grim silence.

A scream pierced the air and the capsarius instinctively glanced toward the source of the sound, instantly wishing he hadn't. One of the contubernia from Nasica's century was walking dead-eyed down a line of kneeling villagers, placing the point of his sword at the back of their necks and driving down with all his might, willing the blade faster and more accurate every time, trying his best to give them the quickest and least painful death possible.

Nasica was, Cervianus knew, taking his own career or even his life in his hands just with that. Vitalis had instructed that the priests, leaders and nobles be crucified and that the rest of the population be beheaded, burned or have their throats cut. Nasica had changed the order as it passed through his command, granting the enemy a soldier's death. The blade would sever the spine at the neck and death was almost instantaneous, particularly compared to the slow agony of burning, the drawn-out choking of throat-cutting – or worse still, beheading, which, with short swords, involved more sawing than chopping.

Cervianus, his gorge rising, turned away from the grisly scene, trying not to notice the crucifixes being assembled back near the main temple. Nasica had done what he could within the bounds of his authority, but crucifixion was hard to circumvent, being blindingly obvious as it was. At least Nasica would break their legs and cut them to speed them on their way.

The primus pilus had been unapproachable for the last hour, storming around the complex with a face like thunder. Worse even than the simple butchery itself, which Nasica considered to be far beyond acceptable, Vitalis had overturned his deal with the locals and reneged on his promises. The tribune had made the centurion into a liar, a fact that was readily apparent in every accusatory Kushite stare they saw, even those that looked up unblinking from the dusty ground.

Especially those.

After the last few days of relief, believing that, despite omens, premonitions and simple bad feelings, everything was turning out alright, now all those fears for the future came crashing back in on the men. Few of the executioners' victims spoke or screamed, accepting their fate with silent hatred. Those that did speak did so in low, dark voices and, incomprehensible as their tongue was, it was clear that they were cursing the victors with every last dying breath.

Ulyxes shoved him in the shoulder. "Stop looking. It won't help. Just be grateful we're not on execution detail."

It was a good point. For all Cervianus' complicity in the systematic destruction of Napata, at least he wasn't one of those poor soldiers taking life after life after life in a seemingly endless line of death. Such acts brought on nightmares that could plague a man for the rest of his days. Cervianus had seen such effects before.

As he turned his gaze away from it all toward the wall in the middle distance, he frowned and grabbed Ulyxes' arm. "What do you suppose is going on there?"

The shorter legionary, his face sour, followed his gaze. Half a dozen of the auxiliary horsemen were gathered, almost hidden in the lee of a temple, apparently re-equipping.

"Who cares?"

"I do," replied Cervianus. "Come on."

Ulyxes shrugged and turned to Petrocorios. "We'll catch up with you."

The rest of the unit, hollow-faced and unhappy, plodded on as Cervianus and Ulyxes turned and jogged toward the small knot of horsemen. As they moved, curiously, the auxiliaries ducked back around the corner of the hut.

"Strange."

Ulyxes nodded and they picked up speed, glancing around to make sure they weren't seen and not entirely sure why they did so. A few heartbeats later, they were at the wall of the building, sidling along it.

At the wall's end, Cervianus took a deep breath and peered around the corner. Arms in white linen grasped him and pulled him round into the shade and he found himself face to face with Shenti's junior officer, a heavy-set and powerful man he had first met many weeks ago while running in fear through the night-shrouded camp of the legion. The big man put his finger to his lips. Cervianus blinked as Ulyxes joined them. Shenti was there, helping one of his men rearm. The capsarius shook his head in confusion. What was going on?

The partially armed horseman reached round and grasped the sword proffered by Shenti, sliding it into the sheath at his side. For a moment, his eyes caught Cervianus' and the capsarius saw the fear in them.

"Shenti? What in Hades are you *doing*?"

The enigmatic decurion shrugged. "What do you think?"

The priest of Amun, only a small man, looked almost lost, engulfed in the white linen and mail shirt. The other two priests behind him, both also dressed as auxiliary soldiers, stared at him in fear.

"Shenti, you can't *do* this!"

The officer gave him a humourless look. "Watch me."

"Shenti? Look, I appreciate what you're trying to do, and I don't like seeing this any more than you, but when they find out about this, we'll be nailing *you* to a crucifix!"

Shenti rounded on his friend. "The only way we will fail in this is because of the pair of you raising your voices. Be *quiet*!"

Cervianus reeled back and Shenti sighed. "You are almost unique in paying such attention to us. The auxilia are almost invisible to the legions. We are nothing in their eyes and they could not tell the difference between the people of Kemet, or Kush or even of Arabia if they were in our uniform. Our cavalry compound lies a quarter of a mile to the east. Once beyond the gate, these people can flee and be safe."

Cervianus shook his head. "I don't even want to ask how you managed to get them out of the stockade, and you'll probably manage to get them through the gate, yes. But what happens when their absence is noted?"

Shenti shrugged. "I think you overestimate your organisation. Vitalis sees only enemies. He does not categorise or count. He will assume it is all done for him and your centurions and men are hardly of a mind to quibble with numbers. They are as sick of the butchery as you."

He placed his hands reassuringly on Cervianus' shoulders. "All will be well with me, my friend. In the face of unstoppable madness, we must do what we can to preserve the little humanity left in the world."

Cervianus opened his mouth to argue, but the decurion's arguments were watertight. Shenti may have railed against the warrior-thief culture of the Kushites and would readily fight their armies, but the priests were priests to *his* gods. The capsarius could hardly blame him for trying to save them.

"Be safe and lucky, then."

Shenti smiled. "Two things I try always to be."

Ulyxes nodded and clasped his hand. "You are a good man. Be careful. The army of Tribune Vitalis is not a safe place for good men."

The decurion grinned. "I see the look in your centurions' eyes. I fear this will not be the army of Vitalis for long."

Cervianus nodded once, clasped hands with his friend and turned, grabbing Ulyxes and jogging back toward the other men of their contubernium. Had Shenti seen something he hadn't? Certainly Nasica and Draco both harboured deeply negative feelings about their commander, but Shenti didn't know them the way Cervianus did. Nasica was legion to the core. It was distinctly possible that he would put a pugio through his own gut before he would commit mutiny against his rightful commander. Shaking his head at the madness of it all, Cervianus ran back with Ulyxes toward their compatriots who were exiting the large doorway of one of the temples ahead.

As the five men emerged into the bright sunlight, the first crackles and pops of the fire echoed through the building behind them and the doorway belched a cloud of dark smoke. As they caught sight of the pair, the men turned, their torches giving off long, winding ribbons of black.

"One down, three to go," Fuscus said without a trace of humour or joy.

Ulyxes nodded. Each of the fire-setting units had their task. Four contubernia had filled the sixteen temples with brushwood and dried reeds, while another four cut and soaked torches and then went about the task of setting the buildings aflame.

As they converged and made for the next temple on their route, Cervianus was not sure that he wouldn't rather have been one of the executioners than this. For all the horror and sickness of murder, *this* was desecration, plain and simple. The only religious edifice that had been spared the fire was the great temple at the centre, a structure that Vitalis had decided could be bolstered as a small inner fortress in the event of a siege, given the low height of the compound's outer walls. Even then, the cult barque statue had been removed and thrown on a rubble heap.

The seven men approached the next low, short temple not far from the perimeter wall, the structure they had just left finally erupting in a full inferno behind them, a thousand years of sacred carving and painting charring and cracking in their wake. Taking a deep breath, Cervianus lit the pitch-soaked torch in his hand and followed his friends inside.

Much as in many of the minor Aegyptian temples, this smaller outer pylon lacked a ceremonial avenue or cult statues, and led into a colonnaded outer peristyle, though this one was roofed. Stacks of dried reeds had been packed in around the edge.

Crossing through the small copse of pillars and trying hard not to think about what he was doing, Cervianus followed his tent mates into the inner sanctuary beyond. The seven flickering torches easily lit the small room. Two doorways led off into antechambers, probably chapels of connected deities. The painting on the walls in here was bright and clean as though it had been done only yesterday rather than a hundred generations ago.

Cervianus stopped dead in front of the cult statue, his mind screaming at him. Flashes of almost forgotten nightmares assailed him afresh, battering his consciousness. He might have shouted. He wasn't sure. From the undergrowth in the delta to a nightmare dreamscape at Thebes, and finally to Napata...

Thoth stood at a slight lean, half hidden by bundles of sticks and reeds, the piercing eyes boring into his above that long, curved beak, one foot forward, as though striding from his plinth, one hand stretched out before him...

"No!"

The others turned to look at him and then the statue at which he was pointing, their brows furrowing.

"What?"

"No," Cervianus repeated, a cold shiver running up his spine. "Not this. Not now."

The rest stared at him. Of course, he had never spoken of his dreams, of the nightmare at Thebes and the living gods beseeching him. With sudden and dreadful clarity it all fell into place. He could have stopped all of this. One arrow at Syene. One small iron point could have taken Vitalis to Elysium and prevented everything.

"No," he yelled.

"Cervianus," Fuscus hissed, leaning close to him, "will you keep your voice *down*. I don't like this any more than you, but orders are orders. You try and stop this and you'll end up like the poor bastards out there."

Cervianus was visibly shaking. "We can't do this. Think about it. You fear the gods more than I do, and what do you think they're going to do when we've massacred their priests and people and burned their sacred places?"

Petrocorios nodded. "You're right, of course. But what can *we* do about it? We refuse this and we'll land ourselves straight in the shit, and Vitalis will just set someone else to doing it anyway. You can't stop it."

Cervianus backed away and stared at his torch. "I'll not do it. I can't be a part of it."

To his surprise, Ulyxes appeared at his shoulder. "He's right, though. This isn't right, lads."

The roiling smoke from the seven torches was rapidly filling the small sanctuary room and the legionaries began to cough. Fuscus, with a low growl, pushed Cervianus aside and strode out into the wider, columned room. The other men followed quickly, gagging on the smoke. As they entered the larger peristyle, Cervianus dropped his torch onto a clear, sandy area of floor in the centre and kicked sand and dust over it until it flickered and died.

"I don't care if Vitalis skins me; I'll not be part of this."

Ulyxes nodded. "You know that, whatever they might think of him, Nasica and Draco will never turn on Vitalis; it's not in their nature. And the tribune is too much out of our reach for us to deal with."

The others stared at him.

"I can't believe you even said that," Fuscus snapped. "If anyone hears you talking like that, you'll be burned alive."

Ulyxes shook his head. "No I won't."

"Why?"

Ulyxes straightened and dropped his torch to the ground, kicking sand over it. "Because I won't be here. I'm going."

The others stared at him and Cervianus turned to boggle at his friend.

"That's a *real* offence. You know what the punishment is for desertion?"

"Can it be worse than this?" added Fuscus.

Ulyxes nodded as if answering an internal question. "I'm going tonight. After dark. I would strongly recommend you all come too. This campaign is over for me."

Fuscus and Petrocorios exchanged a look and, for the first time, Cervianus realised with a start that the two men had clearly discussed the same thing themselves. "If you're really planning on that, Ulyxes, you'd sure as shit better have a plan. It's no good just running."

Ulyxes nodded as he turned to Petrocorios to answer. "We've easy access to the stores. With all that's going on today, no one will pay any attention while we take extra water and rations. We leave three hours after nightfall. That's an hour before the change of guard. You know how it works: they'll be tired and bored and not very observant at that point. We make our way up the slope at the mountain's base, cross to the west wall and then drop down outside at the corner where it meets the rock."

"And then?" Fuscus' voice carried something eager in its tone.

"Then we make our way gradually downriver. We take our weapons and the important gear, but no armour. As soon as we find any kind of small native village, we barter for or buy local clothes and mounts and then make for Aegyptus. I don't know about you, but I could happily live out my life as a quiet resident of Thebes."

There were a number of nods from the others, though Suro shook his head. "It's insane. Vitalis may be as mad as a bag of wild cats, but at least the legion has supplies and support. You'll never make it as far as Roman lands. Those bastards in black will cut you to shreds before you ever see Syene again."

Ulyxes shrugged. "If it happens, then it happens, but sure as anything, keeping going here is just marching into the jaws of Cerberus, and I'd rather have small hope than no hope. I'm going... shit, I owe Rome nothing; they annexed us, remember? You lot just need to decide whether you're Galatians or Romans."

Kicking the dead torch out of the way, Ulyxes strode from the chamber, back out of the main room and into the sunlight.

Cervianus blinked, aware of the import of what had just happened. He turned to look at the others, realising just what a risk Ulyxes had just taken. Even had they not been sympathetic, the stocky legionary would likely trust Fuscus, Petrocorios and Suro to keep this a secret, but the two remaining men, whose names Cervianus still hadn't bothered to learn, were such an unknown quantity, having only been in their contubernium for such a short time.

Fuscus and Petrocorios exchanged a look and shrugged, dropped their own torches and allowed them to go out before turning and following Ulyxes out into the sunlight. Cervianus eyed the three remaining men keenly.

"I'm not being executed for disobedience or desertion," Suro grumbled, and the other two men nodded emphatically. Ignoring the very existence of Cervianus, the three men blew on their torches, making the orange flames flare anew, and turned, making their way back into the inner sanctum. Cervianus felt sick.

In truth, he felt so proud of his friend he would have loved nothing more than to throw his arms around him and cheer for his stand against the idiocy that was this campaign. Turning your back on Vitalis and the legion might be easy – it might even be relatively light turning on Nasica and Draco. But to leave the army and flee like thieves into the night meant there was no hope of stopping any more atrocities. Only by their very presence could people of conscience actually hope to make a difference.

It was a heroic and proud thought.

It was also a carefully constructed belief that his mind had furnished him with to mask the real reason he found he could not fall into Ulyxes' camp:

Shame.

Even given his peaceful nature and educated ways, Cervianus was no coward. He had been trained as a legionary, after all. But fear and cowardice could be faced and beaten, forced down until it became as nothing. Shame, on the other hand, grew with every attempt to belittle it. Shame could kill a man as easily as any blade.

He couldn't desert, whether he wanted to or not.

But he couldn't pick up a torch and go on with this.

What could a man of conscience do at this point?

Biting his lip, Cervianus turned and walked out of the temple and, his head lowered in thought, almost walked straight into the officer immediately outside.

He looked up in panic and glanced left and right. Of Ulyxes, Fuscus or Petrocorios there was no sign. The man wore the armour and uniform of a tribune, his plumed helmet beneath his arm glinting in the sunlight. The officer had a long face and aquiline features, thick eyebrows that met above his nose giving him an almost feral look, and a five-o'clock shadow that did nothing to civilise his features.

Cervianus' analytical mind, even as he was reeling back and coming to attention, tracked back throughout the journey trying to pick out where he'd seen the man before. Generally, the junior tribunes were just a uniform and a voice to the ordinary men, with whom they hardly ever even exchanged words.

The tribune had been the one that had briefly argued with Vitalis on their arrival at Abu Island. The man looked haggard and drawn, as though he'd hardly slept in many days. Cervianus was familiar with the feeling and the look.

"Sir," he said, saluting.

"At ease, soldier. What are you doing here?"

"Temple firing duty, sir," Cervianus replied dutifully.

"Without a torch? You must have powerful breath, soldier."

Cervianus blinked as his heart sank. Behind them, smoke began to issue from the temple's inner rooms. The tribune looked past him and pointed to his left.

"Your three friends went that way. I suggest you hurry."

Cervianus frowned.

"Now," the officer added, "before I decide what it was that I just heard."

His pulse quickening, the blood pounding in his veins, Cervianus turned and ran.

Near midnight.

The darkness was absolute in the small room assigned to the seven of them in the palatial building. Cervianus stirred as he had done all night. Sleep seemed as out of reach as Alexandria... or sanity.

His mind was in turmoil.

A tribune had overheard at least some of their exchange in the temple and yet had done nothing about it. Cervianus had spent the entire afternoon and evening on edge, waiting for the guards to come and arrest him, but nothing had happened. Instead, he had lain awake in the dark, struggling with the urge to desert and the knowledge that he'd hate himself if he did. The dark shape of Ulyxes at the far side detached itself from the shadow and crossed the room. The man had removed his mail, shield and helmet and merely carried a bag and his sword and dagger. Ulyxes neared his pallet and bent for a moment.

"You're staying?" he whispered.

Cervianus nodded; he didn't trust his voice.

"Then I hope things improve and that I see you again. Stay safe."

And with that the shadow moved away and was gone, two more shapes detaching themselves from the shade and following on. Darkness filled Cervianus, and with it came a sense of loss and hopelessness.

The dreaded moment arrived.

A cornu blasted out the morning parade call and centurions and optios, already standing outside the buildings, began bellowing orders. Cervianus, awake and dressed for the last hour after a night of fitful sleep at best, checked his equipment and took a last look around the room as Suro and the two others hurried out into the early dawn light. Suro looked troubled, as though a night of weighing up the odds had led him to believe he'd made a mistake and missed a vital chance.

Ulyxes', Fuscus' and Petrocorios' empty blankets stared accusingly up at him. Briefly, he wondered whether he would be tortured. It wouldn't be normal practice over such a thing as tracking deserters, but with Vitalis in charge and Draco being inflexible, proud Draco, there was always the possibility.

With a sigh, he strode outside as the second call went up and jogged across the dusty, pale yellow landscape to the large open area before the surviving un-charred temple. The burned-out shells of the victims of Vitalis' purge stood around the town, some still belching small puffs of black smoke, despite an entire afternoon and night having passed. Blackened stone had replaced the local red, testament to the presence of Rome.

Cervianus tried not to look at them. At least he had not done *that*, when he died and the worth of his life was judged.

Horribly aware of the gaps around him where the men of his contubernium should be, Cervianus fell into position in his century, standing to attention. It was there, as his eyes strained to look along the lines of men without his head noticeably moving, that the capsarius realised with a start that the gaps left by his tent mates were not the only spaces in the parade. Here and there other holes were plainly visible in the line-up. Had Ulyxes' plan spread, or was it a spontaneous reaction across the legion to their commander and his plans?

His eyes strayed across the faces of the officers standing out front. Draco's was carefully expressionless, but Cervianus had known the centurion long enough to recognise the burning anger in his eyes that showed nowhere else. Nasica, further along, wore a strangely calm and accepting look, almost as though he had given in, that was strange and unfitting on the veteran's face.

Vitalis, however, was slowly turning a shade of puce, his eyes bulging as he took in the gaps in the lines. The junior tribunes, standing nearby in a small flock, were engaged in a heated yet whispered argument. Cervianus' eyes picked out and rested upon the one tribune, younger than himself, with a monobrow and long face. He swallowed nervously.

The third call went up, and everyone that was likely to attend was clearly there. Each centurion performed their headcount and passed the details to the legion's chief clerk who, wearing only his tunic and mail shirt, walked down the lines marking numbers on his wax tablet with a pointed stylus. His face became bleaker with each shout.

Slowly, in tense silence broken only by the shuffling of aching feet, the occasional snap of admonishment from an optio, and the calling of numbers, the headcount was taken and the clerk, as he totted up the numbers, turned and approached the commanders nervously.

Vitalis glared at him and, without giving him a moment to speak, snatched the tablet from his hands and examined the numbers. The clerk backed away nervously and fell in with the aquilifer, the legion's eagle-bearer, and the signifers and cornicens, where he stood judiciously examining his feet, hoping his part in this was done.

The senior tribune's face chanced colour again as he ran down the lists. When he had finished, he snapped the tablet shut, his knuckles white on the wooden case as he stared into the middle distance in an apparent daze.

Cervianus watched with nervous anticipation as the commander's gaze swept slowly across the ranks of men and rested finally on the front. At least with *numerous* small groups having gone, the capsarius would be much less likely to be singled out as someone with information on the deserters.

Unless…

His eyes fell on the long-faced tribune again. The man was clearly wrestling with some decision, a fact that did nothing to calm the capsarius's pulse.

"Thirty-two."

The senior tribune's voice cut through the silence like a blade.

"*Thirty-two* deserters," he spat.

Silence.

"Does anyone have anything to say?"

More silence. Nervous, tense, horrible silence.

"I have never *heard* of so many spineless cowards fleeing their posts in one night."

Somewhere inside, where Vitalis couldn't hear, Cervianus ran through a list of a dozen or more instances in the history of the Roman military where greater desertions had occurred: sometimes an entire cohort. Vitalis should consider himself lucky there was anyone at all still here to shout at.

The commander turned to the junior tribunes, who were standing back, trying their best to be inconspicuous. Junior tribunes were young men of little military experience, serving a required period simply to advance their political career. None of them were prepared for this.

Vitalis' eyes narrowed dangerously. "I want the names of the men on guard at the walls and on the mountain last night. You will put those names in a pot and every fourth one you draw gets a dozen lashes, including the duty centurion or optio."

Cervianus blinked. Surely that was going too far? Lashing an officer along with the men? The centurionate couldn't stand for *that*, surely? Nasica didn't even blink. What was *wrong* with the man? He should be close to exploding by now.

The tribunes fell into a whispered conversation once more as soon as Vitalis turned his gaze from them. Cervianus watched the monobrowed tribune carefully. The man seemed to have arrived at some decision and was tapping his lip, taking no part in their discussion.

The capsarius's heart lurched again, as Vitalis ground his teeth then opened his mouth.

"And for those of you familiar with the deserters…"

The commander paused as the monobrowed tribune approached him, and the two men went into a quiet, muttered conversation. As Cervianus watched, his heart in his mouth, Vitalis frowned for a long time and then finally nodded. The junior tribune stepped back and the capsarius was panicked momentarily as the officer's eyes met his knowingly.

Vitalis straightened. "Very well. It seems unlikely that we will get to the bottom of the matter at this juncture, knowing the time it would take to track down the cowards, and there are more pressing matters to attend to now. Rest assured that the deserters will be found and punished in time, as will those who knew of their plans or aided them in any way."

He took a deep breath, visibly calming himself. "However, we are at war and the matter must be pushed aside for the moment for the greater need. As soon as the sun starts its descent today, the legion will begin its march on up the Nile to Meroë where the Kandake of Kush maintains her tenuous hold on this land. The eagle of the Twenty Second will stand on the roof of her palace yet and she will kneel and kiss the standards before I have her beheaded."

A low groan issued from the men and filled the air despite the barked commands for silence from the officers. To move on south into further dangers, deeper into Kushite territory, seemed like lunacy of the highest order. Cervianus was willing to bet the instances of desertion would only increase with each day south.

"I have been advised that almost two-thirds of the missing men belonged to the First cohort, and so those men under Nasica's command will remain at Napata as the bridgehead garrison, maintaining our future supply route back to Aegyptus and imposing Roman control on the northern sector. I will lead the other nine cohorts against the Kushite queen."

As his voice trailed off, Cervianus became aware of two

things: the sighs of relief from the men of the First cohort who would stay safely here under Nasica, and the jealous looks of the rest of the legionaries who would be accompanying their *beloved* leader south. Vitalis folded his arms and glared at the men of the First cohort.

"In our absence, I want the temples here dismantled, the stone used to fortify the central structures and bolster the main outer defences. This complex may yet become a legionary fortress if the prefect in Alexandria agrees to my plans for Kush. Use the time to track down and retrieve your errant comrades before we have time to hunt them as deserters and you will be saving their lives. Once this campaign is over, any men still missing will be found and broken."

Silence fell across the square again.

"Centurions, see to your men and then report in one hour for briefing. I want the army ready to move three hours after the noon meal. Dismissed."

The centurions and optios began to shout out their orders and the centuries moved away from the square, some in formation to check on stores, perform mundane tasks or attend daily training sessions, others scattering back to their barracks. Nasica, his face still strangely, unbelievably, calm, was nodding to himself as though he had arrived at some decision. Cervianus could only hope it was a good one.

Draco, his face almost boiling over with anger, took a moment to compose himself before he spoke. "To your barracks and stay out of my sight until nightfall."

Cervianus listened as their cornicen blew the call, and then turned and walked fast away from the square, hurrying away from his irritable commander and making for the nearest building in a roundabout route to his barracks.

He jumped as he rounded the corner of the burned-out structure and almost walked straight into the waiting man. Urgently, he pulled himself to attention as the monobrowed junior tribune, leaning on the wall in a relaxed fashion, regarded him with curious eyes.

"Good. I thought it was you."

"Sir?"

The capsarius's heart pounded with dread and adrenaline. The tribune looked around momentarily to make sure they were not being observed.

"Rarely do I agree with Vitalis, but he is right on one matter: it would be in the best interests of both you and your friends if they were to return to the fold in our absence. Whether or not there is any punishment when all of this is over remains to be seen, but the simple fact is that behind us lie four hundred miles of harsh territory before your friends reach Aegyptus: territory patrolled and controlled by desert tribes who would love nothing more than to stumble across a few dozen starving and desperate Romans."

Cervianus blinked. "Respectfully, sir, I don't even know where they went."

The tribune pursed his lips and folded his arms. "You're not a fool, so don't expect me to believe that. I walked the walls myself this morning and a blind camel could have spotted the tracks they left. They cannot be far away and they must stay relatively local for now until the legion has moved off, to minimise their chances of discovery. If you value your friends, find them and bring them back here. Whatever may occur to the south, I have no intention of living out the last of my days in the Kushite sands, so we *shall* return."

Cervianus frowned. "Sir, the senior tribune—"

He stopped as the officer shook his head. "I offer this little advice in the name of sanity, but Vitalis is our commander. Don't say anything either of us may regret; my patience is not unlimited." He sighed. "Retrieve your friends, fortify this place and gather in all the supplies you can lay your hands on. I have the distinct feeling that when we return it would be prudent to have a well-stocked and well-fortified place to fall back on."

Cervianus nodded slowly. "I hope you're wrong, sir. Not about the returning, but about the need for a fortress when you do."

The junior tribune shrugged. "The Kushites are unlikely to bend and fold beneath a single legion, whatever Vitalis thinks. The land they control is as vast as Aegyptus, and they may still have the head-taking desert tribes working with them. It is, to my mind, simply a question of how soon we run into an unbeatable force. Be prepared, legionary."

Again, the capsarius nodded and the tribune smiled and, turning, walked away. Wandering on a little, musing on the officer's words, Cervianus rounded the next corner and spotted Draco near their barracks, unleashing the full force of his irritation and temper on anyone unfortunate enough to come close to him. Minding the centurion's words to stay out of his sight, Cervianus ducked in through the charred doorway of the desecrated temple.

With a strange, sad sense of loss, the capsarius wandered in through the former temple's outer peristyle. This building had been larger than many here and the outer room had been an open courtyard with a surrounding colonnade. Though the walls were charred and blackened, the room had survived well so far.

The second peristyle had been less fortunate. The enclosed room with its forest of pillars still pinged and crackled with the heat of the furnace that had roared within during the night. Carbon coated every surface and the floor was thick with ash and burned matter, some of it still hot and in parts even smouldering. Sections of wall carving were shattering and falling away.

Pulling his scarf across his mouth and nose to keep the residual smoke at bay, Cervianus wandered among the columns, feeling somehow lost and aimless. He had seemingly been tasked with preventing a slaughter and desecration and he had failed. Despite everything, Rome had come and had desecrated, vandalised, murdered and burned.

He felt sick.

"Pointless," he said quietly as he ran a finger across the blackened surface of a pillar.

It was only when the noise stopped that he realised he'd been hearing it. A quiet, rhythmic scraping sound had died away only when he spoke. Frowning, Cervianus returned to the centre of the room and peered into the inner sanctuary. A low glow was visible at the rear of the charred inner room.

"Hello?"

He was answered with an urgent shuffling.

"Hello?" he repeated as he moved in through the door. A figure at the far end of the room moved to the source of the glow: a small oil lamp standing on a fallen block. It reached out as if to douse the light.

"No... wait," Cervianus said quietly.

Picking up pace, he walked into the room and across the centre, past where the shrine would have stood before being smashed and removed to the rubble heap by the firing parties.

At closer range, the lamp lit the scene and Cervianus almost laughed as he recognised the figure in the green tunic crouched over the lamp, his armour and weapons lying nearby in a pile.

"Sentius?"

The legionary, now in reasonable health and rapidly recovering from the horrible wounds inflicted on him by the crocodile, looked up in surprise. "Cervianus?"

The capsarius grinned as he strode across the room. "I haven't seen you since before Buhen."

The legionary smiled back at him. "I wasn't sure you'd even made it across the desert. It's good to see you."

As the pair clasped hands, Cervianus frowned and glanced around him. "What are you doing?"

Sentius crouched and picked up his lamp, raising it to better display his handiwork. With just a bunched-up scarf and a bucket of river water, the man had already cleaned the carbon coating off an area of painted and carved wall some three feet across. The colours had been irreparably damaged, but there was still enough to show how beautiful they had once been. Cervianus nodded to himself in quiet appreciation, and then stopped as he focused on the detail. The head of the crocodile god stared lifeless along the cleaned area of wall, seated on a throne of some kind, some sort of staff in his hand.

"Sobek?"

Sentius nodded. "It seemed the thing to do."

"You know the tribune ordered us to demolish these temples and reuse the stone?"

Sentius spat into the blackened rubble at his feet. "That prick can march out into the desert and drop dead. I'm done with desecration."

Cervianus instinctively looked guiltily over his shoulder

to make sure no one had heard the remark, and then slowly nodded. "I suppose we should at least each do what we can, eh?" Reaching down, Cervianus grasped the scarf from his neck and removed it, dipping it in the water and adding his own efforts to the cleaning of the crocodile god's temple. Sentius watched him for a moment and then smiled and returned to his labours.

Outside, the heat and the sense of doomed expectancy gradually heightened as the cracked and charred form of Sobek watched darkly from the rubble heap nearby.

V

GARRISON

No one looked Nasica in the eye.

No one dared.

The primus pilus stood on the sandstone block that he had taken to using as a rostrum, his face as calm and emotionless as it had been continually for the past day or more. While the legionaries and their officers stood to attention in ordered rows, their gazes locked unblinking on the middle distance, eyes straight ahead, the chief centurion's swept the complex.

Since the rest of the legion, under Vitalis' command and along with the entire auxilia, had left less than half an hour ago, the dust from their passage still visible as a vague haze on the horizon, the men had been waiting tensely to see what their chief centurion had to say. His peculiar taciturn calmness had everyone on edge. He had argued not a single point with the tribune, which was extremely unlike him.

There had been no commands, reprisals or even questions from the officers regarding the fugitives, a fact that was extremely telling of their opinions, and yet the high instance of desertion from the beleaguered and unappreciated First cohort had brought Nasica, a hero of Rome and veteran of numerous wars, into disfavour and even contempt from the senior tribune. Whether the primus pilus would continue to maintain this calm in the aftermath of the endless stream of dung shovelled at him from above without passing some of it on to his men remained to be seen, since no one other than Draco had exchanged two words with the man since Vitalis' announcements the previous day.

As the senior tribune had set about preparing for his move further south, sending his men hither and thither gathering supplies and animals, he had paid not an ounce of attention to the First cohort or its officers. In return, those officers had generally assigned their men to quarters or to menial tasks away from the bustle, keeping their disgrace and humiliation out of the way of the commander.

The junior tribune with the monobrow, whose name a few carefully phrased enquiries had revealed was Catilius, seemed to be always at Vitalis' elbow during that time, somehow managing to curb the worst of his excesses and calm his temper. Cervianus watched the interaction from his quiet solitude or work and had begun to appreciate the previously unnoticed importance of Catilius to the command structure. The more he thought on Catilius, the more he could picture scenes from Syene, Abu and Buhen where the long-faced officer had been quietly and subtly at Vitalis' shoulder, muttering words of reason. Where most of the junior tribunes seemed feckless and as military-minded as a goatherd, the long-faced man seemed to have a better grip on the situation than even his superior, and the capsarius couldn't help but wonder how bad things might now be, but for the man's influence.

The past day would have been little different, though, Cervianus and his comrades keeping their heads down as they performed menial chores without comment. Parties from the

First cohort had been assigned to take care of raising mounds and monuments over the graves of the men who had fallen in the conflict that had brought them control of Napata. A number of the decorative sandstone blocks from the ruined buildings had had a hasty inscription carved in Latin and were manhandled into position by miserable soldiers.

Others had carried the bodies of the dead Kushites and heaped them up four hundred paces beyond the walls in regularly spaced piles as per the tribune's orders. Vitalis' remit had called for the executed prisoners and locals to be left in heaps in the desert for the scavengers to pick over and as a warning to any surviving locals that this was no longer their land. The other officers' opinions of the dishonourable tactic was plain from the look on their faces as they carried out his orders without open complaint.

The piles of the dead attracted birds and beasts at all times of the day and night and the smell was unbearable unless the wind picked up and blew the stench of heated decay away upriver.

Indeed, a sudden gust carried the reek of death across the centre of the complex once more, causing the men to blanch and hold their breath. Unmoved in the midst of the miasma, Nasica stood and finally clasped his hands behind his back and opened his mouth to address the men gathered before him.

"Our remit is to alter this, the Kushites' holy place, and make it a fitting legionary garrison. I am aware of the general feeling over the tribune's push toward Meroë and, while I cannot say that I hold their chances to be any higher than the rest of you do, I am bound to my duty as long as it can feasibly be carried out."

A few low grumbles issued from the men, though quietly.

Nasica's calm expression remained in place, though careful study of the twitches and movements of his face led Cervianus to the conclusion that relief was slowly suffusing the man. Whatever decision he had reached that had stopped him from defying the commander was now surfacing.

"By my reckoning, it is between ten and fourteen days' march to Meroë. Even allowing for delays and troubles: no more than sixteen. Therefore, if Meroë falls and the campaign is a success, the longest we should have to wait for word is one month; little more than two weeks if a mounted courier is sent. So we will maintain the Napata garrison for one month and one week and will then, if we have no word, raze our fortifications, gather supplies and return to Aegyptus, assuming the rest of the legion to have fallen to the Kushites."

The atmosphere almost noticeably lightened at the centurion's tacit admittance to sharing the feelings and fears of his men, though faces hardened again a moment later at the realisation of what that decision meant. If the army failed to return from Meroë, it meant that the legion's eagle had fallen into Kushite hands, and no man needed reminding of the shame and disgust that would be heaped upon the Twenty Second if that were the case. Only a generation ago, the infamous Crassus had lost three eagles to the Parthians and the ignominy of the defeat was still the greatest shame of Rome. Returning to Aegyptus without the eagle might save their lives, but not their career or their honour. From the look on Nasica's face as he drew breath to continue, the significance was not lost on him.

"However," the man said, straightening, "I intend to maintain our position here not in the disgraceful manner ordered by the tribune, but in a fashion more befitting an army of Rome. Each century will be assigned specific duties for the next two or three days, after which we should be entrenched and settled and a standard roster can be put together."

He withdrew his hands and snapped his fingers; a clerk rushing to his side. Without glancing around, Nasica retrieved a wax tablet from the man and opened the wooden case to examine the list within.

"The First century will be responsible for completing burial detail, including the stinking piles of our unfortunate new 'subjects' out there who deserve more than jackals to escort them to Elysium. You will give them proper graves and monuments, with appropriate ceremony and gravity. Once this is complete, you will turn your digging talents to increasing the defences and providing a new temporary bathhouse and latrine. I want three ditches around this wall, each wider and deeper than the current one, and the bathhouse extra-mural near the river."

A low groan rose from the men of the First.

"The Second century..." Cervianus tensed, waiting for the news, "will survey the burned temples. Any that are truly beyond repair you will dismantle to the foundations, using the stone to build up the perimeter wall and to make the central temple a defensible redoubt in the event that we cannot hold the outer wall against a potential enemy force – this place is hardly an unassailable fortress. Any temples that *are* repairable, you will do so and we may adapt for our own use in time or may leave consecrated out of respect for the local gods who will have to learn to forgive us in time."

The capsarius almost burst with relief. It was better than he could even have hoped for. Nasica's calm had been born from the decision that, regardless of the commands of Vitalis, as soon as the army left, he would be the one to give the orders and could overturn the excessive and dishonourable plans. The man had simply been waiting for Vitalis to leave.

"Third century – you will begin to carry out patrols and circuits of the land downriver to the west. Keep your eyes and ears peeled for any news or signs of our missing legionaries and, should you manage to hook a fish, bring them in without incident if at all possible – there will be no recriminations from the centurionate. Also, any locals you come across – round them up and bring them to Napata peacefully. There are farms and mines and more here that need working and we may yet have need of them. It is time to repopulate Napata."

He stopped for a moment and tapped his finger on the tablet. "Fourth century, you are on the same duty, but in the other direction: upriver to the east. You will also need to find, supply and man outposts several miles upriver to prepare for the return of the legion or the arrival of any other force."

The men began to nod and look up, focusing on their commander. Despite everything that had befallen the army, Nasica retained his ordered mind and air of authority. Such displays of humanity as this were not his norm, but in the face of Vitalis' idiotic brutality, it was all the more important.

"Fifth and Sixth centuries, you will have rotating duties. You will provide a daily and nightly guard for the walls and the plateau. Those of you not required for watch and yet still on duty will alternate between gathering and maintaining supplies and aiding the Second century on building work as directed by their centurion."

The primus pilus appeared to deflate slightly. "Which brings me to the subject of manpower. According to my figures, we are now down to two hundred and nine legionaries in the First cohort, which gives us a figure of thirty-four or thirty-five men per century. By the noon meal I will have a list of reassignments to even out the manpower. However, it appears that we are currently graced with only four centurions and five optios. Therefore, my own optio, Cunorix, will henceforth take command as centurion of the Fourth century, and Draco's optio, Vellocatus, will take command of the Sixth. We will be appointing new optios appropriately and in due course."

He nodded in satisfaction.

"I know that, while I and several of the officers, hail from Latium, most of you are Galatian, and have never set foot in Italia, but whether you secretly count yourself Gaulish or Roman, you are soldiers of the Twenty Second Deiotaran legion, and that means pride and discipline, maintenance of the Pax Romana and, most of all, honour. Remember your oath and whatever comes to pass in this land, the First cohort will return to Alexandria with that honour intact."

He threw out his arm. "Senatus Populusque Romanus!"

In a fitting tribute to the commanding veteran's hold over his men, the legionaries roared out, repeating the phrase.

For the senate and the people of Rome.

A powerful sentiment, given that most of the speakers had been born in Galatia, an independent kingdom that had watched Rome warily as its influence rolled across the world toward them until in the end it had enveloped the east.

"Very well. Fall out and equip yourselves appropriately. Centurions and optios to me."

Cervianus turned to look at Suro, the only other man remaining in the contubernium from the time of their arrival at Alexandria. The shorter, taciturn legionary was frowning.

"Let's hope they can find Ulyxes and the others and bring them back, eh?" Cervianus said quietly.

As the remaining four men in the contubernium wandered back toward the barracks, Suro nodded. "I hate construction duty, but it beats shovelling corpses or digging shit trenches, I guess."

In the midst of a curious atmosphere formed from the difficult mix of hope and fear, Cervianus and the men of his century returned to their barracks via the storehouse near the west gate, where the many tools that had been found in the complex had been gathered. Quarter of an hour later, the twenty-nine remaining men of the Second century lounged around in front of their building armed with gladius, pugio and shield, but also with pick, shovel and mattock, waiting for the officers to return from Nasica's briefing.

The scuffle as they came suddenly to attention raised a small cloud of dust and Draco rounded the corner narrowing his eyes at the brown mist and the rigid figures of the less-than-half-strength century.

"Good. Glad to see you're ready for duty."

Stopping in front of them and allowing the dust to settle, the centurion ran his shrewd eyes along the too-short lines of men and the vine staff in his good hand tapped on the bronze greave that covered his shin.

"You all heard what duties have been assigned to us."

The men nodded silently.

"What's the first priority?" he asked.

The legionaries looked at one another in surprise and confusion. "Surveying the temples, sir?" a man near the back hazarded. Draco shook his head, his expression unchanging.

"Demolishing the unstable ones?" another legionary said quietly.

Again, a shake of the head.

"Breakfast?" a voice hidden near the back called with a note of hopeful humour. Draco rolled his eyes.

Cervianus, sighing, cleared his throat. "Assigning work parties and dividing labour, centurion."

Draco's eyes whipped across and fell on the capsarius. "Precisely. I had a feeling that overactive brain of yours might stand you in good stead here. Alright – for the moment I am giving you a temporary field promotion to the rank of optio."

The other legionaries turned and cast mostly jealous looks at their compatriot, though there was no surprise in Cervianus' face, only reluctant expectation.

"Very well, sir. What are your orders?"

Draco nodded to himself as if confirming his decision, and then scanned the legionary ranks again. "I will take twenty men and begin the temple surveys. You take the other eight and start to clear out the main temple, checking the whole place over thoroughly. You know what to do?"

Cervianus nodded. "Check defensibility of the temple and come up with fortification recommendations and requirements?"

"Exactly. I've already spoken to the primus pilus and he's going to send over a couple of the best engineers we have to join our century. I'll point one of them in your direction. You've got until the noon break and then you'll report to me."

Cervianus nodded. "Yes, sir."

Draco folded his vine staff under his good arm and pursed his lips.

"Right. Everyone to the left of Patucos come with me. The rest are with Cervianus."

Turning on his heel, the centurion strode off across the dusty ground, the twenty men he'd marked out running to catch him up. The others turned to look at Cervianus. The capsarius sighed as he scanned the faces. Eight men, fortunately none from his contubernium apart from Suro, and only half of them veterans of the First cohort; the others were reinforcements drafted across after Buhen. The latter managed to grant him a certain level of respect in their expression, though the four who knew him of old looked as though they might be trouble.

He straightened. Other times he might have been proud of his sudden promotion, but here and now, it just made him all the more tired. How would old Vellocatus, the former optio, have handled this? Simple – he'd only have spoken to knock them into line. He never *had* to do any more. Well, if Cervianus was going to be an optio, he was going to have to try and act like one.

"Stop gawping like a bunch of gormless fishermen and follow me."

Turning on his heel in the same manner as Draco failed entirely to have a similar dramatic effect as he almost fell, a large, sharp stone becoming lodged in his boot. Cursing silently, he strode on toward the main temple of Amun, occasionally stubbing his foot on the floor, trying to oust the pebble. He was aware of the men following on behind, though he dared not check to make sure they were all there; it would look weak.

As they approached the temple that would be his main objective for the next two or three days, he felt a brief surge of regret that he would not be one of the men in charge of restoring the salvageable temples, where he could continue the work he and Sentius had begun on the sanctuary of Sobek. At least it was being done, though.

His eyes ranged over the long structure and he held his hand up for a halt and came to a stop some forty paces from the entrance, where he was graced with a three-quarter view of the temple. The other eight men came to a halt around him, chattering among themselves.

"Quiet," he said, but without the force or authority of an officer; more in the manner of a teacher trying to think through a knotty problem over the sound of an unruly class. Somehow, the effect was much the same and the legionaries fell silent, their eyes following his along the great structure.

"There's only the one entrance, so that's simple enough, but we need to make the roof less accessible. *We* took the place too easily. You know what that means?"

One of the men shrugged. "Means we've got to shift that entire gravel and rock slope away from the rear of the temple?"

"Exactly. We need at least ten feet of clear space behind it. The roof is high and flat, even up on the pylons, which is perfect for defence, but we'll need to fortify the edge, put up a parapet and crenelations, set braziers at strategic points and actually build and affix a door to the entranceway."

He looked up.

"The three sets of pylon towers will make the best positions for both viewing and artillery, and should have access via stairways. Anyone know if we've been left with any scorpions or whether the tribune took them all south?"

The men around him shrugged uncertainly.

"Alright. You…" He pointed at a man he didn't know. "Go find the primus pilus or his clerk. Find out if we have any artillery and, if we have, try and requisition at least two scorpions for the central temple. We'll set them up on the first pylon as it's the tallest and has the best field of vision."

He ignored the blinking surprise around him as the men tried to adapt to this new view of the cohort's medic. Cervianus nodded to himself. This wasn't *combat* command as such, after all, but more organisation, planning and logic, and that was something at which his brain excelled.

"Go," he repeated, and the legionary touched his brow respectfully and ran off toward the headquarters building.

"You two get round the back and start surveying the slope. See if you can lay your hands on a barrow or two. You'll need to find somewhere to dispose of the spoil where it can't be used by the enemy for cover from artillery."

The two men he pointed at looked at each other for a moment, shrugged, and strode off round the side of the temple.

Momentarily, Cervianus turned and looked at the remaining five men. "Come on."

The small work party made their way across the ground and in through the entrance of the temple of Amun, into the colonnaded first courtyard where a few days ago they had gained access during their night-time assault.

Stopping sharply in the open air at the centre of the court, he turned and looked back, two other legionaries almost walking into him as he drew himself up. "You two start checking out the stairways and the roof and towers. You'll have to take note of any obstacle close by that could help an attacking enemy. With the exception of major buildings, we need to clear them out of the way to give us a good defensive field of view."

The men, who had now righted themselves, nodded and made for the entrances that he indicated at the base of the pylon. With a last glance around the court, Cervianus nodded and strode on into the dark, columned room beyond. This place had not been touched since their arrival in the complex, apart from the removal and burial of bodies, and the cloying smell of blood and viscera still filled the room.

"The door to this chamber will need to be fortified, of course, and lamps permanently alight here. This room will have to serve as both barracks and armoury. We could do with assembling some form of bunks inside, around the edges."

As though dictating to a secretary, he strode on through the room. "Stacks of pila and equipment can go at the back in the corners. Then through here…"

The smaller, columned room that lay beyond was in even deeper darkness. Pausing, Cervianus frowned. "Anyone have a light with them?"

"Hang on," one man said, jogging back into the previous room. The burned-out torches from the day of the attack had been left in a pile in the corner and, while the pitch that had coated them was now dry and long gone, the parched, desiccated bundle caught easily as the legionary struck his flint on his steel belt, sparks leaping into the air. Holding a flickering torch high above his head, he strode back into the dark, columned room.

"Yes," Cervianus said, continuing his mental dictation. "This will be the headquarters for the redoubt."

He glanced ahead, into the inner sanctuary. Striding in, he beckoned to the man with the torch, who followed on closely. Amun sat with his tall, feathered crown, in the box aboard the model barque, watching the intruders with apparent distaste. The three doorways that led off from here each revealed nothing but darkness.

"Amun and his shrine will stay in situ. We're *adapting* the temple, not desecrating it. The day we leave here, it reverts to Amun's cult. The side rooms we'll have to examine in a moment, but they won't be over-large. I think they'll make suitable accommodation for the centurion and optio in charge."

His gaze fell on the room ahead. "This place, though, is the most secure chamber in the temple. I imagine the primus pilus is going to want the vexillum and anything of value kept there. This will be our 'chapel of the standards'."

Striding into the inner chamber, Cervianus beckoned once more to the torch-bearer. The last time they'd been in here had been when the hidden priests had been discovered. His eyes locked on the pivoting stone door at the rear, the newly raised optio strode over to it.

"Securest place in all Kush, I'd guess." Reaching back, he took the torch from the man behind him and examined the door, Suro and another man joining him.

"There must be a way of opening and closing this from the outside."

"Just pushing the wall?" Suro hazarded.

Cervianus shook his head. "I don't think it's that simple… unless…"

Placing his hands on the stone portal, he began to press in various places, occasionally pausing to measure a distance in hand breadths from the pivoting hinge. The door steadfastly refused to move with each push, and the legionaries began to shuffle their feet uncomfortably as the capsarius worked. Suro was just opening his mouth to urge them on when there was a grinding noise. Cervianus grinned.

"Well?" the legionary asked, the new difference in their ranks temporarily forgotten.

The capsarius pointed at the door. "It's all about pressure and force. The hinge only works when pressure is applied to certain places."

As if to demonstrate, he put his shoulder to the door and heaved against it in several places with no success. As the men watched with increasing signs of boredom, the capsarius laughed. "Now watch."

His finger carefully picked out a small carved image of a sun disc. As though attracting someone's attention, he gently prodded it with his finger and the huge stone door groaned and swung inwards. Another light poke at a sun disc on the far side, and it closed just as easily.

"Stunning piece of work." The capsarius grinned, opening it once more. "Makes it as secure as a room could really be. Let's see what's inside."

As Suro ran his finger over the sun discs on the stone surface, Cervianus grasped the torch and, holding it out in front, moved through the aperture and into the hidden room. The guttering yellow flames ahead of him ruined his night vision and it took a moment of blinking and holding the torch off to one side for his sight to return. He almost shouted out as he gave a startled jump.

The bronze face of Octavian, great-nephew of immortal Caesar and Princeps of Rome, stared out at him from the recesses of the small room. Blinking in shock, the capsarius scanned the room in the dancing orange light. Not one, but two full and impressive bronze statues stared back at him, with a third that had been beheaded, its bronze torso muscular and perfect, despite the want of a head. Beside the statues, the standards of the Syene auxiliary garrison stood, bloodstained but gleaming, lording it over the boxes and sacks of goods taken from the looted city.

"Bugger me," exclaimed Suro, following through behind him. "The Syene haul!"

Cervianus nodded, unable to find the right words. This couldn't be *everything* the Kushite invaders had taken from Syene, but it would certainly constitute the *best* of it. Presumably they had stored the most valuable goods in the most secret, safe place they had.

He grinned, but the smile slid quickly from his face.

If they had saved the best of the loot and stored it here... Why would the army abandon their best takings in a religious sanctuary if...

He turned to the laughing legionaries.

"Shit! We've got to go see the commander."

"Sir?"

"The Kushite army hasn't left this place alone and gone south, after all... or not all of it, anyway. They're probably even *based* here."

The legionaries regarded him in confusion.

"Don't you get it? The enemy are coming back *here*!"

Cervianus, with Suro and the two other legionaries hot on his heels, ran across the compound, drawing looks of surprise from all around. The large, palatial structure currently serving as the headquarters building was a hive of activity, the clerks of the cohort running back and forth with tablets containing lists and orders, newly raised centurions and optios equipping in preparation for assigning patrols and work parties, men of the Fifth and Sixth centuries arranging guard duties and passwords.

Taking a deep breath, Cervianus drew himself up straight and skittered to a halt a few paces in front of the headquarters' doorway. Two legionaries from Nasica's century stood guard to either side of the door in full dress with crests, shields, cloaks and all, sweating their strength out in the ever-sweltering sun.

"Halt!"

Cervianus nodded at them. "Optio Cervianus of the Second century. It's urgent that I speak with the primus pilus."

The men looked him up and down with narrowed eyes. Despite the ragged appearance that accompanied almost the entire cohort after the trials they had all endured, officers still tended to maintain their uniform at parade quality to stand out above the rank and file. Cervianus realised that he wore an ordinary legionary uniform that had seen far, far better days, no marks of his new rank, and was coated with red-brown dust.

"Newly raised. This is imperative!"

The two legionaries frowned for a moment and then one shrugged. "Wait here."

Turning, the man entered the doorway and disappeared inside. The other guard stood impassive. Cervianus twitched with the delay. He'd have loved nothing more than to take this to Draco first and go through the chain of command, but his own centurion was surveying more than a dozen temples and could now be almost anywhere in the compound.

Suro tugged at his sleeve in a distinctly disrespectful manner. If he lived to be an optio for a full year or more, Cervianus was fairly convinced that people would still treat him with the same level of uncertain disrespect they had done before now.

"Cerv— sir?" he amended quickly, realising they could be in earshot of the commanders.

"What?" he hissed sharply at Suro.

"Are we *really* worrying about them coming back?"

The guard's ear pricked up at the phrase.

"We're not *worrying* about them coming back. We're *sure* of it. We need to prepare for *when* they come back."

The guard frowned. "You expect the legion back soon?"

"I *wish*," said Cervianus with feeling. The guard frowned all the more and began to shift his feet nervously.

"Then what—"

The guard's sentence went unfinished as the other guard reappeared in the doorway, beckoning.

"The commander will see you, but you'll need to be brief."

Cervianus nodded and strode inside. The three legionaries with him tried to follow, but the guard at the door stepped in the way. Cervianus turned to them.

"Go find Draco and warn him."

Grateful for a purpose in the temporary confusion, the men variously nodded or saluted and ran on across the compound. Cervianus watched them go in a tight cluster and shook his head. When searching a wide area for one man, why had they run off in a group? Idiots. Despite the fact that Cervianus would be the first to pronounce himself unfit for command... well perhaps not the first, but close to the front... he could see why Draco had disregarded the rest of them. If Ulyxes had been there, mind...

Ulyxes. Why couldn't he have stayed a little longer?

His attention returned to the guard who was escorting him into the headquarters and he jogged across the room to catch up with him.

"Don't know what all this fuss is about," the guard muttered in a low voice, "but I hope it's as important as you say, 'cause Nasica's been in a foul-arsed mood all day."

Cervianus nodded as they walked. "I suspect it's about to get worse."

The escort opened his mouth to enquire further but at that moment, they arrived at the doorway to the primus pilus's office. The door was open and they could hear raised voices inside.

Peering in through the doorway, he could see Nasica standing behind a large table with a hastily drawn plan of the compound before him, as well as a copy of one of the legion's maps of Aegyptus and the tiny known portions of these lands to the south. The primus pilus's huge, bulging forearms were planted on the table, the fingers of one hand spread wide and the other slamming a pointed digit into the table forcefully. The two centurions and an optio standing sheepishly around the table were looking down at the maps studiously, likely avoiding meeting the commander's gaze.

"We will repopulate the town as we find anyone willing enough to trust us!" he snapped. "There are at least five forges, smithies and carpenters in town and we need to replace all our pila and damaged shields, repair armour and swords and so on. I *know* they're not trained armourers, but it's a simple matter of manpower. How many men can *you three* spare to make spear tips?"

The commander glowered at them, apparently having just drawn an argument to a close. He looked up at the movement in the doorway.

"Legionary Cervianus?"

The capsarius tried not to register his surprise that Nasica remembered his name. "Currently serving as centurion Draco's optio, sir. I have urgent news."

Nasica frowned, the irritation flitting from his face and professional concentration taking its place. "Go on?"

"Sir, in the central temple we've located what appears to be the cream of the goods stolen from Syene by the Kushites, including huge reserves of gold, the auxiliary standards, the statues of the Princeps and more."

Nasica's frown deepened and one of the other centurions, the commander of the Fifth, Cervianus thought, shrugged. "Excellent of course, but hardly urgent enough to interrupt."

Nasica waved a hand to quiet the man and the officer stared in surprise at the gesture and then flicked a gaze of irritation at Cervianus.

"The pick of the takings, all stored here?" the huge veteran said, his eyes narrowing.

"Yes, sir. So I assume..."

"...that this place is central to the Kushite queen's military?" the primus pilus concluded. "A possibility... one of two."

"Two, sir?" Cervianus asked, his own brow furrowing.

"Possibly this is a staging post for the Kushite army on the journey north in much the same way as we have made it one in our push south; a garrison of sorts." He leaned back. "Or possibly it's being used as a store for the loot through a stroke of misfortune. It could be that while escorting the treasure back south, the army was suddenly called upon for something else and had to leave the haul somewhere safe to collect later."

Cervianus nodded thoughtfully. "They've taken the head of one of the statues of the Princeps Octavian, sir. A trophy, you think?"

Nasica shrugged. "If so, then the army that left the haul here was not commanded by the queen. Some officer would have taken it then as proof of his success and given it to his queen."

Cervianus nodded again. "I think there *is* a military garrison based here though, sir, and the more I think about it, the more I'm convinced."

Nasica frowned. "Go on?"

"Well, sir. We faced just over a hundred guards, going from the combined number of bodies and captives. There were forty-six priests..." a brief pause to assure himself he had discounted the three secret escapees from the number, "and fewer than twenty civilians within the complex. That's a total population of less than two hundred all told within the walls."

"Yes?"

Cervianus shrugged.

"The stores in the compound could keep ten times that number going for an entire campaign, sir. Even allowing for the fact that the harvest season has just ended, the stores must account for five times the amount that the local farms could produce. It has to have been shipped in and stored for a purpose and priests just don't need that kind of supply system."

The other centurions broke into a low, hushed discussion until Nasica glared at them long enough to instil silence.

"It's a persuasive argument," he mused.

Cervianus nodded. "There are also three noble palaces here, sir. In Kush, as in other cultures, it seems to be the tradition that nobles command the army. If there is no military presence in Napata, why would three major noble houses be constructed within a religious sanctuary? Even allowing for a noble commanding the compound guards, which is unlikely since they are probably the province of the priesthood, that would only require one."

Nasica was now scouring the map on the table with his gaze, his attention still locked on Cervianus' words.

"Furthermore," the capsarius continued, sure now of his logic, "we found five or six ancillary buildings that were empty and appeared to serve no purpose. They could be indicative of stores that had been emptied when the garrison moved out on campaign. Our men are quartered in rooms in the palaces and houses that are so perfect they might as well have been built to house a contubernium. Why?"

"Because that's what they *were* built for," finished Nasica. He straightened. "Alright. You've sold me on the idea. Napata seems to be the base for a force that is currently out on campaign. So where are they?"

Cervianus stood silent; he had run out of answers.

"They're not to the north or the west," the primus pilus mused, tapping his finger to his lips as his eyes strayed across the maps before him. "We or the rest of the army would have found at least some evidence of them on the journey here. That means they are either to the south or the east."

His fingers traced across the map as he spoke.

"If it's east, Vitalis will march the legion straight against them, and what happens then is impossible to guess without knowledge of the ground and their numbers and capabilities. If they're to the south, they must be on one of the many desert trails we don't know. Why, and what they would be hoping to achieve are equally beyond me."

"They're both east *and* south," said Draco, marching into the room and falling in beside Cervianus.

Nasica frowned at the centurion.

"It's what *we'd* do, sir," Draco clarified. "They've not met us in battle anywhere on the journey, with the exception of small caretaker garrisons, and that's because they're trying to drag us further south and weaken us all the time until we're too feeble to take them on. Once they have us broken and tired and half-dead, they'll close on us and the legion will simply disappear from history without a trace."

The primus pilus nodded thoughtfully. "You think they're split into two armies? A pincer movement?"

Draco nodded. "I'd say that as soon as the army left Aegyptus with the loot, they came south to Napata, leaving small garrisons to meet us en route, and marshalled here for a time. That way they would always know how far south we had come and had the entire army on hand to react appropriately. They must have split their army in two once we were closing on them and sent them south and east in preparation to spring a trap shut on us."

Nasica frowned. "But we took them by surprise? We came by an unsuspected route."

Cervianus slapped his forehead. "They had warning, sir."

The senior centurions turned to look at him questioningly.

"They must have learned of us crossing the desert from the native tribes," Cervianus replied. "*They* knew where we were; they rustled our animals and stole our supplies, after all."

Nasica shook his head. "I thought we'd ascertained after Buhen that they had turned on their Kushite masters?"

"Perhaps, sir. Perhaps not. Mercenaries are hardly predictable, and there are likely more than one tribe."

Draco nodded. "One army, then, retreating up the Nile toward a prepared ground that they know well. Another hidden in the desert that can then come up behind them and... well you know how that'll end, sir."

Every officer in the room nodded silently. They had underestimated the Kushites in almost every way. The legion was likely marching at this very moment into a deadly trap, leaving the First cohort at Napata in the path of the closing jaw.

In the ensuing tense silence, Cervianus examined the map between them.

"The Kushite garrison may have moved out of Napata."
He frowned. "But they must be close; close enough to observe
us, otherwise they would not know when to move again. The
stores and facilities here would support a garrison of perhaps
a thousand. If this second army is of that strength, it explains
why they did nothing about the tribune's brutality…"

He paused, realising that he had just levelled a career-
threatening accusation against the most senior officer in the
legion, but nobody here even raised an eyebrow in dissent.

Nasica nodded.

"A force of a thousand would not have dared move on
Napata when Vitalis was still here. We would seriously
outnumber them. Their job will be to seal off the escape to
the north; to contain the legion in Kush while the main force
annihilates us. The complete loss of the invasion army will
deter Rome from trying anything similar for generations.
Hades, if that's the case, the governor could even abandon the
southern regions to Kush just to strengthen what he *can* hold
with the Third and Twelfth."

Draco straightened, his eyes suddenly glinting with
anticipation. "And now that Vitalis has gone?"

They all fell silent again, contemplating the situation, the
tension building until the centurion of the Fifth shrugged.

"Aren't we taking a lot for granted here, sir? This is all mere
speculation based on a pile of stolen goods and the theories of
a field medic with no command experience."

Nasica turned slowly to the man. Cervianus couldn't see
the primus pilus's face, but the other centurion swallowed
nervously and stepped into the background. As the commander
straightened, he turned back to Draco and Cervianus.

"A little over two hundred men against an estimate of a

thousand. The odds aren't good, especially given our poor level of available ammunition. Not more than half of the men have a shield now, and some of them haven't even had body armour since the march across the desert. I'm not convinced we can hold Napata against the enemy."

Draco nodded and took a deep breath. "Chances are, if they are allied again, that they also have desert mercenaries with them, as well as any locals who saw what we did to the local population. They'd likely join the purge. We could be looking at a lot more than a thousand, and the perimeter's too wide."

He turned to Cervianus. "Have you finished surveying the centre temple?"

The capsarius nodded. "Yes, sir. It could be made borderline defensible in around an hour. Given a day or more, it could be a veritable fortress."

"Good," Nasica replied. "We'll forget the latrines and the rest of the menial work. As soon as the dead are buried, have every man either on patrol in the surrounding area or fortifying the main temple. I want at least two hours' warning of approaching enemies and a solid fortress prepared for them when they arrive."

Draco saluted. "Cervianus – get back to the temple and get to work. I'll send you more men as I reassign them."

The capsarius saluted in turn to Draco and then Nasica and spun on his heel, almost running from the room, his heart racing. It seemed hard to credit that a quarter of an hour ago it appeared that everything had settled and they would be waiting on the sideline for a war they would be no part of. Now, it appeared as though most of the cohort was marching into the maw of Cerberus, while they themselves would be playing Vercingetorix to the Kushite's Caesar, defending a fortress against a superior enemy.

Could they have been wrong? Had that other centurion been right when he said that they were simply speculating? He shook his head. No... that the situation was clear to him was enough on its own. That the strategic and experienced commanders concurred was all but conclusive proof.

As he strode out of the building's entrance, past the two legionaries on guard, he found the three men he had sent to locate Draco standing waiting for him. As he joined them, Suro walked alongside him, staring at him.

"Is it true, then?"

"What?"

"You're sure they're coming back?"

Cervianus nodded as he walked fast toward the Amun temple, the legionaries hurrying to keep up. "Not just coming back, they might already be nearly here. They've only been waiting for the bulk of the legion to move on. We need to make the temple defensible – we can't hold the wall against more than a thousand Kushites."

He strode on for several steps before he realised that he was alone. Stopping, he turned to find the three legionaries standing motionless a few paces back and staring at him.

"What now?"

"More than a *thousand*?" repeated Suro, his eyes wide.

"Certainly not less. Depends on whether those desert warriors in black from Buhen are with them again and whether they've stirred up the local populace."

Suro's eyes widened further and he started to back away, shaking his head.

"Where are you going? We need to get the temple fortified."

"Piss on the temple. We've got to run."

Cervianus stared at him as the other two men started to back away too. "Where are you going to run *to*?"

Suro was still shaking his head. "Anywhere that's not here. Should have gone with Ulyxes when I had the chance... the man was right."

Cervianus grumbled and clenched his fists as he stepped forward. "You *can't* desert now. Every man makes a difference at this point. I'm your optio now, remember. I won't let you run."

"Watch me." Without another word, the three men turned their backs on their temporary officer and ran off toward the barrack block. For a moment, Cervianus wondered whether he should chase them down or report them to Draco, or continue with the temple's alteration as the more important task. He dithered in the hot, dusty square before the Amun temple, unsure of what he should do, until suddenly a distant call went up from a horn.

He frowned, trying to identify the order in the call's notes and his own eyes widened as he heard the second and then third musician join in.

They were not Roman horns.

He was already running before the alarm went up.

It was a mad, panicked hour and a half.

Despite the proximity of the enemy horns, they heralded only the vanguard of the Kushites and even then the sound had been amplified as it rang across the wide, open desert to the south, giving a false impression of the enemy's proximity.

Nasica and Draco had immediately set to work with all the

professionalism one could expect of the senior centurionate. The outer wall had been abandoned and all effort bent to fortifying the temple of Amun, which would be their only protection when the source of the music finally arrived.

In a constant flurry, the men of the Twenty Second Deiotariana ran hither and thither with tools, equipment, stores and materials. Pairs of soldiers heaved heavy rocks onto the wooden platforms where they were hauled up on ropes by more legionaries who used them to complete the parapet. The three scorpion bolt throwers the cohort had been left with were lifted to the high towers above the front pylon and to the rear of the temple roof, below which more men repeatedly lifted and shovelled stone and sand into barrows, wheeling it away from the wall and removing the sloping access, dumping the loads next to a nearby temple.

Amid the exhausting and frenetic activity, men spoke little and prayed a great deal, and it was not uncommon to spot a soldier emerging guiltily from one of the more intact temples, his purse a little lighter from making an offering, before rushing back to work. The knowledge that they had, however unwillingly, taken part in a deliberate desecration seemed to have preyed on the minds of many and the need to undo their abhorrent acts had led to a more immediate show of piety than the traditional prayers to Mars, Fortuna or Taranis.

Though the chaos, Cervianus moved around, dividing his time between relaying the commands of the centurions and carrying out the duties of an optio, helping with the actual labour as best he could, and preparing one of the rear rooms in the temple as a makeshift medical station. He did it all almost in a dream, though, his spirits plummeting in line with those of his comrades, merely going through the motions to prepare a defence against hopeless odds. Every step around the complex brought extra depression and resignation, and every order he gave brought a little extra weight to his shoulders.

The near-autonomy his temporary promotion granted allowed him to move with relative freedom throughout the complex on his own schedule, and yet it was still a surprise when he found himself standing alone outside the partially restored temple of Sobek and no recollection of where he had been heading before his mind had wandered. He peered at the temple's entrance with a mixture of surprise and suspicion and pursed his lips.

After all, the other soldiers had been doing it…

Taking a deep breath, and wishing that even one of his friends was still here with him, the capsarius dipped inside, striding through the peristyle rooms toward the small, dark sanctuary of the god, not sure whether he was here to beg, argue or just observe, or what he would give if an offering seemed appropriate.

Here, inside the heart of the holy structure, the din and busyness of the outside world was almost inaudible and it was almost possible to forget that death was descending on them at a frightening pace. The chipped and battered crocodile god stared at him from the central shrine where he had been replaced this morning from his previous ignominious position on the spoil heap.

The capsarius narrowed his eyes at that knowing reptilian expression. "Why?" he suddenly found himself demanding.

Folding his arms, he stepped into the deeper gloom of the dark shrine. "Why this? Why us? Why *me*?"

He flung out his arm toward the statue and walked slowly

around it, talking as though addressing the senate of Rome: a rhetorician's stance.

"I mean, I've never been a man to fawn over gods or thank you for doing things that I know damn well are just natural or pure chance, I'll admit. I've always been a man of reason. I believe in you all, of course, and fear you appropriately, but not for simple things like rain or the passing of kidney stones."

He shook his head as though denying a truth.

"But then I come to Aegyptus... Kemet as your people call it, and you change me. In a few short months you strip away my reason and my logic and turn me into a superstitious wreck, bordering on some sort of prophet like those among the Hebrews."

He stopped and pointed an accusing finger at the statue.

"That was *your* doing. The gods of *Galatia* and *Greece* and *Rome* all sit in their high mountains or their forest glades and happily accept what happens with aloof impunity and watch and preside, rarely pointing a finger or trying to involve themselves in the works of men, but here in Aegyptus? *No.*"

Angrily he returned to striding in a circle around the statue.

"No. Here in Aegyptus, you won't sit back. You won't leave people alone. And I could have been happy performing the will of the gods if you would only damn well make it clear what it is you want!"

His arm thrust out again toward what he thought was approximately north.

"Haroeris made it clear to me at Syene. I could have stopped it then and I didn't, because a life is a life, even when it belongs to a megalomaniac moron. Haroeris made his wishes known and, though I failed in the task, at least I *knew* what it was he wanted. He promised us pain and death if we went on. Well that's exactly what we've got."

Sobek watched him pass by with dead eyes that still somehow seemed to harbour secrets.

"But the rest of you? Dreams and half-imagined weirdness. I've tried to work out what you wanted, but perhaps I've got it wrong. I thought I would be able to save the temples. I was almost sure that was what I was here to do, but I cannot even conceive of a way that could have happened. Short of assassinating Vitalis myself, I had no control, and you would hardly pick a healer if that was your plan. If there *was* a way, then I clearly failed again. Are you playing with me?"

He stopped again and glared at the god.

"Thoth and Sekhmet and you. Others too. You were all there in that nightmare. Was it just my mind? I think not, given how you've insinuated yourself into almost every step I've taken in this benighted land. Coincidence can only be blamed so far, and then I have to lay it all at your feet. So what is it that you want from me? Why allow us to come this far if there's no purpose for us yet and we're just going to die today? Why allow us to live after we'd desecrated Napata? Unless it was to repair the damage. But then, why bring death to us before we can finish the job?"

He started pacing yet again.

"Because dying is exactly what we're going to do, you know? Those warriors about to cross the river? They're going to skin us when they've finished taking our heads. Is this because I've failed? Is this *my* punishment?"

He spread his arms wide.

"Look at these people. Haven't you put them through enough now? Haven't they *suffered* enough? It was *Vitalis* who holds the ultimate responsibility and he's not here. Or perhaps it's me for not stopping him. Either way, you should punish where the blame lies, not these men who have been good and honest and even tried to save your temples."

A thought struck him.

"It *is* me, isn't it? All this shit you've been throwing has all been at me, hasn't it? But you're like a bad archer, missing the target all the time and felling those around me. They're all suffering because I'm here, aren't they?"

Angrily, he reached down to his belt and untied his purse, flinging it onto the basalt plinth next to the paltry offerings of a dozen other frightened soldiers.

"Here. Not much of an offering, I'll grant you, but it's all I have."

Again, his eyes narrowed and he cocked his head to one side.

"Almost all, anyway."

Turning his back on the glassy eyes of Sobek, he strode from the sanctuary and out though the columned rooms into the bright sunlight. Two soldiers hovered uncertainly outside.

"What?" he snapped at them.

"Sir, the centurion told us to report to you. We're to serve as medical orderlies."

Cervianus shook his head at the madness of it all. As if anyone was going to live through today, anyway.

"Get to the temple, find the room I already prepared and familiarise yourself with all the supplies in there, but don't touch anything on the surgical tool table or the medicine shelf."

The two legionaries saluted and, grateful to have a small task that would take their mind off the larger issues, ran toward the Amun complex. Cervianus watched them go for a moment and then turned and strode off in the other direction, toward the southern gateway in the perimeter wall, where a contubernium of men stood watch, eyeing the growing force beyond the river with dismay.

With a strength of purpose he hadn't felt for some time, Cervianus stormed across the compound to the gate. "What's the situation?"

One of the guards shrugged disconsolately. "There's maybe seven or eight hundred of them gathered now, but at least as many more coming up behind, with cavalry on the edges. Looks like they're waiting for the whole army to mass before they cross."

Cervianus nodded. As soon as they crossed that river, the small force in control of Napata might as well open their wrists and go painlessly to the next world.

"Open the gate."

The soldier stared down at him. "Sir?"

"I said: open the gate. I'm going down to the river for a closer look."

"Sir, that's mad. They've got archers that can just about reach the near bank. You go down to the water and you're a sitting duck."

"Just do as you're told and open the gate. You can close it as soon as I'm through."

Obediently and yet with confusion and consternation, the soldiers swung the large wooden portal inwards.

"If you're doing a runner, sir, you'd be better off going out the west gate."

The man flinched at the look Cervianus shot him and stood to attention silently as the haggard-looking optio/capsarius strode past him and out toward the river. Ignoring the noises of the gate closing behind him and the low, muttered and confused conversation of the guards who watched him intently, the capsarius walked with a straight back and chin raised proudly, arms swinging purposefully by his side, across the short stretch of dusty ground and into the cultivated land.

The division between the two landscapes always struck him as eerily well defined. An irrigation ditch separated dusty brown gravel underfoot from the green stalks of harvested crops, sitting in rich, black earth. His feet sinking into the soft soil, Cervianus made his way across the small strip fields and directly toward the river, where he could clearly see the army now gathering on the far side.

Curiosity struck him as he walked and his eyes strayed across the host on the far bank. The cavalry at the flanks were dressed in white, armed with round shields and long spears, their beaded hair held back by white bands of cloth. The mass of the army in the centre reminded him of the howling warriors they had faced at Abu Island and Buhen, though figures in black could be seen moving around toward the rear, a clear indication that at least some of the head-taking desert dwellers were with them. Half a dozen smaller pockets of archers stood in groups among the infantry, bows already in hand and arrows nocked. The memory of their deadly accuracy when picking off the fleeing auxiliaries of Syene sent a tingle of fear up the capsarius's spine as he neared their range.

The centre, though, was what drew the eye. The leader... the queen, perchance?... sat astride a large white steed, dressed in glittering mail and blue and white cloth, some gleaming coronet adorning its head and holding down a hood of blue. In its hand, the figure held a long spear with a gleaming tip, the shaft decorated with feathers of multiple hues. Around the commander, other nobles clustered in their gleaming armour, a guard of elite soldiers in blue and white and glittering mail tightly packed and eager for blood.

As the solitary figure of the capsarius neared the edge of the water, arrows began to arc up from the enemy force and land with a splash in the slow waters of the Nile, each shot reaching closer and closer to the strange lone target.

Cervianus grunted at the danger and strode ahead toward the falling missiles.

Somewhere across the water, among the leaders, a call went up and the arrows ceased as the entire Kushite force settled in to watch the strange spectacle of this fearless madman marching purposefully toward them.

Without sparing them a further glance, Cervianus stomped down the slight incline to the riverbank, where reeds hid the edge in a mass of green stalks. He barely slowed as his feet plunged into the water and sank into the sucking, deep mud beneath. Struggling to maintain forward momentum, the capsarius heaved his feet up and out of the murk, taking deliberate steps forward, his arms parting the reeds until he came to a halt in the centre of the green mass, some five or six paces from solid ground.

"Come on then!" he yelled at the water.

Nothing stirred, barring the few soldiers across the water who were enjoying the pre-battle entertainment.

"Come on, you bastard. You want a sacrifice? Take me."

Swinging his arms around, Cervianus thrashed at the reeds, yelling incomprehensible threats and demands at the gods until his voice cracked and became hoarse and his arms tired. Finally, he fell silent, staring around him through the broken reeds and the water that lapped his chest.

"Come *on*," he repeated through clenched teeth.

His heart skipped a beat as he turned and saw the beast – one of the largest crocodiles he'd seen, perhaps seven paces in length and so dark as to be almost black, making it difficult to make out the details and edges.

Other than the darkness of the hide and the size of the ridged monster, the only thing he would later remember was the eye. The heavy-lidded, slitted orb was a very pale green, the colour of old jade, a stark contrast to the dark skin, almost hypnotic, and it wasn't until it blinked that Cervianus realised he'd been riveted to the spot while the thing bore down on him, parting the reeds as it came.

Cervianus, former surgeon of Ancyra, adoptive Roman, field medic, junior officer, pragmatist and now, at the end, fatalist, watched the huge creature approach and felt suddenly free of responsibility and fear. In a horribly painful and yet thankfully brief moment it would all be over. He would have atoned for his part in the violence and terror that Vitalis had brought to Kush. Whether the gods would aid the rest of the men when he was gone was not his decision.

He closed his eyes and waited.

The wash of river water as the creature turned sharply knocked him back and he had to pedal in the water to prevent ducking completely beneath the surface.

He opened his eyes, spitting out the cold liquid and fragments of flora from the wash, to see the long, snaking tail disappearing into the green.

And then the crocodile was gone.

Cervianus stared for a long time at the empty space where the magnificent beast had been, the water washing the wavering reeds and lapping at the stalks.

It took a near miss by one of the deadly Kushite archers to draw him back to the real world. The missile units across the river had resumed their assault and shafts fell into the water nearby with repeated splashes and plops. For a long moment, Cervianus wondered whether to simply stand still until one of them found the correct range, but that would serve no purpose. If even Sobek had turned his back on him, what else was there to do but to stand alongside those men in whom he believed and die with them for the honour of the legion? He could at least try to save someone.

Nasica and Draco and Sentius at least deserved no less.

With a sigh of resignation, the dejected capsarius waded slowly and with difficulty from the water and staggered up the bank, his boots sucking into the earth as rivulets of sacred water, the Tears of Isis, ran down his flesh and fell from his garb.

Ignoring the arrows falling behind him, he strode back toward the camp and toward his destiny: to fall with honour beside great men.

VI

FORTRESS

Cervianus leaned on the hastily constructed parapet, ignoring the slight rocking as he put his weight onto the merlon. None of the defences had been mortared into place; there had simply not been time. Beside him, Draco watched with his usual stoic yet sour expression, while the men of the First cohort shuffled their feet nervously.

The reused, charred temple blocks formed a small parapet perhaps three and a half feet tall – enough to aid the temple's defence, but only of partial use against missile attacks as the guardians would have to duck quite low to find enough cover, a difficult task when fully armed and armoured.

The entire temple-fortress was around six hundred feet in length and two hundred wide, a perimeter that afforded a defensive force of one man every six paces along the roof, with half as many in reserve as a second line, a crew of half a dozen on each tower, a dozen more defending the front gate and another dozen plus officers and support staff in the interior. Not much of a garrison, and considerably smaller than any there would have liked to see.

Between, and slightly behind, every man on the parapet and tended by the reserve soldiers stood the depressingly thin stacks of pila, along with piles of stones and braziers kept smouldering on the infinitesimally small chance that they could hold the makeshift fortress until dark.

Now, with all that could be done having *been* done, the men had nothing else to do but wait. It was now, as they had nothing to occupy them and keep their minds from the coming fray, when dark thoughts and despair began to sink into the legionaries of the Twenty Second.

Moans rose here and there, and few officers had enough heart left in them to try and keep it down. The almost continual mutter of desperate prayers filled the air above the temple roof, some in Latin and some in their own, more sacred Galatian language. Taranis was called upon to favour the defenders, for certain, but more often the god's name was invoked to look after loved ones and family thousands of miles to the north and whom they would never see again.

His eyes blinking in the bright early afternoon sun, Cervianus had to admit that if he had any belief, love or respect left for the deities of this world, the sight out there across the compound would have had him offering up a few choice promises too.

The Kushites had crossed the river in a leisurely, almost negligent manner. Slowly, units traversed the great life-giving torrent and formed up on the northern bank, amid the green farmland. They had done so with great show and pomp, granting the frightened defenders all the time in the world to examine the strength and number of their enemy.

Once the cavalry had crossed, they had made a few forays to the walls, riding up and around them, confirming that the Roman commander had abandoned them for the more secure central structure. The horsemen had ridden silently and with purpose. No jeers or threats were needed to frighten the legionaries further, and their leader knew the power of a good display. The Kushite horses were tightly controlled and ordered, more so than the generally disfavoured Roman cavalry; their armour was strong and well kept and the spears, swords and shields they carried of a uniform style. These were not the low warriors that had defended Abu or Buhen, but a force of strong and organised soldiers.

Slowly, and with equally despair-inducing show, units of well-equipped foot soldiers had formed up in small bands, moving into positions around the circuit of the walls but well out of range. After them came the units of archers, occasionally firing a single arrow to test the maximum range and make sure the Kushite forces remained out of missile range of the Romans. Then the bulk of the warriors crossed and formed in less organised, though large and frightening masses.

Finally, saved till the last moment, perhaps to strike yet more fear into the hearts of the defenders, the groups of black-clad desert dwellers had crossed in their own bands, filling the gaps in the force.

And then a time had passed with no activity and no noise: a psychological attack in itself, weakening the knees and bladders of men who watched the seemingly endless ranks of Kushites and their allies who, in turn, watched them.

Now, almost an hour later, while the men were as deep in the pit of despair as they were ever likely to be, something had begun to happen out there. Nasica, standing on top of the tower at the first pylon and with a magnificent view of the whole affair, called out with a confidence that was felt by few.

"Their leader comes to parlay."

A tense, expectant silence fell as he finished, the men uniformly hoping for a way out.

Cervianus continued to watch as a small unit detached itself from the front lines of the enemy force, the leader approaching the walls on horseback, accompanied by two dozen men. The tall character Cervianus had seen across the river made its way into the south gate of the complex and climbed up the steps until it reached the parapet, where it stood alone, some three hundred paces from the Roman defenders, though at the same elevation.

Again, silence ruled.

Slowly, the figure reached up and removed the coronet, allowing the colourful hood to fall away. Cervianus found he was irritated with himself for his assumption that the queen herself would be leading this army. The indrawn breath across the roof told him that most of the others had made the same assumption.

It appeared they would die in Kush without ever seeing the woman who ordered it.

The man had a wide, dark-skinned face with high, chiselled cheek bones and a heavy brow that accentuated the whites of his dark eyes. His hair fell in shoulder-length braids and his neat moustache and beard added a frame that picked out the incredible brightness of his white teeth as he opened his mouth.

What he shouted across the sandy ground was as incomprehensible to the defenders as anything they had heard in the local dialect, though it was hard not to appreciate the fact that his voice managed to remain soft and smooth and deep, despite the volume he achieved.

The long sentence echoed away among the cracks and crevasses in the rock face above them as the sun continued to sizzle and fry the men below. Once more, a long silence fell, soldiers shuffling nervously and gripping their weapons in white-knuckled fists. Then something happened that shattered Cervianus' preconceptions in a way he could never have predicted – the man spoke again, and the capsarius blinked.

"Anyone know what that was?" barked Nasica from the tower above when the enemy commander fell silent once more. "Sounded familiar."

Cervianus, still shaking his head in disbelief, cupped his hands around his mouth and addressed his commander. "He asked if we spoke Greek, sir."

Nasica leaned down over the tower top. "How in Hades would this man know Greek?" Without waiting for an answer, he gestured to Cervianus. "Tell him yes and then get your backside up here."

The capsarius, still feeling flustered by what he considered a display of the most civilised kind in so barbarous a land, turned back to the parapet.

"I speak Greek!" he bellowed, and then stepped back, slipping down the ladder, his feet on either side sliding down the wood, to the courtyard below, where he made for the narrow doorway and pelted up the stairs to the pylon top.

A few heartbeats later he arrived on the tower, his knees wobbling from the climb and heaving in gasping breaths. The three-span torsion catapult stood at the tower's centre, a brazier nearby along with a repository for missiles. Nasica stood beside it, in front of the artillery crew.

"Get up here, Cervianus. He's talking again."

The capsarius staggered over to the commander and tried to concentrate on the deep, smooth voice over the pounding of his own blood in his ears.

"Don't know what he was saying, sir, but it's something about his queen. Missed most of it, but that last part was about her walking on a path of Roman bones."

He fell silent at the look on Nasica's face.

"You tell that shit-pile excuse for a leader that I'll piss through his eye socket before that ever happens."

Cervianus paused, wondering whether to repeat the insult word for word but, sure in the knowledge that he was probably the only Greek-speaker present, he took a deep breath and replied in a clear, calm voice.

"The centurion Quintus Scribonius Nasica, commander of the First cohort and representative of Rome, requests the name of the man to whom he speaks."

Another pause as Nasica narrowed his eyes. "That wasn't what I said, was it?"

"More or less, sir," Cervianus replied without looking him in the eye.

The enemy leader folded his arms.

"I am Kalabsha, chosen warrior of the Kandake Amanirenas of Kush, son of Amun and master of Kaerma. Tell your centurion Quintus that by dark we will control Napata but that I, Kalabsha, am inclined to mercy."

Cervianus narrowed his eyes. Mercy seemed an unlikely proposition at this point. Shaking his head, he turned to the primus pilus.

"A lot of posturing, sir, but he's a general called Kalabsha, sent by the queen. Essentially, he says he will control Napata by nightfall and is offering some sort of mercy."

Nasica frowned. "How does a barbarian like this even know Greek? I thought only rich Roman pretty boys and time-wasting thinkers spoke it?"

Cervianus nodded, not at the sweeping general insult, but at the question.

"There are a number of Greek-founded trading settlements on the Gulf coast that have been there for centuries. And, of course, Greek was spoken in Aegyptus for a long time... still is in some places. It's not impossible that he learned it here."

Nasica took a deep breath. "That dog's cock has as much intention of granting us mercy as I have them. Best find out what he wants, though."

Cervianus nodded again.

"The centurion *Nasica*," he announced, stressing the commander's cognomen rather than the somewhat familiar form of address the enemy leader had previously taken, "will hear your terms."

Kalabsha gestured at the temple with a sweeping arm. "Surrender yourselves to me and I will allow one-third of your men to go free."

Without waiting to translate to Nasica, Cervianus cupped his hands again. "And the others?"

"One-third will return to Meroë as slaves. The officers will all have to die for what they have done to this holy place, but that does not have to be a fate shared by the common soldiers of Rome."

His voice low to prevent the words being heard by the majority of the men on the rooftop, Cervianus repeated the offer to Nasica, who sneered.

"Allow the standards to fall into their hands without a fight and sell ourselves into death and slavery on the off-chance that they actually decide to send a century's worth of men away? Could you answer that for me, optio?"

Cervianus nodded. He himself had been wondering at

the ambiguity of the promised freedom. The likelihood that the sixty or more men would be set free naked and without provision had occurred to him. An enemy blade would be a faster death.

"Centurion Nasica thanks you for your offer, but would like to offer *you* the opportunity to surrender now and disband your forces before we have to do something you might regret."

The spluttering of the general was audible even here, and Nasica turned to Cervianus with a suspicious smile. "I suspect I get the drift of what you just said. Pissed him off, didn't it?"

Cervianus nodded. "A little, sir. Look."

Kalabsha was waving angrily over the wall toward his forces. After a moment, he turned back toward the Romans and started shouting at them unintelligibly in his own language. As he ranted and gestured, Nasica took a deep breath, three steps backward and crouched. The enemy leader's violent invective went on for a few heartbeats, ending suddenly as, with a *twang*, the scorpion by which the primus pilus stood launched an iron-tipped bolt two feet long at a high elevation.

Cervianus watched in stunned awe as the missile rose in a graceful arc, crossing the compound with an incredible accuracy, and plummeted to the gatehouse, smashing into the parapet not much more than a foot from Kalabsha's toes.

A roar of approval went up from the men on the temple roof as the enemy leader leapt back from the sudden danger and almost toppled over the outer side of the wall.

The range and effectiveness of Rome's artillery was often the breaking point of an enemy force. Still, three hundred paces was not far off the absolute maximum range a man could coax from the one-man weapon and even then it had to be loosed at such an arc that real accuracy was nigh-on impossible. Effective accurate range was less than a *third* of that.

Nasica's shot had been the stuff of legend.

Slowly the roar died, giving way to a rhythmic chant of the primus pilus's name across the temple-fortress. Nasica turned to Cervianus.

"Tell our esteemed opposition that the next shot will nail his dick to the gate if he doesn't get out of my compound."

Despite everything, Cervianus found himself grinning as he turned back to the furious, dancing figure on the gate and translated his commander's words absolutely faithfully. Kalabsha shouted a number of curses, some in his own language and others in Greek, before running down the stairs at a very un-regal pace and disappearing outside to his forces. As the defenders watched, new calls went up on the enemy's animal horns and the huge force began to deploy in preparation for an assault.

"What now, sir?" Cervianus enquired of his commander.

"Their cavalry are largely useless. He could dismount them for the assault but that would be a waste, given the numbers he controls. See? They're already moving to the rear. I'd say they'll stay with him and his bodyguard like a Roman praetor, while the rest move."

The capsarius nodded. That was what appeared to be happening. "And the rest?"

Nasica pursed his lips. "The archers will be no use on the walls. They may be good, but even the scorpion only just managed, so they could never reach that far. They'll have to get those men to somewhere within range. That means either the roof of nearer buildings or the top of the mountain."

Cervianus' heart skipped a beat.

"The mountain? They'll have an easy shot down on us."

Nasica nodded. "Not yet, though. He'll only send half his archers up there at most. They'll probably not get up to the top of the cliff before nightfall, and then archers are much less effective. Plus, as soon as the enemy footmen start to attack the temple, archers above will kill as many of them as us, if not more. No. They're not much of a threat until tomorrow morning. It's any that get positioned on the roof of other buildings we need to be wary of."

"Wish we had archers of our own, sir."

Nasica shook his head. "In our situation, it's better to have trained infantry. Never trusted archers all that much myself. Too limited and vulnerable."

The primus pilus folded his arms and drummed his fingers.

"I'd have liked to have demolished a few of these buildings but, given the tribune's actions, I'm not about to emulate him. We'll keep the scorpions picking off any rooftop archers unless anything changes. Between that and every man keeping his shield up and being aware of his surroundings, we can prevent too many casualties to their arrows."

Cervianus nodded and was struck once more by just what an awe-inspiring figure the legion's chief centurion was, indomitable and powerful.

"So we need to keep an eye out above and keep the artillery on the archers. The cavalry are out of it. What of the infantry, sir?"

Nasica shrugged. "He won't commit his good troops until he's sure. First few attempts will be with his base warriors, conscripts and local volunteers, testing our defences. They shouldn't be too much trouble, but we'd best be prepared for surprises anyway. While that lot attack, he'll use the chaos to send his archers in to nearby structures, accompanied by a few of his better men. We'd best be prepared. It's about to start."

Cervianus stepped back and, as he turned, a thought struck him. "Perhaps you should send a contubernium up the cliffs, sir? If we can get a few men up top and hidden, they can seriously hamper any attempt by the enemy to get a view down on us."

Nasica nodded. "Strategic thinking. It's a death sentence, mind, so be careful who you send."

Cervianus blinked. "Me, sir?"

"Burdens of command, *optio* Cervianus. Now get to work."

As the capsarius ran toward the stairwell, returning to his position, Draco appeared and nodded professionally as they passed each other, then strode over to receive his orders from the commander.

Cervianus pounded down the stairs, his heart sinking. His job, his entire purpose, was the preservation of life. It was what had driven him since he had picked up a needle and read the first line of Hippocrates. Sending men to their certain death was not something he felt comfortable doing. For the first time since his sudden elevation, Cervianus realised that an officer was something he categorically did not want to be.

Sadly, he was hardly in a position to change that right now.

Behind him, he heard Nasica beginning his rousing speech, extolling the virtues of Rome, Galatia and the Twenty Second legion, reminding them of what they represented and belittling the enormous enemy they faced, bringing out the lion in every legionary's heart.

It was always a thing to behold when Nasica spoke. Were the senate a battleground, the man would have had Rome eating out of the palm of his hand. This time, however, Cervianus closed his ears to the great words, struggling internally with what he must do.

Down the stairs he went, and then into the courtyard of the outer peristyle, casting a brief glance at the three contubernia that were busy piling up heavy stone blocks behind the makeshift wall that already supported the outer gate. These men were determined that their position would not fall. If it did, the whole exterior was lost.

The plan was simple.

As soon as the enemy breached the gate or scaled the walls, the roof, towers and outer peristyle would have to be abandoned, the men that could do so making an orderly withdrawal, falling back to the enclosed columned room where they had first fought the fanatics in Napata. Then the doors could be closed and they would be both temporarily safe and caught like rats. From that point it was simply a matter of how long they lasted and how they went out.

And that was the crux of it. That was all there was to the defence of Napata: how long they lasted and how they went out. The thought brought a tiny spark of comfort as Cervianus scaled the ladder again and set to his grisly task.

Clambering out onto the rooftop, he looked around the men of the Second century, for no others were his to command. His mind categorised and ticked off men as he passed his gaze over them, curiously missing his friend Ulyxes and that phenomenal memory.

Trying desperately to think like Draco or the primus pilus, he discounted men.

Too slow: little use in a sporadic, guerrilla action.

Leg wound: can't climb.

Clumsy: not stealthy enough for the task.

Good with a pilum: too much use on this wall.

Slowly, he picked out half a dozen men.

Taking a deep breath, he reeled off their names and one by one they ran across to him, reserves moving up to take their places.

"How daring are you men feeling?"

The collection of wiry, fast and dangerous men regarded him with non-committal expressions.

"If the enemy get archers to the cliff edge above us in the light, this is all for nothing," Cervianus stated flatly. "We need a small group of very good, very fast and inventive men up there to prevent that from happening. Think you can make the climb?"

The men looked at one another for the moment and he made the mistake of catching their eyes. The look they shared brought a lump to his throat. Every man there knew exactly what was being asked of them.

"We'll make 'em eat their own legs," a dark-skinned, shorter man said with an unpleasant grin. The others nodded their agreement.

"Good," Cervianus said, trying to keep the emotion and uncertainty from his voice. "Get up there and show them Galatian mettle."

As the men ran off the capsarius took a deep, steadying breath.

Up on the tower a voice rang out.

"Here they come!"

The first wave was enough to break the morale of the unit on its own, without the certain knowledge that this was simply a small part of the force that was to come.

As Cervianus rushed to the parapet again, the front ranks of the Kushite force swept through the compound's east gate opposite him, more approaching via the other two entrances to south and west.

Just as Nasica had predicted, the men rushing for them were the bulk warriors of the army, the same as those they had fought at Syene and Buhen. A mass of very dark-skinned, wide and muscular bodies was broken up by the varied hides of wild animals, shields covered with the same materials, an assortment of axes, swords and spears, beaded hair loose or held back with headbands, white eyes and clenched teeth shining out of the dark, deadly force.

They came in a mad rush with no thought for tactics, their commander, the lord Kalabsha, having not so much *directed* them into an attack as *released* them. The violent, bellowing charge swept in through the walls and across the compound, some of the warriors falling in the rush and being trampled by their peers; others, either confused or working to their own agenda, making for incidental buildings en route.

The scorpions on top of the towers stood silent and still, their ammunition and aim precious, waiting for a target worth the shot.

Cervianus watched them come, waiting for the first command from Draco. They passed the thirty-pace range and all the centurion said was, "Steady…" Frowning, Cervianus leaned closer.

"Sir, shouldn't we ready pila?"

Without turning to look at him, Draco shook his head.

"Save the javelins for the elite. This lot are just rabble."

Cervianus nodded and straightened as the enemy passed

the twenty-pace mark: the best effective range for the thrown missiles. Draco cleared his throat for a shout.

"Remember. Nothing heroic or special. Let them come to you and just keep yourself alive."

Along the wall top, legionaries readied themselves, sword and shield in hand, those men without a shield or armour available having been assigned to scorpion crews or secondary roles.

The tide of the Kushite army crashed against the temple walls like a living, snarling wave, the flecked foam and spittle of their rage cresting the writhing mass. It was, quite clearly to Cervianus, futile. The walls were twenty feet high, with a three-foot parapet constructed above. Even thrusting with their spears, the warriors were barely reaching the wall top. The defenders heaved a momentary sigh of relief and then readied themselves again. This was not a failure for the Kushites, but simply an obstacle to overcome.

While a large part of the force moved round to the south to concentrate on trying to break through the temple's new solid portal, the bulk withdrew a little, leaving dozens of their own men, trampled and dead, by the wall's base. There was barely a moment to breathe before a shuffling reorganisation took place and the warriors with the long spears came to the fore, rushing the wall again, while the bulk of the mob scattered in groups across the dusty ground.

The legionaries had no time to question what was happening and few, except those like Cervianus who were "in the know", spotted the units of archers moving in through the gate behind the fight and streaming across the open ground amid the scattered warrior groups, making for other temples and structures.

Suddenly the air outside the edge of the wall became a moving carpet of gleaming points as hundreds of spears jabbed up at the parapet. A few blows were lucky enough to reach past the stone defences, but the legionaries were calm, prepared, and in good order, and every thrust was turned aside with sword or blocked with shield.

After several attempts, the spearmen withdrew again at a shout from an unknown voice somewhere in the compound. In their wake they left perhaps half a dozen extra bodies, fallen prey to heavy rocks dropped by legionaries too eager to follow the strict order to hold back.

The reason for the enemy withdrawal quickly became apparent as the groups that had scattered throughout the dusty ground began to make their way back toward the wall, several men sharing the load as they carried block after block of fallen, scorched stone and shattered statues.

Above, the scorpions began their rhythmic beat of death as iron bolts shot out under expert hands, whirring through the air above the heads of the mass and onto other roofs with unerring accuracy. The artillerists had been selected carefully.

The first archer to emerge on a rooftop was swept from his feet as the initial Roman missile took him in the chest, hurling him back into the second arriving man and throwing the pair from the roof. Other shots began to devastate the emerging archers, though the artillery's targets would likely seriously outnumber their ammunition.

"Alright. Use the rocks!" bellowed Nasica from above.

As the enemy warriors closed on the walls, carrying blocks and chunks of waste stone, the legionaries in the second line on the walls began to pick up one of the fist-sized rocks in each hand, stepping to the wall and casting them down.

The sight from above was sickening, as stone-carrying warriors' heads exploded like overripe watermelons under the barrage of heavy rocks. Faces shattered and arms broke. The heavy burdens they carried fell from their agonised grasps, crushing the feet and legs of the men helping them. The carnage was appalling, or would have been had the defenders not been horribly aware of what awaited them when the enemy breached the walls.

Still, the warriors and their heavy loads were innumerable, while the piles of rocks were finite and the men throwing them fewer still. The inevitable result was that more and more blocks and chunks were making it as far as the wall's base, forming the bare bones of a ramp. Now, seeing that they were beginning to meet with a little success, the warriors redoubled their efforts, concentrating on several specific areas that had already become a low slope.

As the Kushite infantry gathered up other chunks of stone, along with the blocks that had been discarded by shattered and broken blood-soaked warriors, the spearmen began to assemble in groups.

"Bloody good job they don't know how to make a ladder, eh?" laughed a legionary to Cervianus' left, a warm comment that was followed by a throaty squawk. The capsarius glanced round at the speaker, who had been stepping forward toward the wall's edge with a rock in each hand when a thrown spear had struck him in the neck, tearing through his trapezius muscle and snapping the spinal column.

The soldier was still grinning as the head fell through ninety degrees and hung precariously while the body toppled to the ground, another man nearby having to skip out of the way as the still-attached spear almost swept him from his feet.

"Shields!" Draco bellowed as the spearmen, now aware of their impotence at this juncture, had abandoned hope of stabbing the Romans and begun to cast them like javelins up at the wall.

Most of the men were already in the correct defensive posture and those who weren't quickly adjusted their stance as the deadly shafts began to fly up at them. Here and there along the wall, a man who was too slow or simply unlucky would screech in pain and disappear from the line, his reserve taking his place.

Under the covering shower of spears, the other warriors began to carry their heavy stone blocks closer and add to the growing pile at the wall's foot. Cervianus watched in dismay as somewhere off to his left another officer urged his reserves forward to cast down more rocks, the only result of which was to open up those reserves to the deadly rain. Every death was a disaster at this point.

The ramps were building rapidly now, the defenders unable to do much to stop the warriors without opening themselves to the spear throwers.

The capsarius allowed himself a moment to cast his gaze around and see what was happening elsewhere. His hand-picked squad of men were busy climbing the rocks toward the cliff above and would not take too long, judging by the speed of their ascent. He could only imagine the ensuing carnage if the enemy managed to get archers on that cliff. The walls were holding, with perhaps ten per cent losses. Such a proportion was entirely unacceptable. The battle had only been in progress for a quarter of an hour and it was going to get a great deal worse yet.

A commotion from above suddenly drew his attention and

he glanced up at the tower over the first pylon. Clearly, a good position had fallen to enemy archers, for the tide had begun to turn on the scorpions. The tower on which Nasica stood was being repeatedly struck and passed by black arrows, and cries and shrieks spoke eloquently of the enemy's successes. Indeed, a moment later, the scorpion ceased its barrage and an unarmed man, presumably the weapon's operator, hurtled from the tower to fall into the courtyard below, arrows in his face, shoulder and chest, leaving a thin rainbow of blood as he plummeted.

For a moment Cervianus' heart pounded, until he heard Nasica's angry voice telling someone to man the scorpion. Closer to his own position the struggle had slowed, the majority of the spearmen having cast their weapons and left themselves armed only with long knives.

"Steady, lads," Draco said, reassuringly. "Here they come."

As the men braced themselves again, the Kushite rabble charged, bellowing their hatred and defiance, and this time things were different. As the first men reached the piles of abandoned stonework, warriors began to climb. Reaching the wall top would still be difficult, but it could be possible.

"Make 'em change their mind," barked Draco, as the first tip of a sword blade scraped along the parapet near his foot.

The legionaries settled behind their shields, stepping forward and thrusting down with their blades at any attacker who gained a prominent enough position to make him a threat. Another shriek from the tower announced the death of an artillerist and, as this man toppled from the roof of the pylon, the one-man heavy weapon came tumbling after him, his foot caught in the mechanism's stand. Nasica's voice sounded angrily and then became dulled and hollow as the primus pilus left the tower top, disappearing into the staircase on his way back down.

A glance around behind them at the far side told a similar tale. There was no sign of life on the matching tower, the scorpion standing silent and still, surrounded by bodies. It was at that moment that Cervianus realised how much danger they were all suddenly in.

"Archers," he bellowed.

Many of the legionaries, trained and experienced, instinctively hunched behind their shields, lowering their heads before the rain of black shafts came. Still, a few men had been too slow and the arrows plunged into eyes, arms, legs and necks, picking men out from the line and throwing them back to the ground in a wash of pain and blood.

Other men, pulling themselves down and defending against the hail of missiles, instead opened themselves up to attack from below as enterprising warriors thrust up with desperate sword blows, hacking and stabbing at feet and legs they could barely reach.

Cervianus swallowed nervously. The defenders had been in control of the temple for little more than half an hour and they had lost nearly a third of their men, seen the missile supremacy pass from them to the enemy archers, and the defensive strength of the walls lessened by the makeshift ramps.

They would not hold out much longer. Over the din and the generalised screaming, one particular shriek caught the capsarius's attention, given its source. He looked up.

One of the men he had sent up to the cliff hit the roof of the temple and exploded, spattering the men around him. In a sudden panic, Cervianus' eyes rose to the cliff, where the others were just about to reach the top. As he watched, a black-clad figure appeared over the precipice and threw something down. A legionary shrieked as he was hit in the face, and plummeted back into open space where he fell, turning as he descended, and hit the temple roof head first.

The noise was audible even over the battle and made Cervianus squeeze his eyes shut. Somewhere near the two fallen men came the sound of vomiting. At the top, the rest of the legionaries were being dislodged by a sudden swarm of black figures. He distinctly heard a soldier begging his tormentor just before there was a flash of a blade and the man fell back into open air, screaming and missing both hands. Cervianus looked away and began to fumble at his chinstrap. Removing his helmet, he stared at the optio's horsehair crest and feathers. With a snarl, he cast the feathers aside and began to wrench out the hair. A cough interrupted his self-loathing and he looked up to see Draco giving him a pointed look.

"I can't do the job!"

"Get that helmet on, stop pissing about like a Vestal Virgin, and get along the line, giving the order to cast pila and then withdraw. We're pulling back inside!"

Cervianus was about to question the order, which seemed so unlikely, coming from a man like his centurion, when the point was made adequately by two flying arrows, one of which glanced off the helmet in Cervianus' hands, whistling off through the air, the other smashing into the face of the man behind Draco.

Cervianus nodded and turned, jamming his helmet back on and running along the line, bellowing the order to loose and fall back.

As he ran, it became painfully obvious to him that they had all but lost control of the roof. All three scorpions had been silenced, the only missiles in the air being the arrows of the Kushites. The walls were scalable by a determined man. The defenders on the parapet had halved in number and were now too few to create an adequate defensive line. Worst of all, and likely the thing that had tipped the scales and fuelled the order to withdraw, somehow, the desert nomads serving the Kushite general had secretly taken control of the mountain before the entire enemy force had moved.

Even now, they were beginning to drop heavy stones and jagged shards of rock from the clifftop down onto the defenders below. As Cervianus ran past, bellowing, a falling rock crashed into a legionary, shattering his shoulder into a hundred pieces and smashing his ribs. The man tried to scream, but his lungs had gone and all he could do was hiss as the last breaths escaped him.

Bitterly, Cervianus' mind flashed him an image of his carefully prepared hospital in the temple downstairs. How little he could do for most of today's wounds. Racing around the rear of the temple, where he was blessedly sheltered from falling stones by the overhang, he shouted the order to the rearmost men, who were fighting a desperate action to keep clambering, snarling warriors from the wall. They were failing.

Two legionaries suddenly fell with cries of pain as half a dozen black-skinned men poured out onto the roof, hacking and stabbing. Turning his back on them, Cervianus ran forward again toward the front of the temple, still bellowing the orders. As he passed, those men who could stepped back from the assault and grasped a heavy, weighted javelins, casting them out over the parapet and into the mass of warriors, before turning and running after him.

After a few long moments that felt like a year of peril and

sickness, Cervianus found himself back at the first peristyle with the colonnaded courtyard that was already filled with withdrawing soldiers fighting and pushing to make their way in through the inner pylon doorway and into the interior.

Grasping a ladder, Cervianus slid down it without bothering with rungs and made for the familiar crests that marked out Nasica and Draco. The two centurions were conferring not far from the beleaguered main gate. Pushing his way through the throng of panicked and desperate soldiers, he found himself face to face with the commander and remembered at the last moment to salute.

"Optio?"

"Sir, I've given the withdrawal order across the top. They'll swarm the place any moment. They're already on the roof at the back."

Nasica nodded solemnly.

"Stop panicking!" he bellowed at the top of his voice, and the effect was amazing, as the legionaries stopped pushing and shoving in automatic reaction to the primus pilus's voice.

"Quick and orderly withdrawal inside."

Cervianus turned to the gate. Seven men had their backs braced against a wall of heavy, uncemented stone blocks: all that remained between them and the enemy. As he watched, the blocks moved and undulated as they were struck by repeated blows from outside. A sharp blade appeared between two blocks where a crack had widened, and drew an agonising line across a legionary's arm.

Nasica joined him and addressed the optio who held the centre position among the seven.

"You'll have to hold that to the last, Rautius."

The junior officer nodded solemnly as he strained to control the block wall under the pressure from the other side. Cervianus was at once humbled by the strength of the centurionate as this man accepted his fate with stoic honour, and convinced again of his own unsuitability for the role.

The number of men in the courtyard was thinning as the bulk had now made it inside, the last few men appearing over the edge of the courtyard and dropping down, ignoring the presence of the ladders. Cervianus stared in dismay at what was clearly the end of the First cohort.

Draco's hand fell on his shoulder and turned him around bodily. "Inside."

The capsarius followed the two officers as they jogged across the courtyard and ducked in through the door, following the last of the large group of men. In the doorway, he and Draco paused to look back. The seven men holding the main stone-blocked gate closed had already been whittled down to five. The optio yelled something they didn't catch, but the men beside him echoed the legion originator's name: "Deiotarus!"

Two men appeared on the roof above the courtyard, trying to catch up. The first jumped badly and landed awkwardly on the flags below. The other never even made the jump as hands grasped him from behind and he was suddenly enveloped in Kushite arms, disappearing back out of sight with a scream.

Cervianus lunged forward, making for the man who had fallen. The legionary had picked himself up, wincing and crying out at the leg he could hardly move, the foot dragging behind him at an unhealthy angle. The capsarius, however, found his forward momentum arrested as powerful hands grasped him and pulled him back inside. He watched with infinite sympathy as the doors swung inwards, gradually obscuring the view of the legionary with the smashed ankle shuffling across the courtyard.

The last thing Cervianus saw before the portal slammed shut was the Kushite warrior approaching the legionary from behind, a glinting knife in his hand and a wild grin on his face. Despite the thick, solid door and the general hubbub within, the scream of the last legionary outside sent a shiver up every spine.

Half a dozen men under the command of a lesser centurion barred and jammed the door shut, the heavy beam sliding across it and down into its sockets. An army could break through the door, but it would take considerable time, even with a ram.

Draco turned to Nasica. "What's next, sir?"

Cervianus was impressed again. It was not an admission of defeat or a desperate demand for a way out, but a professional enquiry as to their next course of action.

Nasica folded his arms and frowned. "This Kalabsha is not a patient man. He will not, I fear, have time to cut and build a ram, even if he knows how, and he'll not get through the door any other way for days. There's only one thing he can realistically do at this point, I'd say."

"Burn it?" Draco enquired, nodding.

"Exactly. Even if it takes days to burn the door, he'll know that the smoke will fill the place and kill us in a matter of hours."

Draco ground his teeth in irritation. "Any way you can think of that we can punch through them, sir? Say, in a wedge? Make it out to somewhere we can face them in open battle and die like men?"

Nasica shook his head. "Besides, I refuse to lose all hope for the legion. It is always possible that the tribune will win his fight and come back. If he does, we won't be the officers who allowed the cohort to perish and added our vexillum and standards to that bastard's collection."

The primus pilus narrowed his eyes. "How many men would you say we have left, Draco?"

"No more than a hundred, sir. I'd say somewhat just over ninety."

The primus pilus turned to Cervianus, taking him by surprise. "This secure room where the treasure's stored. Could it hold men?"

Cervianus blinked. "Yes, sir. Perhaps forty or fifty. More if we took the treasure out."

A nod.

"And we would assume that only the priests of this temple and you know how to open it?"

"That's a fair assumption, sir. I certainly can't imagine a general from Meroë to the south knowing, anyway."

"Then as soon as it becomes certain that smoking us out is what they're doing, half the men will retreat to the secure room and take refuge there with the standards. Even if we all die here, the standards won't be taken by Kalabsha. The rest of us will open the door and make a last fight of it here in this large chamber."

Draco nodded. "The standards must be saved, sir."

The two centurions clasped hands and Cervianus suddenly felt horribly out of place standing next to them.

"Cervianus? Who's the god of this temple?"

"Amun, sir."

"And what is he, really? Mars, by any chance?"

Cervianus struggled for a moment to comprehend what the commander was asking, before light dawned. It was a curiously Roman trait: to accept any and every god, but to assume he was just a local guise of a good, hearty Roman god.

"Err. I think you'd say he was Jupiter, sir."

Nasica nodded. "Good. Let's go find this Jupiter and offer him a few prayers, eh?"

The first faint plume of smoke billowed up from beneath the door, the noise of the crackling fire that rushed through the dried reeds creeping through the cracks in the heavy portal. A collective indrawn breath accompanied the sinking heart of the ninety-four surviving men of the First cohort, trapped in their sandstone coffin.

Draco gestured toward the door from where he and Nasica stood at the room's centre.

"Looks like this is it. I'd rather hoped the legion would reappear just in time. Jupiter's obviously busy elsewhere."

Nasica nodded. "Time to make our last stand."

He turned to face the gathered, disconsolate faces in the gloomy corners of the large room.

"Alright, lads. Time's up. The hope is that their commander doesn't know how many men escaped into here, so we might be able to save a few men. Five contubernia of legionaries, along with two officers, will settle into the sealed room at the rear of the temple with the vexillum and the standards, keeping them from the enemy."

He straightened. "With a little luck they won't even know of the room's existence, let alone how to open it. Take a week's worth of stores in with you and wait until all this is over and the enemy has left. Then do your best to get back north. If the gods are with us, Vitalis will be victorious and the legion will come back for you before then."

Squaring his shoulders, he drew his gladius from the ornate scabbard and examined the edge as he continued. "The remaining fifty or so of us have our work cut out. We need to deny them this room to the last man. I expect every man who stands with me to greet Elysium in the solid knowledge that he died a noble member of the best army in the world, and satisfied in the understanding that he took ten of them with him."

The men in the room glanced at one another in anticipation. Faced with the possibility of spending a week in a pitch black, cramped hole in the desperate hope that there would be life at the end, many of them would gladly accept the chance to stand and die as a legionary, quick and honourable.

The commander took a deep breath. "Volunteers, to me."

The bulk of the room's occupants shuffled across to stand near Nasica, sharing looks of simple sad acceptance. The primus pilus regarded his men with pride and then counted the remaining legionaries at the far end.

"Looks like too many men eager for the blade to me. I'm going to need another seven men to join them." He turned with a sad smile. "Draco? You too, old friend."

Cervianus stared. The very idea of denying his centurion the fight was unthinkable.

Draco shook his head. "My place is here, sir."

"Draco, your place is to take command of the survivors. On the slight chance this all works out and they manage to get away, they'll need an experienced and sensible officer. That's you, and you know it."

The primus pilus's gaze rose over Draco's shoulder and locked on Cervianus.

"And your optio will be needed for his medical talents. Who knows what you might be facing, and it's a waste for him to stand with me now and die early. You two: take seven more men, get that safe room stacked with supplies and seal yourself in. You've not got much time before we have to open the door to prevent the smoke doing us all in."

Draco was still shaking his head, but Nasica clapped a hand on his shoulder.

"You should have been transferred out as a primus pilus for another legion years ago, my friend. You're as much a commander as I. Now's your chance. Save the standards and the honour of the cohort."

Cervianus found there was a lump in his throat as he watched the two senior officers, veterans of decades of service together, saying a final farewell. He waited solemnly, his gaze lowered, until Draco turned with a deep breath, his composure regained and his expression all business once more.

"Cervianus – find me seven men worth preserving and then head to the back room."

The capsarius swallowed nervously as he nodded. He'd had a life's worth of deciding who lived and who died already today, and now Draco was ordering him to do it again. Still, given what the centurion was currently going through silently in his own heart, Cervianus could hardly argue.

Trying not to catch anyone's eyes, he looked across the gathered men, picking out individuals. Two engineers and an artillerist, a man who had served as a medical orderly for him, both weeks and a lifetime ago, two men who were calm and accepting... all six men of bulk who would survive for many days on low rations and men of a tranquil mind, despite everything, who would not submit to panic and despair...

And Sentius.

Of all the people he might call friend, the only one here in this place who filled that description was the legionary he had saved from the crocodile attack months ago. His heart went out briefly to Shenti, marching into the jaws of death with the blindly power-hungry Vitalis, and to Ulyxes, out there somewhere, hopefully alive and heading for Alexandria.

His eyes picked out Sentius' arm with its limited mobility and a surge of guilt ran through him. There were better men to choose, but he somehow couldn't do so. With a sigh, he gestured to the seven men and turned to follow the rest, who had gathered the standards and supplies and were making their way through to the hidden room at the rear of the temple.

At the doorway, as the seven went ahead, he paused to look back. Nasica was rolling his shoulders and flexing his fingers ready for the coming fight.

The man was a rock; *the* rock upon which the legion's pride and courage was founded.

Cervianus shook his head, uttered a rare prayer to the Roman gods that the primus pilus went to his rest well, and followed the forty-one men, ready to seal them in.

Nasica waited until he heard the grinding noises at the back and the last, faint shout from Draco that they were secure, and then looked around him. Every man had an expression of grim determination and the primus pilus's heart swelled with pride. He had faced horrifying opponents before, though never with such certainty of failure. And yet the men he had trained and led for years stood like *kings* in this room, awaiting their bloody end.

Less than half of them had a shield and several were unarmoured, and yet they drew their blades and nodded to one another, muttering prayers to their own Galatian gods and the Aegyptian lord in whose temple they would die today, preparing to see one another again in Elysium.

Nasica was Roman through and through, from birth. He had first encountered the Deiotariana when they were a client army under their own king, while he himself was a young legionary serving in the Sixth. The two forces had fought the King of Pontus together and even then he'd been impressed with the strength and discipline of the Galatian army. It seemed somehow fitting that here, at the other end of his soldiering life, he would be leading that very army in a last stand to rival the famous Spartans.

"Don't forget, lads. Ten men apiece, or you'll get an arse-kicking on the other side."

A chorus of low laughs greeted the comment.

"Ready?"

The legionaries of the Twenty Second legion's First cohort nodded grimly and settled into a triple line between the columns. Stepping back to join them, Nasica gestured at the two men standing wreathed in smoke to either side of the door, who braced themselves and lifted the great locking bar with immense strain, heaving it over to one side and dropping it with a crash.

They barely had time to pull back before the weight of the kindling and timber heaped against the far side in a burning orange mass pushed the door inwards, spilling out onto the flags, spitting fire and sparks.

There was a strange pause as more and more charred and orange logs rolled in across the floor, fresh timber which had recently been added following on behind that. No sign of movement could be seen beyond for a long moment.

Then, slowly, the smoke thinned and the flames lowered, revealing the eager faces of Kushite warriors hovering at the far side of the portal, rearing back from the intense heat. Dark-skinned men with bronze armbands and white linen tunics gripped spears and swords and animal hide shields, their beaded hair held back by bands of white. They bobbed up and down, trying to determine what had happened, peering into the pitch darkness beyond the fire where their Roman enemy would wait.

"Let's give 'em some encouragement, eh?" Nasica laughed, and he and those of his men with shields began to bang the flat of their blades against the bronze rims rhythmically. The other men each drew their pugio in their offhand, and bashed that against the gladius.

The thumping had the desired effect. The bobbing figures without began to bounce in a frenzy and finally, as Nasica was beginning to wonder if they'd have to charge the Kushites, a warrior who had reached breaking point yelled a curse in his own language and ran into the embers.

The man had bare feet and in other circumstances watching him dance uncomfortably as he crossed the orange glowing wood on the floor could have been very amusing.

"Yours, sir," said a man to his left, and Nasica nodded.

The warrior had barely crossed the burning mass with sore, sizzling feet, raising his spear to thrust, when the biggest Roman he could possibly imagine, with arms like a side of beef and the face of a demon, stepped out of the darkness and sank a short blade into his chest twice, before smashing it across his jaw. The warrior fell back among the fiery remnants, still alive as his clothing caught fire.

The satisfaction of watching him writhe and scream was short lived, though, as others began to leap across the embers in sandals and boots and bare feet, with swords, axes and spears at the ready.

The next man ran straight at Nasica and he raised his shield, already missing a small portion from an earlier engagement, deflecting the overhead axe blow and wheeling the man aside as he struck twice like a snake, ripping jagged holes in the man's chest and then kicking him over.

Immediately behind him was another screaming warrior, while further men had started to peel off to either side. The sounds of the legionaries beginning the work for which they had trained long and hard filled the room, amid the shrieks and roars of the enemy.

This next warrior was taller and bulkier than the others, bearing a number of copper accoutrements. Perhaps a noble?

As the man swung his sword, Nasica dipped to the side and sliced back, his blade biting deep into the man's thigh. As the warrior screamed, the primus pilus straightened and punched the man with the shield boss before driving his gladius into the torso.

The two warriors that followed him managed to push the dying noble out of the way and Nasica immediately sized them up. Ignoring the spearman, he stepped forward, slamming his hobnailed boot down on the other man's foot. As the sword-wielding warrior screamed and lurched back, the spearman thrust.

Nasica ducked, the point narrowly missing his face and

scraping across the embossed eyebrow of his helmet. In retaliation, he slammed his gladius into the man's gut, using his impressive strength to rip the blade left and then right before pushing the man back and pulling out the sword. The warrior's guts tumbled out and hung down to the floor as he screeched and dropped the spear, trying to gather his intestines and push them back in.

The unfortunate warrior suddenly found himself thrown to one side as more men reached them. The limping swordsman with the crippled foot flashed out with his blade, having recovered quicker than Nasica had expected, and the commander felt a sharp pain in his side. Ignoring the blow, he slammed his own sword into the man's neck.

And now they were everywhere.

Nasica could hear the sounds of his men fighting and dying, curses in Latin and screams of indeterminate nationality, but he might as well have been alone now, his world a mass of ebony enemies coming at him from every direction. He stabbed repeatedly, counting each blow he knew was fatal.

Number six managed to carve a huge piece from his shield with a sword, leaving a long, painful line up his arm and it was with regret that the primus pilus dropped the glorious, eagle-emblazoned shield as useless weight.

Seven and eight went down almost together, though eight managed to land a heavy axe blow on his left arm that had probably smashed the bone. The agony of a lost arm flooded through him, but he was in a place beyond pain now.

Nine was trouble. Nasica's gladius jammed in the man's collarbone and, though he managed to push the warrior away with his foot, the gladius went with him, stuck fast.

As two spear thrusts stabbed home, catching him in the

abdomen and the left leg, he unsheathed his pugio. Eyeing number ten, he leapt forward, slamming the short, wide dagger into the man's face and driving through the eye, deep into the brain.

Suddenly he was falling with his victim.

The floor was a mass of writhing bodies, slick with blood and innards and discarded weapons. His leg had given way, the muscle hopelessly torn by the spear blow. Taking advantage of his new perspective, he managed to hamstring three men before anyone seemed to realise he was down there.

A warrior... number eleven, he realised with satisfaction... tried to push a sword down through his back, but he moved aside and slammed his dagger into the man's groin, using it as a handhold to pull himself upright.

As the wounded warrior howled in agony, Nasica used the man to haul himself to his feet before slashing out with the dagger and cutting the throat.

A sword blow hit him in the back and scythed through chain, bone and muscle, either carefully aimed for a chink in the armour or very lucky. He felt his breath tighten as the lung collapsed and saw the red-coated point emerge from his chest before being agonisingly withdrawn.

With an angry growl, he turned around, tearing the impaling blade from the man's hand, and headbutted him, the ridge of the iron helmet smashing the warrior's face.

An axe blow struck his shoulder and smashed the bone to pieces. As his arm fell awkwardly to the side, Nasica fought the white fog that seemed to be clouding his sight and turned amid the flying fragments of mail, striking out with his dagger and feeling it drive through bone and tissue. The man's howl turned into a gurgle and the primus pilus sagged with a grin.

Thirteen, he thought happily as he felt the blades repeatedly smashing into him from above.

Thirteen! He would be owed a few drinks in Elysium.

Cervianus sat in the darkness, listening to the almost inaudible sounds of the fighting in the large room. Waves of sorrow continually smashed against him as he thought of the great ox of a primus pilus that had made the army his life and ruled the Twenty Second with an iron fist. No one spoke – not for fear of being heard, but fearing what they might say.

Even a quarter of an hour after the last sounds of combat had died away, silence ruled in the hidden room. The men waited, tense. Slowly, they began to hear noises as the enemy searched the temple's rooms for survivors and loot.

It was an eternity of thumping hearts and sweating brows.

Footsteps outside the room... searching the rearmost chambers of the temple.

The capsarius couldn't help but issue a low groan of dismay as the stonework in the wall began to rumble and a sliver of light appeared.

It seemed Kalabsha *did* know of the hidden room, after all.

The occupants blinked as the light of multiple torches blinded them, following their enforced half hour of darkness. By the time Cervianus had blinked and strained, trying to see what was happening, he was being hauled from the room by ebony figures, manhandled as the sword was ripped from his scabbard and his dagger from the far side. The pugio was used to cut the strap on his medical bag and his most prized possession fell to the floor, the sound of bottles and jars within shattering. A dozen or so archers stood around the periphery, their arrows nocked and trained on the Romans.

Draco, nearest the door, tried to fight, his blade already in his good hand, but almost blinded by the sudden light and confined in the cramped conditions, he was unable to do more than struggle as they disarmed him and hauled him from the room.

Cervianus felt rope bite into his wrists as the warrior tied his arms behind his back, and felt the last morsels of hope leave him. Draco, next to him, had the bleak expression of a man who would rather be dead, while they wrenched his broken arm behind his back, undoing all of Cervianus' work as they bound his wrists.

Utterly lost and dejected, the forty-two survivors of the First cohort were trooped out of the room, past the sanctuary of the god, where Cervianus managed to flick a withering look at the tall, feather-crowned statue of Amun, who remained aloof and unconcerned about their fate. Through the inner chambers they shuffled, pushed and hauled by dark-skinned warriors. At the entrance to the large chamber they were pulled up and stood in two lines. The room was lit by burning torches in the sconces on the walls as well as the light from the doorway and the glowing embers nearby.

The floor of the room was a nightmare of body parts, innards and blood, the walls spattered red in a horrible echo of Cervianus' first memory of the place. The smell was appalling. Behind him, a man was noisily sick.

One hundred and fifty heartbeats he counted, as they stood there, Kushite warriors entering and leaving the room, going about their business while archers remained poised, ready to deal with any attempt at flight or fight.

Finally, half a dozen of the impressive Kushite guards in white with glittering mail made their entrance, picking their way across the burned timbers and the charred bodies to stand on either side, reminiscent of the sphinx avenues so popular in these lands. Behind them came the tall figure of Kalabsha, stepping lightly, trying not to dirty his boots in the carbon, blood and brains on the floor, and failing dismally.

Examining the survivors, his eyes roved back and forth along the lines, squinting in the darkness. Periodically he turned to his guards and exchanged words in their strange throaty language, speaking loudly over the groans of the prisoners and the noises of the mortally wounded and not yet dead in the chamber.

A shout from the recesses of the chamber drew the general's attention and he barked a command. Cervianus felt a lump in his throat as he watched Nasica's broken and mutilated corpse being dragged from the darkness into a pool of torchlight.

Kalabsha nodded, snapped out two more commands and gestured to the door. As two men unceremoniously dragged the body from the room, Kalabsha bent and retrieved the centurion's helmet with the unmistakable transverse crest. Spitting into the bowl, he threw it out through the door, after the corpse.

"Is the man who speaks Greek still here?"

Cervianus swallowed and fought the nerves threatening to unman him. "I am. Titus Cervianus, capsarius and..."

The general waved his name aside as irrelevant. "That man was your officer? The one you call Nasica?"

Next to him, even in the fug of pain from his re-broken arm, Draco straightened and opened his mouth at the mention of his commander's name. Cervianus trod heavily on his foot and stopped the centurion from speaking.

"He doesn't know you're an officer, sir. I think you'd be best to keep it that way," the capsarius hissed. Draco's helmet and harness were missing, and few outside the Twenty Second would be able to identify him as a centurion.

Kalabsha nodded to himself.

"Your unholy commander has paid the price for his defiance, but his desecration of Napata demands more. He will be dishonoured and defiled for his actions. The rest of you are now prisoners and slaves of the Kandake of Kush, awaiting her pleasure when she returns. You will go quietly and without trouble to your prison and stay there until you are required and, should any of your number cause trouble, I will have him flayed and pegged over a scorpion nest."

He glared at Cervianus. "Translate!"

The capsarius did as he was bid and, once finished, silence reigned in the room until Kalabsha snapped out more orders in his own language.

A spear point pushed into Cervianus' back, urging him toward the exit.

Without hope, the forty-two men were trooped out of the darkness of the charnel chamber and into the blinding sun of the late afternoon.

VII

CAPTIVITY

Mist billowed through the night-shrouded vegetation, a warm mist, as though the sun had boiled the great Nile dry and wafted it across the land.

A dream again, and Cervianus was curiously aware of it as such, a sinking feeling in the pit of his stomach as he recognised the dreamscape.

He was alone in the field again and the statue stood as it had before: at a slight lean, half hidden by foliage, piercing eyes boring into his own above that long, curved beak. But were the eyes supplicatory? Desperate? Commanding? It was so hard to tell.

Thoth stood with his one foot forward, the statue cracked and shattered and with a pitted, mottled surface, as though that life-changing vision at Thebes had changed the Thoth of dream for ever and he was revisiting the scene at a later date.

Behind and to the left of Thoth, great judge of the dead and resolver of divine disputes, the cracked and ruined forms of Sekhmet and Sobek still reached out plaintively, their fanged features curiously passive, given their militant natures. At the Ibis-god's right shoulder lurked the damaged shapes of Haroeris with his hawk's head, and Amun, the feathered crown soaring.

Even through the fug of dream, Cervianus' logical mind asserted itself. A continuation of that dream, but with new aspects: Amun was a new addition. Was his mind taking facets of recent events and using them to fill in the blanks?

Others still lurked in the shadows to the rear... cat-headed, human, dog, snake...

But only the five stood forth, with the great arbiter at the centre. They all seemed to be reaching for him still, but something had changed. What was it? It had something to do with the five, clearly. All five gods had been influential in some way, and they seemed to have ended their joint supplication and were now... what?

The hands still reached out and he wished he could move, but the memory of that earlier nightmare was still fresh even over the months. Feet riveted to the ground, a heavy weight...

But that was not the case, now. Whatever had changed had granted him freedom of movement. But to do what?

The statues exploded into a thousand fragments and Cervianus blinked, rudely awake.

"Mph?"

The legionary who was shaking him by the shoulder stared at him, wild-eyed.

"Someone's coming."

The dream still fresh in his mind, he sat up sharply, the immediate danger of their situation reasserting itself. Their small jail was hot and dark, bare mud-brick walls with no apertures and a heavy, barred wooden door. Their bindings had been removed when they first arrived, their captors secure in the knowledge that escape was impossible. The forty-two men had been crowded into the room while the sun still hung low in the sky after the battle had ended, and they had remained there, cramped, uncomfortable and unattended, as the sun sank, the moon rose, and the hours rolled by in hopelessness.

In the room it was impossible to tell what the time was, though Cervianus would be willing to guess that the sun had been up again for some time, from the heat beginning to filter through the walls.

The footsteps outside came to a halt and there was a heavy *thunk* and a slow sliding noise before the door opened slowly, allowing enough light to creep in through the gap to flash-blind the occupants.

As Cervianus' sight slowly recovered, he blinked and peered through the door. Three archers stood outside, their arrows trained into the room, several spearmen along with them. The door was being opened, however, not for them, but for one of the higher-class warriors in the white linen and the mail shirt.

"You. Come." The language was Greek, but spoken haltingly in the fashion of a novice at the tongue.

Cervianus wearily pulled himself up to a seated position. His limbs ached to the very bones. He turned to look in the direction of the centurion, who was slumped in the corner.

"How's Draco?"

One of the legionaries nearby leaned over him and then straightened. "Barely conscious. He's sweating and cold. Spent a lot of the night muttering."

Cervianus nodded. "He's not well. I need to medicate him, but I can't do anything without my bag."

He turned to the guard at the door and spoke slowly,

claborating his words with accompanying helpful gestures. "I need my medical bag. I will come, yes?"

The guard looked confused for a moment and then shrugged and gestured out of the room. With a lingering backward glance at the men, huddled and cowering in their prison, Cervianus shuffled out of the door under the watchful aim of the archers and the accompanying spearmen, sharply aware that this could easily be the last time he ever saw another non-Kushite.

His eyesight was still adjusting to the brightness as he shuffled stiffly along the corridor outside the room, light from several small windows illuminating the interior. Along the wall, graffiti from the Galatian and Roman occupants drew his gaze; this building had been a barrack block for several days, eight men sharing the room now allocated for forty-two.

Lentulus is a girl

Nearest whore — one thousand miles

Up yours Frontinus

All along with the obligatory carving of a phallus for luck. On impulse, Cervianus reached out and ran his hand along the carving. Any amount of potential good fortune was important right now. The guard reached out to swat his hand away, but then he and two of the accompanying warriors shared a joke in their own language and sniggered. Cervianus rolled his eyes. Juvenile behaviour was hardly the sole province of Rome.

It was, indeed, late morning. They strode out of the building into the baking heat of a high sun and Cervianus began to sweat heavily as he continued to work out the kinks in his tired muscles.

"See," demanded the guard as they crossed the main open space at the centre of the complex. Cervianus cast his gaze about, trying to identify what it was he was supposed to be looking at. The compound itself was unchanged, though now it thrived with life – guardsmen, warriors, ordinary folk, animals and supplies filling the thoroughfares. The noise was reminiscent of the marketplace in Ancyra, along with a sizzling mixture of sweat and animal dung that assaulted the nose.

It took two passes before his eyes locked on what was being shown to him, yet he couldn't see it clearly enough to make much sense out of it. It appeared to be a crucifixion and, though he wished he couldn't identify the victim, the inclusion of the centurion's transverse crest made it clear who hung there. The capsarius was extremely grateful that the display was far enough away that he could only make out the vague shape. Curiously, there appeared to be some sort of contraption below and around the figure, though it was too far away to see too much detail.

The guard was grinning at him as he turned back, three bad, blackened teeth adding to the vicious malice of the smile. The man struggled to find the right words in Greek, but gave up and rattled something unpleasant off in his own language, finishing with a sharp bark of laughter.

"If I could get my hands on a curse tablet, your loins would shrivel and fall away," replied Cervianus with a warm smile. The guard frowned uncertainly and shrugged.

Moments later they were at the main Amun temple and the guard ushered him inside. The fortified, walled temporary front gate had been dismantled and removed, the open first peristyle beyond filled, in a beautiful, miraculous and somewhat unexpected display, with flowers. Blooms of many colours filled the walkway around the periphery, peering out between the carved pillars to catch the rays of the blazing sun.

Cervianus frowned and considered questioning the guard,

though his lack of Greek and surly demeanour made the capsarius think again. It was only as they approached the room that had repeatedly been at the centre of the killings that Cervianus realised the archers and spearmen had left them somewhere en route before they had entered the temple. Only he and the guard walked through the doorway and it occurred to him that if he had been Draco, Nasica or even Ulyxes, the chances were that he would have leapt on the opportunity to lower the enemy numbers by one.

Instead, he walked on meekly, curiosity and reason sharing control of his mind. The middle peristyle was hardly recognisable as the scene of such earlier carnage. Torches and lamps had been removed so that it was once more plunged into a deep gloom. The bodies had all been removed and the floor and walls painstakingly cleaned to remove the taint of death. Bunches and bundles of honeysuckle and jasmine were packed into the torch rings, filling the room with a heady, sweet smell that blanketed the senses with thoughts of peaceful gardens and meadows. To Cervianus' astonishment, even in these circumstances he found himself smiling.

He nodded to the guard, trying to convey his approval of the way they were handling the grisly scene, but the guard appeared to be uninterested, instead gesturing them onwards. The Roman supplies and equipment had been removed from the third peristyle, and it was once more a sacred room, heralding the entrance to the inner sanctum of Amun. In the centre of the chamber, hard to spot in the gloom, stood Kalabsha with two more guards. He turned his head at the sound of footsteps and dismissed the men with whom he had been speaking.

"Titus Cervianus, if my memory does not deceive me," he said in smooth Greek.

Cervianus nodded respectfully. Nothing would be gained here by pushing his luck.

"You said that you were a cap-something-or-other. I am unfamiliar with this Roman word, but it means medic, yes? My men tell me your bag contained unguents."

Cervianus nodded. "An army medic, yes."

He momentarily considered explaining the difference between the capsarii and the medici, but that would lead to a further explanation of his own peculiar background and status. He would have to ask about the bag.

Kalabsha nodded and tapped his finger on his lip. "You are an educated man. Will you give me your word you will not attempt anything stupid?"

Cervianus shrugged. "For now. I cannot promise in perpetuity, of course."

"Obviously."

Kalabsha turned and gestured to the guard, who saluted and strode away, leaving Cervianus alone with the commander of the Kushite garrison. Flashes of memory battered at him – an arrow at Abu Island that could have done for Vitalis and prevented all of this and which he alone could have stopped, and did. Would one swift stroke now make such a difference? Sighing, he realised that, even if he *could* end all their troubles by killing Kalabsha now, he was no more capable of assassinating a man that was showing him courtesy than he was of allowing a dangerous madman to die when he could prevent it.

The general turned and strode back out of the darkness into the first room, Cervianus hurrying to keep up. "Come with me," Kalabsha said seriously.

As the two men marched out from the gloom of the inner rooms and into the light, through the first pylon, the various

Kushites wandering the compound paused for a moment at the sight of their commander walking calmly alongside one of the enemy prisoners, but soon went back to their work. Staring at Kalabsha could probably be dangerous.

"Tell me," the general said quietly, "about your army."

Cervianus frowned. "I'm not sure what you mean?"

"The bulk of your army has marched on Meroë, where they will meet my queen and she will teach them why even the great Ptolemy never tried to exert his influence south of Syene. Your leader... the one they call Vitalis... he is dangerous, I think? A bad man. He is the man, I think, behind all of this, and the one who must pay the most for your crimes."

Cervianus, walking alongside, shook his head. "You cannot play the innocent, injured party, general. I have seen Syene. I saw what you had done there."

Kalabsha shrugged. "War is like that, medic. Syene has been our city before and will be again. It is in the nature of border cities that they periodically suffer. If they quickly capitulate, the suffering is lessened. Since Rome came, though, they fight to the last. There is no capitulation, and therefore the injury is worse."

He glanced sidelong at Cervianus. "Even at the worst, however, our armies would never desecrate temples. That is beyond reason."

Cervianus sighed again, aware that his argument was weakening. "Not all of us are so sacrilegious."

Kalabsha nodded. "I have been made aware of this. My men tell me that, although your army burned the temples when they arrived, since they left, there is a great deal of evidence of repairs and cleaning. This is the work of your small force? Against the wishes of your Vitalis?"

The capsarius nodded. "What was done was wrong. We are aware of that."

As they rounded a corner near the west gate, Kalabsha clasped his hands behind his back in a manner so reminiscent of a Roman officer that Cervianus almost laughed. "Your army will not return from the south, medic, and you and your friends will end your days in Kush. Your final fate will be the decision of my queen, but I can be inclined toward supporting a merciful course, if you prove to be model prisoners."

The capsarius heard the words, but his reply died in his throat at the sight before him. Nasica hung on his cross above the compound's gate, the only covering left to him his helmet and mail shirt with harness: the marks of his rank. Though he hung some twenty feet from this corner, Cervianus recognised the horrible fact of his shaming. The body was pink; too pink for anything natural. He had been flayed and his face and private parts cut away along with the skin. The capsarius looked away, but an unfortunate gust of wind carried the smell to him. He felt the bile rise and spat on the floor, retching.

"You are frightened?"

Cervianus shook his head, his stomach heaving at the smell. "Not frightened. Appalled. Why would you do this?"

"He defied a general of Kush and lord of many men. He also attempted to shoot me on the wall. Above which, he is your commander and therefore played his part in the desecration here."

Cervianus rounded on him. "Nasica was the man who initiated the *repairs*! He deserved better than this."

"It is as the gods wish. Perhaps his belated piety is the reason he died *before* the unmanning and did not have to suffer *through* it?"

The capsarius glowered at his captor.

"He may be the *lucky* one," Kalabsha reminded him. "Certainly the other two were less lucky."

"Other two?" Cervianus asked, his heart skipping a beat. So many friends out there in the desert...

Kalabsha walked on toward the gatehouse and Cervianus realised with a shock what the contraption beneath the awful display actually was.

Some sort of frame had been constructed from wood and reeds. The two bodies attached to it had been mutilated. The closer he got, the more Cervianus could see and the more he wished he couldn't. The Kushites had clearly begun by removing fingers and toes, and then hands and feet, then the lower arms and legs. Now only the core remained of each body: torso and head, with stumps jutting out, the dismembered parts pinned to the apparatus in approximations of their original position.

Cervianus, unable to stop himself analysing the scene as they walked ever closer, recognised the figures of Suro and one of the men who had fled along with him. It saddened him about the state of his soul that his initial thought was not sorrow or sympathy for the two men, but gratitude that neither of the dismembered men was Ulyxes.

He almost jumped as one of the torsos moved and groaned. They were still alive!

Closing his eyes and fighting once more against the rising bile, Cervianus turned to Kalabsha. "Why *that*, then?"

"Simple necessity. We captured them less than two miles from Napata, fleeing their post. We needed to know everything about the defensive force, and they had the information. They were very noble and defiant for half a day. As the sun started to bake their wounds, though, they became quite talkative. It is possible that we would never have found your hiding place without them."

He sighed. "Still, I agree that they have now served their purpose." He cleared his throat and shouted a command up to the men on the gatehouse, who saluted and drew swords, moving over to the half-men and cutting their throats to end their suffering.

Cervianus wrinkled his nose as another gust of wind carried the corruption that was Nasica to his nostrils. "Is this what you brought me out of the room for, general? To parade your masterful cruelty before me? If so, I am suitably sickened, though not impressed. And now, I think I would rather return to my cell."

Kalabsha smiled curiously. "It is clear that you are a medic first and not a soldier. A soldier would recognise the value and necessity behind this. A medic sees only the pain. Come."

He turned away from the gate and its grisly decoration and marched back along the main thoroughfare toward the Amun temple.

"Until either the queen comes here, or we are ordered south, we will remain the garrison of Napata. You and your companions have two options. You can be defiant sons of the north, refusing my orders. If you will not be accommodating, however, we will be required to take steps as required."

Cervianus nodded quietly. He could imagine what Draco's answer would be.

"Or you can earn yourselves better quarters, better conditions and even some small comforts."

The capsarius frowned. "Go on…"

"You began the work of cleaning and restoring the temples here. I grant to you and your men leave to continue the task.

You will continue to repair the damage done to Napata by your legion and it may stand in your favour when the queen returns." He turned to Cervianus. "This is, I feel, the fairest treatment I can give you. You work for the betterment of Napata and you will live and live more comfortably. Will your men agree to this?"

Cervianus nodded slowly. "I believe so, general. It is a generous offer."

Inside, he pictured Draco's face when confronted with the option of working willingly for the enemy who had defiled Nasica's body. Still, that was a problem that could be overcome later.

"Good. I will have a guard escort you back to your men and food and water will be brought to you. Rest and recover, and tomorrow morning you will begin work."

Cervianus cleared his throat. "May I ask, general, if I can have my kit?"

"Your 'kit'?"

"Yes, sir. The leather bag that contained my medical instruments and salves and so on. I have a number of men that require my ministrations. If it has been preserved, would it be possible for me to have it?"

Kalabsha pursed his lips. "I will have it found, checked through for anything dangerous, and then returned to you."

Cervianus nodded. "Thank you," he said quietly, his mind listing his beloved surgical tools that would be removed and confiscated, likely along with several of his jars.

His mind raced as they walked on. A cruel end seemed to have eluded them again. How long could they go on surviving in the face of such odds and, given the situation, was it even worth trying? Again he pictured Draco's response.

Still, only a *living* soldier stands any chance of escape and redemption.

He straightened his shoulders as they approached the centre of the compound once more. Time. Again, they had bought time.

Draco grasped Cervianus by the arms and hauled himself up to glare into the capsarius's face. "Get... out... of the way!"

Cervianus ground his teeth. "Sit back down and rest, sir. You're still fevered."

A low rumble issued from the centurion's throat. "Some bloody medic who can't even fix a broken arm without making it worse."

The grinding of irritated teeth became louder as the capsarius spoke through them. "This has nothing to do with your arm. This is something entirely different that you've contracted since we arrived in Napata. Could be from the water, perhaps. Whatever it is, you need to rest and stay wrapped tight and warm, keep up the purging and take down as much barley gruel as you can cope with."

Draco shook his head angrily. "We can't go on like this!"

It had been three days since Kalabsha had released the prisoners to their building and restoration duties. The men of the legion had taken to the opportunity with relish after a disconsolate two days shut in a small, hot room, and their work had been both fast and of unsurpassed quality. One of the men had even displayed some artistic talent, mixing up a palette of paints and touching up the soot-damaged wall frescoes.

Kalabsha had been so impressed with not only the work, but also the attitude of the prisoners, that on the second day he'd had them moved to more spacious quarters with open windows. Draco, his fever running as high each day, had been too ill on the first morning to put up any sort of argument. He had spent all three days in their prison, sweating, groaning and muttering, despite all Cervianus' medications. This afternoon, however, the fever was showing the first signs of starting to break. Yesterday he wouldn't have had the strength to do what he'd just done.

"We *have* to go on like this, sir. There's nothing else we can do at the moment. You can't hope to manage *anything* until you've recovered, and that'll be days away yet."

Again, Draco tried to heave Cervianus out of the way, but the strength in his arms gave out and he slumped back. Cervianus sighed. "Two days and you should be a lot stronger. The fever seems to have broken overnight, but you need to recover before you can even get out of the building."

Draco exhaled slowly and painfully and shuffled into a better position as Cervianus tucked the blanket around him again.

"It's still possible that Vi— the legion will return, sir."

He'd had trouble not mentioning Vitalis' name, but had managed so far. The warriors who stood outside the door and all the windows, keeping a continual guard on the prisoners, spoke no Latin, so conversation was generally safe, but certain names would draw the wrong kind of attention.

"Cervianus…" another pause for a laboured breath, "you know as well as I that there is little… chance of that. We… have to proceed as though… we are alone."

Somewhere deep inside the capsarius, something that he refused to believe was cowardice, objected that their current conditions as workers in Napata was as good a situation as they could hope for, and that any attempt to change that could have disastrous consequences. All he managed to say was, "I suppose so."

"Then we have to... put a plan together."

"Escape, sir?"

"What else. How's the mood among... the men? Have they still got the balls for it?"

Cervianus glanced back at the door through which the rest of the men had just left, returning to their labours after the noon break. The fact that most of the work was being undertaken inside heavily walled temples meant that they were among the coolest and most comfortable occupants of Napata at the height of the day's heat, despite their labour.

"The men are starting to recover from everything, sir. I'm not sure whether they've contemplated escape themselves, but I'm fairly sure that if you suggest it, they'll be behind you."

Draco nodded wearily. "We need to have at least the bare bones of... a plan before we open it up to them. The centurionate... are seen as always prepared, and we can't... allow that belief to falter. We need... every man on side."

Cervianus shrugged. "I can't even conceive of how we can go about it, sir. If only Ulyxes was still here with his memory."

"Forget your... deserter friend. We need... to work out how to neutralise... the guards outside this room first. Then... we need to rearm and reequip as... best we can. We need a solid plan... for getting out of the compound. Finally... we need to have an idea of what... to do next unless we plan... on ending up like Suro and his friends, stretched... on a rack and cut to pieces."

The capsarius sat back on his heels and frowned. "I think I have something that might help, sir."

Draco nodded expectantly, saving his precious breath.

"Well, sir. It might be best if you don't ask how they came to be there, but about thirty paces from the rear of the main temple, there's a cache of five pugios buried. They'll be easier to get to than the weapons locked away in the stores."

Draco's brow knitted. "Pugios?"

"Yes, sir. Officers' pugios. Brand new and quartermaster sharp, sir."

Draco continued to glare at him suspiciously. "Five. It's a start. I'll work on the... rest. You get those daggers. We'll... approach the others tonight."

Cervianus sighed and sat back, grasping an acrid-smelling earthenware bowl and pushing it toward him across the dusty floor. "In the meantime rest, recover and keep drinking this. The guards have orders to call for me if you need anything."

Draco grumbled quietly and Cervianus smiled.

"We'll be back at sundown otherwise."

With a last look at the centurion, he rose and left the building.

The white-tunic'd guard shouted the familiar halt to the day's work. This afternoon, once he had returned from the noon meal, Cervianus had shifted the soldiers' focus to two smaller temples that backed up against the cliff of the great mountain, all but neighbouring the Amun temple. The prisoners had split into two groups, half working on each of these temples which had suffered less damage than others, due to their proximity to the main building.

All afternoon, while he had scrubbed and heaved, lifting fallen blocks back into place with the aid of other soldiers, and others mixed good Roman mortar to affix the stones, he had run through a thousand plans in his head before finally settling on something he gave a little less than a fifty-fifty chance of success. It was still better by far than anything else he had considered.

Finding the opportunity to broach the subject to half a dozen likely prisoners was a tough enough job in itself and two men had flatly refused to be part of the plan, a fact which had sowed the seed of doubt into Cervianus' mind. Would they really support Draco when the time came?

Around him, at the call, legionaries rushed around gathering their paintbrushes and dipping them in the jar of water, slapping any excess mortar in to fill large gaps so it would not be wasted, washing out their cleaning brushes and rags.

Within a hundred heartbeats the entire troop of prisoners was ready, gathering outside the two small temples for the headcount before returning to the barracks. The glowing, orange disc of the sun slid slowly toward the desert in the west as one of the two white-clad guardsmen stood with the dozen warriors assigned to watch the prisoners, while the other walked back and forth, performing the count. Once he was satisfied the number of prisoners was correct, the guardsman gestured toward the large structure that housed their prison, back past the central square.

Carefully positioned within the group and close to the front, Cervianus and his six confederates shared glances and nods of readiness. As they moved off, the capsarius was grateful to note that the guard on his side was the man who spoke a little Greek and who knew Cervianus for a medic. That would make things easier.

As they approached the main temple of Amun, the capsarius

kept his gaze locked on the ground ahead. Ulyxes' hiding place was enough to escape the notice of any average observer, but a dead giveaway to a man in the know. Despite the stocky deserter's best efforts to blend the site in with the ground all around, there was a telltale circular dip where the dirt had settled over his digging pit. Cervianus had heaved a sigh of relief when he'd seen it after lunch. Without it, he'd have had great difficulty locating the hidden pugios.

The dip came into view exactly where he'd anticipated. The column of men under guard would march past it at a distance of about six feet. Indeed, the accompanying warriors would walk right across the top of the cache.

Taking a deep breath, Cervianus achieved a passable impression of a man choking on dust. The guards never even flicked their eyes toward him, though the half-dozen men with him took note of the signal and scanned the ground ahead until they spotted the depression.

At a steady pace, the prisoners shuffled on toward the site and Cervianus tensed ready, trying not to appear apprehensive or overly alert.

"Stop treading on my pissing ankle!"

Too early, Cervianus thought to himself, his heart sinking. Should know not to trust anything complex to a man who had been taken off paint-restoration because of his ham-fisted approach. Damn the man!

"Naff off, Cautex."

The supposed transgressor gave the complainer a shove between the shoulder blades that sent him staggering forward into another prisoner.

"Right!" the stumbling man bellowed. "That's it. Your arse is mine!"

Cervianus heaved a sigh of relief. The transgressing man had spotted the error and his extra hard shove had launched the small group ahead to the right position. As the first punch landed, Cervianus stepped two more paces forward and then glanced to his left to see the sunken dirt that identified the resting place of the stolen pugios.

In a series of moves so perfectly played out that they might as well have been choreographed, the other four men joined in the scuffle, laying punches on one another and screaming threats and insults. The timing was so beautiful that Cervianus stepped aside just as the instigator, apparently felled by a powerful uppercut, launched himself out of the now-halted column, landing heavily and flat on his face, right above the depression. The man may have bad timing, but apparently his aim was spot on.

"Bastard!"

"And your mother!"

"Up your tunic, shit-head!"

The sounds of punching and vitriol grew from the column as a number of other men, who were entirely oblivious of the manufactured nature of the argument, weighed in on one side or another, fighting and hurling genuine abuse. The Kushite warriors, unwilling to involve themselves in such a humorous dispute, watched on with grins.

The Greek-speaking guard turned to Cervianus and nudged his shoulder, pointing at the man on the ground, face down and immobile. "No dead?" he asked in his stilted, heavily accented Greek.

Cervianus crouched by the body of the man who was clearly having difficulty breathing face down in the dirt. Making a few fake examinations, he slowly turned the legionary's head and pulled open his eyelids, staring into his eyes. The man tried to blink in an automatic reaction, but Cervianus held the lids up.

"He'll live," he said loudly, and unshouldered his medical bag, digging around within.

Just as he'd hoped, as soon as it was confirmed that the prisoner was alright, the guard lost interest in him and stepped away to intervene in the growing fracas. It was amazing how, among the non-medically inclined, the simple act of opening the bag was enough for them to assume that subsequent events would be complicated and dull. Indeed, as the guard stepped toward the fight, even the native warriors nearby moved to join in, paying Cervianus no further heed.

For a moment the idea passed through Cervianus' head that he and the other man were, right now, completely unsupervised and that here, near the mountain's base and between the temples, they could quite easily slip away unnoticed.

Instead, he took the opportunity to carry out the plan as intended. Using the large man's prone form and his own back and medical bag as cover, he dug down into the dirt for what felt like hours.

As the loose grit slid constantly back into the pit he dug, his eyes began to dart nervously back to the column. The fight was already almost over. As soon as the guard and his warriors had decided to intervene, it had not taken long for the punches to stop flying, nine men being pulled apart by grinning warriors, blood and dust coating them.

An enterprising legionary, noting that Cervianus was still feverishly working away, managed to pull himself from a warrior's grasp and delivered a mighty kick to another man's genitals. With a squawk, the injured legionary disappeared to the ground amid the crowd, the unprepared, shorter Kushite warrior that was holding his shoulders sprawling in the dust with him. The natives erupted into laughter, poking fun at their unfortunate friend.

A second round of violence erupted in the wake of this, and it was only when the guard bellowed an order and warriors hefted spears and stretched bow strings that the brawl began to subside again.

Cervianus panicked. He couldn't *possibly* have got the wrong spot! He was almost precisely thirty paces from the main temple wall. The sunken earth denoted a spot where it had been disturbed. It *had* to be the place. With a lump in his throat, he realised what must have happened. Someone had already found them.

Could it have been when the Roman garrison was still in control of Napata?

No. If it had been, the matter would have been brought up and he'd know. A small fortune in buried officer's blades? Someone would have been beaten close enough to Hades to feel the breath of Cerberus if that was the case.

The Kushites, then. It must have been some random warrior who recognised their value and kept it to himself. If Kalabsha had found out about them, he would likely have raised the matter with Cervianus.

But either way, it meant that...

His hand closed on the cloth of the sack and the capsarius felt a lake of tension sluice out as his heart thumped away in his chest. Shouting from above him indicated that the column was back in line. Desperately, knowing how short on time he was, Cervianus thrust the dusty sack, heavy contents and all, into his leather bag and shoved the dust back into the dip. The big man began to move, trying to fake stirring from unconsciousness and managing instead to look like a cheap ham actor running out a scene from Menander.

"Up," bellowed the guard in his thick-accented Greek, and Cervianus and his "patient" hauled each other upright, using the motion to kick the pile of dust around.

A moment later he was helping the man, limping in the centre of the column, back toward the prison building, a feeling of immense satisfaction filling him at the reassuring weight swinging around in his medical bag.

As he walked, his eyes strayed around the complex and fell upon a statue, standing forlorn in the centre of a thoroughfare. Horus, or Haroeris as he preferred to think of the bird-headed god, stood at a slight lean, surrounded by piles of gravel, pots of pigment and tubs of cement, currently undergoing restoration before being returned to his temple. It was with shock that he realised the statue was reaching out in his direction with an empty hand, its cracked and pitted surface unbearably familiar.

His heart sank as he strode back toward the barracks, his erstwhile elation at locating and securing the first step to their freedom fading to be replaced by the unpleasant realisation that this was probably not a good idea. Somehow, despite everything, their destiny... or *his* at least... was tied in with the gods and with this place. Abandoning Napata was not the answer. There was still something to be done here, he was certain. His face beset by doubt, he marched on with the column, the weight in his bag now seeming a millstone around his neck.

At the door of the building, the warriors moved off into their positions outside the windows or by the main door, while the two white-garbed guards entered, ushering them into the large bunk-room now assigned to them. Draco was seated on the low bunk opposite the door, wrapped in his blanket but, as he looked up, Cervianus could see the gleam in his eye.

The centurion was on the mend and his mind had been working through the fever.

Behind him, the door was closed and barred. He waited for a while until the guards were safely away from the door, back out at the front of the building, and then heaved a deep sigh.

Almost a dozen men moved into one corner of the room where the labrum of tepid water had been placed for their use. The stink of the chamber reasserted itself after the relative fresh air outside. The three wooden buckets in the opposite corner that constituted a latrine for forty men were overdue an emptying. Cervianus decided he could hold his bladder for now, and strode off toward the centurion, as far away from the latrine corner as they could get, close to the blessed relief of a window.

Draco had his brow furrowed as he watched the men at the labrum dabbing split lips and washing out cuts and grazes. "Talk to me, Cervianus."

"Bit of a scuffle, sir. To cover this up."

Crouching next to the centurion, he undid the leather bag's catch and withdrew the dusty sack from inside, brushing it off onto the floor before upending it and tipping the contents out onto the bed.

Five pugio daggers clonked, glittering, onto the rough blanket. Draco picked one up and turned it round and round, drinking in the decoration with hungry eyes.

"Jove, Cervianus. This one alone's better than even mine! It's worth a *fortune*; they all are."

"I said it was best not to ask too many questions, sir."

"This has your dubious pal Ulyxes all over it. Still, can't say I'm not glad in the circumstances."

Cervianus cleared his throat. "I'm not sure how to say this, sir, but..." Nothing else for it but to dive straight in. "I don't think we should be trying to escape."

Draco flicked him a look that was in equal parts surprise and disappointment. "Don't be an idiot."

"Sir," the capsarius insisted, "the time's just not right, yet. Don't ask me why, but there's something we have to do here still. I don't know what it is, but we're not supposed to leave yet. Something's been keeping us here all this time. Even the crocodile god wouldn't let me leave."

Draco narrowed his eyes. "Since when did *you* become such a religious nut, Cervianus? If I remember rightly, you pissed off your entire cohort by denying the gods and telling everyone their gifts and miracles were just 'natural'?"

Cervianus sighed. He had to admit that it really didn't sound like him. If the Cervianus of three months ago met him now, he'd give him a kick in the shin, a poke in the eye, and tell him to stop being superstitious and read a damn book once in a while.

"I realise it sounds a bit strange, sir, but the fact is that even I can't fight the weirdness that's been going on in southern Aegyptus and Kush."

"The fact remains," Draco replied in a low voice, "that it is the duty of a soldier to escape his captors and return with vengeance and the full force of Rome. Whatever your 'weirdness' is telling you, every day we spend faffing about here, painting walls for the enemy, we're one day further away from freedom and one day closer to the bitch who rules this country coming back. You know what's going to happen when she gets here, don't you?"

Cervianus nodded slowly. He'd given that some thought himself. For all Kalabsha's big talk, no amount of good behaviour was going to save them from the Kandake's executioners.

"Still, sir… can we not delay it just a few days? I'm absolutely positive there's something just around the corner."

"No, Cervianus, we can't. The thing that's just around the corner is the army of the Kushite queen. Tonight we plan. Tomorrow we prepare…" the centurion clenched his fist around the hilt of the pugio and drew it from the scabbard with a satisfying rasp, "… and tomorrow night we leave."

Cervianus leaned against the window frame and tried not to breathe too heavily. Next to him, Draco gave the signal, every man in the room moving into position.

The Kushite warrior with his lion-skin wrapping and colourful shield, a long spear in hand, returned from his regular check around the building's perimeter and took up a bored position some three feet from the window, his gaze locked in the middle distance as his mind attempted to occupy the vast emptiness of a night on guard duty.

Cervianus leaned out to look through the heavy, wooden slats that formed the prison's bars, making sure that the man was paying no attention to the building's dark interior. The moonlight glinted off the spear tip and he could hear the Kushite rattling out speech in low tones. A prayer? A song? Who knew?

Better be a prayer, he thought bitterly.

No amount of wheedling, persuasion, argument or cajoling had come close to changing Draco's mind about tonight's move.

The centurion had spent much of the previous night looking thoughtful, between the shivers and groans, and Cervianus had begun to hope his arguments about leaving had had some effect, but tonight, as soon as they'd got back from the day's work, Draco had begun to outline his plan.

Cervianus gritted his teeth. Well, *part* of his plan, anyway.

At the next nod from the centurion, he grasped the wooden window frame and tugged with as much force as he dared, willing it not to make a sound.

The centurion had spent his last two days of isolation in the prison working at the window with a pugio. The short-sighted Kushites had been sure of the security of the timber frame. It was strong. Even working with a knife, it would take many weeks to dismantle part of the frame. The wall surrounding the window, however, was of mud-brick. Half an hour of scraping had loosened one of the bricks and, with two days on his own, Draco had worked the entire surround free. The big trick, since they were not mortared in place, was not to release pressure above the window, or the bricks would simply fall.

Cervianus carefully and quietly tipped the bottom of the window in toward him, keeping the top in place and jammed against the loose bricks. Once he had it open by about a foot, he paused. Draco, ever a man to take the danger unto himself, ducked beneath the wooden frame and came up in the empty aperture, pugio glinting in his hand.

With surprising dexterity for a man of his years, size and general state of health, the centurion hopped over the low threshold of the window and threw his arms around the Kushite guard.

His left hand went over the mouth while the right came round with the knife, drawing a deadly, deep line across the man's throat. Draco held him tight for a long moment as he convulsed and bucked, a spray of liquid black in the night air spattering the ground. As soon as he was sure the man was dead, he gently lowered the body to the ground and gestured back through the window.

The forty-one men of his unit quietly clambered over the window ledge and dropped to the dirt outside, the front four wielding the beautifully crafted pugios. Cervianus crouched, his hands free, having declined the option of the daggers.

"What now?" he mouthed at the centurion.

This was the trouble. When Draco had announced his intention to escape the prison, the men had greeted him with mixed reactions, perhaps shaking his resolve. Certainly, he looked at a number of the men with suspicious eyes now, as though by their dissatisfaction with the idea they had all but sided with Kalabsha. It had resulted in a general unwillingness to reveal his plan to the group, and Cervianus found himself wishing he had at least an inkling of what the centurion planned. After all, the man was still suffering the after-effects of a fever.

Draco gestured toward the large building some thirty paces along the road and directly across the wide thoroughfare from the main temple.

Cervianus blinked.

Was the man mad?

The building was, for certain, the main store in the compound for the valuable goods, and would be where their weapons, shields and armour were kept, along with the captured standards, but it was also the home of several guard rooms, as well as the headquarters of the general and his senior men.

Cervianus' heart sank as he realised what Draco was planning. It was not good enough to merely escape. To lose the cohort's standards and vexillum was to heap dishonour upon them, so the man actually intended to raid their main store and retrieve the unit's standards. A number of the others had seen the gesture and were sharing equally disbelieving looks. Draco must be *crazy*. The fever was still in control of his brain.

A few of the men hesitated, but soon fell in line and rejoined the group. The simple fact was that they were now committed to whatever insane plan of action Draco's febrile mind had cooked up. Soon the guard's death and the open window would be discovered, and the whole compound would be on the alert.

Two hundred heartbeats at most, Cervianus gave it.

Nothing for it now but to join in and hope.

A hand signal from Draco sent them off at an angle from their building and the Roman prisoners darted across the street like thieves in the night, diving into the moon-cast shadow at the far side, lurking in the pool of darkness beneath the wall of the temple of Haroeris. From here it was a short run toward the centre of the complex and the headquarters building that was Draco's unbelievable target.

The entrance to the large building was off to the far side, facing the Amun temple as they approached from the rear, and Cervianus was unaware of any ancillary doorway. Two men in white habitually stood guard at the main door, and the likelihood of other Kushites being awake in the central area of the compound was high, in the capsarius's opinion.

As Draco led the men on at a low run and dropped into the shade at the rear of the headquarters, Cervianus could hear the restless mutterings of the men. Few were happy about the direction they were taking. Even Draco's hold over his men would only drag them so far into what appeared to be an idiotic raid on the centre of Kushite power in the compound.

As the last of the men dropped into the lee of the wall, Draco motioned them to silence with a stern look and used his hands to split them into two forces, directing each along one side of the building toward the front, where he mimed a guard having his throat cut. The men with the daggers moved to the corners, ready. Another signal and they were off.

Cervianus, having been directed left, away from Draco, ran with the two dagger-wielders along the wall of the building and to the next corner. He and the man beside him risked a quick glance around the front.

Sure enough, two men in white stood, blinding in the moonlight, to either side of the door, perhaps ten paces away. Beyond them, another fifteen paces or so into the distance, they could just make out Draco's head bobbing out for a look.

Another gesture from the far end: Draco was wasting no time in the assault. Cervianus barely had time to gather his wits before the dagger-wielding man with him turned the corner and ran quietly at a crouch. For a moment, Cervianus paused, aware of how much rode on the quick, silent dash from the corner to the door and the unnoticed death of the guards. Given Cervianus' record with stealth, he wondered whether to wait in the shadows until they came back out with the gear. Surely that would be better for them all.

Across the square, another building apparently warranted a dual guard, though they were far enough away that, if they were suffering the standard ennui and tedium of a night-time posting, they might not spot the action.

After a moment, Cervianus realised that the rest of the men had stopped behind him, waiting for the order to move out round the corner. Draco's men at the far side were already on the move. His eyes flicked to the guards across the square. If they saw anything amiss, this was all for naught.

Urgently, Cervianus motioned the men to follow and ran out along the front after the knife-man, who was already at his target. Behind him, as well as at the far corner, men were now swarming out, desperate to make their way inside before they were spotted running in the moonlight.

The two sneaking knife-men had managed to make short work of the guards and as Cervianus reached them they were wiping a dark red slick from their glinting blades, the still-spasming bodies at their feet pumping lifeblood out into the dust.

The capsarius motioned to two of the men behind him and mimed his intentions. The men nodded dubiously and, crouching, removed the guards' white tunics, slick with blood, donning them over their own dirty, faded green garments.

Within a few heartbeats, two men in white were standing at attention by the doorway, holding spears and shields rigidly. From a reasonable distance, and by moonlight, they could be mistaken for the real thing.

As the rest of the legionaries poured into the doorway between them, Cervianus ducked into the shade and peered back out across the square, narrowing his eyes, a look of concern and suspicion falling across his face. Alright, they *had* been quick. A few moments from lurking in the shadows to having killed and replaced the guards, all crowding into the doorway and out of sight.

Yes, it was dark and only moon and stars lit the activity.

Yes, it was the middle of the night, and guards were traditionally at their least perceptive at this time.

But it was almost inconceivable that they had achieved all that without the two guards across the open space at the other building noticing *something* amiss. If they *had* seen anything, though, why had the alarm not gone up, and why had they not moved?

His heart began to pound faster as he turned and ran inside. The mass of legionaries were milling about in the main front room from which two passages led off into the heart of the building. He scanned the crowd desperately and spotted Draco looking directly at him and beckoning.

Running across, he pushed his way between the soldiers. "I've a really bad feeling about this," he said quietly, yet with a tone that made a number of heads turn to him, worry clouding their expressions.

"Stop pissing about, Cervianus. You know the layout of just about every building in the complex, so I guess you can lead us through this one?"

"Sir?" the capsarius said desperately.

"Yes or no?" snapped Draco.

"I know the *rough* layout," Cervianus replied desperately, pointing off to the right-hand corridor. "The place they'll be storing the Roman equipment and standards…"

"Screw the standards. We're not here for them."

Cervianus stared at the centurion, his mouth flapping open and closed. "Then what…?" But he knew what. He already knew. His eyes closed in disbelief as Draco confirmed his worst fears.

"I'm not leaving Napata in the hands of this slave-driving shit-for-brains. Where will Kalabsha sleep?"

The sudden realisation of what Draco was attempting sank into the legionaries and, to a man, they turned to stare at him.

"Glory for the Twenty Second, lads. Let's rip the general's spine out and tie it to the standard before we march out of here."

The response was mixed. Less supportive than Draco probably hoped, but considerably more positive than Cervianus expected.

"Listen. I think we're in trouble!" Cervianus snapped.

A few of the men turned at the warning, but Draco shrugged. "Then we'd better be fast. Which way, *optio*?"

Despite Cervianus' worries and objections, he found the commanding voice and the use of his rank had him rattling out the answer before he'd even thought it through. "Left-hand side at the far end is the only multiple-room apartment. It's around a small peristyle garden, almost like a Roman house," he found himself saying.

"Good. Half of you stay here on guard. The rest with me. You too, Cervianus."

The capsarius shot a look left and right in near-panic. This was not right. Everything was poised to come crashing down around their ears and no one seemed to be listening to him. Worst of all, now that they were here in the building there wasn't much he could do about it. He was as committed as the rest of them. Committed and...

Trapped?

Was that why nothing had been done? They were waiting to get all the prisoners in one place? Desperately, he ducked back through the press of soldiers to the doorway and glanced to left and right. For a blissful moment his panic began to subside. The two legionaries in their stolen white tunics still stood to attention to either side of the door.

Pinned.

His mind reeled as he took in the half-dozen arrows that affixed each man to the mud-brick wall. Even as he tried to think his way out of the situation, another two arrows whizzed through the air, one jamming into the door frame next to him and the other disappearing into the gloom of the doorway behind.

There was a squawk from the legionary it struck and Cervianus, the panic beginning to build to unbearable levels, ducked inside again and pushed the doors closed, dropping the bar just in time to hear the thud of three more arrows driving into the wood outside.

"They're on to us... it's a trap," he shouted, as he returned to the main room, which was already in a state of chaos. Two legionaries thrust their wounded companion at him, an arrow jutting out of his lower back near the hip. Cervianus grabbed the man in surprise, and then passed him back to them, pushing onwards. Draco was already gone from the room, several legionaries with him.

As he moved to the doorway he'd indicated and through which they'd left, he heard the first scream.

"Wait," he bellowed.

Running into the passage he could see, silhouetted in the corridor, the figures of perhaps eight soldiers, one of whom would be Draco. As he watched, the half-dozen Kushite archers standing beside the torch at the end of the corridor released their arrows again, and three of the eight figures fell.

"Stop," he shouted, running toward the action. He could hear moans and gurgles. The fact that Draco was not bellowing defiance suggested that he must have been one of the casualties.

Changing tack as he ran, he called for a halt to the arrows again, this time in Greek.

The voice of Kalabsha rang out from the end of the corridor in his own language, and the arrows ceased, though the archers nocked ready to loose again on command. The general, fully armed and armoured and backed by two of his guards, strode forward, taking up a stance in front of his archers.

"I gave you every opportunity," he said quietly. "I gave you the chance to atone for your crimes and I treated you well; better than Rome would have treated us, I think. And yet not only do you plan to escape, but you plot my death into the bargain. This is most saddening." He straightened. "Fortunate it is, though, that I took every precaution I could, having you all watched and followed and buying the loyalty of your surprisingly malleable men wherever possible."

Cervianus shook his head. Treachery from their *own men*? If Draco had spoken Greek, and if he was still alive, of course, his blood would boil at the thought.

"Why?" the Kushite leader asked quietly, in genuine puzzlement. "Why would you jeopardise your own well-being and comfort?"

"Cervianus?" barked the centurion in a wheezy voice from somewhere at ground level, and the capsarius heaved a small sigh of relief.

"Sir?"

"What's this shitbag saying?"

Shuffling forward and joining the small group of Romans who were variously standing, crouched or lying on the ground, several with arrows jutting from them, the capsarius repeated the general's question in Latin. Draco's face hardened and he pulled himself a little more upright, clutching the shaft of the arrow jutting from the shoulder of his already-broken arm.

"Tell him it's because we are soldiers of Rome, and he is the enemy."

Kalabsha frowned as Cervianus translated into Greek. "But you are beaten! You are prisoners, not soldiers."

Draco waited for the reply, and then pointed a finger threateningly at the Kushite. "You will learn one day, general *Piss-Pot*, that Rome cannot be beaten. You cannot destroy us or contain us. All you can do is delay us."

Cervianus shook his head again. Stupid. Don't rile the man now.

"Translate it," Draco said quietly, noting Cervianus' reluctance. "Word for word."

"Sir, you'll just make it worse."

"Do as you're ordered, optio."

Taking a deep breath, Cervianus repeated the words in Greek and, sure enough, Kalabsha's jaw clenched.

"You are foolish, espousing your superiority when it is clear that you have lost. Rome is not the power people say. The lands of Kemet may have bowed beneath you, but we know of your failure in Arabia. Merchants from their lands bring us goods across the water. Do you not even recognise the armour and blades you face? Many of them are Arabian, or even Indian... the same shirts that foiled your army there. *Two* legions could not take Marsiaba from the Sabaeans, and they are traders, not warriors. The people of Meroë are warriors born, and you send only *one* legion to deal with us? *Three* would not be enough to take Kush. You have lost, Roman, and you have yet to comprehend to what degree..."

Cervianus had been interpreting as the man spoke and now he paused as Kalabsha drew a sword from his side and gestured toward them.

"My queen has sent word today for us to travel south and join with her army. Your Vitalis has been defeated more than a hundred miles from Meroë and the survivors of your legion have fled into the desert, where they will die. I go to help her finish the task and then, when the last trace of Roman blood has boiled away from our land, we will march north and take Kemet from you, returning it to a ruler who understands its people."

Draco struggled to stand, but his strength was waning rapidly from the combination of the arrow wound and the fever still coursing through him.

Cervianus closed his eyes sadly.

Shenti and his men, gone. Catilius, the monobrowed junior tribune who had tried to temper the commander's rule, gone. *All* gone into the wastes of the desert for the vanity of Vitalis, curse the man.

He realised Kalabsha was talking again and rushed to translate.

"If you are so set on following your Roman leaders, then you shall have your wish. You can pursue Vitalis into the next world."

The general barked out a series of orders in his own language to the men behind him and swords were drawn.

"What was that?" asked Draco and Cervianus shrugged dejectedly.

"I don't know, sir, but I guess it's the execution orders."

VIII

PUNISHMENT

Cervianus tried to exercise his wrists a little, though the manacles chafed with every slight movement. As another patch of raw skin scraped away beneath the warm iron, he hissed through his teeth.

The thirty-nine survivors of the First cohort stood wearily in the corridor, roped together, and manacled in some cases. Only half a dozen sets of iron cuffs had been found, so the rest had their wrists rubbed red by rope instead, the iron being used on those prisoners Kalabsha considered most troublesome. Needless to say, Cervianus had somehow become first on that list, despite his intent to prevent any of this from happening.

Two days now they had been roped and bound and locked once more in a room too small to comfortably accommodate even half their number. Two days during which the Kushite army prepared to move out and complete the annihilation of the Twenty Second legion.

Once more, spirits had plummeted and even Draco's stalwart strength had failed to arrest the decline. The news that the army had been defeated had meant the end as far as most of them were concerned.

Despite the fact that no one truly believed Vitalis capable

of achieving his insane conquest, they had lived on clutching to the glimmer of hope that a victorious legion would return to Napata and take them back to Nicopolis in righteous glory. Now that last flicker of light had been snuffed. Whatever survivors there were from the main army had disappeared into the desert, and Cervianus, having made that disastrous crossing from Buhen, knew exactly how much chance *that* gave them.

The nature of their end had not yet been revealed to them, a fact that had made the execution-bound prisoners all the more disconsolate. They had little reason to expect even the slightest mercy. A groan issued from somewhere near the back of the line.

"Stow that muttering," barked Draco, whose fever had continued to recede over the last two sundowns and now seemed much his old self, despite the stub of the arrow shaft still protruding from his shoulder. The skin around the wound was puckered and discoloured. Cervianus regularly eyed the wound for infection, yet none seemed to be setting in, astoundingly. Could it be that even disease and illness were frightened of Draco?

There was a muted rattle and a *thunk*, and the door at the head of the column of condemned men swung open, bathing them in early morning light.

"Time," snapped the guard with the passing knowledge of Greek. "Come."

More groans rose from the men, and Draco spun his head, his teeth grinding. "Shut your faces. Remember you're legionaries of the Twenty Second, not some auxiliary elephant farmer. Act like it, or when this is over I'll tan your hide again in Elysium."

Even in the face of death, the centurion's threat was enough to curb the murmur, and the man at the front of the column shuffled through the doorway and into the light, blinking at the blinding sun directly ahead.

Disconsolately, the line of men began to trudge forward, the tunics that constituted their only apparel soiled and drab from the days without ablutions or latrines, roped together as they were even through the night.

Eighth in the line, and three men ahead of Draco, Cervianus emerged blinking into the light. The complex looked all but deserted again, as it had once Vitalis had marched the legion south, leaving a depleted cohort to guard the place. The bulk of the Kushite force was gathered outside the complex, by the river, preparing to march, various wagons and support units alongside. Perhaps a hundred warriors, a dozen archers, three guards and the general himself remained in the centre, near the temple of Amun.

Briefly, Cervianus wondered if the centurion had another plan: a sudden idea to free them from this and launch an attack on this diminished group of Kushites. It was wishful thinking of the most ridiculous sort, of course. Even if they could manage to escape their bonds, they were unarmed, variously injured or unwell, and still outnumbered almost three to one. They would be dead before they had moved two steps. No. They would just walk out and be executed.

Kalabsha waited until they were all out of the building and twitching under the heat of the morning sun and then rattled out a series of orders in his native tongue. Four of the warriors stepped forward and untied the knotted rope around the front man's hands with some difficulty, it having pulled tight with each movement over the past two days.

The man was led away from the column by the warriors,

his shoulders slumped, already apparently having accepted his fate. As four more warriors stepped out to untie the second man, Kalabsha walked forward and folded his arms. "For your repeated violations and the damage you wreaked in the holy places of Napata, it is clear that there is no option left to you but death."

A low groan rose from the column but as Draco cleared his throat meaningfully it died away. A number of the men even managed to hold their head high with traditional legionary pride.

"Many gods are worshipped here, but Napata is the birthplace of Amun-Ra, he who creates and rules in the sun, and it is he who shall deliver you to the next world."

The second man was now being led away and as the next four warriors came to untie the third prisoner, Cervianus turned his head to follow the activity. The first man from the line had been led to the wall of the large, mud-brick palace/ headquarters building they had tried to infiltrate that ill-fated night. As the capsarius watched, a wooden stool was placed by the wall and the man forced to climb it. Now, some three feet from the ground, the warriors hammered a wooden peg into the wall and used a length of rope to bind his wrist tightly to it. The job was repeated at the far side and then, without ceremony, the Kushites stepped back, removing the stool as they did so.

The legionary screamed as his support vanished and he dropped toward the ground, still hanging so that his feet were a foot from the dirt. The sound of dislocating shoulders and tearing muscles had been audible. The man continued to yelp and struggle for a moment and then, mercifully for him, blacked out, slumping against the mud-brick and hanging limp.

Cervianus closed his eyes.

"Amun-Ra will parch your skin and leech the life from your bodies until you are a dry husk, your eyes burned out by his glory. If you are lucky, your body is weak and you will succumb to the pain before you parch and starve. If you still have any respect for the gods, pray to Amun to end it for you before the scavenging cats find you and begin to eat your feet."

Another groan arose and this time no amount of Draco's acerbic comments and threats could stop it. Cervianus shuddered, remembering the tone in the voice of the auxiliary officer back at Syene all those weeks ago as he'd spoken of the survivors of his unit being pinned to the walls of the Abu fortress so they could watch them die.

The stool was moved along the wall just far enough that, when the second man was attached to it, his fingertips were a foot away from his neighbour's. This time, Cervianus saw as the stool was whisked away and the man dropped, his right arm wrenching from the socket and extending by six inches or so in a sickening way. The legionary was tall and, with his arm so stretched and dislocated, his toes brushed the dust of the ground in a tantalising manner, though not enough to relieve the pain or pressure. He yelped repeatedly, trying not to move, as every twitch sent agony coursing up and down his arms.

By Cervianus' estimate there should be just enough prisoners to cover the entire wall-circuit of the main building. He watched with dread as the process was repeated with the next man; then the next, and the next.

Suddenly, far sooner than he had anticipated, his hands were being unbound.

Panic began to rise in him. How had his fellow soldiers allowed the ropes to be removed and walked quietly away with a resigned look? It was one thing to march or run into battle. The odds were often stacked in favour of the legion, and at least they had protection and a good chance of survival. But to walk quietly to certain and very painful, drawn-out death? That took something that Cervianus was rapidly becoming aware he didn't have.

He was fighting them off as soon as his wrists were freed, despite desperately wishing he had the strength of character, the sheer willpower, to hold himself straight and proud. He was vaguely aware of disapproving chatter from Draco behind him, but the comments met with the wall of his panic and were lost.

It was all to no avail, of course. His flailing, red-raw wrists were grasped and gripped tightly enough that the blood flow to his hands was restricted; blackened, dirty fingernails bit into the flesh. He gasped in pain, horribly aware that this was nothing compared with what was yet to come.

Struggling impotently, the capsarius was half led, half dragged across the dirt to the wall. As he looked up in fear, he was just in time to see the previous man drop as the stool was removed, muscles tearing as he screamed. Somewhere deep in his brain the logical, methodical part of him began to assert itself through the fear.

Don't sag, his mind told him. *Keep tensed and ready. A moment of strain will save so much pain.* Something to focus on: preventing what had happened to the preceding eight men from happening to him in his turn.

The new-found focus took control and he stepped onto the stool unbidden. The warriors lifted his arms into position, measuring their place and then hammering the wooden peg deep into the wall. Taking a length of rope, the warriors bound his wrist once more, looping the rope and twisting it round the peg and then yanking it so tight that he bit his tongue with the pain. As they tied it and began to repeat the process on the far side, he toyed with the rope.

A moment's playing and he realised it was possible. Though it tore yet more skin from his wrists and rubbed him raw, he could actually grasp the peg itself. There was no way a man in this position could find the leverage and strength to remove the peg and escape, or untie the rope, so getting out of the situation was clearly impossible, but gripping the peg would give him one great advantage over the previous victims.

The warriors finished tying his other hand and began to step back. As the next prisoner was brought to the wall a few feet away, Cervianus desperately and hurriedly grasped the peg with his other hand. Turning his head, he spoke urgently to the next victim.

"Watch what I do and copy it. Then tell the next man."

The legionary frowned and examined him, noting how he held the pegs. The Kushites reached for the stool and Cervianus tensed, pushing out with his arms so that his feet barely touched the stool, his muscles taking his weight as though exercising in the palaestra of the great public baths in Ancyra. Grunting and gritting his teeth, he stayed in perfect position as the stool was whisked away.

"See?" he hissed to the watching legionary as the stool was moved along the wall ready for the man. The nervous man nodded. "Now I lower myself gently and nothing dislocates or tears."

It was less smooth and pain-free than he'd expected, and he gasped as he dropped the last few inches, but the exercise had done the job. No jerk in the fall meant no dislocation. Not yet, at least. It would likely happen slowly over the next day or two, if they lived that long. The legionary next to him nodded again as he was urged up on to the stool.

"Make sure you get it passed on and we'll save as much pain as possible."

Realising that blood was filling his mouth from his bitten tongue, Cervianus spat heavily onto the dust and settled as comfortably as he could. On the bright side, his arms would numb in less than an hour and he would probably hit delirium by sundown. That would be good, since the scavengers would start to come at sunset.

Next to him the legionary grunted as the stool was removed and he lowered himself into position without serious wounding. The Kushite warriors began to chatter concernedly among themselves. He couldn't understand them, of course, but they were probably trying to decide whether this was relieving too much suffering.

The argument seemed to conclude with a collective shrug and the next legionary was placed in position and let hang, his arms taking the strain as the word was passed on. Cervianus offered up a quick prayer to both Haroeris and Taranis that he withstand the pain and discomfort like a man.

Draco was next up against the wall, climbing onto the stool while spitting invective and bile at the warriors. As the legionary passed on the instructions, the centurion nodded grimly. Gripping the two wooden pegs, he took the strain, incredibly, given the recent break and the arrow wound, and, as the Kushite warrior stepped forward to remove the stool, he used his impressive, muscular arms to swing his torso out, his legs wrapping around the warrior's head. Suddenly, the man found himself with his head jammed between this insane prisoner's knees. Draco grunted and twisted, gasping with the pain as he used his knees to snap the warrior's neck.

The body fell away limp, its head at an unpleasant angle, and Draco returned to hanging limply, heaving in deep breaths and fighting the pain in his arms. It looked from the angle as though the centurion had now re-broken his arm. The other three Kushite warriors were gathered in a shocked huddle, staring up at the prisoner, who spat at them defiantly.

"Any other arsehole want to come have a go?"

There was a brief discussion and, in a move that would have been funny in other circumstances, one of the warriors approached slowly at a crouch until his fingertips touched the fallen stool. Gingerly, making sure he was out of reach of the centurion's feet at all times, the warrior grasped the stool and retreated, preparing for the next victim. Draco sagged unpleasantly, his ruined arm unable to take any further punishment.

And so it went. No one else had the strength of either body or will to attempt something like that and, as the moments passed in pain and sweat, the work continued on around the corner of the building, the hammering of pegs into the walls coming as an echo around the buildings of the complex.

All the time, Kalabsha and his archers looked on impassively. Slowly the column of waiting men dwindled until the last legionary was led off to the wall. Occasionally there had been a shriek as a man had failed to find enough strength to hold himself up and had fallen heavily, tearing arms out of sockets, but many of the men went to their place of execution and endured it in silence.

Finally, the warriors returned to the general with the stool, a coil of rope, and mallet and pegs. Kalabsha nodded to himself and held a short conversation with his guards. Finally, he stepped forward and began to chant and mutter in his own language, throwing his arms up to the sun.

"He cursing us?" asked the man next to Cervianus breathlessly.

"Can't understand him, but I think it's a prayer."

A few heartbeats of muttering and chattering, and Kalabsha lowered his arms and folded them.

"We go now to hunt down your legion's survivors and end their time in our land. When this is over and we march on Alexandria, we will be sure to hold your standards high while we take them home for you. Those of you who were led into this disaster against your will, I hope die well and quickly. I have asked Amun-Ra that he help you do so. Farewell, soldiers of Rome."

Cervianus spat on the ground, his mouth filled with blood from his cut tongue once more, and Draco seemed to take it as a defiant gesture, joining in. Kalabsha shook his head sadly and turned, walking away and making for the east gate, the guards at his shoulders, archers and then warriors turning and filing away after him. They watched in silence as the master of the Kushite army left with his prime troops to rejoin the bulk of his force by the river.

For the first time in days, Cervianus felt a jolt of hope. If they were left alone to die, there was the possibility of escape; only the very *slightest* possibility, but a morsel of hope. If someone, probably Draco given his fortitude and sheer willpower, could manage to get free, then he could help the rest.

They would be moving down the Nile in a matter of hours, fleeing back to safety.

It was possible...

* * *

It was *not* possible.

He watched with a sinking feeling yet again as the last thirty or so warriors closed the gate behind the departing force and set guards on the walls and near the building where the Romans hung limply. There was to be a caretaker unit making sure that they did die after all. Of course, Kalabsha was unlikely to leave anything to chance; the man was too shrewd for that. Once again, as he felt the sun drying him out, his mouth parching despite the rich, tinny blood inside, the capsarius found himself analysing his situation.

Why?

Why had the gods continued to show him portents and dreams if he was to die here? Why the warrior gods and the healers? It hadn't occurred to him before but now, as he hung here on the wall, waiting to slowly desiccate, he realised what at least the *grouping* of the gods in his new dream might mean. Sobek and Sekhmet: the two warrior deities that Shenti had explained to him. The two that they had sought out for aid and protection before marching south at all. And on the other side, Haroeris the "Good Doctor" and Amun, the creator: creating and healing. And the balance of Thoth between them. What were they asking? What did they mean?

He was still puzzling over the meaning as the last dust of the departing Kushite army disappeared over the eastern horizon upriver.

Hours passed in blurred, sizzling discomfort.

It wasn't the pain that really caused him to suffer. It was

the sheer strain of the position as his arms continued to throb, muscles beginning to tear. His mouth had dried a long time ago and the matted blood inside made it dreadfully unpleasant.

For a moment, he dreamed of eating dates, or even fresh fruit like that he'd seen in the markets of Memphis. He would happily do without his left arm right now for a taste of an apple.

Sometime just after noon, he had realised that the Fates, being the bastard crones they were, had placed the thread of the last few hours of his life in the direct line of an ant trail. Almost an hour he had struggled with the regular tickling of the creatures crossing his ankle and occasionally stopping to bite it. But then, if the worst thing that bit his ankle this day was an ant, he could consider himself a lucky man.

What had woken him again?

He realised he had drifted into unconsciousness during the worst heat of the afternoon. Couldn't be the light or temperature. The sun was still up, though descending toward the horizon at a good pace.

Then the whooping sound came again.

Some sort of desert predator or scavenger. He thought he knew what that noise was supposed to be, but for some reason his mind didn't seem to be working properly.

His mouth was too dry and it took great effort to unstick his tongue from his palate. He should try and produce more spittle. It wouldn't save him, of course. Some people thought that if you could put a pebble under your tongue you would produce enough saliva to survive in the desert.

Some people were morons, of course.

Since the body was continually losing fluid, where did people think the spit was coming from, the gods?

But it would help with temporary lubrication and reduce the discomfort, at least.

Where would he get hold of a pebble with his hands affixed to the wall like this?

He sighed and sagged a little more, grunting at the pain that brought.

His mind wandered through what he had left. Tunic, of course. They'd left the signet ring that his father had passed on, though that would be of precious little use. Jewellery wasn't really his thing and in the circumstances...

His brow creased.

Jewellery.

With a small, pained smile, he inclined his head to rest on his chest. The extra strain this put on his arms was unbearable, but he ignored it as his lip worked away, trying to move the neckline of his tunic out of the way. With difficulty, he unstuck his sore tongue from the roof of his mouth and dipped further forward, straining in agony. It was like a nightmare version of the old child's party game: bobbing for apples in a bucket of water.

Again and again his lip curled and his tongue probed. The pain and exertion were becoming too much, and he began to see white flashes in front of his eyes, recognising that any time now, he would pass out again, but then he had it. He felt the warm, almost burning metal on his tongue and before it could escape, he clamped his teeth around Ulyxes' lucky coin, the leather thong on which it hung just long enough to allow him to lift his head again with the coin beneath his tongue.

Within moments, he felt the saliva rising unbidden in his mouth until it became a torrent. He smiled with relief, making sure not to open his mouth and let the coin fall away.

At least his last few hours might be a little more comfortable.

He glanced left and right, but the men to either side were either dead or unconscious.

With a sigh, he sagged back against the wall and waited for the inevitable.

The jackal whooped again, much closer to the compound now.

Hopefully it wouldn't find *his* feet first.

It was morning.

It *must* be morning, since it was his turn to be torched and seared by the face of Ra, and he was pegged to the east-facing wall of the building.

Scavengers had come last night and had picked at the hanging banquet, though there was too much fight yet left in the meal, and after a few tentative nips and a number of struggling kicks, the jackals had pulled away, slinking off into the dark, where their luminous, unearthly eyes peered out expectantly, waiting for the strength of the hanging banquet to finally ebb.

A quick roll of the eyes skyward that seemed to take almost every ounce of strength Cervianus had left allowed him to confirm that the vultures had moved in when the jackals had retreated, and were circling hungrily.

The man to his left that he had helped overcome the initial jolt groaned and muttered something about a woman or a girl called Palla, invoking Taranis, Teutates, Jupiter and Amun just to be sure. The man to his right had died sometime during the first night. Cervianus remembered vaguely being woken by the death rattle. He'd have liked to confirm that Draco was still there, but lacked enough strength to turn his head and crane forward to look past the praying legionary.

His mouth was so dry it felt as though he'd never experienced moisture. His lips were cracked and split already and it hurt to move them, though he hadn't really the strength to do so anyway. His eyes burned with the brilliance of the sun even when his lids were down, which was most of the time. They didn't prevent the sun from searing his retinas; they just turned the brightness a pinky colour.

Had it been two days?

Three?

Certainly he must have been here more than a day. What had happened the first night? Had the jackals come then? Or was it only one night after all, and he was getting confused? The periods of painful light were certainly seeming to blend into one.

The meaning of the dream had become immaterial now, given some of the nightmares and peculiar visions he'd been granted while he hung here. If *they* were supposed to be prescience then clearly his life-changing "god" dreams had been a torrent of drivel that he'd been swept along in, caught up in the heady mysticism of this peculiar land.

It would have been better for everyone if he'd never left Galatia; if he'd never joined the royal army that became the Twenty Second; if he'd never taken on that boy as his patient in Ancyra and failed to live up to his reputation. When the lad had died despite his ministrations, the woman had kicked up enough of a fuss to put the matter through the courts. His practice in ruins and all but penniless, Cervianus had been left with little other choice.

Still, had he decided to flee to somewhere more rural and set up again, unknown and without the stigma he carried, instead of chancing the army, he would have been unlikely to have ended up here, pegged to a mud-brick wall at the southern end of the world and waiting to die.

Indeed, the invasion would never have happened.

Vitalis would be dead, Kush would be—

He realised with a start that he might have been over-simplifying things since the very start. Vitalis might have died and the legion may not have marched south, but Kalabsha had stated a clear intention to march north and take Aegyptus.

Would that have been any different?

Cervianus' head was now thumping with the effort of so much thought and he found himself consciously blanking his mind. Concentration took just too much effort, the strength of which would be more useful if the jackals came again. Better to die of exposure and starvation than being slowly eaten from the feet up.

He sighed as, with even the thought of the eating process, his mind furnished him with an image of a stuffed hare in wine, cumin and vinegar, parsnips and leeks.

Sigh...

Thunder?

Did it ever rain here? It was hard to believe.

Slowly and painfully, Cervianus prised his eyelids apart, the crusted saltiness causing him to blink rapidly. The world was still too bright to countenance, but the sun was not visible. It must be somewhere behind him. Afternoon, then.

Sun?

Thunder and sun?

Forcing the last dregs of energy from his tired muscles, he squinted and peered at the horizon.

Nothing.

The complex and its walls… and then blue sky with distant brown undulations of land. Perhaps the storm was also behind him. If it was as powerful as the one they'd met crossing the high lands to get to Napata, it would finish them all off. Of course, that would be a blessing.

Nice and quick.

Sigh…

The vulture must be pecking at his arms.

Perhaps sitting on his shoulder and head? It certainly felt uncomfortable.

How many last reserves of strength could he find?

With another monumental effort, his eyes stuck together with crusty matter, he thrashed left and right with his head, trying to dislodge the thing that was feeding on his wrist.

Vultures. Had to be. Jackals wouldn't be able to reach.

"Ow. Cut it out, Cervianus, you knob!"

Something familiar.

The name?

"Cervianus". So familiar. Who was this Cervianus?

A suspicion began to nag at the cloudy grey in the back of his mind.

Neither vultures nor jackals spoke Latin.

Did they?

With extraordinary difficulty, he prised open his eyelids. A blurred shape moved around in front of him, dark against the bright gold of the world.

Suddenly, his arms were free and fell to his sides with earth-shaking agony.

He screamed and slumped forward over something that smelled of spices and cheap wine.

"Fuscus," the familiar voice said quickly, "you and Petrocorios get Draco down and get the others on to any more survivors. Let's get them inside."

Fuscus?

Petrocorios?

Names he knew almost as well as "Cervianus".

Some time, a thousand years ago, they had meant something.

Pain battered at him as he bounced along on the sharp-smelling animal, through the bright heat and suddenly into darkness.

"Let's get you somewhere comfortable."

He felt himself sliding off the beast and falling.

A soft thud.

Sigh…

Sweet smell and cool, relaxing feel.

Cervianus' fugged head reeled.

A familiar smell.

Why was it dark but with no moon and stars?

Horizontal?

Fuscus?

Petrocorios?

His eyes flicked open suddenly and in surprise.

A deeply tanned face, almost as dark as the Kushites', with bright white teeth and sparkling green eyes hovered above his face. His eyes rolled in panic, taking in everything he could.

The room was lit with low oil lamps and filled with people, mostly lying down.

Ulyxes put slimy hands on his head and slowly forced him back down to the warm, comfortable animal pelt beneath him.

"Calm down, you idiot."

"Ulyxes?"

His friend, deeply tanned and weathered, went back to rubbing the oily liquid over his wrists, arms and neck.

"Wha…?"

"Don't speak yet. Not for an hour or two and until you've had plenty of water." The stocky man grinned, the bright teeth against the mahogany skin strange on the northern frame. "Look at *me* giving medical advice to *you*."

"Wha…?"

"It's amagdalinum oil mixed with honey, the root of lily and Cyprian rosewax."

Cervianus' mind reeled again and he managed a look of utter incomprehension.

"Found your bag inside the building. I remember you applying this for sunburn and general exposure damage when we were on the way across the desert. Looks like you need it, but I'm being quite sparing. There are twenty-two others that need a go."

Cervianus blinked and suddenly a man was next to him with a flask of water, a flask that bore strange pictorial designs of fantastic, impossible animals. Fresh, wonderful water was tipped between his lips and he swallowed eagerly, choking in the torrent.

"Slowly, Abbar. Slowly and carefully," Ulyxes said, soothingly.

Cervianus tried to focus on the water-bearer. He wore a grey robe wrapped around him and white baggy breeches, his head shaven and his feet bare. His skin was more ebony still than the Kushites', and his face flat and wide. The capsarius flicked a perplexed look at Ulyxes, who grinned.

"I'll tell you all about it later. Get some rest now."

As though the command went straight to his body without passing through his brain, Cervianus went out like a light.

When he came to once more, he started and almost banged his head back on the ground. Draco's face was inches from his, a look of impatience spread across it.

"Good. He's coming round. I hope he's clear enough to deal with this damned arrow, now."

Somehow it didn't surprise him at all that the centurion was already back to his old self.

"Need... need to rest and recover first. Eat. Drink," he said quietly.

A strange figure appeared as if from nowhere in the low lamp light. Wizened as though by great age, he moved with the litheness of a young warrior, almost snake-like. His white robe and turban were familiar, as was the curved knife at his belt. An Arabian? The man proffered a plate of fruit and sweetmeats. Cervianus blinked, and Ulyxes leaned down.

"Go on. They're fine. Hama is good with fruit."

"Hama?"

"This is Hama."

The Arabian grinned at him and Cervianus felt a fresh swell of confusion. Struggling into a seated position, he reached for the plate and the cup of water that was being proffered alongside it. Hungrily, he gobbled down melon and dates, pomegranate and apple, washing it down with water and wincing as it all passed his chapped lips and slid down a throat that felt as though it had been ravaged with blades.

Finally, swallowing with difficulty and shaking his head, he frowned. "Ulyxes? How did you...? Where have you been? Who are these people?"

His friend grinned that infuriating grin again. "It's quite a long story, but I'll give you the short version. We were heading west and north, but we only went out two days. See, all the routes back north are guarded by Kushite garrisons. We couldn't really sneak round them or hope to take them on. There were only three of us, after all."

Cervianus shook his head. "There were other deserters..."

"Not with us. Can't say where they went. They're probably dead. There's Kushite armies, garrisons and patrols every-where." Ulyxes sat back on his haunches. "So we stayed in the area. For a while we lived off the pickings of small villages, theft from orchards – that sort of thing. But we got really unlucky and really lucky at the same time. We were spotted by a patrol and had to flee into the desert to escape them. It was bloody awful. We got turned round and lost and spent two days out there until we chanced on a merchant caravan."

"A *sucker* caravan, you mean," shouted the familiar voice of Fuscus a few paces away.

Ulyxes grinned. "We introduced them to a few new dice games, and before we knew it, they owed us a small fortune. We took three horses, two camels, four slaves and a whole bunch of supplies from them."

"Slaves?"

"Yep. Hama and Abbar you've met. Then there's Ula and Anaadi. You'll like them. They're not slaves anymore, mind."

Draco frowned. "You've *freed* them?"

"Only fair." Ulyxes shrugged. "The caravan masters got a little reluctant to part with their goods when we tried to leave the next day. Our new slaves helped us fight our way out, so now they're friends instead."

Cervianus shook his head. "So you've been around this area all the time?"

"Here and there. Did a bit of trading. With the clothes, animals and goods, you'd be amazed how easily you can move about. We've passed right under the noses of Kushite patrols. Not tried heading north past the garrisons, though. They run checks on anything heading to Aegyptus."

Draco nodded. "Not a surprise, given that they're planning to invade."

"What made you come back for us?" Cervianus asked quietly. "I thought you'd be staying well away from Roman or Kushite forces, either way?"

Ulyxes grinned. "Opportunity. We saw the Kushite army leaving here, so we assumed the place would be more or less empty. The guards were easy enough to take out. They were mostly watching the interior, to make sure you didn't escape, I suppose. Our new friends have proved to be quite proficient with weaponry. We were actually coming to see if there was anything left in the stores worth taking."

Draco shook his head. "Thieves and deserters. If there was anything left of the legion and its discipline, you should be beaten to death."

Ulyxes gave the centurion a withering look. "We didn't desert the Twenty Second, Draco. We deserted tribune Vitalis, and you know that." He turned back to Cervianus. "We need to amass a small fortune, then we're heading to the coast along the east trade route. There's a big port there called Limen Evangelis. We passed the route to it on the way south to Napata, if you remember? If we have enough money we can buy passage there on an Indian ship, right the way back up to Arsinoe up at the delta, no questions asked and right past the Kushite border. I guess we'll need a lot more cash if we're going to add twenty-three men to the journey."

Cervianus could almost have predicted the next move as Draco's hand suddenly clamped down on Ulyxes' shoulder. "No ship north for you, Ulyxes. You're back with the eagle again now, lad."

"I think you have me wrong," the stocky man replied with an uncertain smile. "We're just passing through. Stopped to do a good deed."

Draco grinned unpleasantly. "Do you remember your oath, legionary Ulyxes?"

"Of course I do."

"Good. Then you can administer it to the four new recruits. Nasica is gone, so I am assuming the rank of primus pilus in the Twenty Second." He glanced down at Cervianus with what almost looked like sympathy.

"The capsarius here has been serving as my optio, but it's a position he's not really cut out for. Too much pacifist in him, I think. Can't give the tough orders. I'm giving you a field promotion to optio, Ulyxes. Now get those foreign bastards enlisted."

Ulyxes was shaking his head. "It's a nice thought, centurion, and I appreciate the offer, but think about it – we're deep in enemy territory. The Kushites are closing on what's left of the legion somewhere south of here, near the 'heart of Kush' trade crossroads and, when they catch them, we'll be the only non-Kushites left for a thousand miles. Now might be a good time to get out of here, while we still have our skins. Promotion or no promotion, I'm not up for playing 'rats in a trap' against the entire forces of Kush. I've been hearing things about their queen that'd make your blood run cold."

Draco's grip merely tightened. "Problem is, Ulyxes, that they're going to march north and swamp Aegyptus. You think the Third and Twelfth can stop them in their current state? If the Kushites march north, being back in Alexandria won't help you."

Ulyxes sighed. "Being somewhere like Tarsus and living as a merchant might." He sighed as he saw the look in Draco's eye. "You really intend to try and stop the Kushites marching north with thirty men?"

The centurion shrugged. "I'd try if I was on my *own*."

Ulyxes crossed his legs and settled down, reaching for a plate of fruit that sat nearby on the ground. "You're serious? Chances are that the legion won't survive the next few days, you know? The talk on the merchant trails is that they're down to about half strength after the first clash and floundering about in the desert. And we know that two Kushite forces are closing on them."

"When have I ever been noted for my sense of humour, Ulyxes?" the centurion said quietly. "Now find yourself an optio's crest, a staff or something like it, and get that oath administered to the new fellers."

Ulyxes grinned. "You know you're a mad bastard, sir, yes?"

"You still here?"

The shorter legionary reached out and grasped Cervianus' hand. "Good to see you again, my friend."

"Go!" barked Draco, and the newly assigned optio laughed and clambered to his feet to go and break the news to his friends.

The centurion waited until Ulyxes was out of earshot and slumped next to Cervianus. "I think there may be something wrong with my wound. I'm going numb and it's all puffy. I need you to get it sorted out. Take the arm if you have to, but make sure I'm able to lead this lot in the next few days."

Cervianus nodded slowly. "I'll have a look in a moment, sir."

Draco nodded and rose, crossing the room to speak to the others and leaving Cervianus slumped on the pelt.

Well, he could never accuse life of tedium. Somehow the arrival of Ulyxes seemed to have changed everything. The man moved through the world like a trireme, making large waves and leaving a wake that rocked and undulated and turned lives upside down. They were thirty men, many wounded, some newly conscripted foreigners who spoke no language they understood. They were all tired and broken and sore, badly armed and equipped.

And yet, suddenly, the prospect of facing an immense army of Kushites seemed less frightening, as though it were even possible to stop them. Across the room, he could hear Ulyxes explaining the oath to the newcomers.

The world was about to change again.

"What the shit is that?"

Cervianus concentrated on the centurion's wound, examining the puffy skin puckered around the shaft of the arrow, his tongue protruding as he probed, the object of Draco's exclamation held at table level in his left hand.

"This," the capsarius replied casually, his eyes never leaving his work, "is called the spoon of Diokles. It is specifically designed for arrow extraction."

Draco eyed the metal device with suspicion. "You don't need anything fancy. Push the bloody thing through and pull it out of the back. That's how I had the last three removed."

Cervianus nodded. "I can quite imagine, knowing Albinus and his bunch. Doing that can cause so much more damage in the process. I prefer to remove the arrow without inflicting further internal injury." He prodded the puffy skin and leaned round to look at the centurion's back. "Besides, it's lodged just under your clavicle. If I wanted to draw it right through, I'd have to push it through your shoulder blade. I think you'll agree my way is better."

Ulyxes, standing to the other side of the centurion, who lay on his side on the makeshift examination table, reached out his hand and gestured to Cervianus, pointing at the item.

"Lemme see?"

Cervianus paused for the first time. It sent a little shudder of discomfort up his spine to allow anyone else to handle his tools. Fighting down the urge to refuse, he gingerly handed the device to his friend. "Take it by the handle only and don't touch the other end."

Ulyxes nodded and held the thing up to the lamplight. The "spoon" was around eight inches long, shaped like a hollow sausage with one side cut away, a tiny hole in the enclosed business end, the other flared into a handle.

"So you have to push this thing into the wound?"

Ulyxes thrust the gadget into an imaginary chest cavity, grinning at Draco.

"I'm beginning to wonder whether you're optio material, Ulyxes," the centurion snapped irritably, his eyes following the movement of the spoon.

Cervianus reached out and snatched the device from his friend. "This is serious, if you two are done mucking about with my delicate equipment."

Draco and Ulyxes shared a look and Cervianus took a deep breath, calming himself and steadying his hands. It occurred to him that two months ago he would not even have opened his mouth in front of Draco without waiting for permission. How much circumstances had changed the dynamic of the unit was fascinating.

"Alright, sir. On your back. Take a deep breath and bite down on the thong."

Draco gave him one last glare and then clamped his teeth around the leather strap proffered by Ulyxes, settling back down and closing his eyes tight. Cervianus reached out with his right hand and selected the scalpel from the tray without even looking. An organised surgeon laid out his tools precisely and could select any item necessary at a moment's notice and without taking his eyes off the patient.

Without further examination, he sliced a neat line both up and down from the arrow shaft. Draco merely grunted, but the sweat stood out on his brow and he tensed. Ulyxes leaned over him and gently but firmly held him flat.

"This is going to hurt, I'm afraid," Cervianus warned. "I'd give you something to numb and dull the pain, but the Kushites broke most of my pots and phials."

Draco gave him a look that said "get on with it", and Ulyxes exerted pressure once more, holding the man down.

Taking another steadying breath, Cervianus grasped the Diokles spoon by the handle end, used his last two collyrium sticks to probe the incision, and then, with a force that surprised Ulyxes, pushed the metal "spoon" into the wound, sliding the tip down the shaft of the arrow for a guide.

Draco yelped even through the leather strap and bucked on the table, despite the hands pinning him down.

"Hold him *still*," hissed the capsarius, and Ulyxes flashed him an apologetic look.

"Shit, that must hurt."

"You *think*?" snapped Cervianus sarcastically, his tongue protruding as he worked the spoon down into the chest, continuing to use the arrow as a guide.

"Why'd you push so hard?"

Cervianus rolled his eyes. Why did people always want to ask questions when he was engaged in the most delicate parts of a procedure. "The arrow is jammed between the second and third rib. The barbs are inside the rib cage. He's damn lucky not to have lost a lung. Had to push hard to drive the spoon through the ribs."

Squeezing his eyes shut, Cervianus measured the finger-widths of the spoon that stood out from the chest and frowned. "Hold him tight, now."

"He's passed out," replied Ulyxes.

"Not for long. Hold tight."

With a frown of concentration, the capsarius waggled the device around for a moment. Draco returned to consciousness with a shriek that was only partially muffled by the leather thong. Suddenly, the spoon stopped moving. Cervianus smiled and gave it a tentative pull. The arrow shaft wobbled. Draco's eyes widened and Ulyxes exerted yet more pressure.

"That's it. Here goes."

Gripping the handle of the spoon, Cervianus swiftly and smoothly pulled the entire thing out, followed by a welling up of blood. The centurion passed out once more. Ulyxes stared at the result. The device was slick with blood, but the arrow, shaft and head perfectly intact, were contained within the hollow of the spoon.

"So you can pull it back out without the barbs ripping him to shreds."

"Precisely. Now let's get him poulticed and bound. There are still at least a dozen wounds I need to look at, before I think about infections, illnesses and the rest."

The rest of the morning passed quickly with a great deal of wound stitching and binding, administering the few drugs that had survived the Kushites' rough treatment, and doling out medical advice to people he knew would almost instantly forget or ignore everything he told them.

Ulyxes helped for the first three trickiest wounds, and then left him to it, heading off to carry out the onerous duties of an optio, keeping the men busy, seeing to the stores and equipment. It was with a huge sigh of relief from both of them when they met at noon in the room designated as a mess hall for a bite to eat.

As they sat and tucked into the excess mutton and bread that had been left in the stores when the enemy left, they greedily eyed the precious watermelon awaiting them for dessert. Petrocorios and Fuscus sauntered over to join them.

"So what's the situation?" enquired the newly raised optio.

Fuscus, whom he'd sent to the armoury, pursed his lips as he ripped a chunk from the bread. "We're short of everything, but then you knew that. Thirty men…"

He dipped the chunk of bread in his barley gruel and took a mouthful as he snapped open the wax tablet he'd brought in.

"Twenty-eight helmets; twenty-one shields. Enough swords and daggers to go round. Nineteen mail shirts, plus two quite badly damaged ones that'll be serviceable with a few hours' work. Eleven pila. One scorpion, but only two bolts that we've located. I've got three men working on making new shields and two more searching the whole complex for pila and scorpion bolts. Hoping we can turn up some more."

Ulyxes nodded. "Take a walk afterwards round the back of the Amun temple. I saw a half-buried shield in the gravel and three intact bolts there a few hours ago. How's the food situation?"

"Good enough to eat reasonably well for a week, I'd say. I've sent a couple more of the lads into the settlement to see what extras we can drum up there."

Again, a nod from the stocky optio. Cervianus watched him with interest. He would never have seen Ulyxes as officer material a few months ago. He'd pictured *himself* as the perfect optio, not often having to lead charges like the centurions, but being given the tedious tasks of organisation and planning. It would suit him, he'd thought.

The reality of his brief time as Draco's second had made him painfully aware both of his shortcomings in the role and his general unsuitability for command. He'd been relieved when Draco had reduced him back to his *immune* status.

Ulyxes, on the other hand, had taken to the role with aplomb, as though born to it, and, given the fact that Draco had spent most of the day unconscious and in recovery, the stocky, moustachioed legionary had, in essence, assumed the temporary position of centurion. He had been everywhere throughout the morning, issuing commands and supporting the men. Astounding, really.

"I've not had a chance to discuss it with Draco yet," Ulyxes said quietly, "but we're going to have to come to some sort of decision as to what to do. We don't have enough men to hold the outer wall, or even the Amun temple now. Besides, I'm not keen on us being trapped in a building again, remembering what happened to you lot. We might be better not tying ourselves to a defensive perimeter. What d'you all think?"

Petrocorios wolfed down the bread and mutton in his mouth and shrugged. "Frankly, I can't think what we'll do if the enemy come back for us. We couldn't fight off a drunk Syrian catamite with the shits. There are merchant caravans passing the trails near here that are better armed and defended than us."

Cervianus nodded. "Then whatever you decide, it'll have to be using our heads and not our strength, since we don't have any."

"What d'you mean?" asked Fuscus, pausing while reaching for the watermelon.

"Well, we don't stand a chance against anything other than a small patrol if we simply meet them in battle. If we can't win a fight, we need to make them unwilling to start one."

Ulyxes narrowed his eyes. "Sounds like you've got an idea?"

Cervianus shook his head. "Not as such. I'm starting to dream up possibilities. Quite literally, in fact. I'll think on it for now, but I suggest you all put your powers of deduction into planning contingencies for our near future."

Ulyxes nodded and returned to his meal as the door at the far end of the room opened.

"Ulyxes!"

"*Optio*," stressed the stocky officer as he turned to face the newcomer.

"Sorry, optio. Column of dust to the south-east, sir."

The four men at the table shared a look and quickly rose from the benches, scraping the wooden legs back across the ground and rushing to the door.

"How big a column?"

"How far away?"

"Can you see anything else?"

The group of men, still chattering away, emerged from the building into the blistering noon sun. Cervianus shaded his eyes and glanced toward the south gate as Ulyxes crammed his helmet back on, the optio's crest marking his rank. Without waiting for the legionary to usher them on, the four men rushed across the compound to the gate in the southern stretch of perimeter wall and clambered up the steps to the wide walkway above.

There was, indeed, a dust cloud, and it was closing rapidly. Past the place where Cervianus had walked into the river in the face of a vast enemy, challenging the gods to take him as a sacrifice, a force was approaching.

Judging from the size of the cloud it was unlikely to be more than a small scouting unit, likely of riders, given the speed of the approach. The question that rose to the tip of every tongue was: Roman or Kushite? Was it a small independent force, or merely the van for a large army?

The watchers tensed.

"Better send someone to wake Draco," said Ulyxes, squinting into the distance.

Cervianus shook his head. "Not unless we have to. He's just had chest surgery. Let him sleep."

"You realise how pissed off he'll be if something important happens and you let him sleep through it?"

The capsarius was still shaking his head. "If it's an attack, what can a drugged, temporarily crippled officer do?"

"He can kick your arse, for a start." Ulyxes leaned down to Fuscus. "Go wake Draco and tell him where we are."

Cervianus glared at his friend, but turned back to the approaching cloud. It really was moving fast. Moments passed in tense silence, the only noise the sound of the birds and wildlife near the riverbank and the pacing of men back across the compound as they scoured the dust for missiles and spare equipment. Slowly, shapes began to resolve themselves in the beige cloud. Horsemen, but what sort?

A moment later they heard Draco's voice behind them, and turned to see Fuscus helping the centurion across the compound to the gate, though the commander seemed to be largely ignoring the help, marching strong with the legionary tagging along, trying to provide support.

"Can you identify them yet?"

"Not quite, sir, but any time now."

As the centurion was helped up the stairs to the gate, Cervianus and Ulyxes watched the cavalry force bear down on the green strip beside the river. Gradually, as the riders moved into the cultivated area, the dust cloud dissipated and by the time the first man reached the riverbank they were visible.

Riders in white, with mail shirts and helms and long spears. The tense silence of held breath gave way to an explosive communal exhale as the vexillum, the unit's flag, reached the open air at the front. The eye of Horus glittered in gold on a blue background.

The cavalry of the Nome of Sapi-Res.

"Shenti!"

Draco, arriving on the walkway at last, frowned. "What's a Shenti?"

"Auxiliary decurion, sir. That's the cavalry that rode south with the legion."

Draco leaned on the parapet, almost collapsing. "About bloody time. Let's hope the legion is right behind them, eh?"

As Cervianus sighed with relief, leaning on the wall and watching the auxilia preparing to cross the river, he became aware of the commotion in the compound. News had somehow got back to the men already, and jubilation was the theme of the garrison of Napata.

The riders descended the far bank and plunged into the water, a rare location on the great river where the shallowness of the water and the accumulated sandbanks made crossing feasible except during the inundation. Arriving on the near bank, they assembled in turmae, small units of thirty-some men under a decurion. As each turma rallied to its standard, it became clear to the observers that the cavalry had suffered serious losses, few of the groups achieving even half strength. Finally, after almost half an hour of manoeuvring, the entire force was across, the cavalry numbering a depleted two hundred at most.

Cervianus watched tensely, but could not identify the individual men and officers at such a distance. By the time the force was moving again across the green band and toward the walls of the compound, quite a reception had gathered around the south gate.

The cavalry commander, a Roman prefect dressed much like a legionary tribune, rode at the head of the men in blue and plain white linen. Though he sat proud and commanding as he reached the walls and passed between the open wooden gates, he was clearly exhausted, troubled, and possibly wounded. Dark circles beneath his eyes gave him an anxious look. The legionaries of Napata gave a rousing cheer as the cavalry entered the compound, an honour that no auxiliary soldier would normally expect from the legions.

The cheering died away as the prefect at the head of the column reined in and, in an attempt to gracefully dismount, slid from the saddle and fell to the ground heavily. One of the legionaries ran across to help the man up and, as the white cloak fluttered, the burgundy-coloured bloodstain on the tunic beneath became visible.

The cavalry commander was followed by the standard bearers of the unit and then by the first turma. As the officer of that sub-unit reined in and slipped from his mount, rushing over to help the prefect, Cervianus felt his heart soar. Shenti looked surprisingly well.

As the legionary and the decurion helped the wounded commander to his feet, other officers began to dismount, their soldiers waiting for the order.

"Prefect Gnaeus Lentulus, commander of the cavalry of the Nome of Sapi-Res, reporting. Who's in command here?"

Draco, halfway down the steps once more with the aid of

a legionary, threw out a salute and then winced, regretting the action. "Publius Draco, now the primus pilus of the Twenty Second, Napata garrison."

The two men eyed each other with weary respect, taking in the belly wound that had clearly been festering in the prefect for many days and the broken and slung arm and fresh bindings on the centurion.

"Hard to say who's had the worse time, by the looks of it, centurion."

"I'd have to say us, prefect, but let's get your men settled and then our capsarius can have a look at your wound while we update each other on the situation."

The prefect nodded and turned, gesturing to his standard bearer. The man waved the vexillum in a circle and the rider next to him drew out a short horn and blew three short blasts with a high note at the end. The cavalry began to dismount and lead their horses to patches of shade where they could be corralled.

Cervianus took a quick look toward the wounded prefect and then glanced across at the weary smile of Shenti, who was approaching, leading his horse.

"It's good to see you, Shenti. *Really* good."

"I am pleased to find you intact, my friend. We should talk."

Cervianus nodded. "I'll have to see to your commander, then I'll come and find you. If Ulyxes can spare some time from his duties I'll get him to come along."

Shenti nodded and grinned.

"*Really* good," he repeated, as the capsarius turned and rushed off after the wounded officer.

IX

OVERTURE

"You have no idea, my friend, of what it was like."

Cervianus nodded encouragingly as Shenti paused and took a short draught of fruited water.

"The entire army could have been obliterated in one move; *should* have been, really. Despite many warnings, Vitalis kept the army marching in a tight column along the valley. Scouts were limited to riding ahead and behind along the cultivated lands. Idiocy."

Ulyxes nodded seriously. "And that was not where the danger came from?"

Shenti sighed. "The great force of the Kandake came pouring down into the valley from the high lands to the east. They had been so easily hidden by dunes. If we'd had scouts ranging across the desert, we would have been prepared, but we were blind to the dangers until they were on top of us."

Cervianus frowned. "I thought the whole reason Vitalis was taking the cavalry with him was so that you could scout for him? He doesn't really trust the auxilia, you know."

"There was an... incident. My commander called him a number of things that did not sit well with the tribune's inflated self-image. Once he'd had my prefect put in his place, he relegated us to the rearguard and ignored us."

Ulyxes nodded again. "So you marched straight into a trap."

"The Kandake gave no warning and offered no terms. Her army swept down into the valley and killed as fast as they could swing their blades. While the infantry crossed the few hundred paces of open ground, their archers began to loose from the hills. Vitalis tried to send out orders and pull a defence together, but he was too late. By the time he realised he was in trouble, hundreds had fallen to the arrow storms and there was time to do nothing more than throw a shield wall up."

The dozen or so legionaries in the tent sat in rapt fascination at the tale, but the voice of Draco cut through the tense expectation. "How did you and others escape?"

The centurion had attempted to debrief the cavalry prefect, but the man's condition was almost critical and his chances of surviving the night, let alone regaining lucidity, were narrow.

"Vitalis fell."

"To an arrow?"

There was a long pause and finally Shenti shrugged. "I cannot be sure. One moment he was standing, throwing his arms about in the manner of one of your senators with the endless speeches, screaming at his men and blaming them for his shortcomings. The next, he was gone."

Draco nodded. "Sounds like an arrow caught him mid-speech."

The soldiers settled back, seemingly satisfied at the news that a stray missile had ended the career of the man who had marched them into Hades.

Cervianus, however, narrowed his eyes. *He* had seen the look on Shenti's face as he had finished speaking. Other questions would have to be asked later.

"And you fled?" Draco asked without a hint of accusation.

Shenti smiled, this time with genuine satisfaction. "Astoundingly, no. The army was in disarray and being cut to pieces. The Kandake had sealed off the valley ahead and behind and her main force was coming from the east. One of the junior tribunes, a stone-faced man with a great black snake for an eyebrow, stood in his saddle and took command."

The decurion leaned back and slapped his balled fist into the palm of his hand. "He was like the pharaohs of old. Like a Thutmose, or a Ramses. He was bold and decisive. In moments, legionaries were formed into defensive lines and rearranged so that the wounded and the auxilia could begin pulling back away from the archers. We retreated up the west bank and into the sands beyond. The cavalry were spread out west and ahead to make sure the way was clear, and the rearguard of legionaries were lessened with every quarter-mile so that, in the end, some two hundred men were holding off the whole of the Kushite army while the rest pulled back."

He shook his head sadly. "They gave their lives and they did it willingly. Without them holding back the enemy, no retreat would have been possible. We left over a thousand bodies in the valley and even as we moved into the heart of the desert we could see the vultures gathering miles back. A terrible day, but it could have been a great deal worse. Those men who stood and died to protect the rest… if anyone ever doubted the courage of your legions then there is the proof, lying in fields north of Meroë, peppered with arrows and spears."

"And they just let you go then? They didn't pursue you?"

Shenti shook his head and took another swig of cooling drink. "We were harried until we were truly in the deep desert. I do not think they intended to kill us then and there as we would have cost them too many of their own troops. They urged us on, knowing that the desert itself would kill many. There were signs for days that they were pursuing us, but they were doing it at their own pace, using known trails and making sure they were well watered and supplied while they watched us die."

He took yet another appreciative swig. "They knew that every day out in the sands killed many more of us without them having to risk a single life. Why would they wish to attack?"

Cervianus frowned. "General Kalabsha marched his force south days ago. I suspect the queen was driving you into a trap: the open arms of the waiting general. But instead, you're here. How is this possible?"

"The new commanding tribune is not a man to under-think a manoeuvre." Shenti grinned. "He has managed to stay a step ahead of the Kushites at all times since that battle. We found signs of a merchant caravan – fresh… only a day old. My unit was sent to track them down and from them we learned of the trade routes and nomad trails, paying well for the information. Then we made use of their trails and water caches, leaving appropriate repayment at the sites, as is only proper. Soon we were back in good form, sending out scouts and a van and moving like an army with a purpose rather than a ragged, beaten force fleeing for its life."

He drained the last of the drink, looked into the spout in the skin with disappointment, and dropped it to the table. "We became aware of your Kalabsha's army early the day before yesterday, firmly set in the way, blocking our path north. It also appeared that the Kandake had begun to hurry her forces to catch us up. The tribune spent an hour in consultation with his new maps and then sent us out to the west and north. It was a great gamble; there were no trails that way, and the army would suffer at least two days without water, but we would circumvent the forces waiting for us."

He patted his chest and grinned. "And so we are here. We survived a potential slaughter, a long journey through the desert, and managed to side-step a pincer attack."

"And the army are close behind you, then? You are the van?"

The smile in Shenti's eyes slipped for a moment. "We hope. It has been the best part of a day, but the last time we saw signs of life behind us the dust cloud was slightly eastward of where we expected the legion to be. It could be that the Kushites have corrected for our manoeuvre and are already ahead. It now all rests upon the throw of a die."

Draco stretched his shoulders and winced at the combined pain of the arrow wound and re-broken arm. "So both the legion and the full Kushite army are on their way here and there will likely be not more than half a day between them either way?"

Shenti nodded. "Then we'd best get ourselves prepared to receive the enemy."

Draco gestured at Ulyxes. "Have you finished the defences yet?"

The stocky legionary shook his head. "We're still at least half a day from ready. I've limited the use of the pitch, mind, so that'll save us a few hours' work. I thought it best we keep some with us for last-ditch situations. You realise that if our army gets here first we'll be packed tight up there?"

Draco nodded. "It may be that the new tribune will have no

use for a good defensive position, but we've been through this before and I'm not going to have us caught with our tunics up again. Get to the redoubt and check on progress. I want that mountain top as secure as a Vestal's tits by morning."

Ulyxes saluted and groaned as he hauled himself to his feet. "Remind me why I accepted this job again?"

"Because the alternative was to feel my boot up your arse. Get up there and do some work."

Ulyxes grinned at the centurion and hurried out of the room. As he left, Draco stood.

"I suggest the rest of you get back to your assigned duties too. Decurion, I gather you're the serving officer of the First turma now?"

"I have that honour, sir."

"Then that makes you interim prefect. I know it should be a Roman, really, but you know how to handle your men and they trust you. Cervianus tells me that your prefect will certainly not be up to carrying out his duties for some time."

Shenti bowed. "Then it is my honour to deliver the cavalry of the Nome of Sapi-Res to your command until the army returns, sir. What are your orders?"

Draco pursed his lips. "No point in having scouts at this point. We'll see an army of that size coming from miles away, and we can't risk sending men to check them out. Have all your horses tethered somewhere safe with a full supply of food and then get your men up to the mountain top and join in the preparations. Optio Ulyxes will know where to assign them."

Shenti bowed again and turned to leave. Cervianus stood hurriedly. "I'll walk out with you. I've got to go check on my patients and see if they can be moved up the mountain yet, anyway."

Leaving Draco mulling over the situation, Cervianus left the room and fell in beside his friend as they walked out into the warm evening air. This time of the day was the most comfortable of all at Napata. Further north the lack of air, despite the fading heat, made it stifling and uncomfortable. Here it was so dry, with a breeze that blew down the valley from the eastern highlands, that the air moved and brought a warm freshness. Cervianus took a deep breath, relishing the opportunity, and prepared to ask the delicate question.

"What did you not tell Draco?"

"My friend?"

"About Vitalis. I saw your face."

Shenti's face hardened. "It does no good to talk of it further."

"Tell me."

The decurion sighed and slowed his pace, glancing around to make sure they were alone. "Few saw the truth. The cavalry were away from the officers when the attack began, playing rearguard. My prefect sent me forward to find Vitalis and tell him we were going to need infantry support to hold the flank. I was almost at his side when it happened."

"When *what* happened?"

"Vitalis. He… he seemed to have lost his mind. He was shouting contradictory orders; screaming at his officers and calling them cowards. Suddenly he fell silent and stiffened. It could so easily have been a stray arrow shot, but I saw the truth of it. I saw two of the tribunes grab his falling body and lower it to the ground and I saw the other wipe his red blade on Vitalis' cloak before he sheathed it and stood again."

He turned and delivered a meaningful glance at his friend. "You understand? No good can come of the truth. He was felled by an arrow. Better for everyone."

Cervianus nodded quietly. If word of such a heinous act reached the powers-that-be in Alexandria, more than one young tribune's hopeful career would be cut short before they could move into their comfortable civil positions. And along with them, the rather promising military talent of the clearly capable and pragmatic, if unethical, Catilius, now commanding the legion and dragging them back from the gates of Hades, into the light.

"I suppose you're right. You know that even if they get here ahead of the Kushites, unless we pack up and run north like the winds of Aeolus, we're still done for? And Draco won't countenance leaving, probably not even in the face of Tribune Catilius."

Shenti nodded. "What must be, will be, my friend."

The pair walked on in thoughtful silence into the centre of the compound, where Shenti would make his way over to the cliff behind the Amun temple, while Cervianus would enter his makeshift ward.

"Don't wear yourself or your men out faffing around for Ulyxes," Cervianus cautioned. "You're all still exhausted from your journey. Make sure you're all resting long before midnight, or you'll be no use to anyone tomorrow. You may be unharmed, but you need to be rested mentally too to be whole."

"Spoken like a true *swnw*, my friend. You fear for my ka − my soul − as well as my body."

Shenti wandered off toward the cliff with a wave.

"I wouldn't go that far," Cervianus said with an indulgent smile.

He watched for a moment as his friend went to work, shouting for his men, who rushed to his side as he walked on, gesturing at the lift. Ulyxes' men had constructed an A-frame at the clifftop and a platform on ropes big enough to carry a contubernium of men up the cliff at a time. If he was on schedule with his plans for the mountain's defences, it would be the quickest and easiest route to the top now.

The capsarius smiled and entered the hospital. Pausing briefly to nod in respect to the image of Asklepios that had been hastily carved into the stonework by the door, he wandered inside.

He'd never had such a full ward. Seven men still lingered in the first room following their attempted execution, suffering from torn tendons, dislocated limbs and general exposure damage. A few of them could return to duty in the morning, really. It went against the grain to discharge a man before he was truly in full health, but in the face of constant imminent demise, that hardly mattered.

Beyond them, in the second ward, eighteen cavalry troopers lay quietly, all suffering from wounds that had been inflicted many days ago in the heat of battle and which had festered during the long journey through the desert. They were unevenly spaced, with twelve on one side of the large chamber and only six on the other. None of them had thought to question why, for which Cervianus was grateful.

The six men would be dead within a day and a half at most. Some were almost at the gates of the underworld by the time they'd arrived at Napata, barely able to stay in the saddle. Others were slowly succumbing to rot and he had given them a potent compound that would ease the pain while giving them a gentle push toward the next world.

Better not to have the still-living corpses dropping away spaced among those who would recover in time. Morale made a surprisingly sizeable difference in the ability of the body to heal itself.

Then, beyond the two large wards, four small rooms led off the corridor, once storerooms for this large, palatial structure; the wards had originally been some sort of reception room and dining room. Cervianus had taken one room for himself, one for an office, and used one for storing his supplies.

The chamber he made for, however, held the shuddering body of the cavalry prefect, another man who would be unlikely to see dawn. He sighed. The prefect had suffered an unpleasant stab wound to the gut: apparently a long spear with a wide, leaf-shaped blade. The blade had been slightly rusty, as had been evident from residue in the wound, but the iron shavings would be helpful and saved him dipping into his own almost diminished supplies.

At least the blade had not been barbed. If it had, then the withdrawal stroke would have ripped half the man's intestines out and he would have been dead days ago. He *could* pull through, though the chances were small.

As Cervianus had tried to explain to that damn mother who had ruined his career in Ancyra years ago, even the best doctor in the world was not able to heal *everything*. Sometimes half of any chance of success lay with a combination of pure luck and the patient's will to survive.

He wondered briefly why, when he knew none of these men, he found himself desperately wishing the man would pick up, but the answer was simple – Shenti held the man in great respect. It was for his friend that he put every effort into helping the prefect.

Curious, really. The auxilia were almost uniformly under the command of a Roman citizen of good rank, while they themselves could only hope to achieve citizenship and a small settlement on their discharge. This tended to lead to a great chasm between the commander and his men, a chasm over which respect passed with great difficulty. An auxiliary officer had to be truly exceptional to gain such devotion as this man seemed to evoke from his men. A sort of Draco or Nasica for the auxiliaries, he supposed.

Standing and staring at the officer, who still writhed in his fevered struggle against death, Cervianus arrived at a decision. The man who'd been assigned to him as an orderly would be in the temporary medicus's office.

"Aduatix? Come give me a hand!"

The legionary strode in slowly, closing a writing tablet as he did so, a stylus in his teeth. "Mmph?"

"Leave the records for now. We may never need them anyway. We need to start moving the wounded up to the top early in the morning, so we need to categorise and prioritise, but first I need your help moving prefect Lentulus in there."

"Moving him now, sir?"

"Yes, but not up the cliff. Get the other end."

The man had been in such bad condition that Cervianus had been unwilling to attempt moving him off the stretcher upon which he'd been brought to the room and had simply worked on the wound while he still lay on it. In the end, it had stayed there.

Aduatix grasped the handles at the head end and Cervianus took the feet, turning to face away from the patient.

"Carefully, now. Follow me."

Slowly, and taking care not to jostle or tip the stretcher, the two men carried their unfortunate burden out of the room, along the corridor, through the two wards and out into the open air. Outside, Cervianus paused for a moment and then set off again, his junior hurrying to keep up and hold the stretcher level. Moments later, they arrived at the doorway to a building and the orderly frowned as they stopped.

"A temple, sir?"

"Yes. His recovery's out of our hands now. It's down to him and to the gods. Come on."

Without further comment, they carried their burden deep into the temple, past the first, soot-blackened and partially restored peristyle, through the second, where the fresh bright colours spoke of the considerable effort that had gone into repairing the damage here, and finally, into the heart of the temple.

The central sanctuary was almost returned to its original glory. The great statue of Horus, or Haroeris the "Good Doctor", sat in all its falconine glory, the cracks and damage inflicted upon it painstakingly repaired with good Roman mortar and painted back to its original colourings.

"Haroeris, watch over this man."

Carefully, they lowered the stretcher onto the plinth upon which the image of the god rested, laying the prefect beneath its piercing gaze and curved beak. Cervianus became aware as they stood back up that his new orderly was watching the statue with a look of awe.

"Something wrong?"

"These Aegyptian gods put the shits up me sir. It's not right, with them having animal parts an' all."

"You said you were interested in medicine?"

"Yessir. I sort of wanted to train as a capsarius, but I was told I was too clumsy and was denied duplicarius status."

"Well if you want to move into the medical service, you

need to open up that mind and be accepting of all sorts of ideas," Cervianus said, while secretly chiding himself for his inability to practise what he was preaching. But then, Aegyptus was changing him. Even Shenti had said he was starting to sound like a *swnw*.

"This is Haroeris, who is Horus. He's a god of all sorts but, among other things, he is the master of medicine – the 'good doctor' they call him. And here's your chance to get to know him. Stay here with the prefect and try to get comfortable. I'll take over in the wards and I'll send someone with blankets and food in due course. Come get me if there's any change."

The legionary nodded, looking up nervously at the statue. Cervianus smiled as he turned and left the room. Time to start putting these gods to the test. They seemed to be badgering him all the time. Were they responsible enough to do him a favour in return?

"Mmmh?"

Cervianus woke to a rhythmic shaking.

"Sir... wake up!"

Blearily, he peeled his eyelids apart in that first fuddled moment when the brain tries to remember where, what and who it is. Slowly, the pink blob coalesced into the shape of an eager, grinning face.

"What?" he snapped, rubbing his eyes and cursing the lack of locks on the chamber door.

"You wanted me to let you know of any change!"

Instantly alert, Cervianus' eyes widened and he rose to his feet, his tunic rucked up around his midriff. "The prefect?"

"Yes, sir. He asked for water. I think he's on the mend, the sweat's receded a little."

"Is there any seepage or discolouration around the wound?"

"Sir?"

"You never thought to check?"

The man stared. "I'm just an orderly, sir. You'd tear me a new one if I messed with your patients!"

Cervianus opened his mouth to deny it, but the man was absolutely correct. "I suppose so. But on the basis that we may yet make it through this campaign, I'm going to need people around me who can be more use than fetching and carrying. Come on – I'll show you how to check over a wound for infection and how to apply a fresh dressing."

The legionary grinned and hurried after him. Still pulling his tunic straight, Cervianus grabbed his medical bag from the table by the door and strode briskly out of the rear rooms, through the wards, trying not to lose his sudden positivity at the sight of the six terminal patients and trying not to count how many of their chests were still rising and falling.

Three.

Damn it.

Brushing potentially depressing thoughts from his mind, he rushed out into the daylight, the orderly at his heels. The compound was a hive of activity. Legionaries rushed around, ferrying goods toward the makeshift lift that would carry them to the fortified mountain top. Small groups of men were emptying storerooms and loading items into barrows and crates and others rushed around carrying entrenching tools.

The prefect was still alive, and by the sound of it on the mend. The gods of Aegyptus were, it seemed, as active participants in the world of men as Cervianus had begun to suspect. He could have little doubt but that the "good doctor" had taken a personal interest in the prefect's well-being. Certainly there was no real reason for him to have survived the night other than him being a tough old bastard and Haroeris lending a hand.

Amid the chaos, as he walked toward the temple of Haroeris, it took a moment for Cervianus to spot the figures moving on an intercept course. Petrocorios was hurrying toward him from the south in some excitement, waving an arm and ducking and weaving between workers. At the same time, a legionary he didn't know was bearing down on him from the mountain's direction, also waving his arms and shouting something that was lost in the din.

Damn it.

Briefly, he wondered whether he could outpace the other two men. It was imperative that he get to the prefect as fast as possible. If the man truly had turned a corner and begun to climb the steep slope back to health, then this was the most critical time to observe and monitor his progress and, with the best will in the world, he would rather not leave the task to a novice aspirant medic. He glanced at the two approaching men again. It was no use. They had clearly both seen him, so he would have to make quick excuses.

As they converged on him, Cervianus stopped and "harrumphed" irritably.

"Sir!" one shouted as he approached, while the other more familiarly cried out, "Cervianus!"

"What?" he snapped, his head swinging this way and that. "I'm in a hurry!"

The legionary approaching from the north stopped suddenly

and threw up a salute. "With respect, sir, the optio said you'd..."
he closed his eyes as though remembering a speech word for
word, "... 'waffle and bluster and be all self-important' and
that I was to tell you he needed you and drag you by the throat
if necessary."

"Tell Ulyxes he can jam it up his arse. This is more
important!"

As the soldier began to chatter at him, flustered, Petrocorios
grinned. "I'll say it is! Guess what—"

"I wasn't talking about you!" Cervianus barked. "I've a
patient in need. *That's* my concern!"

Petrocorios shook his head. "Not more important than this.
Dust on the horizon, and moving at a bastard of a pace!"

Cervianus shrugged. "You don't even know who it is yet.
It'll be hours before they get here, so why bother me?"

"Because Draco said to fetch you in case it was the enemy,
what with you speaking Greek and all that."

Cervianus sighed. Pointless. He would spend a couple of
hours standing in the sizzling sun on the gatehouse waiting
for a force that might be Roman anyway. Did Draco think he
had no duties at all? Still, a centurion's order simply wasn't
ignored. He frowned.

"What does Uly— the optio want from me?"

"We've almost finished the mountain defences, sir, and he
wants to ask you some questions. Says you've got a clever
brain, sir."

Cervianus rolled his eyes. "Go back to Ulyxes and tell him
I have to see Draco first and I'll be along as soon as I have a
few moments."

The man bit his lip, shuffling from foot to foot.

"Stop dithering and go tell him."

"Yes, sir," the man said unhappily and ran off toward the lift up the cliff face.

Cervianus turned to find Petrocorios nodding in satisfaction. "And Draco should know better than to interrupt a doctor in his work for something as pointless as that, especially with his wounds. Tell him when you found me I was in surgery, but I'll be along presently."

His tent mate started to shake his head, but Cervianus glared at him and set his jaw firm. "I've got urgent medical business. If you really want to take me now, you'll have to knock me out and drag me!"

For a moment, as Petrocorios frowned, Cervianus wondered whether the man might actually do just that, but finally he nodded.

"Don't be long then. He's hot and his arm's itching, so he's not in a good mood."

As Petrocorios turned and ran off back toward the south gate, Cervianus walked on toward the temple of Haroeris, his orderly grinning as he ran to keep up.

"This is what the medical service is all about, Aduatix. It's not glamorous or glorious. It's having endless responsibility with no authority. It's like being the ox. You get to pull the cart but you can't direct it."

A moment later they entered the temple, moving from the bright morning sunlight that was already making the sand sizzle to the deep shade of the huge stone structure. Cervianus gave an involuntary shiver; the thick walls of the temple still held the night cold and it occurred to him too late that the conditions here last night must have been less than ideal for a recovering patient. His medical tutor back in Ancyra would have slapped him for making such an elementary mistake.

Ah well. No one here to do that, and the play-off between unhealthy cold and divine influence seemed to have swung the right way. Trotting through the rooms and into the inner chamber, he found the prefect lying where he had been laid, beneath the statue, his chest rising and falling raggedly.

"Prefect? Can you hear me?"

There was a snorting noise and then a cough and the man's head rose an inch or so from the stretcher and turned to face him. "Medicus?"

Too tired to explain, Cervianus simply nodded. "How do you feel?"

"Like someone's been using my belly to store ballista shot."

The prefect tried to pull himself up to a seated position, but collapsed back with a grunt as Cervianus rushed to his side to keep him back down safely. "Don't try to move yet. Good grief, man, you've got a major belly wound."

The prefect smiled weakly. "Made it through the desert with it, though."

"Barely. If I were a betting man, I'd have put the money down last night on you greeting Hades by now."

"I'm not that easy to kill." The man sagged back, breathing heavily. "Alright, medicus. Am I allowed to drink wine in my condition? And eat, say, lamb?"

Cervianus shook his head not in denial, but in exasperation. "The only wine you'll find here, prefect, is the vinegar I use in poultices. I wouldn't drink it, even if I was desperate. I'll have some hibiscus tea brought for you, but be very careful with it. If you experience any ill effects you'll have to switch back to water. And certainly no food for a few days."

"A few days?" the prefect protested. "I'm ravenous."

"Eating with your wound is what's done half the damage.

The spear that went in your belly cut a hole in your ileum – part of your intestine. Matter has been leaking into your abdomen every time you eat or drink and has caused inflammation, aggravating the wounds. I had feared for blood poisoning, given your fever, but if that were the case, I would be wrapping your funeral coverings right now."

The prefect went pale as the description of his troubles rolled out. "Am I still in danger?"

Cervianus shrugged nonchalantly. "Such injury is never good. I'm hoping you've turned the corner. Certainly all signs are very hopeful now."

Somehow his comforting words seemed not to have the expected reaction on the prefect, who paled further.

"Don't worry. I've repaired the damage from the spear, stitched up your intestines and cleared out the abdominal cavity. The continued course of medication I'm prescribing should take care of the inflammation and bring you back to rights."

Briefly, he wrestled with the idea of staying on to monitor the prefect and re-apply the dressing, but a call from the centurion really could not be ignored for long.

"Aduatix here is my assistant. He will stay with you and look after you. I will come as often as I can. If you feel anything unusual... any slight change, no matter how small, you will need to tell this man, and he can find me."

He turned to the legionary. "Hibiscus tea in small amounts. Water as required. I was going to show you how to change the dressing and probe the wound, but we'll do that a little later. It's probably best that he drinks a little and regains some strength now anyway. Come find me if anything happens. You know where I'll be."

With a last glance at the patient, he smiled. "You're a very lucky man, prefect Lentulus. Another day in the desert without medical aid, and you'd only be helping the vultures."

Again, this uplifting and positive comment seemed to have a less than desired effect on the man, and the capsarius turned and left with a sigh. The glare and sizzling heat of the sun struck him hard as he emerged from the cool darkness of the temple to a strange sight. Amid the general busyness of men running hither and thither about their tasks, a legionary was making his way slowly across the compound, weighed down by a burden.

Cervianus frowned. The man had an expensive-looking belt with decorative gladius and pugio hanging over his shoulder in addition to his own weapons, his left arm straining as he dragged a large, heavy sack through the dirt, stirring up dust. It was his right hand that interested Cervianus, though. The helmet he grasped with some difficulty, continually juggling it, held the transverse crest of a centurion, and the mail shirt chinking in his grip and trailing on the ground was accompanied by a leather harness covered with phalerae.

"Hang on," he shouted as he jogged across the dusty thoroughfare to the sweating man. The legionary stopped gratefully as the shout drew the brief attention of other soldiers who quickly decided that the scene was unimportant and returned to their tasks.

"What are you doing?"

The legionary shrugged. "'S my job. Empty out all the stores. Put weapons and armour to use, send other metals to Diorus to melt down for scorpion bolts, dump the rest."

"You realise that's a centurion's gear."

The man nodded. "Optio Ulyxes said rank didn't matter.

Everything's to be made best use of. Mind, this shirt's full o' holes, so I guess it should be melted down with the medals too."

"Give me that!" snapped Cervianus, grasping the harness and its jingling silver discs.

The mail shirt was indeed beyond repair; the man who'd worn it had died hard. The legionary stood opening and closing his mouth. Though Cervianus technically outranked him, the difference was minimal, and an optio had set him to the task, even though that optio was the infamous Ulyxes.

"I gotta get this stuff where it needs to be."

Cervianus ignored him, slinging the harness over his shoulder while allowing the mail shirt to crumple to the ground. He grasped the sack and yanked it from the man's hand, opening the top and peering into it. The sun's rays glanced off something small and reflective and filled the bag with light.

"This is Nasica's kit!"

"Yes. Found it in the enemy headquarters."

"Find the next pile, you ghoul, and leave this with me. You can have the shirt, though."

Leaving the legionary staring down at the ruined mail shirt in the dust, the capsarius strode off toward the south gate, carefully folding the harness and stuffing it with some difficulty into the heavy bag as he walked.

Draco was standing on the highest point of the gate, shielding his eyes from the sun as he peered off to the south. The men nearby, who had been on a variety of duties, had stopped to stare anxiously off into the distance from the wall top. Cervianus clambered up the stairs, beginning to sweat under the weight of the large sack. As he reached the walkway and strode over to the centurion, Draco turned at the footsteps and, his attention no longer riveted on the horizon, noticed for the first time the still forms of the tense men waiting, watching.

"Any man I see not back to work in ten seconds gets trenching duty 'til we see Alexandria again!"

Suddenly the wall and gate area burst into life again as the legionaries hurried about their business. In a tribute to Draco's reputation, even the men who were on guard duty and had nothing to do other than stare from the wall top managed to look suddenly busy.

"Cervianus... good. If that shitbag of a Kushite general is in that lot, I want you out front to translate."

Cervianus nodded, wishing he had the authority or the guts to point out how little use diplomacy would be if the Kushite army was about to descend on their small force. History seemed to be repeating itself.

"Sir? Ulyxes wants me to go help him with the defences on the mountain. It'll be a while before there's anything I can do. Should I go help him and return shortly?"

Draco turned to him in surprise. "You've been asked for help by an optio and given a direct order by your primus pilus. I'll leave you to ponder on what you should do, eh?"

Cervianus swallowed nervously and walked over to the wall, resting his burden on the low parapet and making sure it was far enough from the outer edge that it wouldn't fall away.

"What's that?"

Cervianus looked up in surprise at the centurion. "It's centurion Nasica's effects, sir. A man was going to recycle them, but I thought..."

He was unable to finish his sentence, however, as Draco reached across and grabbed the bag. "You've found his kit? Why did no one tell me?"

The capsarius frowned, confused at the sudden excitement in the commander's voice. "I think it's only just been found, sir. I was going to go through it and have the important things packaged to send to his family."

Draco was paying him no attention, rummaging through the bag's contents. As he searched, he withdrew a variety of items and cast them aside on the wall walk: wax tablet case, torc, comb...

Finally, he hissed with satisfaction as his hand closed on something and he withdrew it. His fingers unfurled and in his palm lay a burning glass, a convex lens in an iron ring that could be used on a sunny day to light fires – an expensive and uncommon item, for certain, but deserving of special attention?

"Sir?"

Draco seemed to suddenly remember that he was there. "Nasica showed me this a while ago."

Cervianus shrugged. "It's a burning glass, sir. I used to have one when I was in private practice. Sold it before I signed on."

Draco nodded. "But they can be used for more than that. Watch."

As Cervianus frowned in confusion, the centurion held the lens up to his left eye and squeezed his right tightly shut, peering into the glass. Cervianus leaned round to look at the centurion's face, his brow furrowing. Draco clucked irritably and shoved him back away.

"Sir?"

"A burning lens can make things far away look a bit bigger. It's not too clear, but I think... yes."

He dropped the glass from his eye and opened his other, blinking.

"You look. Tell me what you see."

Cervianus, still frowning, mimicked Draco, placing the glass to his left eye and shutting the right. He started and pulled the thing away from his face, staring at it.

"See," Draco said with a smug grin. "I thought you know-it-all Greek science types would know about this."

Cervianus blinked, turning the glass over and over. "I can see how it might work, but I'd never even thought..."

"Nasica said he learned the trick from a Phoenician. He used it occasionally, but only when it was desperate, 'cause it makes your eye ache like a bastard for hours afterwards!"

Cervianus repeated the procedure, this time aware of the strain he felt in his eye and trying to focus the somewhat blurred image by moving the glass back and forth a little. Finally he settled on the most comfortable position and moved his head, scanning the distance until he located the dust cloud.

"Green."

"Thought so," confirmed Draco. "Looks like it's our boys. Don't remember any green Kushites."

Cervianus was nodding, once again blinking his aching eye and examining the glass as he turned it over.

"Right," said Draco with a grin as he snatched the glass back, "now you can take the rest of that and do what you have to. And get up to Ulyxes and tell him the news."

Cervianus smiled as he gathered up the fallen items and stuffed them back into the bag, once again having to move his head as the signalling mirror within caught the sun and nearly blinded him. As he ran across the compound, the heavy sack bouncing on his back, he heard the call for muster go up. Draco would be preparing his men for inspection by the legion's new chief tribune.

★ ★ ★

It was far from triumphant.

The diminished remnants of the Twenty Second Deiotaran legion traipsed through the south gate of Napata in relative silence, the steady tramp of feet and jingle of armour the only sound. The tribunes headed the column on foot, weary and coated with the ever-present brown dust, Catilius with his monobrow furrowed at the fore. Behind the tribunes came the aquilifer, bearing aloft the silver eagle that they would later discover bore three dents and a sword slash, quickly followed by the legion's signifers and musicians. The command party and the standards moved off to one side as they entered the compound, allowing room for the remaining cohorts to enter, which they did in perfect march formation.

Cervianus stood with Ulyxes and Draco at the front doorway of the headquarters building, where he had been summoned in the likelihood that his talents would be required. It was with dismay that they realised not only how many men were missing from the column, but the conditions of the men who had survived. Starved and battered by the elements, exhausted from endless desert travel, the nine cohorts nevertheless managed to maintain a good, proper formation as they came to a halt in neat lines, many still bearing their shields and wearing helms.

Catilius stepped forward, the aquilifer marching out to stand at his shoulder as he approached the small command party by the door.

"Nasica?"

Draco simply shook his head. The tribune, hollow-eyed and already showing vast strain, nodded sadly though with no visible show of surprise. "You had the second force attack here, then?"

Draco cleared his throat. "Beg leave to report to commanding officer. First cohort of the legion is reduced to twenty-eight men and two officers, one newly raised. Napata is not defensible, though we are making every effort to secure the mountain top, and there are numerous little surprises waiting for any assaulting enemy, sir."

Catilius smiled bleakly. "Nasica would have been proud – *was* proud, I expect. I take it you have assumed his role?"

Draco stiffened. "I have temporarily taken on the position, sir, though it is your decision to make."

Despite the situation and his weariness, Catilius gave a small laugh. "Consider the promotion given, Draco. Nasica always considered you his replacement anyway. Did he die well?"

Cervianus tried not to picture the mail shirt with so many rents in it, or the figure on the crucifix above the west gate.

"That he did, sir," Draco replied. "Gave his all to save the standard and a few of the men, sir."

"Of course, of course."

The tribune looked for a moment as though he would collapse, or possibly nod off, but shook his head as if to clear the fug and clasped his hands behind his back. "The cavalry?"

"Arrived safe and sound yesterday, sir. I've put them to work helping with the mountain's defences."

"Very good."

Draco gave him an odd look. "Begging your pardon sir, but where's *your* horses? It's not right for the officers to walk."

Catilius smiled. "Every non-cavalry mount gave his all to fill empty bellies on the journey, Draco. I hated to lose my beloved

Aias, but his passing probably saved a dozen men, and we'll need every man in the coming days."

The centurion nodded. "They're right behind you, then, sir?"

"Close enough that they can smell the sweat of the legion and hear our marching songs, centurion. If they push as hard as *we* did, they will arrive before nightfall, though I think we will have a night's grace. They will want to take it steady. They now know they cannot stop us before we reach Napata, so they will want to be well-rested and arrive in the morning without the threat of night-time hanging over them."

Again, Draco nodded.

"Would you and your companions join me in the headquarters, centurion?" the tribune said quietly.

"Sir," he replied. "I have Cervianus here standing by to deal with any wounded."

Catilius cast a quick glance at the other two men and smiled. "I see you found your wayward friend. Come inside. Medicus Albinus is exhausted and badly equipped, but he can look after the legion for a little longer. To be honest, it's food and water and a sit down they need more than anything else."

Draco turned to a small knot of legionaries standing by the wall nearby. "You two – fetch food and water for the lads of the other cohorts and direct them to the bunk rooms."

The tribune nodded his thanks and turned, raising his voice. "Twenty Second. Fall out and wait until you're allotted space, food and water. Senior centurions and signifers to me." Turning, he gestured for the three men to walk ahead, and Cervianus shadowed Draco and Ulyxes inside, the staff of the legion following on behind.

Moments later, the trio and the dozen or so tribunes and

chief centurions of the other cohorts reached the large chamber that served as a headquarters. Catilius paused at the door and turned to the signifers carrying their heavy burdens. "Take them down and lodge them in the vault, then get yourselves water, bread and a lie down."

The look of relief that spread across the red, sweating faces beneath their animal-pelt-covered helmets made Cervianus smile. It was one thing for a legionary to survive such an ordeal across the desert in his armour and helm and with his kit intact. To do so carrying a heavy standard and wrapped in the pelt of a great wildcat was nothing short of miraculous.

Finally, the group settled into the room and chairs and benches were found and pulled up so that all present could be seated. Once the officers were all relaxed and had removed their helmets, shields and cloaks, Catilius leaned back against the wall, his hands behind his head, fingers interlocked.

"Decision time, gentlemen."

There was a respectful silence.

"No need to stand on ceremony now. We represent the command staff of the legion. It's for us to hammer out the plan. I am not an autocrat."

Again, silence reigned. They were all used to Tribune Vitalis ruling the roost with his inflexible attitude to command.

"Very well. I'll start, then. The way I see it, there are three options. Option one: we gather together as many supplies as we can, and we march back to Aegyptus as fast as our legs will carry us." The tribune's lip quirked into a half-smile as he caught the look on Draco's face. "Option two: we make use of the fortifications that the First cohort has put in place and try to defend the mountain top against the army of Kush."

A series of sour looks passed round the centurionate.

Defensive siege-play was not the way of war Roman officers preferred. It did not suit the tactics of the legion.

"Option three: we rest and recover, rearm, and then file out as a legion and meet them in battle on the open ground and hope that our discipline, training and superior armour goes some way to negating what I have calculated to be a twelve-to-one action."

The men smiled at the forced humour of the comment. No amount of "edge" was going to negate those kind of odds.

"Thoughts?"

Draco leaned forward and slapped his hand on the table. "Can't run away, sir. Better the standards fall in battle than flee like cowards from a bunch of howling barbarians!"

"I'm not sure that's true, Draco, but I take your point. A legion fleeing is never a popular move. Likely it would signal the end of the Twenty Second anyway."

The centurions nodded and Draco slapped his hand on the table again. "Not just that, sir, but Kalabsha told us…"

"Kalabsha?"

"The general of the army that swamped us here. He told us that the queen had set her sights on occupying Aegyptus again. We leave here and run north, and we might as well just invite them in."

Catilius nodded. "I was not aware of this, but it certainly makes sense. The Kandake already outnumbers the entire Roman garrison of Aegyptus and, by the time she's gathered allies from the desert, she'll outnumber any force the governor could even hope to call on. You're right, of course: she has to be stopped here, before her power and force grow any more."

Draco, his face registering satisfaction, leaned back in his chair again. "Then we need to decide how we are to meet them."

Ulyxes cleared his throat. "With respect, sirs, I think Cervianus might be on to something."

The capsarius's head whipped around to stare incredulously at his friend. "What?" he mouthed.

Ulyxes shrugged. "We had a planning meeting a few days back, sir, and Cervianus said," his face took on that faraway look he seemed to always achieve when he delved into his impeccable memory, "whatever we decide, it'll have to be using our heads and not our strength, since we don't have any."

Catilius narrowed his eyes at the pair and Draco turned to stare at them, his eyes carrying a combination of question and accusation as to how they might have had some sort of meeting without him.

"Go on?" the tribune urged.

Cervianus suddenly became aware that Ulyxes was gesturing for him to say something, while Draco glared at him and the rest of the officers looked on in anticipation. Panic began to settle in. What in Hades did Ulyxes think he was doing?

"Erm…"

Ulyxes gestured at the room while looking at Cervianus. "You said you were 'dreaming up possibilities' and that you would 'think on it'."

Cervianus shook his head at his friend. Had he? He'd had a few thoughts, yes, but that was as far as it had got. Certainly nothing he'd consider detailing for the staff.

"You said: 'If we can't win a fight, we need to make them unwilling to start one'."

"Very helpful," he mouthed back angrily, and turned to the

officers, his mind racing. "Well, there's…" He hesitated, really not sure of what he was supposed to say. His mind drifted back through little-trod alleyways, where he had begun to formulate an idea.

Gods. The healer and creator gods, balanced with the warlike figures of Sobek and Sekhmet. That was where the idea had started. It was all about what they represented.

"Religion," he said at last, and the others collectively frowned at him. "And war," he added, as though it helped to explain what he meant. Damn Ulyxes for putting him in this position.

"Religion and war," repeated Catilius encouragingly. "Yes? Go on."

"It's what the Kushites respect, sir. They're the *only* things they respect and the only reason they would ever invade or, conversely, call off an invasion."

The tribune was nodding, and suddenly Cervianus found he'd hit his stride. The thoughts were rushing forth, filling his head with possibilities. "The reason they're invading, sir, is war. They think the Roman hold on Aegyptus is weak. After the debacle in Arabia that left the province virtually defenceless, the Kandake marched as far north as Syene. Why stop there, sir? Why did she not go any further?"

The tribune nodded. "She was testing the waters? Dipping in her toe? I can see that."

"And the governor's reaction, sir, was to send south a force that had little chance of defeating her. I don't think that the former commander's decision to march into Kush would have made much difference, sir. Once she realised she could win, she'd have marched north anyway." A thought occurred to him and he narrowed his eyes and raised a finger.

"And the Kushites trade with the Sabaeans in Arabia. They have links with them. They are far better informed than we thought, considerably more powerful, and certainly more belligerent. So they took Syene to gauge the Roman reaction. Everything we've done since we came south has simply reinforced the clear fact that she could walk into Aegyptus and snatch it away from Rome with relative ease."

Draco frowned. "And what's religion got to do with this?"

"Don't you see? The Kushites are powerful and a large empire. Why are they not expanding into the tribes and the wilderness to the south and west? Why did they not try and annex Arabia, which is not far across the water? Why go north and pit themselves against a potentially powerful enemy?"

The officer looked at him expectantly.

"Because of the *gods*!" he explained as though speaking to a child. "In a way, Aegyptus is like their parent country. Aegyptus is where they found their gods and their culture. The same Amun and Horus are worshipped right here as they are way up in Alexandria."

He stood and pointed at the map drawn on the wall. "They plan to invade Aegyptus because they *can*, they know they're strong enough to achieve it, and because they think they *should*, to liberate their gods from Roman domination. Might and religion. The causes."

Catilius nodded slowly and stood, wandering over to join him, a finger tapping his parched, sandy lower lip. It was only so close, as the man stood next to him, that Cervianus realised how tired, emaciated and filthy the officer was, and yet he'd committed straight to this without rest. Such a man was worth a hundred Vitalises.

"It's a persuasive argument, capsarius. In fact, it leaves little room for doubt. The question still remains, though, what do we do to stop them? You believe the answer lies there too?"

Cervianus nodded, though suddenly doubt was flooding him again. His inspiration had run dry after the sudden epiphany. "I fear optio Ulyxes may have been a bit previous, sir. I'm sure I'm on to something, but the solution's not quite presented itself yet."

Catilius pursed his lips. "Better an unfinished good plan than a completed bad one. You think the answer lies in a show of military might, backed with something religious?"

Cervianus nodded again.

"Then you just earned yourself free time. Albinus is here to take care of the wounded. You bend all your time to trying to work out a way to turn the tide. In the meantime, we will work on the best way to meet them in battle and show them we're not ready to let them walk across us back to Aegyptus."

Cervianus stepped back, relieved in the extreme not to have been expected to come up with some amazing, inspirational idea with no notice. The tribune sat back down.

"Alright. We cannot hope to hold the complex against them. There are too few of us and too many of them. If we try and hold the mountain top, is there a likelihood that we can break out back down to the plains if need be? We really don't want to be trapped there with no way out."

Ulyxes nodded. "I've dealt with the defences myself, sir. Between the winch-lift and the three defensive approaches we've left on the northern side, we could put a century of men on the ground every few moments so long as the enemy give us room to do it."

"Good. So we hold the mountain for as long as we can. A few days might buy us the time we need for young Cervianus here to have his burst of inspiration. Certainly we can use a couple of days to thin their numbers down a little. I have a unit of archers and a unit of slingers with the auxilia that can play merry havoc with the enemy from a nice secure high place. Plus, we still have nine scorpions to have a go with."

The tribune glanced sidelong at Cervianus and gave a strange smile. "And if no inspiration comes, and it's down to the use of force, we'll just have to sally forth and kick their backsides all the way to Meroë."

The silence was broken by a few coughs and the quiet muttering of soldiers conferring.

"Very well. Draco, the other officers are going to need an hour to recover. Then I want you to brief every last centurion, optio, auxiliary officer and engineer as to the precise situation here with respect to defences, supplies, equipment, scouts and so on. We've no camp prefect, so you'll need to take charge of setting watches and passwords and so on, too. We reconvene here in an hour."

He turned to the two friends. "Cervianus, you can go about your business. If you have any thoughts, come and find me. Ulyxes, take me up on your lift. I want to see the defences."

As the officers began to file out of the room, some looking interested or relieved, but most simply looking tired, Cervianus grasped Ulyxes by the shoulder and dragged him aside. "What were you playing at? That was just *mean*. You knew I didn't have a solution to present him."

Ulyxes grinned and patted him on the cheek condescendingly. "And I know that it's when you're under pressure that you think best. I swear if I'd taken a swing at you, you'd have had the answer on the spot. You're close. I can feel it."

Cervianus stifled a retort.

The man was right. He *was* close and he *could* feel it too.

X

MEN AND GODS

The dream was different again. There was no vegetation this time, no mist. Instead, just a dreamscape of unremitting, unforgiving yellow-grey grit, and the obfuscating cloud was of dust not mist. The gods were not the same this time, either, or rather, there were more.

Thoth reached out, hand grasping, imploring, as he stepped forth at the centre of the group, and now all the shards of his erstwhile stony exterior had gone, with dark, shiny muscle and flesh undulating as the god moved forward, leading his small pantheon. At his left shoulder the crocodile god swayed forward, unblinking eye fixed on Cervianus, the lion goddess beyond, fierce and powerful. Beyond Sekhmet, another figure, the head frighteningly lupine as it coalesced from the dust, a terrifying and belligerent-looking figure.

The dream was changing, adapting to all that had happened. No longer were the gods in the lush vegetation of the river valley, but in the hard lands of Kush, the new gods he had encountered here part of the changing dream, and bringing further deities with them.

To Thoth's right shoulder came Haroeris once more, wisdom in those avian features, with great Amun beyond, radiating

*peace and power. Beyond Amun, though, a new figure again –
a ram-headed figure that moved with grace and ease.*

Seven, Cervianus noted, shivering even in his restless sleep.
Seven was a number sacred in many ways in the lands of
Aegyptus, as he had learned during one of his many lessons
with Shenti. Seven gods. But the changes were not over yet.

*The gods continued to step forth, closing on him, and
though he was no longer restricted he still felt no urge to run.
As he looked down, the ground beneath him had changed. It
remained a vast expanse of dust and rock, but there were half-
buried shapes in the surface: the shapes of men and beasts in
deathly repose. He could see them clear enough, and for some
reason rather than the horror he felt should flow through
him at the sight, all he could feel was an immense rush of
sadness.*

Seven gods in a field of bones, imploring him.

*His gaze was drawn to the bodies. They were the men of
the two armies, but not Galatians and Romans. The bodies
through which the gods stalked were the warriors of the
Kandake's army, and those of the native auxilia. All Aegyptians
and Kushites. There, a few paces before the arbiter god, a shield
bearing the eye symbol... the cavalry of the Nome of Sapi-
Res. With immense sorrow, Cervianus' gaze wandered over the
remains, searching out the figure of Shenti.*

*A howl of sheer malice from behind made him spin, and
across the field of bones strode a new figure, tall and malicious,
with a blade in each hand. He trembled, even in the dream, as
that figure, the warrior queen of Kush, raised her two swords.*

Cervianus woke with a start, and this time he felt different emerging from the dream. The earlier trepidation and bafflement were gone now. This was the culmination of those night-time forays, and he could feel it. The dreams had changed and grown with his journey, but this was where they had been leading. Here and now.

Seven figures, with three warlike deities and three of peace and creation, anchored by the great arbiter of the gods at their centre. Seven was, to Shenti and his people, the number that symbolised perfection. Seven was important. The seven gods were important. He wondered whether the earlier three and five had significance too.

Hurriedly dressing, he emerged from his room and out into the corridor to find with surprise that bright light was already pouring in through the windows. He'd assumed it to still be night. Why had no one woken him? Jogging along the corridor and out into the already baking hot day, he shaded his sleep-tightened eyes with a flat hand and looked this way and that. Shenti, he needed Shenti. Instead, he could see Ulyxes with a group of legionaries nearby, close to the lift and deep in conversation. Other than that, work parties were moving about their jobs, men standing atop the walls on guard, and no sign of the Nome of Hapi-Res.

Cervianus, already sweating from the heat as he knuckled the sleep from the corners of his eyes, hurried over to the lift, which was being loaded with sacks. Ulyxes turned at his approach, a strange look crossing his face, something like a combination of worry and sarcastic humour.

"About time, Lord Morpheus. Thought you were going to sleep all day."

"Why did no one wake me?"

Ulyxes shrugged. "Tribune's orders. No one is to interfere

with you until that brain of yours presents him with a solution. Surprised the horns didn't wake you anyway."

"I was having a dream. An important one, too. What horns?"

"Sending everyone to their positions. Our scouts spotted the Kushite army at dawn just a few miles from here."

Cervianus blinked in shock. "How far? Are they imminent?"

"I'm surprised we can't see them yet. That close."

"Damn it. I'm onto something, but I need time. I need to talk to Shenti about it. Have you seen him?"

"His lot were out on patrol earlier, but I think they're back. Check the west gate."

Cervianus nodded. "How's the mountain fortress?"

"We could hold it for a while now. Not forever, but it's better than this place."

The capsarius glanced over at the work party. A contubernium of men were just dropping the last sack on the lift and beginning to haul on the ropes, the counterweight still a small dot high up at the clifftop. The man directing the operation turned and waved, and Cervianus felt a small flicker of gratitude to see that it was Sentius. His arm may not yet be up to such work as hauling on ropes, but he was clearly working hard regardless. The capsarius waved back, nodded to Ulyxes, and then headed off to the west gate.

The horses of Shenti's unit were corralled near the wall, and the building that was being used as a combined stable, tack shed and barracks was filled with life. As he approached, Shenti stepped out of the doorway with a raised hand as though expecting him.

"Greetings, my friend."

"I need to speak to you," Cervianus replied, gesturing across to an area of the compound where there were no signs of occupation or activity, just one of the many spoil heaps of dumped rubble. The cavalry officer followed him, and the two men stopped in the shade of the nearest building.

"You told me some time back of the perfection of the number seven," he said without preamble.

Shenti smiled. "The enemy close upon us and we find time to discuss mysticism and mathematics, yes? You have come a long way from your rigid world, my friend."

"I think that's part of the point," Cervianus said. "Back home, and in Greece and in Rome, the gods sit on high and control things, though they are said to intervene on occasion when it pleases them. But in ancient days there are tales of the gods interfering with everyday lives repeatedly. That's what happens here, and it's taken me some time to get used to the idea. The gods of these lands are interfering now."

"Seven of them?"

Cervianus frowned. "Sort of. In the dreams I've been having for weeks now. Originally there were three gods, and they were statues just coming to life. I think that was me beginning to see them as something more real and present than just a name on a mountain top. Is three important? I knew those gods, you see. Thoth, Sekhmet and Sobek."

"Triads are important, just as they are for your land. Thoth is the thrice great god of wisdom. The ankh and the knot of Isis have three loops. In the *Tale of the Doomed Prince*, an ancient story, he is destined to die three times. Interesting that Thoth the wise is in the company of two warrior gods for you."

Cervianus shivered. Again, things were oddly falling into place. "Perhaps that was because we were marching to war at the time. Once we were in Kush, the gods in my dreams had come to life and now as well as warlike Sekhmet and Sobek, there were Amun and Haroeris, with Thoth at the centre. I think that was because we were here, where Amun and Haroeris are so prevalent."

Shenti nodded. "This mountain is said to be the birthplace of Amun himself. Even the Kandake would bow to Amun, for he is linked to Napata like no other. And five is a number close to both Haroeris and to Thoth."

"And now there are seven, as of last night's dream, and I know seven to be the perfect number. I think seven is all there will be. A ram-headed god and a wolf came this time."

"Wepwawet and Khnum, I think. You have a pantheon of powerful gods in your dreams."

"What are they all? Thoth is the arbiter of the gods. Why he is at the centre I can understand, and I think that I am in some way to play the role of Thoth. But the others? Sobek is a god of crocodiles and of war, Sekhmet of battle and protection. Amun is the creator, is he not? And Haroeris the healer."

"That is something of a simplification. Our gods have many aspects, but yes, these are some of their provinces. Khnum is the divine creator and the Nile is his domain. Wepwawet is the opener of the ways, who stands on the horizon between life and death."

"This is about balance," Cervianus said, chewing his lip for a moment. "Thoth is the balance here, with three gods of war and death and three of creation and life. Balance. All about balance, and I think there is a way to apply it to our situation."

Shenti leaned back. "I fear that the tribune is fooling himself that there can be a solution to this other than war. I know you feel you can do something, but the Kandake will not stop wading through Roman bodies until she has sated her thirst, and her thirst for blood is legendary. I fear it will take the gods themselves walking among them for her to see anything other than conquest."

"And I think that's part of it," Cervianus muttered. "What will you do now? Are you riding out once more?"

Shenti shook his head. "The enemy is almost here and there is no longer a great need for scouts. Cavalry will be of little use on the mountain top, too, so we will put our shields and spears to use as infantry."

"Well, good luck. I think we will all need it. I may call on you again shortly for a favour, if the idea that is forming is possible." Turning away from the rider, Cervianus stalked back toward the centre of the compound. Time was almost up and though he was hovering on the edge of an idea, it wouldn't quite fall into place.

The Kandake and her people respected only two things, as he had told the tribune when Ulyxes had put him on the spot: war and the gods. But the gods were trying to tell him to be an arbiter. To be the bringer of balance? How could he do such a thing? He could hardly make the gods walk up to the Kushite queen and demand that she halt. Even Shenti did not believe this could be resolved without a fight.

He paused next to another temple – the temple with the Haroeris statue and the wounded cavalry prefect. Perhaps it couldn't be finished without a fight, but perhaps it *shouldn't* anyway. Half the gods in his dreams were deities of war, after all, and any peace that could possibly be forged here would never hold as long as the Kandake dreamed of blood and of conquest and felt that Rome could not hold against her. The Kandake's only experience with Rome so far was her almost total victory over Vitalis in the southern lands. She could hardly respect Rome after that. She had to be stopped, but it had to be with both words and blades. Was that what the balance was? A slow smile spread across his face. Yes. Fight to get her attention, and then show her the will of the gods. That was it.

Catilius was not going to like this.

Taking a deep breath, he moved around the compound, glancing up at the walls until he spotted the officers above the south gate, peering out into the desert. For a heart-stopping moment, he wondered whether the Kandake and her army had arrived, but reasoned that warning signals would have rung out had that been the case.

A few moments later he was at the gate, a legionary barring his way. A brief discussion as to his right to approach the tribune ensued, which ended when Catilius turned and looked down at the raised voices, motioning the man to let Cervianus past. The capsarius bounded up to the top of the gate, finding the monobrowed tribune peering expectantly out into the endless gold-grey. He looked tired. Almost certainly he had slept in brief snatches last night if at all. Catilius turned wearily to him.

"Have you an ingenious solution for me, Cervianus?"

The capsarius winced. "I think so, sir, but it's not without its risks, nor without a fight."

"I do not find that hard to believe," the man sighed.

"The Kandake respects only war and the gods, as I said. But we have to give her both. I think I can end the war, but if it ends without us showing our strength first there will be no respect in the resolution. She has to come to understand that Rome will not bow down. That Rome will fight her for our lands. She has to experience enough respect that she abandons plans to conquer, and that she is content to draw the old borders once more, with her in Kush and us in Aegyptus. It's all about balance and about the status quo, sir. Between the two lands, between war and peace."

"You want me to fight them? Your grand plan is to fight a superior army and make them back down?"

Cervianus sighed. "I don't think we can beat them, sir, but if we avoid battle altogether, we might as well invite her into Aegyptus as you yourself noted. We have to make her agree to draw the line. We have to hold our own for a while and engender the respect that she cannot feel after trouncing Vitalis' army. And once we have put a good show on, once we have her attention, I think I can end it and bring her to terms. All I ask is that you give me half a dozen men, and give her reason to respect our armies."

"That will not be easy from our mountain hideaway."

"Then," Cervianus winced again, knowing how this would sound, "perhaps we should meet them in the field?"

Now half a dozen lesser officers and a dozen legionaries in the vicinity all looked around at him, wide-eyed.

"I fear your brains have cooked in the sun, Cervianus," the tribune murmured. "We number little over two thousand all told. The Kushites will field at least three times that number, are better adapted to the conditions, are well-supplied and uninjured. We are exhausted, wounded, unfamiliar, troubled by the heat, and with poor provisions. If we face them in the field it will be over in half an hour. On the mountain we might last days."

"You must do as you see fit, sir, and I can only say once again that I think I can end this, but only if we earn their respect in battle. Am I at liberty to continue my work, sir?"

Catilius nodded. "One man will make little difference here, I fear, even one who can patch up the wounded."

Saluting, and hoping that the tribune would find some way to make this work, Cervianus left the gate once more. He had to see Shenti again, but on the way across the compound, he paused outside the great temple. Hurrying inside, he found his way into the inner room. This, he knew, was the temple's "Holy of Holies", the sanctuary where the god would manifest and where his cult image would be kept shrouded in darkness. When they had first arrived, this room had held the model barque which carried a stone box. Inside that box was the statue of Amun himself, said to have been born from the great mountain that loomed above the temple. During the desecration under Vitalis, that holy cult symbol had gone, cast out blindly. Amun was the master of Napata, and it was him Cervianus needed to end this.

Back outside, he ran across to Ulyxes. "Do you remember that barque from the great temple?" he asked hurriedly.

The optio's brow furrowed. "A replica boat, about four feet long, with a stone box on top."

Cervianus nodded, grateful once more for his friend's incredible memory. "When the temples were raided and burned, the great temple was stripped out to be reused. Do you know what happened to the barque?"

Ulyxes shook his head. "I was gone the night after the temples were fired, but I remember since I came back seeing a whole bunch of statues half buried with broken stones and the like, off in a spoil heap near the cliff. I suspect it was probably dumped there."

Cervianus sagged. "And under Kalabsha's command we had not got as far as digging out and restoring many of the statues. I need that statue and the barque."

"Can't help you, Cervianus. Got too much to do here and the tribune has me on a tight schedule to be ready."

"I can't dig through a spoil heap on my own."

"Then get your cavalry friends to help you. They won't be doing much."

Cervianus grinned. "Of course. Thanks, Ulyxes."

The riders from Sapi-Res were where he'd last met them. Shenti had his men practising using their spears underarm while carrying their shield on foot, an unfamiliar mode of combat for the light cavalrymen, and Cervianus skittered to a halt, sending up a small shower of grit and a tiny dust cloud.

'My friend?' the decurion said, crossing to him and leaving his men to train.

"I have it, Shenti. I really do. The gods want the status quo back. When the priest of Haroeris back in the north told me 'make Syene your end', he was not talking about the campaign or the army, d'you see? He was talking about Rome itself. Syene needs to be the edge of Rome's lands. Kush must remain separate. The gods of Aegyptus and the gods of Kush are the same, and they are watching their peoples kill one another. Not us, because the Twenty Second is peripheral to this. It was your bones and those of the Kushites I saw in the dream."

Shenti nodded sagely. "The gods are wise."

"We need to make the Kandake respect us militarily, so that the border can be drawn at Syene and the second cataract once again, and then we need to make her fear the gods enough to stop the fight. All I can hope is that Catilius can do the former. It's my task to do the latter, with the aid of great Amun. We *are* going to make the gods walk among them, Shenti, after all, but I need to find the barque and cult statue of Amun that was removed from the temple. I think it's buried in one of the spoil heaps. Can you and your men help me?"

Shenti straightened. "Are you planning what I think you are planning?"

"It will be dangerous, and I'm going to ask for six volunteers, but yes, I think so."

The cavalry of the Nome of Sapi-Res dug through the spoil heap with furious speed and yet also with an almost reverential care, for they could not countenance even the slightest accidental damage to the many images of gods that lay half buried, shattered or scratched, in the dust and rubble. It seemed that many of the soldiers who had carried out Vitalis' orders to destroy the temples had done so with efficiency, caring little about the damage they were inflicting upon such religious icons in the process.

Already, three statues had been removed and put carefully aside. Finally, quarter of an hour ago, they had uncovered the tip of what could only be the model ship, the barque that had sat in the "Holy of Holies" of the Amun temple. Since then they had been working feverishly and had managed to clear almost half its length.

"It'll need restoration," Cervianus noted with irritation. "There's so many scratches, and the paint has come off in many places."

Nods came from those men working who understood him. They all appreciated how important it was that this sacred item be presented in its full glory. Fortunately, as Cervianus could testify from his work on restoration during the brief control of General Kalabsha, in this intense and very dry heat, paint only needed to be applied and left for enough time to down half a canteen of water before it was dry. Restoration should be quick.

It was then, though, that the big problem arose. "Where is the statue?" he breathed. They had cleared enough now that if the stone box containing Amun had been in place they should have found it. Cervianus cursed silently. The barque was of no value without the god himself.

"It is likely close by," Shenti replied, still pulling away pieces of broken, carved stone from beside the ship. "The destroyers will have been careless about their burden, but the two will have been brought out together and therefore presumably dumped together. We will continue to search."

The unit continued to dig through the immense heap of sacred spoil and Cervianus, his green tunic now hopelessly filthy and dust coated, worked feverishly until, a few heartbeats later, the entire party was interrupted by the frantic honking of a cornu. The cavalry of Sapi-Res stopped what they were doing and started to straighten.

"What are you doing?" Cervianus asked desperately.

"That is the call to arms," Shenti reminded him. "You may not be required, my friend, but my men will be."

Cervianus, spirits frayed, looked about urgently. The majority of the compound's occupants were racing for the walls, only those men working on the lift and the mountain fortress continuing about their business.

"Ulyxes and his men are still working, so we can too."

Shenti shook his head. "We are expected in place, my friend."

"Keep digging," Cervianus shouted, pointing at the heap of rubble. "I will clear this with the tribune, I promise you, but please, find that statue."

Shenti, brow furrowed, wrestled with the choice for a moment, then nodded and gestured for his men to get back to their work uncovering the ship. The capsarius, his heart pounding, turned and ran through the gathering crowds of soldiers for the south gate from whence the call had gone up. Men were gathering at their standards on the dusty open ground inside the gate, centurions and optios barking commands, the horn still blowing like mad above them on the gate. The walls were rapidly filling with men, stooks of pila being manhandled up there as a potential defence line, despite the focus being on the mountain top. Cervianus felt fresh dismay at the sight. To win the respect of the warrior queen they would have to show their mettle. That would best be done in open battle. It could *possibly* be done from the walls. It would be a difficult proposition while hiding away on the mountain top.

Tribune Catilius was standing with his fellow officers pointing out into the landscape, and as Cervianus reached the wall top and gestured for that same guard as before to let him pass, his gaze strayed out to the south, catching sight of what the tribunes were looking at. His heart began to pound faster at the nightmare sight.

The army of Kush was enormous. The forces stretched out into the immense dust cloud that obscured the southern horizon, the front lines having now reached the river. The Kandake herself was in the van, presumably with Kalabsha, given the size of the force – a colourful party in chariots of blue and gold, with standards raised that showed stylised suns, feather crowns and roaring lions. More chariots followed in ordered lines, with cavalry beyond them.

The infantry were not yet visible, lost in the dust cloud as they were, but on the reasonable assumption that chariots and horsemen would constitute a relatively minor part of the army, the infantry contingent had to be huge. With the confidence of people born to this land, the chariots made for the shallowest slope of the bank and plunged into the water, creating V-shaped waves as they ploughed on without losing a great deal of momentum.

Suddenly Cervianus was less sure of the military aspect of his solution. Clearing his throat nervously, he approached the tribune, who turned at a gesture from one of the other officers. Cervianus stood respectfully, not too close, and saluted.

"Ah, the capsarius calls once more," the tribune said without a trace of humour in his tone. "Have you come to advise me to ride out against them again?"

Cervianus winced. Having witnessed the size of the force, which had to outnumber the legion by more than five to one at the very least, it now seemed a ridiculous proposition. He straightened. "Respectfully, sir, all I can say is that we have to show our strength. How we achieve that is for a strategist, not a medic, sir."

"Quite. So if you've not come to offer me the benefit of your military wisdom, to what do we owe the honour?"

"If I am to achieve what I hope, sir, I cannot do it alone. I would ask that you release the cavalry of the Nome of Sapi-Res to help me."

Catilius shrugged. "The Aegyptian cavalry are of great value in the field but since, as I've already said, I have no intention of marching out to meet that lot, have your cavalry. They'd just be under-trained spearmen in a siege."

"Thank you, sir. We're working as fast as we can."

"With luck there will still be some of us left when you are ready to perform whatever arcane trick you have devised."

Cervianus turned to go, but stopped as the enemy's lead elements swept to a halt, the wheels of the chariots sending up clouds of dirt, the standards and armour of the men aboard them gleaming blindingly in the morning sunlight. The capsarius chewed his lip. He really should be helping Shenti and his men, since that was his project, yet he couldn't resist the chance to see this, to find out more. After all, he would need to be prepared when the time came.

As the enemy commanders waited, letting the dust settle, the rest of the chariots and the first lines of cavalry lined up in ordered rows behind, wave after wave of infantry now reaching the river and plunging down into the waters to cross. Cervianus studied the closest chariots. General Kalabsha he knew all too well, but the Kandake was another matter entirely. Tall and as powerfully built as any warrior, she was armoured in bronze scales and her hair was brushed back in tight black braids and tucked beneath what appeared to be a white skullcap decorated with a rearing cobra at the brow. A neat line of an old wound ran down one side of her face, leaving a V-shaped dent in her chin and an empty eye socket that she had made no attempt to cover. At her side two swords were sheathed, freeing her hands for the chariot's reins and for the red spear decorated with feathers that she carried. She was truly a chilling sight.

She rattled something off to Kalabsha in their native tongue, and the general nodded. At a gesture, the line of chariots behind them opened up at the centre, and half a dozen naked slaves brought forth their charge, a sight that sent waves of shock through the watchers. Each slave held the end of a chain, and at the conjunction of the six lines a collar sat around the neck of a full-grown lion that snarled and jerked, almost pulling the six burly slaves from their feet.

"What strange show is this?" Catilius murmured, though the purpose became dreadfully clear in moments. A second group of slaves led forward a man in a ragged green tunic. One of the survivors of the battle in the south, clearly, Cervianus realised with a chill. The man was a centurion, as the leather medal harness on his chest proclaimed. Cervianus watched in sickened horror as the man was dragged forward without a word, closer and closer to the snarling lion. As he reached a position just out of reach, his slave escort stepped out to both sides, keeping their chains tight so that the centurion was anchored in place between them, their muscles heaving, the prisoner's arms almost pulling from their sockets.

The first slave group let their leashes slacken and the lion, unleashed, leapt at the centurion. Cervianus watched the initial swipe of a great paw that tore the midriff from the captive Roman, sending blood and entrails across the dirt as the man screamed. The capsarius turned away, unable to watch the grisly execution, though he couldn't block out the sounds, and each noise told its own horrible story. When it was over and all he could hear was the snapping of bones and the sounds of an animal feeding, he turned back, trying to blot out the sight of the carcass being consumed. Soldiers along the wall had gone white with shock.

Catilius held himself proudly, his face betraying no sign of what he was feeling. Cervianus found himself recalling stories of how the Romans entertained themselves. It was said that criminals were treated thusly in their great arenas, something to which the men of Galatia were unaccustomed, though likely the Roman tribune had seen this sort of thing before.

The Kandake straightened in her chariot. "It is my understanding that Roman nobles are taught the tongue of the Ptolemies, and so I am sure that at least your officers understand me," she announced in flawless Greek.

"I understand you," Catilius replied. "Say your piece."

The Kandake drew herself up to an impressive height. "Apedemak feeds upon the fools you left behind to die, and in time he will feed upon fresh morsels from this place. I am Amanirenas, Kandake of Kush, daughter of kings, wife of kings, mother of kings, beloved of Atum of the curved horns, living embodiment of Iusaset, rightful pharaoh of all the lands of the Nile. You have dared to invade my lands and have affronted the gods and for that I will scour the land of your kind, leaving nothing but bones. I have no ultimatum to give. There is no offer of terms. I state only your destiny – you will all die here before the sun falls."

With that, she cast that colourful spear, which plunged into the sand between her chariot and the walls, juddering and standing proud, the feathers fluttering.

Tribune Catilius nodded soberly. "Your intentions are noted. You will not find Rome a coward to roll on her back and show her belly to such might, though. The man responsible for the desecration of your holy places is no more. He lies dead in the sands to the south, where we first fought. It was his decision to bring the army into your lands, and he has paid the ultimate price for his hubris and his impiety. Rome's intent was to drive your forces beyond the border of Aegyptus and to reinstate that border at the second cataract, chastising you for your wanton destruction and thievery at a crucial time. Anything beyond that remit was the sole decision of the tribune Vitalis. I now command and, without a plea or demand, I inform you plain that the restoration of this holy place has been allowed to continue, and the gods are being honoured. I do not seek the annexation of your lands, nor the extinction of your gods and, given the opportunity, the legion would now be returning to Aegyptus. However, I am fully aware of your intent to bring war to our lands in response, and I will not allow that to happen. If every man here must fight to the death to prevent your advance then that shall be so."

The queen of Kush, her one good eye narrowing, pulled the two swords from her side and hefted them, peering appreciatively along their lines. "I look forward to ravaging your corpse, Roman, but your speech was well made. You shall not number among those destined to feed Apedemak."

"You will not find us so easy to dislodge," Catilius said in a matter-of-fact tone.

The Kandake smiled a horrible smile, that scar wrinkling. "You believe you can play your children's fort games by securing yourself on the mountain and holding us off? Think again, Roman."

A chill rippled through Cervianus as, along with every figure on the wall, he turned to see where she was looking, far above their heads and behind them. The distant green figures of the small garrison unit who had been working on the mountain-top fortress were lined up along the top of the precipice as though on parade.

Cervianus closed his eyes for a moment. Gods, no.

At a gesture from the Kandake, the entire mountain-top garrison stepped out into the abyss, their shapes plummeting through the air to land with a scattering of thuds somewhere out of sight behind the temples at the base of the cliff. Where they had been, black shapes now swarmed.

They had lost the mountain top to the desert dwellers. The import of that struck Cervianus in two waves. They had lost the place of refuge on which they had worked solidly for two days, but far worse than that, the feared black desert tribes now held the heights and had ready access to the compound.

"Secure the damned lift," snapped the tribune, and Cervianus realised that the platform was at the clifftop and being pulled in. The tribesmen might be able to work their way down the cliffs in the same way the Romans had done, but they would be at the mercy of the defenders, now that their presence was known. But they could land dozens of men at a time on that lift.

"I'll see to it, sir," he said, with a salute, and turned to run. He had to get back to the rear of the compound anyway to help Shenti and his men. Time was running out. He took a last look out over the wall top. The Kandake was simply watching Catilius as her army continued to mass on this side of the river behind her. For a heart-stopping moment, General Kalabsha looked at Cervianus and frowned, but then shook his head, apparently dismissing the notion that this could be a man he recognised.

Ducking out of sight, Cervianus ran down the steps and hurtled across the compound, past the lines of men at attention, feet pounding on the dirt, breath coming in gasps. Ducking around two buildings, he laid eyes upon the lift at last. There was a momentous struggle in progress, Ulyxes and his men hauling on the ropes, attempting to bring the platform back down even as black shapes crowded onto it high up, preparing to descend and assault the defenders. Unfortunately, the lift was well designed, and at the top it could be swung in onto a timber walkway for stability while loaded and unloaded. Dislodging it from there was proving to be more than a little difficult, and every moment, more and more black shapes filed out onto the lift.

Cervianus rolled his eyes as he ran. Why did no one think things through logically. Faced with a simple solution, the soldiers were engaged instead in a troublesome tug-of-war. Ulyxes turned, bellowing a call for any archers in the vicinity before noticing the gangly figure of Cervianus pounding toward him.

"Cut the damn counterweight," the capsarius shouted between heaved breaths.

Ulyxes frowned for a moment, then broke out into a grin, slapping his head. "Good to see you, my favourite over-thinker."

With that he ran over to the work party, and moments later there were two men standing on the enormous boulder that had been wrapped in a web of ropes to act as the lift's counterweight. Cervianus needed to get back to the diggers, but could not tear his eyes from the scene, his heart fluttering as the entire apparatus suddenly shook, dust falling from it in waves as the platform high above was dislodged from the ledge and swung out over the drop, filled with black figures and glinting blades. Even as the capsarius watched, the counterweight started to rise, the platform descending as men atop the cliff hauled on the ropes like madmen.

The two legionaries on the boulder stopped their work, clinging on to the ropes for dear life as they started to rise. One of the pair, panic overtaking him, leapt from the counterweight, rolling in the dust and cursing at some hurt. The other man howled in panic as he continued to ascend.

"Cut the rope," bellowed Cervianus to the terrified legionary as a dozen men, all that remained of a depleted unit of archers, fell in nearby.

"Sir?" one of them said, addressing Ulyxes.

"I don't care what your orders were," the optio told them, "you're my men now. I want you to wait until that platform is in reasonable range and then put arrows into the black bastards on it. Then you stay here and watch for any of them trying to climb down the cliff and pick them off as they come into range. Got it?"

The archer saluted, and Cervianus and his friend returned their attention to the lift. The platform had now descended almost a quarter of the way, while the man clinging desperately to the counterweight was rising, shaking.

"Cut the damned rope and jump," Ulyxes shouted, though both he and Cervianus knew that a jump from such a height would almost certainly result in at the very least a broken limb, and potentially far worse. To the legionary's credit he clenched his teeth, clung tight to the rope with his left hand, and began to hack at the cord once more with his sword. It was fraying, though Cervianus quickly lost sight of such detail as it rose, the platform almost halfway now. Soon, the legionary would be level with the black shapes, and there was the slight possibility he might be within their sword range.

The archers began to loose now, their arrows arcing up and mostly either thudding into the timber underside of the lift or clattering uselessly against the cliff. Two found targets, one victim pitching out from the platform and hurtling to his doom, the other clutching his arm and moving back from the edge. Cervianus held his breath, watching the legionary on the boulder. He was clinging tight to the rope above him with his good hand in an attempt to not fall, though that would only mean rising rapidly toward those black shapes on the mountain top.

The rope gave very suddenly, and the result unfolded in a single heartbeat, with anticipated results. The enormous boulder fell sharply, slamming into the dirt so hard that it buried itself up to a third of its depth. At the same time the rope, released of the weight, hissed upwards at an astonishing rate. The legionary stood no chance. He clung on for a fraction of a moment and then fell with a cry, his sword falling away. In one small mercy he spun in the air and hit the ground scalp first, his head bursting like an overripe watermelon. Horrible, but at least his suffering was over in an instant, and from that height he'd have only lived a painful lingering hour or two of shattered bones anyway.

The black-clad killers on the platform fared no better, at least. As the rock fell away and the rope slithered upwards, so the platform fell. However, with the loss of the anchored stability, long before the timber lift hit the ground, it pivoted and pitched and spun, the men falling from it with a chorus of panic. The desert dwellers hit the ground like strange black hail in a tumult of thuds and crunches, ironically close to the green and glistening-red shapes of their erstwhile victims. An angry howl arose from the other black figures atop the cliff, and already men began to attempt the descent.

Ulyxes smiled unpleasantly as he turned to the archers. "Take your time and enjoy it. Make sure every shot is a hit."

Cervianus nodded and heaved a sigh of relief. The immediate danger here was now over. Steadying himself, he turned. The sea of Kushite military strength was about to break in waves on the compound wall, but the tribune was as prepared as he could be. The mountain top had fallen to the nomads but, against all expectations, Ulyxes had it under control. Now it was down to Cervianus and to Shenti and his men to try and finish this.

It was a strange little world that Cervianus and the horsemen now inhabited. Caught in an otherwise deserted sun trap with blazing light and sizzling heat, surrounded only by the stark golden walls of ancient temples as they rooted and dug into a dusty heap of rubble, continually uncovering images of gods and pharaohs, discussing, though admittedly with some urgency, the requirements of the items they sought and how they might be restored swiftly and precisely. It felt like some great and fascinating expedition of discovery in the presence of experts.

But for the sounds.

In their pleasant, sunny, dusty little enclave there was nothing anyone could do to blot out the sounds of approaching disaster. The periodic barking of an order from the site of the ruined lift, the thud of a bow string snapping taut, the whirr of missiles and the screams of the more intrepid black-clad desert dweller as he was plucked from the cliff face with an arrow and hurtled to a wet, crunching death in the dust below. The bellows of frustrated rage by the rest of the figures atop the mountain as they rained down all the goods the legionaries had taken up there, in an attempt to kill Ulyxes and his men, who ducked out of danger each time, returning only to pick off another climber.

But those sounds Cervianus could cope with. What truly chilled his blood were the sounds from outside the walls. For the first quarter of an hour, he'd felt a small surge of hope as the coming conflict was subjected to the inevitable delays of organisation. As the small team of men dug feverishly, all they could hear from outside were the sounds of signals being given and of huge numbers of feet, hooves and wheels pounding and churning the land as units moved into position ready for the battle. From the walls, in Latin, very little came. Just words of hopeless encouragement from officers, nervous jokes from the men, each of which was stamped on by their commanders in a trice, and occasional muted prayers.

Then the sounds had changed. At some signal that passed him by while he worked desperately, the Kushites moved to attack. The sound that had drawn his attention to the assault taking place had been the arrows. Cervianus had been in battles. Even recently, at Abu and Buhen, he had encountered archers both allied and enemy, releasing their storms of flighted shafts. Nothing he'd heard before had prepared him for this, though. He could hardly imagine how many archers there were out there, for though in his small haven he saw nothing of the attack, the noise was like a thousand snakes slithering and hissing, the volume so deafening that it drowned out everything else, even the hack and clatter of their tools as they dug. What it did *not* blot out, unfortunately, was the cacophony of screams that followed. In truth there were not as many as there should have been for such a dreadful onslaught, but still perhaps twenty men or more fell to that shower of shafts. Clearly the officers had been prepared for it, the men ready to drop behind the parapet and lift their shields at the moment of release, else the death toll would have been in the hundreds.

And as Cervianus heaved aside a piece of charred stone carved with the indecipherable writing of the Aegyptians, guilt plagued him again and again. He was a legionary, and he was a capsarius. As the former, his place was on those walls, weathering the arrow storm and facing the wrath of the one-eyed warrior queen. As the latter, his place was in the compound behind the walls, dragging the injured out of danger and tending to their wounds. No aspect of his role in the legion required him to dig through rubble and paint statues while a battle raged nearby.

But even the guilt had swiftly been subsumed over the following quarter of an hour by simple horror. That arrow storm had been the first of many. The Kandake was methodical and was clearing as many figures from the walls as she could before the main assault. Naturally, the subsequent barrages had less effect as the men on the walls, now more prepared and alert, managed to shelter better each time, though still sporadic screams announced a lucky shot or a foolish legionary.

Then, not long ago, as Cervianus helped the men lift the uncovered ship to flat ground, the arrows had stopped and, with a roar, the battle proper had begun. Since then there had been only the constant din of battle, roaring and crashing like steel waves on brick walls.

Trying to blot out the sound of the world ending not far away, Cervianus concentrated on his work. Irritably discarding what looked a little like the Kandake's serpent crown made of some hard stone, he fumed at the time they were wasting, and then looked up sharply as one of the riders barked something out in his native language. The capsarius had no idea what he had said, but the aura of excitement in the tone was unmistakable. Hurrying across to him along with Shenti, they crouched. The stone box was on its side, the open side looking out to the east. He could just see the edge of the feather crown sticking out of the dirt inside.

"That's it," he hissed in relief and excitement. "Come on, let's get it out."

All hands now bent to the task and in a matter of a few heartbeats they had uncovered enough to haul the statue from the rubble pile. Holding the box face down, Shenti caught the image as it tumbled out, preventing it falling to the ground as all the sand and dirt drained from the container.

As the decurion lifted it, standing once more, Cervianus examined it, wide-eyed. "It needs so much work," he said in exasperation.

"But it is unbroken, my friend," Shenti pointed out.

"Such a complex job to repaint it, though."

"Yet against all odds the ship, the box and the statue have all survived while much else we have uncovered is wrecked."

Cervianus nodded. It was true, and that was more than he could have realistically expected. Another odd truth struck him. "I have no idea what the colours are supposed to be. It's so worn."

"We can do this, and make quick work of it, I think," Shenti said, then turned to his men and spoke rapidly in Aegyptian, pointing at the collection of paints and brushes they had gathered from the temples that had been part renovated. As the riders scrambled around, grabbing brushes and paints and preparing to undo all Vitalis' damage, the decurion turned to Cervianus. "How do you expect to do this? The enemy will not part like long grass for a hunter, even when they see this. The soldiers the Kandake will be throwing at the walls now will be desert tribes who owe her fealty. She cares little about their survival, but they follow their own gods and may not even know who Amun is."

The capsarius nodded. "We will have to fight our way in. I think that was always the likelihood. But once we're into the Kushites and we have their attention, that is when we stand a chance, I think."

"And you still wish to take only seven men, against an army?"

Cervianus nodded. "It's what the gods want, I think. It's symbolic."

"It will take four of us just to carry the barque. You realise that means only three blades at work?"

"Yes."

Shenti pursed his lips. "Then we had best choose my best man to join us at the fore."

"That won't be necessary," cut in a new voice. Cervianus and Shenti turned to see Ulyxes and Sentius standing at the corner of the nearest temple wall.

"You don't know what we're planning," Cervianus murmured.

"Oh, I think I do. And the simple fact is that Shenti and his men here are fearsome in the saddle, but grunt-work is not their style. They've no training in what you're asking of them. Me, though? I *live* to break heads. And Sentius here? Hades, but the man's a trained legionary who even survived a crocodile attack. Sobek seems to watch over him now. And even you, for all your scalpels and unguents, I've seen you at your worst. Remember Buhen? I watched you on that wall top like some sort of berserk war god. I honestly thought you were unstoppable. You, me and Sentius. We're the swords you want. And don't you think it sort of fits that Shenti and his men carry the barque? They are Amun's people, after all."

Cervianus frowned his uncertainty, turning to the decurion.

Shenti looked troubled, but after a moment nodded his head in agreement.

"Alright, then," the capsarius said. "It's settled. But I want the three of us dressed in the same whites as the cavalry. This is all about show, and we don't want them dismissing us as just another three legionaries. Can we borrow three of your shields?" he asked Shenti, who nodded again. "Very well. Ulyxes and Sentius, get three uniforms to fit us, three shields, and get yourselves ready. Shenti, get your men restoring those items as fast as you can. I have to see the tribune one last time."

"I'm not sure they have white uniforms in gangly bean-pole size." Ulyxes grinned.

Rolling his eyes and leaving them to their work, the capsarius dipped around the corner of the temple and ran for the centre of the compound. The open space where the cohorts had so recently been falling into formation was now largely devoid of men. When the arrow storms had started they would have been directed to the nearest cover, and since then they had been assigned defensive positions around the perimeter. Indeed, the walls were so crowded with men that barely a foot of the mud-brick parapet was visible between them, and the only figures inside the compound were the reserves and the medical staff. One of the many ancillary buildings had been assigned as the hospital and in there Albinus, the legion's medicus, would be hard at work sawing off limbs and stitching wounds, his various staff bustling around aiding him. Outside that building stood a large red-and-white striped awning beneath which the shapes of groaning and yelping men waited to be seen – limbs broken or hacked, blood staining black patches on their green tunics, the smell of urine and viscera wafting even to where Cervianus emerged from between two buildings.

The reserves waited in the lee of another structure, four hundred men under a single centurion, awaiting assignment when they would plug gaps on the walls as men fell. A *thunk* above him made Cervianus look up to see that the tribune had positioned two scorpions on a temple's pylon towers, where they enjoyed sufficient height to loose over the men on the wall and indiscriminately into the mass of enemy warriors beyond.

As he closed on where the commanders had gathered, he peered across at the south gate. It had been not only closed and barred, but blockaded with crates and sacks and timbers and blocks of stone. Anything that could be found to help secure it. Likely the east and west gates would be the same, but it was almost certainly the south he would need anyway, the one closest to the enemy leaders, where the main attack had struck. Crossing to the command position, he looked up at the officers. They had retreated from the dangerous walls, where they had been at far too much risk, and now occupied the roof of a building in the compound, a makeshift stairway rising to it formed from boxes and sacks.

Waving at the legionary guarding them, Cervianus began to lope up the temporary steps. The same guard he had encountered twice before did not even bother to check with the tribune this time and simply stepped aside with a nod of recognition.

"Ah, Cervianus," Catilius said wearily at the sight of the approaching capsarius. "Any news?"

"I think we are almost there, sir," he replied as he stepped out onto the roof and turned, taking in the battle with a nervous swallow. He could not believe how *many* of them there were. The walls were being directly assaulted by a rabble of men in animal hides wielding the occasional axe or sword, but mostly armed with rough spears. The trouble they were having approaching the ramparts, and their height relative to the wall top as they neared, spoke eloquently and terribly of just how many of them lay dead beneath the feet of their countrymen, creating a ramp of corpses climbing the wall. The legion had been doing brutal and efficient work. For just a moment, Cervianus wondered if there was actually a possibility they might win this anyway.

Then he saw the ordered rows of gleaming Kushite warriors moving slowly but inexorably forward behind the rabble. The archers had been withdrawn now, and remained at the rear with the impotent cavalry and the chariots that raced this way and that, bellowing out commands and exhorting the army to an ever greater frenzy.

"There are so *many*," he said, almost breathlessly.

"In truth we are holding far better than I had hoped," Catilius noted. "I suspect we lost most of the shirkers, the cowards, the poor officers and the simply unlucky in the south. What we have left are the survivors." He turned an arch look on Cervianus. "And the plotters. What do you have for me, capsarius?"

"I think the queen can be brought to terms, but only by her gods, sir, not by Rome."

"Do you ever speak straight, or is it always in riddles, soldier?"

"Trust me, sir. I need to go out and face the Kandake."

Catilius stared at him, his mouth open in disbelief. Cervianus leapt in before the officer could refuse. "The queen will never bow to Rome, but she will bow to Amun, who is the god of import in this place and a sort of Saturn of their pantheon. There is nowhere else this could work, but I think that here at Napata I can get her to call off the attack. The legion has held and held well. She has to respect that. I hope she respects it enough that she will call off all plans for invasion. But," he took a deep breath, preparing, "I and a small group of men need to make our way through the enemy to meet her face to face, and that means we need to open the gate."

"Are you mad?" snapped one of the other officers, staring at him. "They have been pressing on that gate for half an hour. The moment we take the bar away this compound will fill with the enemy and we'll be fighting our last stand."

"There's no other way, sir. We have to get seven men and a heavy burden out into the enemy. That has to be through a gate."

Catilius' eyes narrowed. "Draco, have a party of men stand by the *east* gate." He turned to Cervianus. "I cannot decide whether you are inspired or insane. Possibly a little of both. But I can spare seven men against the possibility of ending this in any other way than annihilation. The east gate is also under siege, but with much less pressure than the south. In fact, it is the least pressured point on the circuit. It can perhaps be opened briefly to let you out and then forced closed. We will bolster the force there ready and do what we can." He fixed Cervianus with a meaningful look. "I pray this works, for the enemy are beginning to get the measure of the walls, and within an hour all that will be left of us will be carcasses."

Cervianus saluted as he turned to leave.

Gods, but he prayed that too. And to a surprising pantheon of gods.

XI

THE ONE-EYED QUEEN

Shenti shuffled along, gripping the front left underside of the monumental stone barque, grunting and sweating under the impressive weight. Cervianus could understand just how hard their task was, for he'd struggled just to lift the thing out of the rubble pile and move it to flat ground, and there had been six of them on that occasion. Now four men carried the heavy stone boat, with the box containing the patron god of Napata atop it.

But he also knew that his Aegyptian friend revered his burden, and that it was not the effort that had brought the sour expression to the man's features. That was the result of what he considered an unfinished job. The capsarius had fled the command position and the beleaguered walls and hurried back to the work party to find that miraculously the barque, box and idol had been painted up, as far as he could see to their original standard. He'd been so relieved that he picked the god up to examine it and immediately streaked still-wet paint, blurring two colours. The riders had snapped angrily at him, though Shenti had told them that it mattered not. They would repair the smudge when they did the back of the statue.

"To Hades with the back of the statue," Cervianus said,

which immediately had all the Aegyptians present making warding signs against evil.

"It is incomplete," Shenti said, resolutely, "and needs much detail adding."

"It looks good to me, no one will see the back inside the box, and men are dying with every brush stroke. Blow on the bloody thing to help it dry and let's move."

And so they had. The riders waving boards at it to aid the drying process, it had taken only moments for the paint to harden and the apparently incomplete job to be completed. Cervianus, frustrated at the wait and the disapproving looks of the men who wanted to do a more thorough job, had hurried over to Ulyxes and Sentius, dropping his leather bag and shrugging out of his green tunic. The white garb of the cavalry riders was comfortable and airy, and it seemed a shame when he came to cover so much of it with a heavy and already steaming hot chain shirt. Still, he could take no chances with this. As he armed up and tested the grip on the round cavalry shield, he looked over his two friends, both now with sun-darkened skin and looking oddly at home in the Aegyptian garb.

It seemed odd. A few months ago, arriving on that ship at Alexandria, friends had been a thing that happened to other people. Cervianus had been comfortable with his unpopularity, even though it occasionally steered him into trouble. He'd believed himself a natural loner. Then had come Ulyxes, like a ballista ball of dangerous lunacy thundering into his world, and smashed apart the unhappy dynamics of the unit. And despite everything they had been through, Ulyxes remained closer than ever, willing to put himself in mortal danger to support what, Cervianus had to admit, sounded like a suicidally idiotic notion born of superstition and weird dreams. Gods, but a few months ago he'd have slapped himself for even thinking like this.

And Sentius. A man who'd been unknown to him, from another century entirely, but who had survived an attack by the vicious Nile crocodiles and in doing so had brought Cervianus into the temples of Sobek and Haroeris and somehow triggered all of this. Sentius who, thanks to the losses of men and the contraction of command across the legion, was now working alongside him, and who, like Ulyxes, was willing to risk his life on the mere say-so of the capsarius. Two men who would walk into the maw of Cerberus with him in just moments.

And Shenti, too. A native Aegyptian who had saved his life on more than one occasion since they had met in Memphis, that first time he'd owed everything to the decurion, hiding out from tent mates with murder in mind. Shenti, along with his three bravest and most powerfully built men, were prepared to walk out into certain death for him, carrying only a stone statue and unable to defend themselves.

"I hope you're right about the Kushites," Ulyxes murmured, gripping his sword.

"One thing they seem to have in common with the men of Aegyptus is a level of piety we can only dream of. I'm right. I know I am."

"I just hope you're not deluding yourself. It's going to be brutal enough getting through the desert levies. If we manage, and the Kushites decide they don't like the look of us, then it's all over."

Cervianus fought down the quiver of uncertainty that continually threatened to unman him, and nodded resolutely. "It will work. The gods of Aegyptus and Kush are not like ours. They play around with the world. They're among us and influencing us. I find it hard to explain, as it's not something I'd ever considered likely, but it's true. I'm right. I just hope we can get far enough for me to prove it."

The east gate was ready for them. Despite it being only peripherally important, the main focus of the Kandake being the south gate and the walls close by, it was still under pressure. Occasional arrows whipped over the top, though they were mere opportunistic shots, the enemy archers being held far enough back to keep them out of danger. But Cervianus could see how hard the fight was going even here by the struggles of the men on the wall, stabbing out and ducking back from blows constantly, fighting even now to stop the enemy flowing over the walls like ants.

The gate itself was under solid attack, as thuds and crashes from outside confirmed, along with the dust that continually pattered down from the top with each blow. The stones, sacks, barrels and beams that had been blocking it had been removed and stacked to each side, and now the gate was held fast only by its bar and by two single beams wedged against it and braced into dips cut in the ground. It could be opened remarkably swiftly. How quickly it could be closed again under pressure remained to be seen, and the greatest danger in all of this was that the party of seven intrepid idiots might make their way out into the mob while the Kushite army flowed into the compound behind them and destroyed the legion before Cervianus could do anything.

He just had to trust Draco. He had served the implacable centurion through the best and the worst, and the man was a stalwart. He desperately hoped Draco believed enough in him to give this his all.

A hundred or so men were gathered behind the gate, and another half as many atop the wall. As they neared the scene, Cervianus noted strange preparations that had been made. Not the archers – they were a natural choice, for they could pepper the force near the gate and hopefully thin their ranks before the gate opened – but the amphorae leaning against the wall top, covered with sheets. They were an oddity, for sure.

Draco stepped out toward the group, waving his vine staff at their burden. "So this is sort of like the statue of the Magna Mater in Rome?"

Cervianus looked at him blankly. Sometimes the Roman-born officers forgot that the bulk of their legion were Galatians and had only been part of Rome's forces for a few years. Cervianus had never been to Rome, after all.

"Cybele," the man explained. "During the Megalensia, her statue is carried out from the temple and down the hill to the circus for the sacred races."

The capsarius nodded. "I suppose so, sir. And how do the people react in Rome?"

"To be honest, I'm not sure it's approved of. I think the citizens are a little embarrassed about the Greekness of it all."

Cervianus snorted. "Then I think we have to be grateful that the Kushites are a lot more superstitious than the Romans. Pray for a more impressive reaction, sir, or we might be in the shit."

"I can give you the space of about a dozen heartbeats once the gates are open, before they get closed again and you're on your own. We'll clear you a path, but it won't last long."

The capsarius's eyes narrowed, wondering what the man had planned, but Draco just nodded to Ulyxes, wishing his optio luck, and turned to the gate guards. "Be ready. On my first command, arrows. On my second, everything else. Third, the gates are opened, and the moment this lot are through, they're closed and barred again." He turned to Cervianus. "Are *you* ready?"

A prickle of fear ran through him. No. No, he wasn't ready. And now that he was at the point of no return, all the doubts rushed in to assail him. What in the name of all sense and logic was he doing? Dreams were just dreams... the mind playing out desires, fears and a thousand random notions. Why would anyone put their life on the line for a dream? Idiot. But there was still time to abandon all of this. After all, they would be cut down the moment they left the compound. He shuddered. No, this was foolish, and he wouldn't do it.

"We're ready," said Ulyxes at his shoulder, giving him a sidelong warning look that said "don't mess it up for everyone now". Beyond him, Sentius gave a firm nod. Well, at least if Cervianus was going to die, he would most unexpectedly do it among friends.

"We're ready, sir."

The centurion turned back to the gate, raising his whistle to his lips. A single blast, and the dozen archers on the wall top nocked and released four times in quick succession, not bothering with careful aim. All they had to do was hit something in the crowd outside the gate, after all. Barely had the fourth shot left before Draco blew two blasts on his whistle, and groups of men at the parapet grasped the sheets and wrapped them around the amphora handles. Only when the sheets were removed did Cervianus see the ripple of heat emanating from the open tops. The men gripping the handles to each side leaned away from the intense heat.

In moments the men lifted their white-hot burdens, four amphorae spread across the gate top, and tipped them, scattering their contents over the walls. Cervianus winced at the sight. What was pouring from the containers was sand – *heated* sand – a resource they were certainly not short of, and something that Tribune Catilius had likely planned for the rampart's defence all around, but which had initially been diverted here in support of Cervianus' insane plan.

The screams from outside the gate were other-worldly as men were cooked where they stood. Draco's three blasts were hard to hear over the horrible wailing and shrieking of the burning men, but the soldiers inside the gate quickly knocked the bracing beams aside and lifted the locking bar, swinging the gate inward.

Moments earlier, a tide of rabble with spears and ox-hide shields would have poured in the moment the gate gave way. Now, as the party of seven began to run, Cervianus could see that an area perhaps fifteen feet in diameter was filled not with angry warriors, but with agonised men staggering this way and that, clutching melting faces and red-raw, blackening, blistering arms. As a medic the sight was abhorrent, and Cervianus had to swallow the bile as it rose in his throat. As a method of clearing the gate, on the other hand, it had been a work of genius.

They ran. Sentius dropped slightly back to his left, and Ulyxes the same to his right as per their plan. They had to create a front like an arrow. Cervianus was the point, his friends forming the barbs of the head, protecting the shaft constituted of four Aegyptian riders and their heavy load.

The initial charge was simple. The enemy were holding back, howling with rage but unwilling to risk approaching the gate once more. The only figures in their way were more concerned with their own horrific injuries than with the party of men emerging from the gate, and Cervianus and his companions simply stabbed and slashed at them, pushing them out of the way as they surged forward. Despite it all, the capsarius tried to make every blow he landed a killing one, which would be a mercy for these men.

Then, as they crossed that open space of dying men, they were into true danger. The desert tribes that had been levied by the Kandake for her war were the front line, the most expendable, and had been butchered repeatedly by the defenders, but there was still a healthy force of them being driven at the walls by their more important counterparts from Kush itself. Cervianus could see the Kushite warriors behind a narrow screen of the desert rabble and prayed, as Ulyxes had, that he was right about them.

Pushing the last of the burned figures aside, Cervianus paced forward at a deliberate forceful step, the four men with their burden coming up behind him. He could hear now that the cavalry had begun to chant in a strange, sing-song melody in their own language. Some kind of prayer, he presumed, and their four voices together, raised in song, managed to cut across the general din of the battle.

"*Waben su hir snetrn su dhuti, rirtiht nebt nefret wabt. N'Imn-Ra nbus wt-tawy. N'Imn-Ra nub hubusr heps heft renuwr waf nabu staw hapur msuf.*"

Cervianus considered himself an educated man. As well as his own Galatian tongue, he spoke both Latin and Greek like a native, and even a smattering of the Persian language, but if he lived to be a hundred he would never get to grips with the mouth-mangling speech of the Aegyptians. The effect the chanting had on those who understood it, however, was profound.

As Cervianus threw himself at the wall of desert tribesmen, shield out to take their blows and sword back for the first stab, he could almost feel the shock and reverence from the bulk of the army beyond, spreading out in waves like the ripples from a rock thrown into a pond. He had been right, and in that moment, he knew it. The native Kushites were almost spellbound by the god being praised as it bobbed toward them.

Unfortunately, the desert levies had no idea what this strange procession was about, praying to their own obscure gods and with no grasp of the Aegyptian tongue. Unaware of the strange reaction of their masters behind them, the levies knew only that enemies were among them, friends of those who had thrown the burning sand from the gate top. They pressed at Cervianus, howling their fury, and he felt blows raining against his shield. In moments, Sentius was there to his left, Ulyxes to his right, both with shields up, both with teeth bared and swords ready. Ulyxes, somehow, was already spattered with fresh blood and his sword looked as though it had been dipped in a vat of the stuff.

Together the three men hacked and stabbed at the poorly armoured desert tribesmen, heedless of the danger. Cervianus felt white-hot pain as a spear tore away flesh from his shoulder and then, less than a heartbeat later, another blow carved a chunk from his right calf, making him totter and almost fall for a moment. Clenching his teeth against the pain and willing himself to stay up, he stabbed the man before him again and heaved with the shield. The three men were now not so much carving a path as barging one with their shields, stabbing out as the opportunity arose.

Another blow landed, and Cervianus felt certain, with grim misery, that he had just lost half an ear. The side of his head burned with agony and tears rose in his eyes. A howl of pain came from his left and with horror he turned to see Sentius staggering back, a sword lodged in his side, blood pouring from both it and half a dozen other brutal wounds. The legionary gave him a sad smile, blood coming from his lips in gobbets.

"I paid Sobek... in the end," he said, his voice little more than a whisper as a spear slammed into him and another sword knocked aside his shield. Somehow, the cavalry must have reorganised, with three men now shouldering their great burden, for even as Sentius fell away Shenti was there, pulling the shield from his dead arm, taking his place and throwing himself against the mob before them, helping drive them back.

Cervianus stabbed out at another man, grief and agony together threatening to overwhelm him. He had lost sight of Sentius, but still he had a true friend to either side, the three of them heaving and forcing a path forward.

Relief came unexpectedly. Suddenly, the weight pressing back at their advance melted away, and the capsarius risked looking over his shield, something he'd not done since he'd had his ear torn with a spear point. The Kushite regulars had stabbed out and killed their own levied allies from the rear, pushing them out of the way, aiding the passage of the god and his party. As the last blow fell away, Cervianus lowered his shield, sword held exhaustedly down by his side. The Kushite warriors had parted to form a wide corridor through their ranks.

Cervianus felt the most incredible sense of relief at the sight, and paused for breath. Glancing across, he saw Shenti and

Ulyxes bend and collect the ravaged body of Sentius from the dirt. Ulyxes shouldered the corpse like a sack of grain and the two men rejoined the capsarius.

"Seven men," Ulyxes breathed. "You said it was important. And I don't want him left on the battlefield for the scavengers, anyway."

Cervianus nodded and, exhausted, staggered forward, leading the small group into the unknown.

The sheer audacity, and perhaps the idiocy, of what they were doing became more and more apparent to the capsarius as they stepped out from the wide passage between the ranks of the Kushite infantry. The units of archers were not visible, stationed as they were around the rear, but to each side, though a line of implacable and dangerous-looking chariots sat facing them in brightly coloured martial glory, and horsemen in white, who looked extremely reminiscent of Shenti's cavalry, sat in ordered groups around the army's rear, watching them intently.

Silence reigned, with just the impatient snorts, stamps and breaths of horses, the creak of the wood and leather from the war chariots, and the steady crunch of six men's boots on gritty sand. Cervianus found himself listening intently to the silence for some time before he realised what was truly odd about it. It was absolute. The silence covered all of Napata. The battle had stopped.

Perhaps it was more realistic to say that the battle had *paused*. The Kushite army had been so stunned by the appearance of the statue of the great god Amun, carried by devout men who waded into an army without blinking, that they had simply halted their forward momentum, the walls of the compound temporarily forgotten as the army, to a man, turned to watch this strange procession. Between them and the walls, the various desert levies who had no reverence for these gods in particular had also paused, aware that the main force behind them had stopped, and fascinated by what was happening.

And on the walls, the Romans stood pensive, ready to drop behind shields and battlements at a moment's notice and resume their fight to the end, yet watching the peculiar event with amazement. Here and there along the ramparts one of the tribesmen would occasionally take advantage of the stillness and leap at a defending Roman, but each time they were easily put back down, and the small scuffles were distant enough that any sounds of combat from them were simply lost in the huge, all-encompassing silence.

Before the small group, two chariots sat ahead of the others. The Kandake Amanirenas stood tall and dangerously impressive, her twin swords at her side, that one empty eye socket glowering, while her good eye seemed to stare somehow deep into the soul. Aboard the next chariot General Kalabsha stood, frowning. Cervianus quickly glanced at those around him. Ulyxes kept pace with him, Sentius' body draped over his shoulder. Shenti had not yet drawn his sword, but matched his pace on the other side. The three remaining white-garbed riders huffed with effort as they trudged along behind, bearing the sacred burden with silent, reverent fortitude. It was only now that the fighting had ended and he had a chance to look at his friends that he could see exactly how they had fared in their crazed advance and how incredible it was that they had made it through this far. Shenti was wounded in half a dozen places, though none of them were apparently debilitating, and each of his three men bore red lines and blotches here and there among their white cotton uniforms.

Each of them appeared confident, resolute, which was more than Cervianus now felt, uncertainty rising with every step that brought him closer to the dreaded warrior queen of Kush and the conclusion of a plan he'd not entirely finalised in his mind. He knew what needed to happen, but even in his own head he'd not yet found the words.

How had he come to this?

Months of misery and pain, driven by strange dreams and the disastrous decisions of others. From a statue buried in undergrowth to a crocodile attack miraculously survived to a warning from a temple to this great birthplace of Amun, all guided by dreams of gods.

Closing his eyes, he felt himself slipping back into the memory of that most recent dream, and unexpectedly resolution suddenly flooded through him. His feet crunched through gritty sand as the gods' had in the dream. They had crossed a dusty, gravelly landscape covered in bodies of natives as the gods had in the dream. Cervianus was at the centre. With a strange smile, he opened his eyes once more. To his left he could just see Ulyxes, Sentius and a white-clad cavalryman – Amun carrying Haroeris, with ram-headed Khnum following on. To his right, as he spun to look, were Shenti and two of his men – Sobek, with Sekhmet and Wepwawet at the rear under that heavy barque. And when he turned to face the chariots once more, he was calm and prepared, for he was Thoth, arbiter of the gods.

The Kandake's face was unreadable, blank. Kalabsha's expression was one of concern. Of confusion, even, particularly when his eyes fell upon Cervianus.

"Who are you to bear sacred Amun from his mountain?"

the Kandake growled in Greek. "For all your companions, you are not of the two lands."

"I am here to bring an end to this," Cervianus replied, coming to a halt not far from the chariots. "The gods, who speak in dreams and who walk this land even now among us, revile this war." He raised his voice for as many as possible nearby to hear. "The Kandake drives her people from the south, and they kill the men of Kemet. The tribune from Rome drives his people south, and they kill the men of Kush. In all of this, neither the tribune nor the Kandake have achieved anything and nobody wins, but whatever those leaders do, the gods lose, for whichever force is ascendant it is still the gods' people who die."

"You are a Roman. You know nothing of our gods."

Cervianus gave her a smile. "I am a *Galatian*, of the blood of ancient Gaul, and the gods of Rome are as new to me as the gods of Kush, but that does not mean I know nothing of them. In fact, I know them well. Over these recent months better even than I would wish to."

He held his arms out to the side, gesturing to his companions. "Mighty Sobek has travelled with us on our great journey. He marked this man," a gesture to the draped body of Sentius, "and spared him long enough to bring him here so that his sword arm could carve a path to you. Wise Haroeris set me upon my path at the temple of Ambo with prophetic words. Thoth himself pointed the way from the very start near the end of the Nile, when he found this man in the wilds." Pointing now at Ulyxes. "Wepwawet has come to open the way, and it is our choice whether we step through. Khnum has sustained us with the water of the river even when the desert threatened to finish us, and great Sekhmet has given us the fortitude to stand through all disasters and battles to reach this day."

He stepped aside to give centre stage to the great stone barque. "And Amun-Ra has brought us here, now, at this very place, to end the war that kills only his people."

It was a powerful argument, and now that he heard the echoes of his words fading, he could almost feel the shock throughout the Kushite army. To hear that the gods themselves had taken a hand in matters and were demanding an end changed everything. Cervianus was surprised, and gratified too, to hear a few weapons dropped to the dusty ground. Some of the nearer enemy warriors had sunk to their knees now in the presence of the idol of Amun. The capsarius focused on the two people who mattered most.

The Kandake was still unreadable. Her fingertips danced upon the hilts of her swords, though, and she had made no hint of obeisance to the god. Kalabsha, on the other hand, looked thoroughly unhappy. He had gone slightly pale, and his eyes were wild.

"Rome had the audacity to invade our lands and ravage our holy places," the Kandake said finally. "The gods will allow me my revenge, for *my* revenge is *their* revenge. Rome will be driven back to the sea she has the temerity to call her own."

"Then all along the course of the great river, the gods will weep, as the land for a thousand miles will be strewn with the bodies of their people. And your revenge will be short and bitter, for it will simply engender the further vengeance of Rome, and instead of one legion foolishly transgressing, ten legions will come next, and the name of Kush itself will become naught but a whisper on the wind for the rest of time. Is that what you wish for your descendants? The gods demand that the status quo return: the two lands as they were before, and none of their people suffering. This is the time to end it, and it is the *only* time. This opportunity will never come again, just eternal war."

Cervianus felt eyes burning into him and switched his attention to Kalabsha, who was wide-eyed now. "Yes, you know me, general."

The Kushite commander turned on his chariot platform, addressing his queen. "Great Kandake, this man is favoured by the gods. To dismiss him is to dismiss Amun himself."

"Amun no longer controls the kings and queens of Kush," the Kandake spat. "You know our history, Kalabsha."

"But he did, my queen, and not so long ago. This is his mountain. His sacred place. And this man is *his* man. I realise it now, but you must heed, my queen, the *Tale of the Doomed Prince*, who was fated to die in three ways. This prince before you walked into the deep desert where even the army of great Cambyses was lost entire, and he survived because Amun protects him. With a pitiful force he held Napata against my army, and when his leaders were slain, he survived because Amun protects him. And when we marched south to combine the armies, this man and all his companions were pegged to the temple walls for the sun and the predators to finish, and yet here he stands, having walked through your army to speak to you, *because Amun protects him*. This is the doomed prince and a chosen man of Amun. His words have power."

The general bowed his head at the small party carrying the barque, and the gesture seemed to spread out from him across the army. In a matter of heartbeats half the Kushites sank to one knee in a wave. Cervianus felt his skin prickle. This was right. This was fate. This was what was supposed to happen.

He drew himself up to his full height, one matched on this field only by the impressive Kandake herself, and cleared his throat.

"The army of Rome, the Twenty Second Deiotaran legion and its support, will leave Napata today. It will travel along the river, taking only what supplies it needs, and will return without loot or slaves to Aegyptus, which is called Kemet. The army will pass the second cataract and make for Syene, and there border garrisons will be established and the war will end. The army of Kush will not harry them on this journey, nor attempt to stop them. Your army, Kandake Amanirenas, will not pass the second cataract, and from this time the border will stand. Neither people will cross it in war henceforward. This is the will of Amun and of all the gods. Cross them at your peril."

He turned and nodded to the rest of his friends.

"No," snapped the Kandake behind him. "Your army will not leave Napata."

Cervianus took a deep breath and ignored her. He heard her vault from the chariot, heard her footsteps crunching across the gravelly ground, and then heard a second set of boots. He turned slowly, calmly, to see General Kalabsha standing between him and the queen.

"You must not, my queen."

That one good eye peered past the general and bored into Cervianus, who simply nodded. "Listen to your general, Kandake Amanirenas. He is thinking of your people."

With that he spun once more and began to walk back through that corridor between the Kushite masses, Ulyxes and Shenti at his shoulders, the three riders struggling to turn that great weight but managing to bear it back toward the compound, this time leading the way. Cervianus could hear behind him the argument between the queen and her general.

The words were in their native tongue, but the tones were unmistakable. She was defiant, her general resolved.

As they walked slowly away, Ulyxes leaned a little closer. "Do you think she will submit?"

Cervianus looked about them and gestured with a sweeping arm to the forces of Kush who were now, to a man, kneeling before the god. "I think the time of the queen having dominance over Amun is over. She is a terrifying woman, but this is a god, and I do not think this army will follow her to war any longer."

Even the desert levies who had no connection to these gods were silent and staring, watching the procession and aware now of its importance. The way was clear right back to the gate in the compound wall, and the small party made their way between the enemy forces and across ground strewn with burned corpses. They had met the army of Kush with blades and with the will of gods and it looked as though they had survived.

The legion's commanders were now at the gate. Cervianus could see the Twenty Second's eagle and the various standards beside a small knot of men in plumed helmets on the wall top above it. As they approached, the gates swung inward and the six men tramped through. Behind them, the guards shut and barred the gate once more. Just inside, Draco stood, arms folded, shaking his head. "Just when I think you can't do anything less soldierly, you do something like this."

Cervianus gave the centurion a weird smile. Two legionaries carefully took Sentius from Ulyxes' shoulder, and Shenti gave his men instructions to return their sacred burden to the temple where it traditionally resided. Turning, accompanied by Ulyxes and Shenti and with Draco following on, the capsarius climbed to the wall top and approached the knot of officers.

Tribune Catilius had one eyebrow raised quizzically. "Looked like an interesting little chat you had with our enemy. Couldn't hear a word of it from here, of course, but I suppose it's too much to hope that you accepted their surrender?"

Ulyxes snorted at Cervianus' shoulder, earning narrow-eyed warning looks from several officers. As if the heavyset optio would care, Cervianus smiled. He rolled his shoulders. "I offered terms, tribune."

Catilius' eyebrow lowered again now, along with the other, into a frown. "Employing your immense authority as a century's combat medic, I presume?"

Cervianus nodded. "Something like that, sir. I informed them that we will return to Syene along the river and garrison the border as before, and demanded of them that they neither interfere with our withdrawal nor cross the border after us."

The tribune chuckled. "And the warrior queen obeyed you?"

"General Kalabsha certainly seems to be in favour. The Kandake was less accepting, sir, but look at the enemy."

Catilius did so, turning to the sea of Kushites and their allies outside the walls. "They certainly do not look prepared to recommence the assault."

"They believe the gods have told them to halt. I think that whatever the Kandake herself wishes, she will have immense trouble persuading her army and its senior general to join her. It is my hope – my belief, even – that this is the end of the war. If I might suggest, sir, maintaining a warlike posture on the walls might push them where we do not want to push. The legion should be making ready to march north. We can take with us what we have recovered here, but should take no loot, nor slaves."

Catilius chewed on his lip. "It is a great gamble stepping down from the wall, soldier. If we abandon the defences and the enemy have decided that they can still win here, we'll be overrun in moments."

"Sir, if it comes to a fight we've lost anyway. Thus far we've only fought their rabble. The rest of their army are uncommitted. We need to follow the plan, sir."

The tribune wavered for a moment, then gestured to the cornicen nearby and the gathered officers. "Sound the call to stand down. Muster the men in the open. I want all our supplies, the recovered booty and everything we need for the return journey gathered and ready to move within half an hour."

As the blast went up from the cornu, Catilius glanced sidelong at Cervianus. "Pray to whichever gods will listen that you're right, man." He seemed for the first time to notice the leather bag at Cervianus' hip. "And you'd best get down there and help the medical section get the wounded ready to move, since you're a capsarius."

The legion left Napata early in the afternoon with no fanfare or pomp, but still proud and with heads held high rather than slinking away like a defeated foe. The Kushite army had not so much withdrawn as pulled back from the walls, and sat between the compound and the river, glowering at the Romans as they emerged. There had been an initial chill of nerves through every soldier present as they deserted the walls and brought down the scorpions, each man knowing full well that at a single command the forces of the Kandake could quite easily have rushed forward and secured the ramparts for themselves.

They did not. Neither, though, did they leave. On the few occasions during the preparations for departure when Cervianus found himself in a position to look out at the enemy force, they were drawn up as though ready for a fresh battle, and the two leaders, the warrior queen Amanirenas and her general Kalabsha, remained deep in conversation, visible at the rear of the silent, immobile force in adjacent chariots.

No one could say with certainty what was going on among the Kushite leadership, but Cervianus was privately convinced that the Kandake continued to harbour dreams of conquest and the desire to crush the legion. Kalabsha, on the other hand, had been quite convinced of the necessity to end things and not anger the gods, and the vast majority of the army supported him. Briefly, the capsarius wondered whether there might be a coup in the offing – Kalabsha would make an excellent king, after all. But in the end he decided that, despite current events, the queen's rule was still absolute.

The Roman column exited the west gate and marched in detail along the right bank of the Nile, heading in a north-westerly direction. Shenti and the other auxiliary cavalry units created a screen between the legion and the enemy force which sat watching from a distance.

Fears over the long-term intent of the Kushites and their bloodthirsty queen continued to grow as the legion moved further and further away from Napata and the enemy force began to follow in their wake. Still in a battle formation, the Kushite army set off in pursuit of the departing Romans, with what appeared to be a small garrison peeling off from them and moving into the compound that had just been deserted to take control. The Kandake was consolidating her territory once more as Rome pulled back. Would that be as far as she went?

As they marched, with the cavalry screen protecting their rear and the animals there carrying supplies, the tribune and his senior officers issued preparatory commands that filtered through the entire column in readiness for any belligerent move by the army trailing them along the riverbank. The Kushite force matched their pace, but kept back at a secure distance, and though the Roman force continued to stay alert, nothing seemed to be forthcoming.

When they reached the end of the day's march, a full temporary camp was constructed with ditch and rampart and fence of stakes, for fear that the Kandake simply meant to catch them off their guard. Cervianus, working with the medical section and dealing with the many walking wounded, confided in Ulyxes his belief that the plans of the following army were not yet set, and that they depended upon whether the Kandake could convince her general and the army that conquest was still an option.

The stocky optio, in his usual irritating fashion, merely rolled his eyes and suggested that he would quite like an opportunity to kick the smugness out of the warrior queen of Kush.

Cervianus' major worry was not that the Kushites would suddenly turn on them as they retreated down the Nile, for as long as nothing had seriously changed, the enemy would be unlikely to alter their plans. The queen was apparently simply escorting Rome from her lands, and almost certainly setting garrisons in any strongpoint they passed.

The main issue, as far as he could see, was what would

happen when they passed the second cataract and entered Aegyptus. That would be the critical point. At the moment they were still the interloper in lands belonging to Kush, and there was nothing to stop that army moving about with impunity. When the massive Kushite force reached the border and the site of that dreadful fight at Buhen, on the other hand, would the queen be able to convince her army that they need not stop there? The sight of the legion retreating deep into its own territory might give her sufficient ammunition to persuade the army to invade regardless. And if the Kushites crossed the border and were not immediately assailed by vengeful gods, perhaps that would be enough to convince her army and its general that she was right.

The journey was nerve-wracking, and Cervianus could feel the tension in everyone as they marched north, coming ever closer to that all-important border at the cataract. On the twentieth day out of Napata the waters of the Nile began to change again, as they had eight days earlier on passing the third cataract, moving from a deep and wide flow to shallow and white waters. The second cataract with its all-important border was near, and the Kushite army remained less than half a mile behind the legion.

As if to presage disaster, as they neared the border, which lay in some nebulous position between the cataract and the nearby fortress of Buhen, the form of the trailing army began to change. That last morning as they broke camp and moved off, the difference in the Kushite forces was clear. For the bulk of the journey the enemy commanders had led in their chariots, with the rest of the vehicles in a group behind them and then their infantry, the cavalry scouting out to the sides and bringing up the rear. Now, the chariots were moving in lines, as though preparing for a charge, and the enemy horse, split into two wings, moved close to the front on both flanks, the infantry lost to sight behind them.

It escaped no one with an ounce of military sense that the new formation would be perfect if the commander suddenly decided to pounce. The cavalry could plunge ahead on the wings and effectively box in the much smaller Roman force while the chariots engaged them from the rear like a deadly tidal wave. Both those units would be fast, and the shock attack would seriously damage the column before the tribune could even deploy ready to face them.

Tension continued to build.

Passing the cataract, the enemy persisted in shadowing them, and the legion marched now in tense silence, each man half expecting to be chased down by charging chariots at any moment. That the Kushites did not pause even for a moment at the cataract was a worrying sign. If the legion passed Buhen, which would be in sight shortly and would be behind them by noon, and the enemy did not stop there, then they were in breach of the deal Cervianus had struck at Napata. If they did not stop at Buhen, then the Kandake intended to carry out her planned conquest after all in spite of her gods.

Cervianus chewed on the inside of his cheek in worry as they marched.

Buhen first appeared as a small block of golden brown stone by the river ahead. Cervianus marched along with the men of his century, tense and expectant. Even the irrepressible Ulyxes, who had marched along at the rear of the century with his staff of office and had taken every opportunity to smack the back of Cervianus' legs and grin wickedly, had stopped such tomfoolery and now merely walked in dour silence.

The message came back down the column from the tribune, passed to Draco, who then filtered it through the rest of the centurions. In the face of potential aggression from the following Kushites, plans had altered. The legion would quarter for the rest of the day at Buhen. At the next signal, the entire column would shift to the difficult, but ground-consuming pace-and-a-half, and if a further signal was given then it would be double pace, making for the heavy fortress. The enemy might outnumber them significantly, but the powerful fortifications of Buhen would make a solid difference to their chances.

As that small brown block grew with proximity, and gradually resolved into the fortress they remembered with a shiver, so the call went out and the legion picked up the pace to the awkward step-and-a-half. A rumble arose immediately to the rear and nervous backward glances revealed that the Kushite chariots and horses had also picked up their pace. More, they were now moving faster than the legion. Unless things changed, they would overtake the Roman force before they reached Buhen and could potentially cut them down in the open.

In response, Tribune Catilius swiftly put out his second call and the Roman force dropped into the more comfortable, yet more tiring, double pace. Cervianus took a brief opportunity to look back as they hot-footed it toward the dubious safety of the great fortress. The enemy had not changed pace at the same time as the legion, though even without a fresh burst of speed the enemy were still already moving at roughly the same pace as the Roman column, perhaps even faster. They may not have the marching discipline of the legions, but they were more familiar with the terrain.

He looked ahead again. The heavy bulk of Buhen was

tantalisingly close, yet now he realised with only the most elementary calculation that they were not going to make it inside the gates before the Kandake was upon them. This realisation had clearly also surfaced among the commanders, for the next call that rang out but a moment later was for a charge. Every man now put everything he had into a run, desperate to make the walls of Buhen. It was a futile gesture.

Behind them, he heard calls from native instruments, and the rumble and thunder of wheels and hooves increased twofold. They would never make it in time to close the gates on the Kushites. With dismay, he realised that the auxiliary cavalry were no longer moving alongside them and knew that Shenti and the others had dropped back, prepared to sacrifice themselves against the Kushite charge in order to allow the rest to reach Buhen.

No. He turned his sad gaze away from the empty land beside them. *Shenti.*

His eyes fell upon the great mud-brick fortress ahead, their sole hope for salvation, and he saw the change at the same moment as the commanders at the head of the desperate, charging force. The walls of Buhen were not empty as they had expected, but were lined with men, gleaming spear tips and helmets flashing in the afternoon sunlight. But it was not the gleaming metal that truly drew his attention, for those could mean anything, including that somehow the Kushites had managed to send a force around ahead of them. There was something else. Amid the glinting spear points and helmets, he could see the telltale shapes of legionary standards and vexilla, and in addition to steel and bronze, he could see a profusion of madder-dyed red.

Buhen was garrisoned by Rome.

Without the need for a call the entire legion slowed, eyes wide at the unexpected but most welcome sight. Cervianus couldn't estimate quite how many men there were watching them from the walls but it had to be a legion at the least, either the Third Cyrenaica or the Twelfth Fulminata, both of which would probably be at full complement by now. Even as the column reeled, taking in the astounding sight awaiting them, the gates of Buhen opened and auxiliary cavalry poured out into the dust, gathering in large groups. At a call from an unseen cornu, there was a chorus of clicks and the strains of both wood and torsion cable so numerous that it could be heard all across the sands. Ballistae and scorpions by the dozen were primed and ready to release along the walls.

Cervianus marvelled. Mere moments ago, they had been racing for their lives, hopelessly outnumbered and endangered by the Kushites on their tail. Now Rome had the edge in firepower, in manpower and even in terrain with the heavy fortress in their hands. An attack by the Kushites now would be futile and costly and would only result in them limping south in defeat.

As the Twenty Second, sweating with exertion and almost crying with relief, approached the gate they had fought so hard to open a few months earlier, Cervianus was surprised to see the figures gathered on the horses inside the fortress gateway. Gaius Petronius, governor of Aegyptus, sat beside the senior tribune of the Twelfth Legion, a man Cervianus had last seen in a house in Nicopolis sporting a black eye. At that time he'd not have cared if he never saw the Twelfth or their commander again. Now, oh how things had changed. And as the prefect and the tribune watched the tired and injured ranks of the Twenty Second pour through those gates, there was no trace of the earlier spite about the Twelfth's commander, just respect and sympathy, especially at the sight of the standards and flags of lost units that they had reclaimed in Napata.

As the legions assembled, the forces of the warrior queen pulled up some distance from the walls, no longer lined up for battle, but with the leaders' chariots out front once more. A stance for negotiation.

Petronius smiled at the officer by his side and, as Tribune Catilius saluted and reported in as acting commander of the Twenty Second, the prefect of Aegyptus straightened in his saddle. "You can tell me everything shortly, and I shall need a full debrief. The last I know from the reports of the Twelfth and Third was that Vitalis marched you off on some fool campaign deep into enemy territory. First, though, let's go and deliver our unconditional offer of terms to the queen of Kush."

Twelve days after the settling of the border at Buhen and the sullen withdrawal of the Kandake to her own lands, the battered cohorts of the Twenty Second settled in for the night at Ambo, little more than a quarter of the way back home yet. Prefect Petronius was travelling with them, while the tribune of the Twelfth had been left at Syene to organise the garrisoning and fortification of Upper Aegyptus against any future belligerence on behalf of Kush.

Cervianus seemed to have retained his excused-duty status, no longer required to dig ditches and latrines or take guard duty, which no longer seemed to irritate the men of his century. At a loss, he had reported often to the legion's medicus, upon each occasion being told tersely by Albinus that he did not need the help of a combat medic and that Cervianus' place was with his unit. And so, at Ambo, he had milled around bored as the men settled the camp, until his eyes had fallen upon that great temple on the hill above the water and he'd known then what he needed to do.

Approaching the gate of their temporary camp, he prepared for an argument with the guard. He had the correct watchword, of course, but doubted he'd be released from camp without written orders. Such was the esteem he was apparently currently held in, however, that the guard simply saluted and let him past on the strength of the password alone.

With aching legs, but with a true sense of peace in his heart for the first time in many months, he climbed the sloping road to the temple. Passing beneath the great arch, he could see the sun now only as a low, golden half-disc above the western horizon, and a temple attendant moving silently around the sacred compound lighting lamps. The capsarius was not entirely sure whether the temple was supposed to be open to visitors at this time, but since the gate was open and the attendant did not seem surprised, he simply walked on. Entering the shadowed hypostyle hall, he chewed on his lip. Sobek and Haroeris shared this temple, yet each had his own inner hall. Casting his mind back, he recalled heading into the right side the last time he was here.

On that occasion he had made his offering to Sobek in the form of the crocodile-tooth amulet he had brought all the way from Nicopolis. With it, he had bought the favour of the crocodile god, who had seen them through everything, and given him Sentius until the very end. But it was at this place that Haroeris had also first spoken to him, through a priest, where he had learned the core of what had needed to be done. Make Syene your end.

Passing through the left-hand doorway, he made his way into the dark chamber at the heart of the temple. The falcon-headed god watched him wisely from his position of honour at the centre of the room, and Cervianus felt a shiver of the unnatural run through him. Gone was his resistance to what he had once seen as superstition. In its place was... understanding. It did not have to be either science or the gods. They were not mutually exclusive. He, like the animal-headed Haroeris before him, was something of both, now.

He bowed his head.

"In Rome, when a man returns from somewhere perilous, it is the habit to raise an altar to the god responsible in thanks. I understand that is not the way here. I have little to give, but what I have, I give in thanks to you, Great Haroeris, patron of my profession, who guided me through peril to unexpected success in Kush. All is as it should be once more. The status quo has returned."

He reached into his tunic and drew out the leather thong inside. Untying it, he slid Ulyxes' lucky coin from the cord and dropped it into his hand, gripping it tight.

"This saved my life in Napata. I have only recently come to see the value of good fortune. May this small offering be found worthy."

With a sigh, he dropped the coin onto the offering plate.

The war was truly over.

EPILOGUE

Cervianus reached the bluff above the water and dropped to the rough sandy rock with relief, laying his bag carefully to one side. The waters of the sea looked glassy and dark as night truly fell, and he squinted out to the north as if he could perhaps see the coast of Asia, which harboured his native Galatia so far away.

Behind him, the sounds of masonry and carpentry were dying away to nothing as work on the new legionary fortress of Nicopolis once more ended for the day. Excused duty and still viewed with suspicion by medicus Albinus, Cervianus had again been devoid of anything to do since they'd returned. Tomorrow he had leave to visit the city, and would spend time wandering Alexandria and finally drinking in its ancient sights. Indeed, he could see the city perhaps four miles along the coast, the great Pharos lighthouse shining out across the black waters, the harbour's arms reaching out to embrace the world. Perhaps tomorrow he might climb it and look back along the coast at the new, growing Nicopolis.

Yet somehow the edge had gone from his initial need to explore and examine this ancient world. After all, few tourists could possibly see ancient Aegyptus at the level he had now experienced it. There had been a brief argument yesterday with Albinus about setting up an altar and a statue to Haroeris in the new hospital complex that would be part of the fortress. Albinus was set against it, clinging solely to Asklepios, but the capsarius suspected that Tribune Catilius, still currently commanding the Twenty Second, might back him. It seemed only right and fitting after all.

He sighed and sagged onto the warm rock, fishing out the bag of dates he'd purchased that evening from one of the endless sea of street hawkers trying to fleece the legions of their wages.

That dreadful time in the south seemed so distant now, almost like a dream he couldn't quite shake. It appeared certain that Aegyptus had seen its last invasion from Kush, and if the latest rumours to come out of the south were true, then somehow the tribune of the Twelfth, in reorganising the defences, had retained the services of a certain tribe of black-clad nomads in maintaining the border. That brought a smile to his lips, imagining how the Kandake would feel about her former allies now being lined up ready to keep her out.

It was over. Vitalis had been posthumously honoured for leading a valiant campaign deep into enemy territory. His family were rich and with hooks into many sectors of high society in Rome, and to leak out the truth of his foolishness and rashness would only cause political troubles, so his true involvement had been glossed over. Indeed, Prefect Petronius had taken on the greater responsibility for the disaster, carefully couching it in terms that painted it in the best possible light in his missives to Rome. What had been a near catastrophe on the scale of Arabia had apparently been a heroic chastisement of the Kushite queen, resulting in a strong victory and favourable peace terms being forced upon the warrior queen. The recovery of the standards and much loot from Syene, including two of the three bronze statues of the Princeps Octavian Augustus, had been seen as a resounding success, after all.

Had it not been for the loss of good men like Nasica and Sentius, Cervianus might even have considered it all worthwhile in the end. At least plenty of worthy men *had* survived. Draco had had his field commission as primus pilus of the legion confirmed and now strutted around Nicopolis like a gravelly and bad-tempered peacock, picking at any failings he could find, no matter what legion was responsible.

And Shenti had been raised to the command of an entire cavalry ala and assigned to somewhere on the far side of the delta, roving protection against potential nomadic raiders from the peninsular mountains, or even Arabia, or the Nabataeans beyond. The man had smiled at Cervianus as they'd prepared to depart and noted that he was owed quite a number of days' leave, and would make sure to spend it in Alexandria so that he could show his friends more of the sights of the ancient city than the average visitor would normally become aware of by wandering around.

The capsarius almost leapt out of his skin as a hand clapped on his shoulder, and he was still swearing under his breath, pulse racing, as Ulyxes sank to the gritty stone next to him. Cervianus' eyes narrowed as they fell upon the staff of office that the optio laid across his knees. The bronze knob on the top was freshly polished, but he could see the telltale signs of drying blood around the join where it met the ash staff.

"Optios aren't supposed to go around beating men senseless," he muttered.

"Just a friendly disagreement with a prick from the Twelfth who refused to show respect appropriate to the rank. He's fine. Might have a banging headache tomorrow, though."

"Gods, but you never change, do you?"

"That's what makes me a lovable character," Ulyxes grinned. "Anyway, we're golden at the moment. Recovering the standards and loot from Napata bought us a cartload of goodwill. I reckon I could pound a centurion from the Twelfth into the ground, walk away with his purse and all I'd get would be a light telling-off."

"Try not to."

Ulyxes laughed. "It's over, mate. It was a shit-bath of a few months, but it's done, and we've come up smelling of rose petals. It's been good for us."

"Speak for yourself. Nothing's changed for me."

It wasn't true. *Everything* had changed for Cervianus, but he wasn't about to admit as much in the face of his friend's irritating optimism. *Having* a friend was a change, for a start...

"I reckon you could apply to be instated as a legion medicus now. You know more than most surgeons, and Albinus must be due for retirement soon. The old coot had already lost his hair when Vulcan was a boy."

"That's not how it works. I'm a soldier, a medicus isn't."

"*Cartloads* of goodwill," Ulyxes said again. "You could probably be a senator now if you pushed for it hard enough."

"I don't want to be a senator. Or a medicus."

"Just miserable?"

Cervianus turned a sour look on the optio. "What, rise in the ranks and miss all the fun of fighting homicidal tribesmen and being repeatedly smacked in the calves on the march by you?"

Ulyxes laughed again. "Just a thought."

The two men lapsed into silence, looking out across the inky water in the sultry night air. Cervianus opened his mouth to say something pithy that suddenly occurred to him, but was interrupted by someone calling his name. Both men turned to see a breathless legionary staggering their way. They waited long enough for the man to heave in a healthy supply of air before addressing him.

"What's up?" Cervianus asked as the two men clambered to their feet, grabbing staff and leather satchel.

"Tribune's calling for you. There's been an accident."

"What sort of accident," the capsarius sighed.

"With any luck a column fell on Draco." Ulyxes grinned maliciously. "Dead man's shoes is the best promotion. This time tomorrow I could be primus pilus."

"Primus pillock is about the best you can hope for," glowered Cervianus, patting his medical bag for reassurance. "Nothing ever changes here. Come on, let's go and dress a wound or two. And try not to hit anyone with your stick on the way."

Ulyxes simply laughed, and smacked him on the back of the calves.

AUTHOR'S NOTE

A few times in my life I have found myself in the desert. In Morocco, I encountered a man with a snake and a pipe, which I had always thought to be the stuff of Hollywood, but it turns out actually exists. I also met camels and foods that would turn a vegetarian green. In Egypt, I rode a camel, which is essentially a mobile hairy sack of coat hangers with no suspension system, or so it feels when you sit on one. In Israel and in Jordan, I watched brown rock and dust go past for seemingly endless miles and met wizened men with names like Abdullah or Moshe, who would very shrewdly sell me a bottle of pre-owned water, that could well carry dysentery, for the price of a Volkswagen Polo because I knew I was close to my thirst limit. This is the desert.

In Egypt of old, the Nile was all. Civilisation relied upon the river. It became central to life in the land. Other than the river, the only habitable parts of Egypt were the scattered oases. In *Bellatrix*, book two of the Legion XXII series, our heroes depart from the river to begin a dangerous crossing of open desert, a journey of some two hundred miles as the crow – or the vulture – flies. And such a crossing is not a thing to be undertaken lightly. Some of you will be old enough to remember the movie *Ice Cold in Alex*, where John Mills is pitted against a war in the desert and finally crawls into a bar in Alexandria for a cold beer. Van der Pohl, at the end of the movie, announces that their war was not against their human enemies but against the desert itself. And that is truly where the start of this book comes from. Because the desert can kill at least as easily as a war. The Persian King Cambyses II lost (according to Herodotus) an army of fifty thousand in the Egyptian desert east of the Siwa Oasis in a sandstorm. On the way to Napata, Cervianus and his friends encounter a series of problems and disasters that might seem outlandish, but are all very real and regular dangers in such a crossing.

Heatstroke and sunstroke begin to take their toll, and then snakes, which are an endemic pest in the region. Burning by day, freezing by night, scorpion stings, sandstorms and more, Cervianus gets to practise his craft again and again on the journey. This is something of an eye-opening journey for Cervianus, yet, despite so many troubles, eventually our heroes reach Napata. Indeed, the journey of Cervianus and his friends across the desert is my take on a line from Strabo that references the Roman advance: "*after passing through the sand-dunes, where the army of Cambyses was overwhelmed when a wind-storm struck them.*"

The world of the Kushites is still a relatively unexplored one. The peoples of Nubia in that era have not enjoyed the level of fame and excavation as Rome or Egypt. Yet what we have is tantalising and extremely intriguing. The Kushites were almost a twin culture of Egypt for many centuries, sharing gods, the reliance upon the Nile, an expansionist culture and even architectural similarities. The land had spent half a millennium under Egyptian rule, while later Egypt was ruled by the Kushites for more than 50 years. There had been conflict and competition between the two throughout history. By the time of our story, all these conquests are in the past, but their history creates the grounding for this story.

After the Kushite capital, the field of pyramids called Meroë, Napata is probably the most investigated site, and yet still it is largely buried and holds many secrets. To the Kushites this holy site, a collection of temples in the lee of a massive mountain, the Jebel Barkal, was the birthplace of Amun, the chief god venerated by both Kushites and Egyptians. The place was as sacred to the people of the time as Jerusalem to the Abrahamic religions or the Kashi Vishwanath Temple to Hindus. My portrayal of Napata is based upon the archaeological remains thus far logged and the geographical and geological data for Jebel Barkal, expanded using the life-saving tool (in a world of Covid) that is Google Earth, and with all the blanks filled in with plausible educated guesses. We know that Napata was sacked by Romans in 23 BC, and that is the scene in this book. The strange cult that has formed, filling a weird absence of gods in a world where the Roman emperor has become pharaoh, are entirely my own creation.

Strabo tells us that Napata was not only captured, but razed. He tells us that the Romans took their booty and slaves and made to leave, only to have to turn around and meet the Kandake again, who had marched against his garrison. He tells us that the matter was finally settled not by war but by ambassadors. Cassius Dio tells us: "*Petronius, finding himself unable either to advance farther, on account of the sand and the heat, or advantageously to remain where he was with his entire army, withdrew, taking the greater part of it with him. Thereupon the Ethiopians attacked the garrisons, but he again proceeded against them, rescued his own men, and compelled Candace to make terms with him.*" What led to my addition in the tale of a Roman march south, beyond Napata (which is not mentioned by either of the above) comes instead from Pliny, who tells us that the "*extreme distance to which he penetrated beyond Syene was nine hundred and seventy miles.*" Even following the wide loop of the Nile from Aswan (Syene) to Napata would be less than seven hundred miles, so where were these other three hundred? The Kushite capital of Meroë lies around two hundred miles south of Napata, and with some twists and turns lost in the desert, this was an appealing notion, that a rabid commander might decide to press on and finish the job. Additionally, I have made our heroes the garrison that the Kushite army moves against, and Napata the site of that garrison, since the location and details are not directly identified in the sources. And that the survivors of the expedition south are the Romans who come to the garrison's aid was a conceit of the tale.

But when it comes down to it, the duology that is Legion XXII is not really a story of war, despite all appearances. It is a story of a struggle between science and superstition, and how the two interact. It is about Cervianus coming to terms with the fact that his excessive knowledge of medicine and physics does not answer every question. It is about men, and about gods, and it is this conflict that resolves the tale. Cervianus and the gods of Egypt and Kush become, in essence, the ambassadors spoken of in the sources.

As well as the works of Cassius Dio, Pliny and Strabo, which tell us of this campaign, there are a number of fascinating confirmations that this campaign is more than mere fiction.

The *Res Gestae Divi Augusti* (the monument that records the achievements of Rome's first emperor) tells us:

MEO IUSSU ET AUSPICIO DUCTI SUNT DUO
EXERCITUS EODEM FERE TEMPORE IN
AETHIOPIAM ET IN ARABIAM QUAE APPELIATUR
EUDAEMON MAXIMAEQUE HOSTIUM GENTIS
UTRIUSQUE COPIAE CAESAE SUNT IN ACIE AT
COMPLURA OPPIDA CAPTA. IN AETHIOPIAM
USQUE AD OPPIDUM NABATA PERVENTUM EST
CUI PROXIMA EST MEROË. IN ARABIAM USQUE
IN FINES SABAEORUM PROCESSIT EXERCITUS AD
OPPIDUM MARIBA.

Thus, in the words of Augustus himself: "*On my order and under my auspices two armies were led, at almost the same time, into Ethiopia and into Arabia which is called the Happy, and very large forces of the enemy of both races were cut to pieces in battle and many towns were captured. Ethiopia was penetrated as far as the town of Nabata, which is next to Meroë. In Arabia the army advanced into the territories of the Sabaei to the town of Mariba.*"

If this tale has captured your imagination, and you have not the wherewithal to visit Aswan, Napata and the lands in between, I invite you to visit the British Museum, where you will find the physical evidence of these events. One of the museum's highlights and most famous exhibits is a bronze head of the emperor Augustus in room 70, a haunting portrait that is believed to have been manufactured in Egypt, but which was excavated at Meroë in Sudan – spoils, clearly, of the Kandake's invasion. In room 65 lie two less famous and less visited exhibits, but which shed the light of truth on this expedition: a piece of unique leather armour and examples of Roman military footwear unearthed at Qasr Ibrim, just sixty miles from the now-vanished fortress of Buhen.

Cervianus' journey – physically, metaphorically, and literarily – is over. Perhaps he will return some day in another story, but I hope you have enjoyed this two-book foray into a little-known era and region. Thank you for coming with me on the journey.

Simon Turney, June 2022

ABOUT THE AUTHOR

SIMON TURNEY is from Yorkshire and, having spent much of his childhood visiting historic sites, fell in love with the Roman heritage of the region. His fascination with the ancient world snowballed from there with great interest in Rome, Egypt, Greece and Byzantium. His works include the Marius' Mules and Praetorian series, the Tales of the Empire and The Damned Emperor series, and the Rise of Emperors books with Gordon Doherty.

Follow Simon at www.simonturney.com
and @SJATurney